this
much is
true

Jane Sanderson was born in South Yorkshire. She studied English at Leicester University, then after graduating she became a journalist. After a series of jobs with local newspapers she joined the BBC where she worked as a producer for Radio 4, first on the *World at One*, and then on *Woman's Hour*. She lives with her husband, the journalist and author Brian Viner, in Herefordshire. They have three children.

Also by Jane Sanderson

Netherwood
Ravenscliffe
Eden Falls

this much is true

much is

true

Jane Sanderson

First published in Great Britain in 2017 by Orion Books,
an imprint of The Orion Publishing Group Ltd
Carmelite House, 50 Victoria Embankment,
London EC4Y 0DZ

An Hachette UK company

1 3 5 7 9 10 8 6 4 2

A CIP catalogue record for this book
is available from the British Library.

ISBN 978 1 4091 6823 2

Typeset by Deltatype Ltd, Birkenhead, Merseyside

Printed in Great Britain by Clays Ltd, St Ives plc

www.orionbooks.co.uk

In loving memory of my mother-in-law,
Miriam Hyams
1925–2017

Acknowledgements

Thanks to Andrew Gordon for keeping the faith, to Jemima Forrester for picking up the manuscript and to Ben Willis and the Orion team for running with it so seamlessly. Thanks to Carolyn Baker for helping come up with a title that everyone loved, and to Anne Sanderson for her red pen and eagle eye at the proof reading stage. I'm grateful to Rob Orland (and his fascinating Historic Coventry website) for advice on the River Sherbourne and other aspects of 1950s Coventry. Any inaccuracies are mine alone. And finally, to Brian Viner, a thousand heartfelt thanks for your boundless love and support.

'You are fettered,' said Scrooge, trembling. 'Tell me why?'
'I wear the chain I forged in life,' replied the Ghost. 'I made it link by link, and yard by yard'

A Christmas Carol, Charles Dickens

I

Every Wednesday morning, Annie Doyle walked her dog, Finn. She'd done this now for the best part of two months, since the day Josie and Sandra – well, just Josie really – asked her to join them. They were at the reservoir car park and they all happened to be loading their dogs into the cars at the same time, and although Annie had kept her eyes down, Josie had said a bright hello and made an almighty fuss of Finn, a certain route to Annie's heart. Even so, she'd been taken aback by the offer of joining them the next week, because really, she hardly ever came here and the last thing she was looking for was friendship. But Josie had been so chatty, so sunny, that although Annie was about to shake her head no, she found herself nodding yes instead.

So it began, and now, on Sunday nights when she considered the week ahead, she felt immediately brighter about all her dull and dutiful chores: visits to Vince, appointments with his doctor, errands for Michael – nothing, in truth, that she actually *chose* to do, only things that had to be done. No, her Wednesday walks meant the world. Michael mocked her for it, but she didn't care. She and Finn had a new shape to their week and the dog loved it as much as she did: more, probably.

Other days, Finn didn't get much of a walk. Oh, she might put him in the car on her visits to Vince, because she drove past the reservoir then, and it was no trouble to stand a while and let him rootle through the undergrowth at the water's edge. But usually she just took him five minutes down the street on his lead to the rec – or rather he took her, dragging her along while he lunged ahead – to sniff the air and do his business and lope around, getting in the way of joggers and boys on BMX bikes. On Wednesdays, though, Finn woke up knowing in his bones that today was the day, and from moment to moment as Annie pottered on, he kept her in his sights. That wasn't difficult, mind, because by anyone's standards the house was small – six good strides from the bottom of the stairs and you were already at the kitchen sink – so he made a nuisance of himself, trailing behind her from kettle to toaster to hob to washing machine to front porch and back again, as if he was certain that without his vigilance she'd just nip off out without him.

Today, as always, Annie was trying her level best to leave as silently as possible. Michael was still upstairs, and he hated to be disturbed. All his life he'd been a light and fractious sleeper: even as a baby he could never surrender completely to a good night's rest. So Annie crept cautiously round the kitchen in her socks, ran the tap as softly as she could, rinsed her cereal bowl as if it were Lalique, because the ordinary sounds of domestic plumbing had the power to ruin his day.

At the sink she stared through the kitchen window and saw the sky was a solid gunmetal grey. It might be an idea, she thought, to warm up the Nissan, so she knotted the belt on her cardie and made for the front door. Finn plodded along too.

'I'm only going to warm the car up,' she whispered, but he fixed a determined, purposeful gaze on the front garden through the double-glazed porch glass and his tail thudded rhythmically against the telephone table, making it wobble on its four thin legs.

'Shush,' Annie said, and she slipped out, then shut the door on him and scooted down the garden path in her rubber-soled slippers, clutching the car keys. Mournfully the dog watched her go.

She climbed stiffly into the car and put the key into the ignition. Her face wore a small frown of anxious concentration, as if the task in hand – inserting the key, turning it – was a delicate, uncertain operation. Somehow she always expected the battery to be flat, but the engine coughed obediently into life so she pushed the heater switch to high and the fan to full before easing herself out of the car again. Then she left the little Nissan rumbling in a cloud of fumes, and darted back to the house. When she opened the door again, Finn took a few clumsy steps backwards then rushed at her with reckless joy, as if she'd been away for a month. He was a big, heavy-set golden retriever and she was only five foot three so they were mismatched, though they couldn't have loved each other more. She clucked at him and scrubbed at his ears and he closed his eyes and smiled. Before Finn, she hadn't known a dog could smile, but he did, and often: the soft black edges of his mouth curving up at the corners when he looked at her, or when she petted him, or when his biscuits rattled into his bowl.

'Now then,' she said, batting him away.

He gazed at her with mute devotion and followed her once again to the small kitchen, where she washed her hands and dried them on an old tea towel, which showed a faded parade of beach huts and a recipe for Cornish pasties. Andrew had given it to her years ago and it'd been so long among her kitchen possessions that she didn't always even think of him when she used it. This morning, though, she had a sudden, sharp image of him solemnly handing it over, still in its candy-striped paper bag, at the end of a wet few days in Padstow. He was such a generous boy, she thought now; so steadfast in his love for her. From the youngest age he would save up his pennies to buy presents for Annie at Christmas and on birthdays, and they were always his own ideas. And always, too, there would be that moment of awkwardness when Andrew proffered his little gift and Michael's face took on a closed and sullen look; the look that he sometimes still had, even though he was a grown man of fifty. Annie knew she hadn't always thanked Andrew as fulsomely as she should have done, trying to appease Michael, trying to keep the peace. She sighed, feeling sad all over again at these long-ago events, then she tutted at her own foolishness, snapped out the tea towel and draped it over the chrome rail of the oven door to dry.

Annie left the kitchen still followed by the dog. There was an old-fashioned five-prong coat-stand in the hall: two for her, three for Michael. He had a grey wool coat, a lightweight green anorak and a Day-Glo orange cycling jacket and she knew whether or not he was in by whether one of these garments was missing from the stand. He never left without a coat, and then, on his return, he never left a coat anywhere other than its correct place.

4

Now, as always in the mornings, all the coats were here because the other thing Michael never did was spend the night elsewhere, being the sort of man who valued home comforts above the unpredictability of the outside world. He was a little like Annie in this respect, although even she sometimes wondered why a man his age had nowhere more interesting to be than his own single bed. Still though, she appreciated his presence in the house overnight, because it was just the two of them. Three, if you counted Finn, which she did.

She unhooked her navy fleece from the coat-stand and put it on, then patted the pocket to be sure the whistle was there. Behind her the dog made guttural noises of glee and bounced his big yellow front paws on the hall floor so that his claws rattled on the tiles. Michael said Finn was too large for a house this size and Annie supposed he was right; it was true that when she got him she hadn't known how big that sweet golden puppy would grow. Mind you, she sometimes thought – and she thought it again now – that she'd sooner get shut of Michael than Finn. She smiled and reached for the broad flat plane of the dog's forehead, enjoying for a moment the firm, silken warmth. Then she turned back to the coat-stand for his lead, and found it gone.

'Where's your lead?' she asked the dog. Finn trotted jauntily to the door, ready to leave.

It was always on the coat-stand, always: only, this morning it wasn't. Annie stood for a moment, looking at the space where the lead should have been. Finn had his nose in the crack of the door, ready for off.

'We're going nowhere till we find it,' Annie said.

She made for the kitchen again and after a second's

hesitation the dog galumphed after her, barging ahead, so that a hot wave of annoyance washed over her, though it was prompted as much by the missing lead as by Finn's bad manners. Upstairs she could hear Michael walking into the bathroom, and this annoyed her too, because she'd meant to be on her way by the time he appeared. She stared crossly at the worktops. Tea caddy. Kettle. Toaster. Michael's fruit bowl and, next to it, Michael's banana stand, which she noted was empty. There was no sign of the lead and in fact she would have been amazed to find it here, where it didn't belong.

Back they went to the coat-stand, and down came Michael, descending the stairs straight-backed as if he had an invisible tray of china teacups on his head. His black hair was wavy and a little too long, just as it had been since he was sixteen. Here and there it was greying. He had grown it long when he decided to apply to music college and ever since then it'd been in his eyes. It was thinning now and looked to Annie as though it could do with a brush, or a wash, or a short back and sides. She smiled.

'Hello, Mother,' he said, in the way he had of sounding disappointed to see her. 'Dog Day again? How it does come around.'

'Hello, love, have you seen Finn's lead?'

He stopped on the bottom step and looked at her with his head cocked. 'Why? Did you hang it in the bathroom?' he asked, facetiously. Annie and Finn, side by side, were both looking at him but Michael looked only at his mother. He never included Finn in a conversation, although for his part Finn maintained a generous interest in Michael, as if at the smallest signal he would be happy to love him, in spite of past slights.

'No,' Annie said. 'I just thought—'

Michael continued on his way, stepping onto the hall floor and rounding the newel post in a tight, fluid movement.

'Well you thought wrong,' he said. 'Damned dog's nothing but trouble.'

Oh, thought Annie, that isn't nice. But she let it pass.

The lead wasn't in the car either so as Annie pulled away from the kerb she was discombobulated: too preoccupied by its loss to notice the white van directly behind her that had to slam to a halt to avoid a collision. Only at the T-junction, when she looked left and right and then glanced in the rear-view mirror, did she see the angry driver behind her, his face contorted with contempt, his right hand making a gesture Annie had never fully understood but which she knew to be obscene. She looked away at once and made a careful right turn into Park Road and then again into the main road, keeping her eyes fixed ahead and praying that the white van would turn left towards Sheffield, not right towards Barnsley. She drove steadily, perfectly, regally, but her hands, clamped on the steering wheel, were white at the knuckles. She wasn't prone to road rage herself. If anything, the mistakes of other drivers only served to make her feel kinder towards them, so to have her actions provoke this sort of instant apoplectic loathing made her feel truly wronged. She would have thought the benign presence of Finn in the boot and her own curly white hair, which puffed up above the top of the seat like a meringue, would be enough to grant her a little kindness, not to mention respect. She didn't even know what she'd done wrong.

At the crossroads she was aware at the periphery of her vision that the van had slid alongside her. Good, she thought; he's turning off left. But he'd opened his window and she heard furious, shocking expletives raining down on her like shrapnel. She kept her eyes rigidly on the road ahead, and when the lights turned to green she managed to pull away with a smooth, textbook action as if to demonstrate once and for all what a fine driver she was, and how harshly she was being judged.

'Has he gone?' she asked Finn. The dog was silent in the boot, although he sat up at her voice. Annie risked a swift glance up and across and saw in the mirror the bonnet of the white van still just a hair's breadth away from the Nissan's rear bumper. Her heart hammered in her chest and in a panic she braked when she'd intended to accelerate. Behind her the van driver slammed a hand on the horn and held it there. Annie wailed. She wished Finn was in the passenger seat and not in the boot, but then thought it was a comfort to have his bulk placed between her and the furious man, whom she now assumed had had no intention of turning left and had only wanted to shout at her. She felt bewilderment as well as fear. His anger was inexplicable to her; was he actually chasing her? It seemed unlikely that his destination was the very same as her own.

There were no more shops now between here and the reservoir where she was meeting the others: nowhere safe for her to run inside and seek sanctuary. She considered the primary school, but there were secure keypads on the doors these days, to keep out paedophiles and gunmen. She pictured herself arriving at the reservoir – first, as always – and having to face her tormentor alone. She felt an urgent need for the lavatory and underneath her fleece her blouse was damp with perspiration. Then she thought of Sandra, whose cottage she'd seen but never visited, and which lay – with a small detour – between Annie and the car park, so she made a snap decision to turn right, up Wheatcommon Lane. She did this without indicating, spinning the steering wheel like a getaway driver, and the van turned too, so she pressed on up the lane the few hundred yards to Sandra's house, and tilted the rear-view mirror off at an angle so there was no danger of inadvertently seeing the whites of the angry man's eyes.

When Annie's little hatchback hurtled up the driveway, Sandra Moloney's first impulse was to laugh, but this was immediately quelled by the sight of a dirty Ford transit in dogged pursuit. Sandra, dishevelled and not yet quite dressed, was at the kitchen window, leaning against the sink, chewing a cold crust from a piece of toast. Ordinarily Sandra didn't dash anywhere for anyone, but this morning she made an exception; Annie's precipitous arrival was unprecedented and a short, beefy man in baggy jeans and a Motörhead T-shirt was unloading himself from the van in a menacing fashion. Without shoes or socks, the crust dangling from her mouth like a damp cigarette, Sandra bolted for the door and rounded the corner onto the drive, where she arrived at Annie's car only shortly after the bullet-headed brute. His hands were splayed on his knees as he bent close enough to Annie's window to steam up the glass. Annie, round-eyed, had locked herself in and now threw Sandra a look of fathomless despair.

The man hadn't seen Sandra; his focus was only on

Annie. 'Stupid bitch,' he shouted through the glass, loudly enough that mild-mannered Finn gave a sharp bark of retaliation.

'Stupid old bag, you're a fuckin' liability.'

He banged on the window with his fist one, two, three times and Annie started to cry, her face in her hands. Sandra, temporarily ossified by shock, sprang into sudden life. She hurled herself at him, thudding into his stocky frame and shoving him backwards and sideways, away from the car. She was taller than he was, and just as solidly built, and he staggered with the force of her attack, then lurched back towards her with a roar, a bovine bellow. Sandra planted herself between him and the car, as fixed and sturdy as an oak tree. Behind the glass Annie watched in mortal fear and Finn, fired up by the turn of events, barked and bounced so that the Nissan rocked from side to side.

This was the scene that greeted Josie Jones when she arrived at the end of Sandra's driveway, holding Betty on her plaited leather lead. Betty, a serene and graceful collie, stepped a little backwards and a little left, so that she stood behind her owner, in a position from which nothing could be asked of her.

'Sandra!' Josie shouted. 'What are you doing?'

Sandra shot her a savage look. She had one hand on the car and another on the man's chest, clutching a twist of T-shirt and somehow keeping him at arm's length from his quarry. He was a short, fat, beast of a man, whose irrational anger threatened to consume him. His face was dark damson purple and the veins in his neck stood out like electric cables. At his left temple, another smaller vein pulsed visibly with hot blood. He flailed at Sandra, who in this moment was magnificently invincible.

'Fuckin' lunatic!' he shouted.

'Sandra!'

This was Josie again, marching towards danger, dragging a recalcitrant Betty on four unyielding legs. The little dog left channels in the gravel where she passed. Then the passenger door of the car flew open and Annie clambered out, ungainly in her haste, shaking with shock, her ashen face the very image of despair; Josie and Betty stared and inside the car Finn agitated noisily for release, his gentle brow puckered with bewilderment.

Annie, who now had the car and Sandra between herself and danger, mustered a deep, shuddering breath and shouted, 'Please stop!' Miraculously this did the trick. The man stopped his flailing and Sandra dropped her arms by her sides and stood panting, keeping her unblinking gaze on his face. The fire was leaving him; he glanced left and right, as if uncertain where he was, or why. His T-shirt had ridden up to expose a swathe of white belly.

'What's going on?' Josie asked, looking from Annie to Sandra and back again.

'He followed me,' Annie said, in a sort of injured wail. 'All the way from Beech Street.'

'You cut me up,' the man said. 'You never even bloody looked.'

Sandra said, 'Oh just eff off, you big buggering bully.'

Josie laughed, she couldn't help herself, and Annie, desperate now to broker peace, said, 'Whatever it was I did, I apologise.'

'No you don't,' Sandra said. 'If anyone should be sorry it's him.'

'You're all fuckin' mental,' said the man. He rubbed

his ear then moved his head left then right and the bones in his neck clicked. 'You,' he said, pointing at Sandra, 'should be fuckin' locked up and you' – pointing now at Annie – 'shouldn't be fuckin' drivin'.'

'And you,' said Josie, narrowing her striking green eyes, 'should be ashamed of yourself, terrorising this lady.' She pulled Betty along behind her and walked right up to him, staring into his face as if committing every detail to memory. 'I don't like the look of you,' she said, 'and I *never* forget a face.' For a moment the man looked likely to resume hostilities, opening his mouth and drawing a single long breath as if there were more insults to hurl. But then he closed it again and, like a wounded grizzly bear, lumbered unsteadily to his van where the driver's side door still hung open. He hoisted himself up, shut himself in, started the engine and reversed away down the drive, scattering stones and dust and flicking one last rigid middle finger at them as he went. Sandra whooped and shouted, 'Girl power!' and Josie grinned, folding her arms and watching the van's retreat. Annie, frail with utter relief, only closed her eyes and tried to calm her breathing.

2

They sat in Sandra's kitchen, the women and their dogs. Finn was possessed by post-incident excitement and he skittered and spiralled idiotically across the floor with his tail in his mouth. He looked like a mutant crab. Betty sat primly looking the other way and Sandra's elderly Alsatian paid nobody any mind. He lay on his big stained cushion in an alcove that had long been his alone, and snored. Now and then he emitted a silent gust of foul wind that even Sandra noticed.

'Jesus, Fritz,' she said, and wafted a hand ineffectually. Annie sat mute and pale and Josie only smiled.

Breakfast detritus was all across the table, including a bottle of milk and an open plastic tub of butter, its surface soft and littered with toast crumbs. A late wasp, survivor of the recent Indian summer, performed listless sorties through the clutter. Sandra didn't apologise for the mess because she didn't see it. Josie saw it but didn't mind it. Only Annie, whose own domestic life was rigorously ordered, noted the squalor and felt uncomfortable. Her tea was untouched because there were traces of an earlier brew on the rim of the mug; dried droplets of someone else's brown drink. And although Josie and Sandra were talking nineteen to the dozen about the drama, Annie only sat, consciously quiet, wondering if they'd noticed she wasn't joining in; wondering when they could leave. Then Josie said, 'So Annie, he followed you all the way?'

Annie looked up and nodded.

'And what do you think got his goat?'

'You see, I couldn't find Finn's lead.'

This was no answer at all.

'Nutters like that don't need much of a reason to blow their tops,' Sandra said.

Josie nodded. 'It's true,' she said. She rubbed Annie's back and Annie managed a watery smile.

Sandra gave a sudden spurt of laughter. 'Your face,' she said to Josie. 'You thought I'd gone mad.'

'I couldn't believe my eyes,' Josie said. 'And you, a librarian.'

Sandra smiled grimly. 'What a brute though! He called Annie a bitch.'

Annie winced.

'He thumped her window as if he wanted to smash it.'

'What if he'd hit you?' Josie said. 'What if he'd had a knife?'

Sandra shrugged.

'He could've hurt you.'

'Well what was I supposed to do?' Sandra was starting to feel nettled now, and she looked at Annie, expecting some form of support, if not actual acclaim, but Annie was hunched in her chair feeling sorry for herself and even when Finn crashed into the dresser and rattled the plates on his mad progress round the kitchen she just sat on, silent and suffering.

'Annie,' Sandra said.

Annie looked up again, slowly, as if it required an

effort. Her pale blue eyes were rimmed with red.

'You okay? You're not saying much.'

Annie stared at Sandra.

'You haven't even said thank you,' Sandra said.

'Oh, but didn't I?' said Annie, startled into finding her voice.

'Nope.'

'I'm sure I did.'

'Well then,' said Sandra. 'As long as you're sure you did, I suppose that's the main thing.'

She stood up and stomped to the sink, where she jettisoned her tea and dumped the mug among the dirty breakfast pots.

'Well anyway, thank you, Sandra,' Annie said, anxious now, and Sandra said, 'Sure, whatever.'

There was a silence, and it might have turned prickly except for a terrific clattering on the stairs and the crash of a door hurled open. A teenage boy plunged into the room then drew back in some confusion when he found the kitchen full of women and dogs. His face coloured instantly.

'You're late,' Sandra said, without turning round. 'The bus comes by in three minutes.'

His blushing face now took on an injured look. 'You didn't wake me,' he said.

'I did, but you went back to sleep.'

'Well, you didn't wake me again.'

'Correct. I said I wouldn't, so I didn't.' She was pulling on some old woollen socks now, which she seemed to have found in the folds of Fritz's bed.

'Hi, Billy,' Josie said. He turned to her and smiled, and Annie could see now what a handsome boy he was, dark haired and brown eyed with a lovely smile that she gathered was reserved at this moment for people other than his mother.

'Hey, Josie,' he said.

'This is Annie,' Josie said. 'And that's Finn,' she added, pointing. The boy nodded pleasantly at Annie, and she nodded back. She could see nothing of Sandra in him, except perhaps his unkempt appearance, and that surely was nurture not nature.

Sandra said, 'Seriously, Billy, you'll miss the bus, and I'm not driving you to school.'

'I'll walk if I miss it.'

'Right, good luck with that.'

Josie laughed and said, 'Billy, just leave, that's your best bet, sweetheart.'

He grinned at her. 'Yeah, right, I'm outta here.' As he passed Sandra he punched her softly on the shoulder and said, 'Bye, Ma,' and Sandra said, 'Bye, hon, see you later,' in a voice that no longer had any harshness in it, only love. Annie, watching and listening, thought about Michael, who even now could sulk for days at the least provocation, and herself, who could never ignore him, only fuss and worry and make him worse.

'Okey doke,' Sandra said, standing up. 'Let's walk the dogs.'

Annie tapped the tub of butter. 'Shall you put this away?' she said.

'I'll clear up later,' said Sandra. She gave Fritz a jiggle with her foot. 'C'mon, Fritzy, stir yourself.'

'But it's melting,' Annie said, because she couldn't help herself.

'It'll be fine – the heating's gone off now.'

She swung out of the room and Annie, easing herself up out of the chair, wondered how Sandra's mind worked. When she'd first met her and Josie, she'd thought perhaps the regular company of younger women would be good for her, stop her turning into so much of a stick-in-the-mud. But if anything, Sandra made her cling harder to her own habits. Oh, it would be a snowy morning in hell when Annie Doyle left a pat of butter to melt half the day on the kitchen table.

Annie and Finn were ahead and Josie, whose car was with the mechanic again, put Betty in Sandra's boot with Fritz. The old Alsatian couldn't jump in these days; Sandra had to heave him up in her arms where he hung, heavy as a sack of wet sand, waiting to be shovelled into the car. Sandra had rescued Fritz when he was a youngster, a malnourished, dull-coated creature who'd been picked up on the hard shoulder of the M1 with bloodied paws and terrified eyes. He was about fourteen now – they could only ever guess at his age – but still he looked at her with fathomless gratitude, as if she could never be repaid. Nobody knew his story, and there were more attractive, less motley-looking specimens in the line-up of rejects at the dogs' home. But Fritz had stepped forward in his cage and pushed his face side on against the bars so that Sandra could scratch the back of his ear. After that, she couldn't leave him there to be spurned again and again by people seeking the more obvious charms of perky terriers and spaniels with liquid chocolate eyes.

Now, when she looked in her rear-view mirror, she could see the sharp white tips of Betty's pointed ears but there was no sign of Fritz and she knew that he'd be lying like a huge draught excluder against the door of the boot.

'She *is* a terrible driver,' Josie said. She meant Annie, who was keeping them to a twenty-five-miles-an-hour creep along a wide, clear highway; she braked at the approach to corners, and she braked at the appearance of oncoming traffic. 'I expect she wound that brute up, driving like she's driving now.'

'The boot of her car is all dog,' Sandra said.

It was true. Annie kept her back seats down flat to make more room, but still Finn seemed to fill all the available space. When she braked, his bulk lurched a little forward before settling back again. He faced Sandra and Josie through the rear window and panted; it looked as though he was laughing at them. Now Annie slowed still further and her right indicator came on, although the turning to the reservoir was still some way off, and on the left.

'I might overtake,' Sandra said.

Josie shook her head. 'Don't,' she said. 'That'd be hostile.' She yawned. 'I ordered five hundred daffodil bulbs from Marshalls and they came this morning in four sacks.'

'God. Five hundred?'

Josie nodded. 'I know.'

'Lovely though. Where you putting them?'

'That bank at the side of the house.'

'The grassy one?'

Josie nodded.

'God,' Sandra said again. 'It's not even soil then.'

Ahead, Annie turned left with infinite care onto the track that led to the reservoir car park. Sandra followed. Josie said, 'I might get Mr Dinmoor to put them in.'

'The old man?'

She said this in the way a person might say 'the clown', as if behind the words was a barely concealed snort of laughter.

'He's not old,' Josie said. 'I mean, he is, but that's not *all* he is.'

'If you say so.'

Josie opened her mouth to reply but Sandra had parked alongside Annie and was already getting out of the car.

The reservoir path was only two miles around and completely flat, but it was still a bit of a push for Fritz so their pace was slow, more a meander than a walk. They passed a row of anglers' platforms, empty at this hour on a weekday morning, and a tatty yellow board erected years ago by the Samaritans, with a number to call before you took the final plunge. The further you walked from the car park the wilder the water's edge, until at the far end the tangle of reeds, bull rushes and low-slung willows formed a mini-reserve for water birds, which nested in the shadowy interior. Now and again coots, moorhens or crested grebes exploded in a maelstrom of fuss and feathers. Often they'd be dodging Finn, who kept charging into the shallows then standing there as if he'd forgotten what it was he'd come for. He wasn't supposed to disturb the birds but Annie didn't like to restrain him on his walks, and besides, this morning she didn't have a lead: a fact she was currently explaining to Sandra and Josie.

'So anyway,' she said at last, 'I'm thinking that it might've slid off my neck in the woods last week.'

Sandra yawned. 'I don't know why you're fretting,'

she said. 'It hardly matters, given how rarely you use it.'

'Well ...' said Annie.

'We can look for it next time,' Josie said.

'Oh it'll've been swiped by now for sure,' said Sandra.

'Still, let's look.' Josie hooked a companionable arm through Annie's. 'You can borrow Betty's today if need be,' she said. 'She won't miss it.' Leashed or unleashed, Betty never left Josie's side. If Betty were a working collie, Josie said, she'd be worse than useless. She'd pick her favourite sheep and stick with it, and all the rest could go to the devil.

There was a wooden bench about a quarter of the way round and without consultation the three women stopped at it, because they always did. The dogs milled about and sniffed the legs of the bench, deciding where to sit. Josie had a tatty woven knapsack, which she'd bought in Kabul twenty years ago and had carried with her, by and large, ever since. Today it held a flask and three small mugs and these she lifted out and placed on the bench. Sandra sat down heavily and the flask wobbled.

'It might be a bit strong,' Josie said. 'I lost count of the dose.' She made her coffee in a scarred metal stove-top percolator that sent a geyser of boiling water up through freshly ground beans and into a jug. It came out like mud, in Annie's opinion. Bitter? She was hard pressed not to spit it out the first time she was given a cup.

'Plenty of milk for me please,' she said now, watching Josie pour.

'Oh Annie,' Josie said. 'I forgot it this time.'

Annie looked at her and wondered how milk could ever be forgotten in the preparation of coffee. But Josie could drink it black or white and she just shot Annie a rueful smile as she passed a cup to Sandra then sipped at her own.

'Sorry,' Josie said. 'Try it without?'

Annie shook her head. She felt inordinately disappointed. If anyone deserved a nice coffee this morning, she did. She cast a glance at Sandra, who she knew liked lots of milk too, but Sandra caught her eye and grinned cheerfully. 'Cheers then,' she said, and though she sniffed the contents of her cup a little cautiously, she drank it anyway. Annie felt excluded, which she knew was silly and which she put down to the earlier horror. It'd left her feeling raw, thin-skinned.

'Look,' Josie said. She pointed across the reservoir. A huge bird sat on a rudimentary wooden jetty holding out glossy coal-black wings to dry in the feeble autumn sunshine. Their great span, together with the bird's long neck and stumpy black legs, gave it a primitive, prehistoric appearance.

'A cormorant,' Sandra said.

Annie shuddered. 'It's watching us.'

'Watching the water, more like,' Sandra said. 'It's after the fish.'

'Aren't they sea birds?' This was Josie. She was standing now, shading her eyes with one hand.

'It's a long way from the sea,' said Annie.

'Magnificent creature,' Josie said.

Annie stared hard at the bird, trying to see something other than its raptor's neck and sharp, curved beak. Then Finn ran pell-mell into the water barking, and even though it was some distance away from him, the bird beat its wings once, twice, then rose into the air with a sort of grave dignity, which only emphasised the dog's foolishness.

'That's that then,' Sandra said. At her feet, Fritz opened one eye, but there was nothing to see now so he closed it again.

3

By the time she drove away from the reservoir Annie felt almost cheerful. She turned on the radio and tapped her fingers on the steering wheel, keeping time with Tony Christie's search for Amarillo and at the chorus she joined in. The reasons for her lifted spirits were three-fold. One, it was Wednesday, which meant Michael had choral practice as well as school commitments, so he'd be out until the evening, leaving her free to please herself: watch a panel game, start a jigsaw puzzle, she hadn't decided yet. Two, she was calling at Fletcher's on the way home for a custard slice or a fresh cream éclair; she didn't know which, she'd see when she got there. Three, apart from the coffee and the vaguely unsettling sight of the cormorant, she'd enjoyed today's walk. In the end they'd just turned around and dawdled amiably back to the car park because Fritz had been lying down too long at the bench, and when he got up again he was dragging a hind leg; it had stuck out behind him, useless as a stick, as he lurched and hobbled on the other three. So the walk was curtailed, which Annie didn't mind because she wasn't one of life's natural hikers: built for sitting, she always thought. She shifted in her seat and trilled along with Tony, dreamin' dreams and huggin' pillows in what Michael called her old lady's warble.

Old lady indeed! There were times when Michael behaved more like an old lady than she did, with his pernickety ways. The trouble with Michael, thought Annie now with a pleasurable shiver of disloyalty, was that he never had to please anyone other than himself. Oh, he thought he was busy, certainly: thought he was pulled in all directions with his music lessons and his choirs. But all of that, really, was for himself. He never – not now, not ever – did anything he didn't want to do. Annie absolutely didn't mind sharing her home with him; she didn't mind it at all. Shopping for him, keeping the house tidy, washing his clothes and his sheets in the detergent he liked – these small services made her feel useful. But oh dear, he had no idea what it was to act unselfishly. And the older he got the more deeply ingrained ran his belief that the world revolved around his needs.

Thinking of Michael made her think of Andrew, who lived all the way across the globe in Australia, in a coastal town called Byron Bay: a name so lyrical, a place so far away, that Annie couldn't hold an image of it in her head, even though he kept posting photographs to her of an azure sea and tropical sand and lush, abundant vegetation. Andrew had gone to Australia aged eighteen and never come back. Well, never come back for good. In fact he did come, once in a blue moon, to visit, but the houses in Beech Street were small, and close together, and staying with Annie and Michael seemed to induce in Andrew a sort of nervous twitch in his arms and legs, as if he needed to stretch but didn't have the space. In Byron Bay he had space. He also had an Australian wife and two little Australian boys, and they all had surnames in place of first names: Bailey, Blake and Riley. Once and once only, all four of them had visited, when Blake was three and Riley nine months. Vince had had gastro-enteritis so none of them had gone to see him for fear of catching the bug, and the weather had been so atrocious that they were cooped up together for a fraught and cheerless week of disrupted nights, early starts and interrupted meals, none of which would have mattered quite as much if Michael hadn't been so difficult. He had either been entirely silent – the sort of silence that intruded just as effectively as noise – or rudely outspoken. 'I'm jiggered,' he had said on the evening of their fourth day, standing at the door of the sitting room in his paisley dressing gown and burgundy slippers with a hot water bottle under one arm, 'and if these two make so much as a peep tonight, I'll wring their necks.' This, to their mother! But being Australian, Bailey had only laughed. Annie remembered a pleasant-looking girl with a high, childish ponytail, a wide tanned face and a scattering of fine freckles across her little nose, like cinnamon on a bun. She laughed a great deal, Annie recalled now. She'd laughed when Andrew swore at Michael and called him – now what was it? Annie couldn't remember. They'd left the next day though, two days before they were due to go.

Annie sighed. At the time, she'd been able to see Michael's point of view. Now, though, while she still had a strong memory of his fury, she found she could no longer understand how he could have been so livid with two sweet, warm, pudgy blonde boys who were, after all, his only nephews. They hadn't been back to England since. Blake was nine now, and Riley nearly seven. They beamed at her from a silver frame on the mantelpiece, two little strangers, her grandsons.

She picked up a new lead for Finn, a sack of kibble and, from the greengrocer's, a bunch of bananas for Michael. Then she pointed the car at Barnsley and headed into the town centre, although before she called at Fletcher's Bakery she had to visit Vince at Glebe Hall. *Had to*. That made it sound as if she didn't want to, which wasn't true because she liked the nurses, who were a merry bunch and always seemed pleased to see her. There weren't any visiting restrictions; you could pop in whenever you liked. Annie only wished she could go without actually sitting with Vince.

The home was a council-run, no-frills establishment and he'd had a long, dull residency here. It was a converted Victorian mansion, a relic from Barnsley's prosperous past, built from great blocks of soot-blackened stone. Vince's room faced a busy main road and buses and lorries lumbered past his window all day long so that there was never any peace. Residents at the back looked out over a small garden where blue tits and a woodpecker came for the peanuts and suet balls. Once, a year or so ago, a room with a view had come free and Annie had suggested to Vince that he move.

'What do you think?' she had said, being pleasant, being considerate. 'A nice room on the other side, Vince? You can watch the birds.' Her husband had seemed to be considering the question, but then had said in a querulous voice, 'She only went out for a loaf,' so Annie had dropped it, left him where he was. Birds, buses; it was all the same to Vince anyway.

At the back of the home there was a visitors' car park, which wasn't quite big enough for its purpose, and Annie's heart beat a little faster as she turned into it. She did so hate having to reverse into a bay that was squeezed on both sides by other vehicles. She felt, on these occasions, that she was taking her driving test all over again, but today there was a welcoming row of three unoccupied spaces so she sailed gaily into the middle one with the blithe spirit of a woman whose day was getting better and better, admittedly from a very poor start.

'Now then, Finn, I shan't be long,' she said. She turned to look at him and he panted stoically. She let down the rear windows a crack, then got out of the car and locked it manually, so that the alarm wouldn't go off if Finn shifted or barked. Then she unlocked it again, put the key back in the ignition, and let the windows down further. She didn't know how much air a big dog like Finn could use up in a small hatchback; she didn't want him to run out of oxygen, didn't want to find him dead, or gasping for life like a goldfish on a carpet. She locked the door again and trotted across the car park, but then the insidious, insistent thought took hold that now the windows were wide enough open for someone cunning to slide in an arm and unlock the car to steal Finn, so back she went. The dog watched her comings and goings with detached calm; he was well used to her rituals, and had no expectations of early release. He knew the score. In fact he was settling down for a comfortable snooze even as she opened the car door one more time, engaged the ignition, and closed the windows an inch and a half. He was shutting his eyes even as she thoroughly tested the gap, trying – and, crucially, failing – to insert her own hand through the opening.

'Righty ho,' she said, finally satisfied. She knocked on the window and Finn opened his eyes.

'See you later, alligator,' she said.

'Morning-Mrs-Doyle-or-is-it-afternoon-already-with-the-way-time-flies-nothing-would-surprise-me.'

It was the Irish nurse, Moira. Annie said, 'You're all right, Moira, there's five more minutes of morning,' and they both laughed. Moira was as short as Annie, but probably forty years younger. Her hair, cut in a sharp bob, was a glorious shade of auburn that made Annie feel wistful about her own colourless curls. Also Moira had the sort of luscious hourglass figure that the Ancient Greeks might have gone to war over and Renaissance artists would have queued up to paint.

'How is he today?' Annie asked, dutifully.

'He's awake, but he's grumpy,' Moira said. 'Threw his cornflakes at the wall.'

Annie blushed for her husband.

'I hope it hasn't marked the wallpaper,' she said.

Moira winked. 'Why do you think it's vinyl? Sure, there's not a surface in this place that can't be wiped clean.'

'Well anyway,' Annie said.

It was embarrassing. He was like a toddler. When Andrew was eighteen months he'd scribbled on the kitchen wall with a red crayon and there'd been nobody crosser about it at the time than Vince, and now look! Flinging food and crockery at the walls in a tantrum. He wore a nappy, too.

'I'll bring some tea through,' Moira said.

'I promise I won't throw it at you,' Annie said, and Moira howled. The sound of her laughter followed Annie all the way down the corridor and into Vince's room where the door was propped open with a rubber wedge. He was slumped in a faux-leather wing chair, caving in on himself like a deflating lilo. The television was on and a man in pressed jeans and a checked shirt was explaining the importance of varying the contents of your compost bin, but he was talking to himself. Vince's eyes were open, but there was nobody home.

Annie touched him on the shoulder. 'Vince,' she said. 'It's me.'

He turned his head and looked at her.

'Who are you?' he said. He hadn't really known Annie for five years or more, except for the occasions when he remembered how much he disliked her.

'Here we go again,' she said. 'I'm the tooth fairy.'

Solemnly he held out a hand and said, 'Pleased to meet you,' and Annie immediately felt unkind, in spite of everything.

'No, Vince, I'm Annie. Annie Doyle. Annabelle Platt as was. Your wife.'

He curled his top lip and turned his empty gaze back to the television set, like a blind man following the sound of voices. How are the mighty fallen. Annie had this thought even now, so many years into his deterioration. When she'd met him he'd been the talk of the town, cock of the walk, but he'd singled her out and taken her dancing, even though she was the least likely girl to catch his roving eye. Oh, he was handsome back then! She almost forgot to breathe, the first time he spoke to her;

29

she had thought him magnificent. But Annie looked at him now – bony white ankles poking out of drab pyjama bottoms, hands curled like big dried leaves in his lap, mouth encrusted with dried spittle, a smell of Sudocrem and urine – and tried to call to mind Vincent Doyle, because this wasn't him. The Vince she'd married smelled of Brylcreem and Old Spice, and when he walked into the Locarno dance hall, heads turned.

'This isn't very interesting,' she said, pointing at the television. 'It's gardening. You never liked it, even when you had your own.'

He looked at her again.

'It's a poor do,' he said.

'It is.'

She picked up the remote control from the arm of his chair.

'Now then, I think it's this one.' She pressed a button, and the screen changed to a menu of inexplicable options. *AV1, AV2, TV, S-Video, Component.*

'No then, not that one.' She had another stab at it, this time choosing an upward-pointing arrow. *Auto Programme, Manual Programme, Favourites,* the screen said.

'Oh pot it,' Annie said, and pressed what looked to her like an off button but in fact it took them to the cockpit of a Lancaster bomber, in black and white. Vince sat up and leaned forwards. He watched with a sort of baffled interest, as if some long-buried memory had partly emerged through the thick fog of his mind, though not quite fully enough to be understood.

'I know him,' he said, pointing at Richard Todd. 'I used to work with him at the National Provincial.'

For a while Annie and Vince watched the film together

in silence. The bombers flew with steady certainty and purpose through German gunfire towards the dam.

'Oh I like these old films.' This was Moira, bearing a tray with a mug of tea for Annie and a beaker for Vince. 'Those were the days, ey, Mrs Doyle? When men were men and women were grateful.'

'Before your time,' Annie said.

'And yours, surely,' said Moira, with a wink.

Annie hadn't drawn her eyes away from the screen. She looked at Guy Gibson with his leather helmet and steady hands, issuing brisk, tinny orders through his pilot's mask, and she felt English to the core and proud of it: a member of the same, splendid club. 'They filmed this not far from here, Moira,' she said, hoping the nurse might stay. 'I think it was the Derwent Valley.'

'Is that so?' Moira handed Annie her tea, glanced at the television. The thrum of the bombers blended with the traffic noise outside Vince's window. Guy Gibson was flying straight at the dam, valiant in a hail of enemy fire. 'This is fine, I can see everything,' he said brightly to his co-pilot. 'Stand by to pull me under the seat if I get hit.'

'They're bombing that dam, Vince,' Annie said.

'No they aren't,' he said, as if she was a fool.

Annie looked at him, then back at the screen. There was something so familiar about all this: his disparaging tone, the television set, the old film, their armchairs side by side. If it wasn't for the way he looked and smelled, they could have been in their first front room, in Coventry.

'I've brought you your tea, Vince,' Moira said, in the loud voice she used for the demented residents of Glebe Hall. 'If you're planning to throw it, wait until I'm out of the room.'

31

'Thank you, Moira,' Vince said, in a precious moment of clarity and appropriate behaviour. He took his tea then pointed at Annie.

'This is the tooth fairy,' he said.

4

Annie Platt wasn't born at home in a tangle of old towels like so many of her contemporaries in their small mining town, but at the Pinder Oaks Maternity Home in Barnsley. She was the first child of Harold and Lillian Platt, who had a car and a detached house with a garden front and back on Hawshaw Lane in Hoyland. Harold was a bank manager, not a miner, and Lillian was the vivacious, highly strung youngest daughter of a prosperous Sheffield cutler. They had only a middling income and not a scrap of illustrious lineage but in the modest context of Hoyland, Harold and Lillian passed for quality.

Their Annie was actually an Annabelle and she was the only one in Hoyland, although something about her – even in early infancy – encouraged the use of the diminutive. She was going to be the first of four children, two girls and two boys, but the other three never arrived, which was a deep regret to Lillian, who liked a crowd, and a puzzle to Harold, who hadn't pictured himself presiding over such a small gathering at mealtimes: hadn't imagined either that he would have no son on whom he could imprint his own narrow version of the world.

Before this disappointment though, they had their

firstborn. Harold drove Lillian home from Pinder Oaks and Annie lay across Lillian's lap, tightly swaddled in a white crocheted blanket. Every time Lillian glanced down on that five-mile journey, the baby was staring up at her, unblinking and expressionless. Lillian didn't take to her. She had a too-round face, as round as a tea plate, small navy blue eyes and a squashed nose with round nostrils that resembled a piglet's snout. Lillian was worried that her daughter wouldn't be pretty. She wondered, too, if she had the right baby.

'This is definitely ours, is it?' she said to Harold as he drove. 'I mean to say, how would we know? We just took what we were given.' Harold, a careful driver, wouldn't take his eyes off the road. 'Well it's ours now,' was all he said.

At home, baby Annie hardly ever cried, which should have been a blessing except that when the time came for smiling, she hardly ever smiled either. To Lillian's surprise, she found Annie neither lovable nor unlovable. The baby inspired no strong feelings either way. Oh well, thought Lillian, she's all right in her own way and anyway there'll be others. But by Annie's fifth birthday, she was still Lillian and Harold's one and only child, and Lillian was wishing she'd paid her more attention, because it was difficult, after five years of indifference, to suddenly find a fresh footing. Lillian tried, nonetheless. She became jollier around her daughter, playful even. She suggested they build a den from the clothes horse and the weekly wash, but it took hardly any time at all to accomplish and then, when they sat inside it, squashed together in their tent of damp woollen drawers and cotton sheets, Lillian couldn't think what to say to the child. Annie sat on, impassively cocooned, long after Lillian had given up and crawled out. Another time, Lillian took Annie outside in the snow and showed her how a snowman was made, expecting her to join in, but Annie only watched, studying her mother's actions with the anxious concentration of a child who, while not especially bright, was certainly willing to learn. Lillian all of a sudden lost patience. She stopped pushing the snowman's body – which anyway was going wrong, turning oblong and picking up mud – and said, 'You just don't know how to have fun, Annie Platt,' then marched indoors to put the kettle on and warm her hands. Annie stood on, alone and solemn in the snow, uncertain how to proceed. Watching her from the kitchen window, Lillian wondered again if her own baby had gone home from the maternity hospital with another woman five years ago. She wondered if somewhere, not very far from here, there was a little girl with angel features and a lively sense of mischief, running rings around a plodding woman with a porcine nose and an inability to see a joke.

In 1950, when Annie was nine, the family moved to Coventry where Harold was to be manager of the National Provincial Bank. This change in their circumstances was disastrous for Lillian, who felt she'd been transplanted from her native soil into new and adverse growing conditions. Harold brushed off her protestations with firm reassurances that soon the new house, a detached 1920s villa with views on the leafy Kenilworth side of the city, would feel as much like home as the old one. Houses, to Harold, were like cars; it was nothing but a treat to buy a new one. This one had a dining room with panelling; he was certain such a house didn't exist in Hoyland.

'But I don't know a soul,' Lillian wailed, sitting in bed as he dressed for another working day. She watched him, suddenly loathing the prissy way he tied a double Windsor knot then tugged at his collar and cuffs until everything was just so. 'I liked Hawshaw Lane and that's where I want to live.'

'Remember, Lillian, that you didn't like Hawshaw Lane when we moved there. In fact,' he paused his activity and looked directly at her tragic reflection in the oval wall mirror, 'you said you didn't know a soul.' Harold smiled, pleased with himself.

'I didn't, but now I do, and I don't want to start all over again. I'm lonely.' She sounded petulant, but she felt her sorrow very deeply. She felt, too, that Harold was an unfeeling monster, by the standards of her own heightened sensibilities. His stolid face registered no sympathy, not a scrap.

'You've Annie for company, after school,' he said, which to Lillian only underlined how little he understood. 'And you can have a daily char. Put an advertisement in the *Evening Telegraph*.'

'You're a brute, Harold. You have less feeling than a clod of earth.' She threw herself sideways across the bed and buried her face in a cushion, spoiling the velvet with her tears. Harold turned. Histrionics made him uncomfortable. Ungovernable emotion was a sign of spinelessness, and even after eleven years with Lillian, he hadn't altered his view on this matter. Backbone was generally what was required in any given situation.

'Lillian,' he said, sternly now because he wished to end the scene, 'there's many a woman would swap places with you.'

'Find me one then, and arrange it,' she said, so Harold left her to stew and on his way out passed Annie sitting on the wooden stairs which curved down in an ostentatious sweep to the hallway. She pressed herself against the posts to make room for him and he stopped and looked down at her pale, round face. She hadn't fussed at all when they'd flitted from Hoyland. She'd got on with it, made the best of things. It was the only trait that Harold valued about his daughter, this silent acceptance of her lot. Unsmilingly they regarded each other.

'Annie,' he said.

She started, surprised to be spoken to.

'Make your mother a cup of tea then sit with her while she drinks it,' he said.

From the bedroom, Lillian's voice came at them like a shrill wind. 'Don't bother,' she shouted. 'I'm not that desperate.'

Harold pursed his lips and dithered for a moment and Annie watched him closely to see what he would do, which turned out to be nothing. He didn't even risk another look at his little girl to see how she'd taken this latest insult, but merely continued on down the stairs, along the hall and out of the front door to the safety of the outside world, where his status as a man to be reckoned with was inviolable. Annie was pleased he'd gone. She was perfectly reconciled to her mother's casual unkindness, perfectly used to solitude.

'Ann-nie?'

Her mother was calling her now in a different, wheedling tone, the one Annie recognised as repentant. She didn't answer, but stood and crept away down the stairs, treading delicately, silent in her ankle socks. At the door she slipped on wellington boots and coat, and took herself off on the long walk to the secret spot she believed was hers alone. She had to walk for ages and the wind was cold and raw on her face, but then she was there, on the fringes of the countryside outside the city, where a shallow, narrow river left the outside world and passed through a culvert to flow in the dark, underneath Coventry. She squatted in her boots and posted sticks and leaves through the teeth of the culvert, and said goodbye to each and every one of them. She wondered where they'd end up. She wondered, too, what it could be like for a river to be sent out of sight, forced underground, away from the sunlight and the sparrows and the tender, dipping boughs of the willow tree.

Two years later, on a dank late November morning, Lillian escaped. On the surface of it, she was merely answering a distress call from her sister Doreen, whose fourth child was due any day and whose husband Bill was refusing to pay for a mother's help, let alone a nanny. In her heart, however, Lillian was making a run for it. Bill and Doreen lived humbly and frugally in a Peckham terrace – she had married him on an impulse before his mean streak had revealed itself – and ordinarily Lillian wouldn't dream of staying with them. But Peckham, truthfully, was only an excuse, a staging post, for beyond Peckham, who knew what adventures lay? To Harold, though, she said she was going to poor Doreen's aid. No, she had no idea when she would be back.

'Well I'm not sure about this,' Harold said, as though he had any bearing on the matter.

'Don't be silly,' Lillian said. 'I'm off and that's that.'

Harold puffed himself up to look bigger. 'And how am I meant to manage in the meantime?' He was thinking not so much of practicalities, because Lillian was as good as useless around the house, but how it would look – his wife absent indefinitely, and no one on his arm at the National Provincial Christmas do.

'There's Annie,' she said. 'And Mrs Binley can hold the fort.'

He gave her a measuring stare and she met it with triumphant defiance. She was offering him their dullard daughter and the charlady, just as he had offered the same to her two years previously. Annie, who was witness to this exchange, wanted to ask about the pantomime. Her mother was supposed to be taking her to see Julie Andrews and Norman Wisdom in *Jack and the Beanstalk* at the Coventry Hippodrome. The tickets were propped behind the heavily ornate mantel clock in the dining room. It'd been planned for Annie's birthday and it was all she wanted – not just to go, but also to go with her mother, on a winter's night close to Christmas, when the street lamps were glowing and the air smelled of fried onions. Lillian would wear her fur jacket and her red court shoes and Annie would wear her frilled tartan pinafore and her plum wool coat. She'd been looking forward to it since August.

'But Mother,' Annie said, 'what about my birthday?' Lillian looked at her, astonished, not because she'd forgotten about the tickets – although she had – but because Annie's voice had a sort of forthright urgency that was quite new.

'What about it?'

'Will you be home by then? It's just, the pantomime...'

'Aha!' said Harold. 'Indeed. Of course. The panto-mime. Just so.' He rocked on his heels, happy that Lillian's trip to London would now be finite: confident, all of a sudden, that his wife would be home in time for the bank's gala night. His smug certainty was maddening to Lillian. Plus, she felt cross with Annie for choosing this particular moment, of all possible moments, to finally speak up for herself.

'Oh that,' Lillian said. 'Mrs Binley can take you.' And then, because she didn't want to give the game away, she added, 'Or I will.'

Little Annie narrowed her eyes as if she was trying to see into her mother's heart, and Lillian felt so uncomfort-able that she had to turn away and make a performance of fastening her suitcase and buttoning her coat and checking the time on her gold wristwatch.

By the end of the second week of Lillian's absence, Mrs Binley was ruling the roost. Annie had always quite liked their charlady, who sang while she cleaned and called Annie 'm'duck'. She had two grown sons she called 'use-less lumps' and a parrot in a cage, and she tried to make Annie smile by telling her the things he said, such as 'much obliged' when she passed him a monkey nut. But now a creeping unease settled on the child as with each consecutive day, Mrs Binley grew perkier and ever more comfortable in those parts of the house that she wouldn't ordinarily inhabit. Her own home was two bus journeys away from the Platts and this was perfectly fine when she came Mondays, Wednesdays and Fridays, ten till three. But Mrs Platt had asked her to do six days a week with Sundays off, and the only sensible way forward was for Mrs Binley to live in. This she had done so eagerly, so *greedily* you might say, that Annie wondered if she'd planned it all along: a sort of domestic annexation, such as Hitler pulled off with Austria. Mrs Binley had been given a guest bedroom at the back of the house on the second floor, but one afternoon Annie crept in from school and found her rifling through Lillian's wardrobe while in the air around her hung motes of fragrance from a recent puff of Je Reviens. Another time she found the bathroom occupied and, issuing from inside, the unmistakable splish-splosh sounds of Mrs Binley wallowing happily in water. But worst of all was the day Annie came home and discovered the char lady comfortably settled in the drawing room with Lillian and Harold's wedding album open in front of her on the coffee table.

'Look here,' she said to Annie, without a speck of embarrassment, only budging up on the couch and patting the seat so that Annie had to join her. 'Your mum picked two fat bridesmaids! Oldest trick in the book that one.'

'This one's Auntie Doreen,' said Annie in spite of her disapproval, pointing at a plump blonde girl who looked hot in her tight pink taffeta. 'She's the one having the baby.'

Mrs Binley looked a little closer. 'Is that right? You'd never know they were related. Mind you,' she said, glancing across at Annie, 'you'd never know you were, either. It's a shame when looks skip a generation. You have a look of your aunt, though.' She licked her finger and turned the page. Arm in arm, Lillian and Harold stared out at them with oddly shocked expressions, as if they were witness to something startling behind the photographer. The picture didn't flatter either of them and Mrs Binley gave a sharp snort of laughter through her nose, then she licked her finger again and drew it across the stiff black paper, leaving a snail-trail of spit and creasing the corner of the page as she turned it. The next photograph was of Lillian alone and this time her face was lively and natural, and no one could say she looked anything but beautiful. She was laughing at the camera and her delicate crown of waxy white flowers looked to Annie as if it had been twisted and threaded by the nimble fingers of woodland sprites.

'Humph,' said Mrs Binley. 'It's cockeyed, that head-piece.'

Annie sat on quietly, but inside she fumed.

5

By the time Annie got to Fletcher's Bakery the custard slices were all gone, so she bought a chocolate éclair, and wasn't sorry to have the decision made for her. She wondered about a loaf, and then remembered that Michael had stopped eating bread. Every morning now he had a large bowl of pale porridge, the leftovers of which clung to the insides of the saucepan like wallpaper paste in a decorator's bucket. The shop assistant was a young girl, who asked Annie if that was all, in a disbelieving tone, as if one éclair was hardly worth spoiling the paper bag she put it in.

'Thank you, yes,' Annie said. 'It's just a little treat for later – I don't make a habit of eating cream cakes and I was thinking about a sliced granary as well but we don't get through so much bread as we used to now my son's given it up.'

This was too much, Annie knew. She had a habit of sometimes running on with a one-sided conversation, words spilling unchecked from her mouth in a torrent of inconsequence. The girl behind the counter said, 'Sixty-four pee,' and held out her hand; then while Annie fumbled in her purse and counted out the coins into the girl's palm, she turned her head and stared moodily out of the shop window.

It felt like a relief to be back out on the street. Annie trotted back to her car and all the things she might have said to that rude young woman ran through her head, so that by the time she unlocked the door and climbed in, she felt all the satisfaction of having actually said them. The inside of her car had the pungent, fishy smell of wet dog so she drove home with the windows down and Finn pushed his head over the back of her seat and closed his eyes in a state of bliss, twitching his nostrils in the wind. In Beech Street she buzzed the windows up again and pulled up outside her house.

'There we are,' she said. 'Home sweet home.'

Annie's house was the only one on the street with a front porch. She'd had it built soon after moving in, because with an extra door she felt safer, more battened down. What burglar would bother picking two locks when he could go to any other dwelling, left or right, and pick his way into only one? But the porch had also brought a dash of unexpected character to the bland little dwelling; its bottle-green eaves were like upward-tilting, quizzical eyebrows. *Home so soon?* it seemed to say.

She let Finn out of the boot of the car, and hung on to his collar with one hand while she fumbled in her handbag for the door key. Once, Finn had shot off up the street after a jogger, woofing and careening about so that the man – furiously silent – had to halt and wait for Annie to catch them up, red-faced with exertion and embarrassment. Now the dog stood docile and patient but she clung on anyway, which meant she had to stoop at an awkward angle while blindly delving through the innards of her capacious leather bag. Gingerly she groped around the éclair, trying not to squash it, and when the door flew open from the inside, it was so unexpected she thought she might die of shock. She let go of the dog and stood up straight, and Michael loomed over her, filling the doorframe with his aggravation.

'Well finally,' he said, spitting the words. 'I don't know where the dickens you were, but you've been gone so long that the nursing home fetched me out of work!' His voice soared high with indignation as he reached the end of his sentence and Annie stared stupidly at him, catatonic with confusion. Finn, released, walked calmly into the house, brushing against Michael's trousers as he passed and leaving a swathe of fine golden hairs on the grey flannel.

'I was only just there, not long ago,' Annie said, finding her voice. 'What's happened?'

'He's had some sort of fit and now he's unconscious. Twitching and foaming when the nurse found him.'

Annie looked sceptical. He must be making up the details, she thought; they never would use that language over the phone.

'So where were you?' her son asked again. 'I have to say, Mother, this isn't part of my brief.'

'Pardon?' She really had no idea what he meant. Brief? What could he be getting at?

'This,' he said, flinging his arms wide. 'Rushing back here because you were nowhere to be found, being interrupted in my workplace by a call that you should be dealing with, my whole day going to pot. I've a lesson in Gawber that starts in fifteen minutes and not a hope in hell of getting there now.'

'Well I only went to Fletcher's,' Annie said. She was standing outside still, and she shivered suddenly with cold. 'And I was at Glebe Hall only just before that. It must've happened just after I left.' In fact, she thought, they probably hadn't even bothered ringing her at home; they would've phoned Michael's mobile phone instead. 'Can I come in?' she asked, stepping over the threshold at the same time. 'It's bitter, this wind.'

What annoyed her was that Michael was here and not at the nursing home. He must have cycled all the way home, when he could have gone instead to the home and been better placed from there to get to Gawber. Oh yes, he was an awkward customer all right; Annie could always rely on Michael to turn a molehill into a mountain. He'd shut the door now and was standing in the porch in a huff, his arms folded, spoiling for an argument. He was so like his father, Annie thought. Vince had always been quick to fly off the handle, too. How strange it was that such things could be genetic, in the same way as the size of your nose or the colour of your hair.

'If you'd only get yourself a mobile,' Michael was saying. 'If you'd only catch up with the twenty-first century.'

'We have an answerphone and, look, it isn't flashing.' They both looked at the telephone; the red light was steady, not blinking.

'So? It doesn't alter the fact that you weren't here to answer it.'

'Do we have time for a cup of tea?' she asked, ignoring his tone entirely.

'Time?'

'Yes, I mean before we go.'

46

'Go where?'

'To Glebe Hall.'

'Glebe Hall!' he said, in the manner of a man pushed to the very limits of his sanity. 'Glebe Hall! I'm not going, you are.'

'Well, but if you can't get to Gawber in time,' she said, 'you could come to Barnsley with me?' She knew quite well he wouldn't, but asking him was her oblique way of letting him know she knew.

'I've to be at choir practice by five,' he said.

Annie looked at the wall clock, which said half past one.

'I'm sorry, Mother,' he said, meaning that he wasn't sorry at all. 'I'm not risking missing another appointment today.'

Annie suddenly felt unutterably weary. She felt every one of her seventy-three years, and more besides. She'd drive back to the nursing home – because how would it look if neither she nor Michael turned up to show an interest? – but she couldn't do it just yet. She walked into the kitchen still wearing her fleece and pushed the switch on the kettle. She wondered if she should change out of her dog-walking clothes; she wondered how she might eat her éclair without Michael seeing; and she wondered, at last, how Vince was, and whether he might finally die.

The traffic lights in Hoyland always seemed to be red, and if they *were* green as Annie approached them, they'd craftily change, barely pausing on amber in their haste to stop her. She knew well enough that this was a fanciful notion, but it felt personal, and if she'd had the nerve, she'd just sail on through in blithe defiance. When she'd first lived in Hoyland, in the big house on Hawshaw Lane, there hadn't been any need for traffic lights at this crossroads because hardly anyone apart from the Platts owned a car. Back in those days their gleaming oxblood Rover had been enough of a novelty to make children in the street tear after it, hooting and squawking like chickens. Annie had a sudden image of the back of her father's head, his oiled hair as dark and shiny as a bowling ball. She was always in the back seat, directly behind him; even if her mother wasn't with them, the front passenger seat wouldn't be offered to Annie but would be occupied instead by her father's hat. Harold Platt drove with a stately unconcern for the riff-raff on the pavement, although Annie always sank low in the seat and tried to be invisible. Imagine, she thought now, if he'd had to draw to a halt at these lights and let the children catch him up. He would have stared rigidly ahead, refusing to be distracted, while Lillian would have fumed at the inconvenience of being told by a system of coloured lights if and when she was allowed to go. Annie's memories of her mother were few, and those she had were probably planted in her mind by old photographs rather than real happenings, but she did remember Lillian's dash, her pizazz, her way of never settling to anything that required her to be still.

The lights changed, and Annie set off, throwing the car accidentally into third gear and immediately stalling. In a fluster she tried again for first, but forgot to put the clutch down and the gearbox made a grating noise that ran up her spine like nails on a blackboard. The cars behind her began overtaking, some of the drivers shaking their heads at her; she could see them at the periphery of her vision though she tried her hardest not to look. Then the passenger door opened and Josie got in.

'Clutch,' she said, and pointed at Annie's left foot.

'Oh!' Annie said. She engaged the clutch and slipped the gear stick smoothly into first.

'But don't go yet,' Josie said. 'The lights are red again.'

She was half-laughing as if this was a funny mistake that absolutely anyone could have made and Annie found this so comforting that she had to rummage for a tissue in her pocket and blow her nose briskly, to prevent tears from coming.

'Why are you here?' she said, which came out a little snippy, unintentionally so.

'I was – I *am* – on my way to the garage,' Josie said. 'The car's ready. I caught a bus to here and now you can drop me off if you don't mind?'

'Yes. I mean, no. I don't mind at all.'

'You?'

Annie looked at her, confused.

'Where you off to?' Josie said.

'Oh, me, I'm visiting Vince.'

'Ah, your husband! Where is he?'

Annie gripped the steering wheel tightly and tried to remember what she'd told Josie and Sandra about Vince in the short time she'd known them. Not much, more than likely, and certainly not the truth. She had fallen into the habit decades ago of smoothly telling lies about Vince: it was hard, now, to break it. The subject of his dementia, his addled existence at Glebe Hall, had simply adhered itself to the layers and layers of shame and shock and sorrow laid down during their marriage like the strata of sedimentary rock.

'Hospital,' she said now. Well, it wasn't an out and out lie, she thought; for all she knew, he might have been moved there by now anyway.

'Annie! You didn't say.' Josie leaned in and placed a hand on her shoulder. 'What happened?'

Annie's face was an artful mask of discreet suffering. 'A stroke,' she said, then added, 'a small one.'

Josie gave a murmur of concern.

'How is he?'

'Poorly,' Annie said. 'Michael says ...' and then she stopped speaking, because she didn't, in fact, mean to repeat what Michael had said.

'Your son?'

Annie stared at the road ahead.

'Is he there already? Or would you like me to come with you? I mean, for company?'

Annie pushed up the indicator, to make a right turn into the garage. 'Here we are,' she said, too brightly. 'And there's your car.' She pulled up and stopped in front of Josie's Citroën, which was facing them on the forecourt. Through the murky window of the office a mechanic saluted their arrival. Annie smiled briskly at Josie and said, 'No, I don't want you to come with me, no need for that.'

'Oh right, well okay then, if you're sure.' Josie hesitated for a moment, as though reluctant to accept Annie's refusal, then she opened the passenger door. 'So, let me know if I can do anything,' she said. 'You know, feed Finn, or whatnot.'

'Oh heavens, I'll be home before dark,' Annie said, and this sounded wrong, too brusque and uncaring, so she added, 'all being well.' She longed for Josie to shut the car door and allow her to drive away, so she looked squarely at her, locking eyes, and said, 'Cheerio then.'

'Bye,' Josie said, a little uncertainly. She was out of the car now and seemed about to close the door, but then she ducked her head down again to speak.

'I do need to get on,' Annie said, heading off any further insistence that she might need company.

'No, I know, sorry, it's just—'

'What?'

Josie pointed at Annie's face. 'You've cream on your chin,' she said.

6

At Glebe Hall there was still the throb of unusual excitement that always followed a drama and Vince had been moved to a room close to the staff office: the room they used for desperate cases. Oh yes, Annie knew the drill all right. There were degrees of sickness in this home just as there were degrees of senility, and you could gauge a person's chances by the sprinting distance between them and the nurses. There was a black rubber wedge holding Vince's door open, so Annie could hear the rise and fall of conversation among the staff, and an occasional swell of canned laughter from a television. The nurses could all see right into the room simply by looking across the hallway, and Annie had adopted a look of grave compassion so they wouldn't think her heartless.

Vince was asleep, his grey features slack against the starchy white pillow. He'd had these episodes before: Tee-Ai-Ays, Annie called them, like the nurses did. She'd forgotten what the letters stood for, but she knew they were mini strokes and that each successive one shortened his life. This time it had lasted longer, the duty matron told her.

'What happens is, they increase in frequency and severity then usually end in a massive stroke,' she said cheerfully. 'More than likely, there'll be a final big one that he won't come back from. I've seen it many a time. He's a poorly man.'

She was a plain-speaking woman but Annie didn't mind; it was only the truth. Certainly Vince *looked* poorly. Annie sat at his bedside and stared at his face; it had a ghastly pallor, like old putty. Why didn't he just get on and die? This drawn-out stagger towards the end of life was such a nuisance for everyone, yet here he lay, neither knowing nor caring who anyone was, snoozing his way on to fight another day. Well he'd outstayed his welcome, thought Annie: outstayed his welcome and cost her all her savings from the sale of that big house in Coventry. She didn't like Vince: hadn't liked him for years. Actually, correction; she *preferred* him in his present state to how he was in his prime, but even so, if it wasn't for how it'd look, she wouldn't be sitting here at his bedside like the grieving wife, she'd be at home with her feet up, watching *Cash in the Attic*.

'Bless him, he looks peaceful enough now.'

This was the matron, who'd stepped in through the open door, almost soundless in her sturdy rubber-soled lace-ups. Annie flushed pink and gave a sheepish smile. Hastily she took Vince's limp hand in hers.

'I was wondering, Mrs Doyle, if you might let your other son know.'

'Andrew? Know what?'

'Did you say he lived in Australia?'

'That's right, he does.' Annie smiled, but she was plainly bemused.

'Well, he might want to say goodbye to his dad.'

'Oh!' Annie said, as if this was a nice thought but a

ludicrous one. 'He doesn't come to England really. At least, not often.'

'I'm just saying, it might be harder on him than either of you realise if he only gets here ...' She paused then, and lowered her voice to a whisper, sparing Vince's feelings. 'Y'know, afterwards.' On his bed, Vince snored peacefully.

This was a new idea entirely for Annie – not Vince's likely demise, but Andrew's possible arrival – and it immediately summoned a legion of small, practical worries, which formed a jostling queue in her head. Front of the line was making the call to Australia, a feat to which Annie had never felt equal. All those digits! So easy to muddle them up and expose yourself to the horrors of a stranger's voice on a wrong number. Then, if you did everything right and got straight through, there was a disconcerting delay on the line, so that you didn't know when to speak and when to listen.

'I'm just saying,' the matron said again. 'At least if you let Andrew know, he could decide what he wants to do. I expect you'd like to see him anyway, wouldn't you?'

This seemed presumptuous on the matron's part, although she was right; Annie very much *would* like to see Andrew, now that his name had been conjured out of thin air. Where he would stay, whether he would want to bring the boys and Bailey, how Michael might react to such a plan – all these concerns took an obliging step backwards to allow her to see her younger son in her mind's eye, clear as day: blonde where Michael was dark, plump where Michael was thin; warm and funny where Michael ... well now, she thought; it wouldn't do if we were all the same.

*

Contrary to what she told Josie, she wasn't home before dark. A doctor had been sent for to have another look at Vince and everyone assumed that Annie would want to wait for his verdict, and so she did. Then he had to see another two patients before finally summoning Annie to the quiet room to explain Vince's prognosis. The doctor was sixteen; at least that was how he appeared to Annie. Traces of acne lingered on his forehead and his brown hair was spiked with gel. But his badge said Dr Hewitt, and he spoke with the detached authority of a medical man, confirming what the matron had already explained. Could she pop in again tomorrow, he asked, at about four? Vince's test results would be back; the picture would be clearer. Annie listened, nodded, asked one or two dutiful questions, but all the while she was thinking about her dog, alone in the empty house. By the time she got away it was past seven o'clock and yet she couldn't hurry, because the street lamps and headlights conspired to dazzle her, and so she drove anxiously, peering through the windscreen at the road ahead as if she was creeping through a blizzard.

Finn's joy filled the hallway when finally she let herself into the house. He crooned at her, a canine song of love, and she stooped to reward his devotion with a hug, pressing the side of her face against the golden heft of his solid head. If she ever had to leave Finn alone in the house she always left the television on for company, and many was the time she'd asked Michael to do the same, but he never did. Michael believed in saving the planet through small economies and also – doubtless more to the point – he didn't like the dog. Annie, who only wanted for

Finn what she would want for herself, couldn't see how a bit of daytime telly could melt a polar ice cap. That this house was Annie's own, that her wishes might overrule Michael's – these were points she never made, although they ran through her mind now.

The answerphone on the hall table was blinking and Annie stared at it. She wondered if it was the home; could Vince have had another turn, so soon after the last? She unbuttoned her coat and shrugged it off, then hung it on the stand. She pressed the red light, and the machine told her she had two new messages. 'Two,' Annie said wonderingly to Finn, who sat by her side to listen. Then a woman's voice filled the small hall.

'Hi, Annie, hope this is you, it's just me, I wondered if you'd like to come for lunch tomorrow, nothing special, just a bit of—' there was a pause here and a laugh, '—well, actually, I've no idea yet what we'll eat, but do come, and if you want to bring Finn that's fine. About half twelve? Call me back if you can't, but just come, okay? Bye.'

Annie looked at Finn, who smiled. 'Who the dickens?' she said. Anxiety rose in her breast at the thought not only of a lunch invitation, but from a person she didn't know. She wouldn't go, of course, but how could she call back to say no? Perhaps the message wasn't intended for her – perhaps it was a wrong number? Except they'd called her Annie. Could there be another Annie, and she herself the wrong one? She patted her heart in consternation, and pressed the light for the second message, and the same voice piped up again.

'Sorry, it's Josie Jones. I don't think I said. Bye then. Oh, and thanks for the lift, and I really hope your husband's feeling better. Bye.'

Oh, it was Josie. Now Annie felt light with relief at the mystery solved, although it still left her with the chore of ringing back to decline. If only Josie had said it the other way round: ring if you can come, don't ring if you can't. *That* was what she should've said. As it was, Annie would have to make up an excuse, and pull it off convincingly over the phone. She felt a little stab of annoyance and resolved to do nothing at all until she'd had something to eat; nobody could be expected to think straight on an empty stomach.

The opening and closing of the two front doors woke her with a jolt. She'd nodded off in front of the news, which she always found soporific. It was the familiarity of it that caused her eyelids to close: politics, the economy, crime and corruption. You could swap one night's news with another and nobody would notice. The one thing that could hold her attention was a really good weather story; that is, a *bad* weather story. Floods, hurricanes, unseasonal snowfall; these things were interesting. Well, and the royals, too.

'Michael?' Her voice, drawn from the depths of sleep, croaked and broke, and it sounded as if she was upset, so instead of just saying, 'What?' as he usually would have done, Michael came into the room. The cold had made the end of his nose berry red.

'Oh, you're not weeping,' he said. 'It sounded like you were crying just then. I thought the old bastard might've popped his clogs.'

'Michael!'

He grinned at her, showing sharp teeth, then bent

double and snapped off his bicycle clips. 'How is the old goat then?'

'They want me to call Andrew,' she said, knowing this would wipe the smile off his face, which it did.

'Why? What can he do about it?'

'Nothing at all, except come to say goodbye.'

'Oh, how touching,' Michael said. He dropped his cycle clips into his jacket pocket, inhaled deeply through flared nostrils – a new thing, the result of recent singing lessons; at last he knew how to breathe correctly, he said, which caused Annie to wonder how on earth he'd managed for the past fifty years – then stretched out his arms and flourished his hands until the wrists clicked. Annie looked away. She wondered why this elaborate ritual didn't embarrass him. On the television the news had ended and a noisy panel show was starting; young men and women, laughing at each other's jokes even before the show had properly got going. Annie tutted and switched them off.

'What I fancy,' Michael said, 'is a cup of green tea.' Annie got up from the sofa.

'So anyway,' she said, as she walked past him to the kitchen. 'About Andrew.'

'You're going to ask me to call him, aren't you?'

Michael had followed her into the kitchen. In fact she *had* been about to ask exactly that, but his tone needled her so she changed tack.

'As a matter of fact I'm not,' she said. She filled the kettle with fresh water, set it on its plastic base and flicked the switch. In Coventry, she and Vince had had a range, and a flat-bottomed kettle that whistled when it boiled. The range had heavy chrome lids to cover the two hotplates, and Andrew used to like to sit on the cooler of them, cross-legged and chubby, like a little blonde Buddha.

'I might ring him, when I've made your tea.'

'Might you?' He laughed, as if he found this idea unlikely.

'It's been a long time since they were all here.'

'Oh, I see. First it's just Andrew, now it's the whole tribe.'

She gave the spotless worktop a wipe. 'I'd like to see those little boys,' she said.

'Well they won't know you.'

She glanced up at him. He looked a good deal like Vince, Annie thought. At fifty, Vince had had the same lean face, with those same deep grooves running from his nose to the corners of his mouth, and when he smiled, he looked cruel, not amused. It was the same with Michael.

She dropped a tea bag into a mug and filled it up with hot water from the kettle. Green tea: what nonsense. There was a box of spearmint tea bags in the cupboard too, and some camomile. Annie viewed them all with deep suspicion, especially the camomile, which had the same stale urine smell as Vince's mattress at Glebe Hall. Now she fished out the sodden bag and dropped it neatly into the compost tin, then slid the mug along the counter to Michael. He took it.

'I'm expecting a delivery tomorrow,' he said. 'Some new sheet music and scores, so if you could make sure you're in to sign for it.'

'What time?'

'Oh, no idea. They never say, do they? Does it matter?'

She was so much smaller than Michael. He had to

look down to make eye contact, and she had to look up. Perhaps, she thought now, this is why he is so ... so ... she searched for the word: *disdainful*. He treats me with disdain, she thought.

'Well I won't be in at lunchtime,' she said, suddenly inspired and emboldened.

He raised a sceptical eyebrow.

'No, you see I'm invited out to lunch tomorrow.'

There was a short silence and then, 'By whom?' he said.

'A friend.'

'But you have no friends.'

'Yes I do,' she said, calm in the face of his cruelty. 'And one of them has asked me to lunch. She's called Josie Jones.'

He shook his head and pouted to indicate that this name meant nothing to him.

'You don't know her,' Annie said proudly. 'And then I'm due back at Glebe Hall at four, so you see it's a busy day. Now, I think I'll ring Andrew.'

She walked back into the little square hallway and Michael stared over the rim of his mug. Finn, warm from a deep sleep in front of the fire, wandered out of the living room and appeared to wink at her, which she took as encouragement. She put on her reading glasses and found Andrew's number in the book: the only one on the D page. Andrew Doyle it said, in Annie's quaintly slanting cursive, and it struck her now that this made him seem like an acquaintance, not a son. He should be under A for Andrew.

'There'll be nobody in,' Michael said, walking past her and carrying his mug of tea upstairs. Annie looked at the clock.

'I should think there will be, at this time of night,' she said.

'Eleven-hour time difference, Mother,' he said lightly. 'Is it beyond your wit to remember that?'

She *had* forgotten, he was right. Still, she went ahead and dialled the number then clutched the receiver to her ear, willing her heart to slow, willing her distant son to answer. It rang and rang, reedy and remote, all those thousands of miles away in Byron Bay, and nobody picked up because there, it was twenty to ten in the morning, Andrew and Bailey were at work and the boys were at school. Annie let it ring on until Michael's bedroom door clicked shut, until her ear felt hot and squashed, until a long, flat tone told her the call had been ended.

7

Lillian Platt's brother-in-law Bill Marshall was on the production line at the Denette Works in Peckham Rye. The company made bespoke baby carriages, so in spite of the family's lack in almost every other material regard, the infant Edward – born quickly and easily at home on 3 December – enjoyed the comforts of a fine white and silver perambulator, which took up a great deal of space in the narrow front hall of the Edwardian terrace. He was Doreen and William's fourth child and the others were all still under five years old. When Lillian arrived – before she'd even taken off her coat – Doreen went back to bed, with a laundry basket for the baby on the floor beside her. Bill Marshall seemed to work all hours, leaving the house each day with an air of weary heroism, as if the manufacture of baby carriages was key to the nation's economic recovery. They had no char – Bill wouldn't pay – and the household existed in a state of permanent and chaotic uproar. But now here was Lillian, onto whose narrow shoulders Doreen had immediately piled an intolerable burden of responsibilities. She was expected to rise with the three older children, give them breakfast, wash, clothe and entertain them throughout the long day while bringing order to the domestic disarray and getting on with a cooked meal for Bill. None of the children were old enough for school. There were two girls and now, with Edward, two boys, which was precisely the combination of offspring that Lillian had once planned for herself, although now, among this unruly crowd of children, she couldn't imagine what she'd been thinking. Doreen's lot were always egging each other on to mischief, and if one child settled down to some quiet activity, another one bowled up and wrecked it. Lillian, unequipped for the challenge, felt a rosy nostalgia for the long, quiet afternoons she'd spent with her own child, when neither of them knew what to say to the other. Looking back Lillian realised there was a lot to be said for silence. Not that she planned to return to Coventry, however. That page had turned; a new chapter had begun, and her grave little girl must do without her. But five days into the visit to her sister she realised, too, that she must look beyond Peckham Rye – and quickly – if this abandonment of hearth and home was to be classified as an adventure.

She took herself upstairs to Doreen, who was sitting in bed nursing the baby. The room had a curdled smell and her sister's face had the pale and plump appearance of an unbaked bap, her dark eyes like raisins embedded in the dough. She blinked them in surprise to see Lillian.

'I've been thinking,' Lillian said.

'Where are the children?' Doreen asked.

'Oh they're all right. I was just saying, I've been thinking I'd like to visit the West End. Seems silly not to, now I'm here.'

'Yes, but where *are* they?'

'Heavens, Doreen, do I need to watch their every move?'

'Susan's only fifteen months,' Doreen said.

'So, anyway, I'm going up to the West End.'

'Yes, you said. You'll need the number twelve bus, but I don't know why you'd want the bother.' She pulled the baby off her breast and hoiked him upright, patting his back briskly with her free hand.

'Can't you give him a bottle?' Lillian said. 'I couldn't bear to be sucked at like a cow in a milking parlour.'

'No, I dare say,' Doreen said.

'It's just so dreary,' Lillian said, returning to her original theme. 'Nothing ever happens.' The baby's face, turned towards her and pressed against his mother's shoulder, looked like a squashed peach, and milk streamed onto Doreen's yellow nylon nightie from one corner of his mouth. Lillian looked away in distaste and wandered over to the window. She lifted the net and accidentally met the malevolent eyes of the Marshalls' ginger cat, staring up at her from the garden wall.

'Nothing going on?' Doreen said. 'You came to lend a hand, didn't you? There's three kiddies wanting their middle-mornings downstairs I should think.' Baby Edward belched wetly and Doreen said, 'Well done my little Teddy bear, other side?'

Lillian dropped the net curtain and turned back to her sister. 'He's already leaking milk,' she said. 'I'm certain he's had enough.'

'What?' Doreen dragged her gaze from the baby's face and looked at Lillian.

'Never mind. So, I'll go tomorrow afternoon.'

Doreen sighed, and said again, 'I don't know why you want the bother.'

'As I said ...' Lillian waved a listless arm towards the window. 'It's drab here.'

'Well pardon me,' said Doreen. She had a second soft chin beneath the original one and Lillian didn't know how her sister could bear it.

'I thought you and Bill lived more of a London life.'

'Yes, Lillian, we do, and it's not that much different from anywhere else. You always did think the grass was greener.'

'He should let you hire a char. I have a char. It frees you up for other things.'

'Not likely,' Doreen said. She busied herself attaching the baby's mouth to her other ample breast. 'Bill saves his money for a rainy day. He'd cut a currant in half, would Bill.'

'Do you ever think of running away?'

Doreen laughed.

'No, I mean it, Doreen. Can't you picture yourself somewhere else?'

There was a fanciful note in Lillian's voice that Doreen found irritating.

'Don't be daft,' she said. 'There's some Rich Tea biscuits in a jar in the pantry. They can all have one to dip in their milk, and I'll have a couple with a coffee, if you're making one.'

Lillian stalked out of the bedroom, although she paused first at the wall mirror to look at her reflection and confirm that she bore no resemblance whatsoever to her sister.

There was a cold snap the next day, colder than was usual in the city, cold enough to create a pleasant camaraderie among the shoppers at Oxford Circus. There were Christmas decorations strung between the lampposts of Regent Street, and on the corner of Argyll Street an old man was selling sweet blackened roast chestnuts, straight from the brazier.

'Warm yer cockles, darlin'?' he said to Lillian, and when she glanced at him he winked and they shared a complicit laugh, even though he was whiskery and almost toothless, while lovely Lillian was dressed to kill in her red shoes and fur coat. She dropped a few careless coins into his outstretched hand and took a bag of chestnuts, then ate them – nibbling delicately so as not to spoil her crimson lipstick – outside the London Palladium while she gazed at the posters for *Dick Whittington* and suffered a tiny pang of guilt about Annie and her birthday panto tickets. It passed, though, because she felt free and glamorous and charmingly impulsive, and she knew almost without looking that gentlemen in the street turned their heads as they passed, letting their eyes linger, taking her in.

On Great Marlborough Street she was drawn like a moth to the bright festive windows of Liberty, and as she stood there, bathed in golden light, a man in a grey trench coat and black Homburg stopped and said something to her in a warm, confidential tone. Lillian wasn't sure what he said, but it was meant to flatter, that much was clear, and he wasn't English, she could tell that too: Italian, perhaps, or French – continental, anyway. He had a bit of a cheek, she thought, sidling up to her like that, but on the other hand he had a look of Cary Grant and a sweet lopsided smile and his teeth, she noticed, were perfectly white. She looked up into his dark brown eyes, and ten minutes later they were side by side on a banquette in the grillroom of the Café Royal, sharing a bottle of Pol Roger. He was from Milan and his name was Arturo; whenever he said 'Lillian' he lingered over the syllables; when he wanted a waiter, he raised a hand and clicked, just once; when a dozen oysters arrived at their table, he fed them to her and licked his own lips as she swallowed.

This was living a London life, thought Lillian. This was what she meant.

They emerged, three hours later, into a dense and hostile freezing fog, and even under the weight of her fur Lillian shivered convulsively with cold. The Regent Street that had earlier been a-bustle with life now seemed treacle-slow and silent as the seabed, altogether eerie. Lillian, hanging squiffily onto the arm of her new beau, had no idea how to get back to Peckham; the stop at which she'd disembarked from the number twelve bus was a world away in these conditions, and anyway that journey and the lumbering vehicle that had brought her here already seemed to belong to another lifetime. Wordlessly she placed herself in Arturo's care, allowing him to lead her to a discreet hotel in Golden Square where she spent a night the like of which she had never known: *Signore e Signora Arturo Bertolli*, he wrote in the book. Lillian lay back and thought of Italy.

She left early the following morning, pleasurably bruised by passion, meaning only to pack her suitcase in Peckham Rye before returning for good to her Italian lover. Arturo's own plans were a little less definite than Lillian's, a little more nebulous. Would he be there, she asked, when she came back this afternoon? He smiled his disarming crooked smile, and she chose to take this as assent. If it was ungallant of him to let her creep un-accompanied from the hotel, then Lillian was oblivious. And even though last night's fog had mingled with the smoke of a million household chimneys so that the city was now shrouded in thick and toxic yellow smog, her spirits remained high, her happiness unassailable, as she inched her way down Regent Street, clinging blindly to the shop fronts, helpless as a lamb.

In Coventry, Harold read aloud snippets from the news-paper at the breakfast table.

'The capital is being choked by a smog so dense that the police are using flares to direct the traffic at Marble Arch,' he said, as if broadcasting to the nation. 'Eleven people have drowned in the Thames by falling accident-ally into the water. The Sadler's Wells theatre was forced to abandon a production of *La Traviata* because the auditorium filled with fog and the audience could not see the stage.'

'Dearie me, fog indoors as well as out? What a carry on.'

This was Mrs Binley, whom Harold now called Agnes. She not only prepared breakfast for Harold and Annie these days, but also joined them at the table. Today, she'd placed herself in Lillian's chair and, unusually for this time of day, she wore make-up: two bright circles of rouge and a vibrant pink lipstick that only emphasised the thinness of her lips. Annie was only eleven years old, but it was perfectly plain to her what the charlady was up to. The child sat in tongue-tied discomfort, chewing and chewing on a piece of toast that simply wouldn't go down, longing for her mother to walk into the room and catch Mrs Binley red handed. She yearned to hear her mother's voice – a laughing, languorous drawl – send Mrs Binley packing.

'Yes, it's creeping in through doors and windows, by all accounts,' Harold said. 'A proper pea souper.' He read on, but silently now. Mrs Binley, unasked, helped him to more tea and he said, 'Thank you, Agnes,' without looking out from behind the newspaper. How had things become so *comfortable* between them? Annie wondered. She swallowed hard, and the wad of toast at last disappeared, scraping the tender sides of her throat as it went.

'Father?' she said in a small voice.

He looked at her as if he'd forgotten she was at the table.

'Yes?'

'When is Mother coming home?'

Harold and Mrs Binley exchanged a brief, adult glance, full of meaning, and Annie felt a bloom of chilly anxiety on her skin. She surreptitiously wiped the palms of her hands on her grey school skirt. Harold cleared his throat.

'You might as well know. We're not precisely sure where your mother is, in fact.'

'She's with Aunt Doreen, Father.'

Harold silenced Mrs Binley's spurt of laughter with a curt shake of the head.

'Your mother went to see the sights two days ago and hasn't yet returned to Peckham Rye,' he said. 'The fog, you see.'

Annie didn't see.

'Do you mean Mother's got lost?'

'I mean just what I said. She hasn't yet returned.' He stared at his daughter without compassion. He believed

Annie to be at the very heart of Lillian's restlessness. It was motherhood that had altered her, not marriage. Now Lillian's behaviour was making him look foolish, but it was Annie he blamed. According to Doreen, who had telephoned the night before with news of his wife's disappearance, Lillian was in a 'funny mood' when she left for the West End: skittish and excitable, and she'd worn her best fur.

'She said she wanted a bit of fun,' Doreen had said. 'I'm sorry Harold, but I think she might have got a bit more than she bargained for. The fog's that bad now you can't see your nose in front of your face. Bill crawled home from work on his hands and knees today, he felt that unsteady.'

Doreen wanted to know if she should let the police know. Yes, Harold had said, certainly she should; but still, he wasn't so much worried as annoyed.

He folded his newspaper with grim precision and placed it on the table, then stood up and left for the bank. Annie looked at Mrs Binley and wondered what she knew about her mother, what grown-up secrets she was harbouring. Mrs Binley caught the child's eye.

'She won't be back, m'duck, if that's what you're wondering.'

Annie, confused by the juxtaposition of friendly tone and hostile words, only stared.

'She's trouble, your mother is. It's written all over her face.'

Annie slid quietly off her chair and brushed the crumbs from her skirt.

'And what do you think you're doing?' Mrs Binley asked, sharply now.

'I have to go to school,' Annie said.

'Not without asking, madam. Sit down and mind your manners.'

Annie sat.

'Well?'

'Please may I get down from the table, Mrs Binley?'

'Yes you may.'

The child slipped from the room. Mrs Binley, alone in the polished comfort of the Platts' panelled dining room, contemplated a future that was increasingly full of interest, full of promise. She'd leave her grown-up sons where they were in the council house, she thought, but she'd bring a few things of her own here; that nice picture of the saucy-looking gipsy girl for the chimney breast, oh and her pet parrot too. He'd be a welcome splash of colour, and a talking point when she received visitors.

8

House keys, car keys, purse, clean handkerchief, Gaviscon in case there were pickled onions. Annie snapped shut the clasp on her best handbag, checked her teeth in the mirror and finally, with a knot of anxiety in her stomach, set off for Josie's house, already fifteen minutes later than the appointed hour. Finn had been waiting in the car for twenty minutes because at the last moment she'd changed her mind about her outfit and had to trot back into the house to reconsider. Three times she got dressed and undressed before settling on a royal blue woollen dress she'd bought for one of Michael's concerts. Then she had had to hang up the blouses and skirts and slacks that she'd tried and rejected. It all took time. She apologised to the dog through the rear-view mirror: explained that she had no idea what people wore when they were invited out for lunch. How could she? In all her life it had never happened before.

What a day, she thought; what a day, and it was only quarter to one. She'd managed to telephone Andrew as well, timing it carefully this time so that after only two rings Bailey's lazy drawl answered with that odd inflection that made everything sound like a question, even her name; 'Bailey Doyle?' she said, as if even she wasn't sure who she was. Annie had said, 'Hello Bailey, this is Annie,' and then, because the habitual delay on the line extended into a longer silence, she added, 'Andrew's mother,' and, after another pause, Bailey had laughed. 'Oh Jiminy, *that* Annie? Hey there! You'll be after Andy? Hang on, I'll get him?' Just like that. No 'How are you?' or 'Nice to hear from you,' just that swift greeting in her laughing voice and then she was off, her voice diminishing in the far-away house, calling for Andrew but calling him Andy.

Still, hearing Andrew had been comforting, and when she told him that his father was extremely poorly and he should think about a visit, he said, 'Ah Mum, what a shame – are you okay?' which was typical of her younger boy, who'd always been considerate, always been kind. Annie had assured him she was fine, but that the matron at Glebe Hall thought Vince didn't have long.

'Right, well, sure I can come,' Andrew had said. 'Should I bring Bailey and the kids? It's high time.'

Annie, tangling her meaning with negatives, said, 'Only if it isn't inconvenient,' so that Andrew hadn't understood, and she'd had to say that yes, they should all come if it suited them.

'Right, good,' Andrew said. 'We're a bit strapped for cash though so we'll have to stay with you again. Better prepare big bro.'

Annie had had a brief premonition of Michael's sour expression when she told him; a glimpse of his inevitable distaste at the boys' paraphernalia – little shoes at the foot of the stairs, colouring books and crayons on the coffee table, plastic animals piled in the shower cubicle.

'I wouldn't want you staying anywhere else,' she said. 'Lovely. But will Bailey actually want to come?'

Andrew had laughed. 'Sure she will.'

'It's just, she didn't know who I was on the phone just now.'

'Jeez, Mum, chill,' Andrew said. 'Sure she knows you, it's just she's been flat out with work, and the boys. Her brain's fried.'

Annie knitted her brow, trying to decipher her son's words. Safer, she decided, to not bother.

'How *are* the kiddies?' she said instead.

'Great, great, brilliant, yeah. Look, sorry to cut you short but I'd better run. I'll Google some flights and get back to you.'

'When do you think you'll call? Only I'm on my way out for lunch.'

Annie had liked the way this sounded, but Andrew only laughed. 'Okay, tell you what, I'll ring you tomorrow with a plan. Same time? Cool. Talk soon, Mum.'

And then he was gone. Google some flights, Annie thought, replacing the receiver; whatever had he meant by that?

Josie lived in a windmill. It stood proudly on a small hill, its sails long gone and replaced by a castellated roof, so that it looked like a stocky Saxon tower standing guard over the village. Before she met Josie, Annie had driven past it many a time, wondering how you'd go about fitting a kitchen in such a place, and now here she was about to find out. There was a curved door, painted the same racing green as all the neighbouring houses, and when Annie knocked, she heard Josie's voice telling her to come on in. She adjusted her dress, checked the shine of her shoes, patted her white curls and pushed open the door, and she knew at once that she'd misjudged everything.

The scene was one of merry chaos. A round wooden table was piled with bric-a-brac, heaps of it, and the floor was cluttered with cardboard cartons. A metal clothes rail was heavily draped with bolts of fabric in bold, earthy colours and on another there were garments, though nothing Annie would call wearable: costumes, rather than clothes; outfits for the stage, for conjurers and fortune tellers. Sandra was there, looking at home on a cracked leather sofa, her feet tucked under her bottom, holding out a glass for a refill from an elderly man in a well-worn flannel shirt and baggy olive-green corduroys held up with black braces, wielding a glass jug of red wine. They all looked at her, clad like the Queen Mother in regal blue wool.

'Wow,' Sandra said flatly, and Annie wished the stone flags of Josie's kitchen would open up to swallow her. She felt like an extra in the wrong play.

'Annie! You look smashing,' Josie said.

She herself was dressed casually – carelessly, even. She had on a man's collarless shirt, striped in blue and white, and a pair of jeans that she'd rolled up above her narrow ankles. On her feet she wore black plimsolls, just like the ones Michael and Andrew used to have for PE when they were at infants' school. It was the oddest get-up Annie had ever seen on a woman, yet she looked charming and dishevelled, and Annie glanced down at her own immaculate blue patent shoes with their sturdy heels and wondered if she had the nerve to simply walk out of this room and never see Josie or Sandra again.

'Glass of plonk?'

75

This was the man, whom Annie didn't know. She looked at him blankly.

'Alf,' he said, smiling and waggling the glass jug at her, although she didn't have a glass to pour it into, and in any case had never tasted red wine, apart from the occasional sip from a chalice.

'God, I'm useless,' Josie said. 'Annie, Mr Dinmoor, Mr Dinmoor, Annie.' She had a box in her arms so she used her head instead, nodding between the two of them in a comical, exaggerated way.

'It's Alf,' the man said.

'You did say today?' Annie asked Josie.

'Yes!'

She placed the box carefully on the floor then walked up to Annie and startled her with a firm, warm kiss on the cheek. 'And I have lunch all ready for us, but it's mostly still in the fridge, and meanwhile Sandra and Mr Dinmoor have been helping me pack up some stuff. Well,' she said, glancing at Sandra, who was curled like a giant ginger cat on the sofa, 'Mr Dinmoor has.'

'Alf,' said Mr Dinmoor.

'Too many cooks, that's my opinion,' Sandra said. 'Anyway I'm directing from the sidelines.' She yawned and pushed her thick red hair away from her face.

'So, Annie, here, sit.' Josie pulled a chair away from the table and patted it. Annie sat, placing her handbag on her lap. In front of her was an unruly pile of gaudy woven napkins and tablemats and a stack of tarnished brass bowls, their sides faintly etched with an intricate Islamic pattern. The room had a fusty smell, like an attic, or the innards of an ancient wardrobe. Annie felt her mouth pucker and she made an effort to relax the muscles in her face.

'Dispatch day,' Josie said. 'Always a nightmare.'

Annie felt utterly at a loss. She suddenly had no idea why she was here, what was going on, or what she might expect to happen next. At home, there were two slices of Yorkshire ham in the fridge, and a wedge of mature cheddar; she should have stayed put and made herself a sandwich. Sandra stared openly from her comfortable nest of cushions on the sofa, not in an unfriendly way, but rather as if Annie was a museum exhibit, an artefact from a different culture, and a curious one at that.

'Will you have a glass of red?'

This was Mr Dinmoor – Alf – whose startling blue eyes twinkled at her. She wondered, did she know him from somewhere? There was something almost familiar about his face, those eyes … and a memory that stayed just out of reach; but then, she thought, this corner of Yorkshire was full of wiry old men. This particular one had an outdoor complexion, ruddy and lined, and his grey hair, which looked as if it could be abundant given the chance, was close-cropped, like a squaddie's. There was soil embedded in his nails. Annie smiled tightly.

'I won't, thank you.'

'There's white in the fridge,' Josie said. 'Or elder-flower.' She was shifting things from the table, clearing a space, and Annie was relieved when the brass bowls went too; she'd feared they might have been used for lunch, and she knew she couldn't have touched a morsel from a vessel so old and so unwashed.

'Nothing at the moment, thank you.' She cast a help-less glance at the laden table. 'Um, what *is* all this, Josie? Are you having a clear out?'

Everyone laughed heartily and Annie blushed. 'Sorry,' she said. 'Have I put my foot in it?'

'No, you're right, it does look a bit like jumble,' Josie said. 'But I import this stuff from other parts of the world then sell it on my website.'

'What other parts of the world?' Annie said, as if she hadn't realised that anywhere else existed.

'Central Asia.' Josie waved a casual hand in an easterly direction. 'Turkmenistan, Uzbekistan, Kazakhstan.'

'Fancy that,' said Annie, more in the dark than ever.

'Believe it or not, Annie, folk're paying good money for this tat.' Mr Dinmoor put down the jug of wine and picked up a hat, a dusty-black felt dome embroidered with flowers in orange, red and yellow. 'You wouldn't catch me dead in summat like this.'

'It's beautiful,' Sandra said. 'Authentic.'

'Aye, if you're an Uzbek camel herder, but not so clever for a trip down Barnsley market on a Sat'day morning.'

'Okay, Mr Dinmoor, so you won't get one for Christmas,' Josie said, perfectly pleasantly. She looked at Annie.

'Did you bring Finn?'

Josie only meant to bring the conversation back to a topic Annie could follow, but the older woman stood up sharply and her handbag fell to the floor. 'Oh!' she said. 'I did! I forgot all about him!'

'Well that's okay,' Josie said.

'I only left him while I said hello, then I meant to pop out and bring him in. Oh my giddy aunt.'

Sandra, watching from the sofa, rolled her eyes. 'Keep your hair on,' she said.

'Now now,' Mr Dinmoor said to her. 'Be nice.'

Sandra glared and Annie, overwhelmed, confused, hot in her blue wool, looked stricken. Josie was at her side in an instant. 'Come on,' she said, 'let's go fetch Finn.' She walked her towards the door. 'Betty's in the garden,' she said. 'He might like to stay out in the fresh air too?' Annie still felt silly about the fuss she'd made, but Josie's enveloping arm was a comfort, so she allowed herself to be led away from the kitchen: away from the central Asian jumble and Sandra's judging green eyes.

Lunch was blessedly and unexpectedly familiar. Annie had feared an array of eastern exotica: food as strange and elaborate as the fabrics and doodads waiting to be packed and posted. But no, there was a cheeseboard with Wensleydale, Stilton and Red Leicester on it; there were thinly sliced tomatoes with nothing stranger on them than salt and black pepper; there was chutney in a quaint stone jar, and a small wooden ladle for serving it; there was a bowl of salad leaves and a long French loaf, warm and golden from the oven. Relief pulsed through Annie's veins and she breathed more easily as she plastered real butter onto a hunk of bread and bit into it, listening to the conversation but not venturing a comment. Words and laughter bounced across the table like ping-pong balls. Mr Dinmoor was helping Josie in the garden, Annie learned. He was planting a host of golden daffodils for her, so the least she could do was feed him, he said. Sandra was mildly drunk. She told stories against her ex-husband, whose name was Trevor. She poked fun at his dress sense – square – and his hobbies – local history and home brewing. 'I mean,' she said. '*Pur-lease.*' Annie wondered why they'd ever got married, from the tone she took. But then, Sandra's boy Billy wasn't exempt from criticism either – a prize pain in the arse, Sandra said, and Annie was shocked. Mr Dinmoor said Billy was a grand lad and Josie said he was gorgeous and she happened to know Sandra was completely devoted to him. Sandra shook her head and laughed and swigged red wine as if it was water. Mr Dinmoor asked her if she was planning to drive home, and Sandra said it was none of his bloody business. Annie was shocked again, but anyway she was beginning to enjoy herself a little and Finn, in now from the garden, was sitting right by her, pressed up against her chair. She leaned into him, as if they were holding each other up, and she felt his warmth and his strength. Now and again she passed him a slice of Red Leicester.

Covertly, Annie watched as well as listened. Mr Dinmoor – nobody seemed to call him Alf, no matter how often he insisted – looked older than her but he was obviously as fit as a butcher's dog: wiry and strong. His rolled-up shirt sleeves showed nutty brown forearms with a coating of fine white hair and, beneath them, the shocking outlines of a small tattoo – two crossed broad-bladed knives from what Annie could make out, although she was trying not to stare. Mr Dinmoor was clearly fond of Josie, and Annie could see why – such a kind girl, no edges or sharp corners. Oh, and so bonny! She especially liked Josie's loose black curls, long and glossy, like the gipsy girl in a painting from her past. It'd hung above the mantel in the dining room after Mrs Binley moved in for good, and had been the only possession of hers that Annie had liked. The girl held a tambourine and wore gold hoops in her ears, and she looked out of the painting with a half smile, as if she knew all your secrets and they weren't necessarily safe with her. Josie's ears were bare in fact, but she had a collection of silvery, tinkling bangles that slid up and down her arm when she passed a dish or poured a drink, and she tilted her head when she listened. Josie's features were delicate while Sandra was big-boned and plain, Annie thought: defiantly plain, though, as if she meant something by it.

Sandra, feeling Annie's gaze upon her, abruptly turned and stared back with cool green eyes. Annie, flustered, swallowed the hunk of bread she was chewing and looked mutely down at her plate.

'So Annie, how's your husband doing?'

This was Josie.

'Oh,' said Annie. 'Not so good.'

'I'd forgotten you were even married,' Sandra said. 'You never mention him.' She took another swig of wine and drained her glass, then stared gloomily at the dregs.

'Oh dear,' Josie said, to Annie. 'Such a strain on you.'

'What's up with him?' Sandra somehow managed to ask the question and convey indifference at one and the same time. She dabbed a forefinger over her plate, collecting crumbs of cheese.

'A stroke,' Annie said. 'I've rung my other son this morning, to let him know. All being well he'll be coming next week.'

'Where is he?' Mr Dinmoor asked.

'Australia,' Annie said, importantly.

'No, no, your husband. Is he in Barnsley General?'

'Oh, I see, sorry, my mistake.' Annie felt her customary hot blush creep upwards from her fluttering breast towards her face and Mr Dinmoor waited patiently for her answer.

'Australia?' Josie said, unwittingly saving Annie from the choice between full disclosure or a downright lie. 'Whereabouts?'

'It's a place called Byron Bay,' Annie said at once. She didn't want to say where Vince was and why – and it wasn't that Vince's dementia was shameful: not at all. Well, perhaps a little. But mostly it was just that having known Josie and Sandra for two months now, it was awkward to embark on the full story, unpicking the half-truths and evasions of previous conversations; and it was hard, too, to break the habit of a lifetime and confide one's woes to anyone other than the dog. 'It's near Brisbane. Well, I say near, but really it's quite a long way; it's a bit further than from here to Durham, and we wouldn't call that local, would we?' She gave a small chirrup of nervous laughter.

'I think I've been there,' Mr Dinmoor said.

Annie looked at him, amazed. She'd assumed – from his accent, perhaps, or his dirty fingernails – that he'd never been further than Barnsley.

'Mapmaking, a long, long time ago. A lifetime. Seems like it, anyroad.'

'Byron Bay,' Josie said, dreamily. 'It sounds romantic.'

'Not so much when I were there,' Mr Dinmoor said. 'Big abattoir is what I remember.'

'Oh shush,' Josie said. 'Don't spoil it. Byron Bay sounds nothing but enchanting.'

'I think it's nice enough now,' Annie said. 'There's no abattoir on Andrew's postcards.'

She was puzzled, but quietly pleased, when everyone started to laugh.

9

Mr Dinmoor didn't linger but went back out into the garden the minute he finished eating. Then Sandra went, defiantly swinging her car keys. Annie stood too, but Josie urged her to sit again and have a cup of tea with her, because it was miserable if everyone left at the same time, she said. Considering this was her busy day, she seemed to be very relaxed, Annie thought. Then, having thought it – practised it, you might say – she said it aloud, and even though it did have a slight ring of criticism about it, Josie only laughed and said, 'Oh well.' She was filling the kettle – a flat-bottomed stove-top kind, just like Annie once had herself – and rinsing the teapot of old leaves, and Annie said, 'It's a long while since I've had real tea. I buy bags.'

'Well, they're less mess, aren't they?' Josie said. Her tea caddy was an emerald-green tin with a gold lid the shape of the roof on an Arabian palace. She spooned black leaves into a china pot.

'It's been lovely,' Annie said, then hesitated before adding, 'but was Sandra cross about something?'

Josie turned. 'Oh, don't you mind Sandra,' she said. 'She's all right really. She's just a bit snippy sometimes.'

I'll say, thought Annie. 'Why?' she asked.

'Oh, well, y'know, single mum, teenage boy, a tendency to overdo the booze when it's offered.'

'But doesn't she work at the library?'

'Annie!' Josie said, in a laughing voice. 'Librarians are allowed a few glasses of red wine, y'know.'

'Yes, I suppose,' Annie said, although actually she wasn't at all sure about that. 'But I mean,' she went on, 'is she unhappy?'

Josie turned now, so that the teaspoon of tea leaves in her hand hovered in mid-air. 'Does she seem it to you?' she said. 'Only, I've known her for years, so perhaps I'm missing something.'

'Oh,' said Annie, a little flustered. 'Well, no, not exactly.' Just bad-tempered, she added, silently. Josie was busy again, making the tea.

'Sandra's one of those people who can't dissemble,' Josie said.

'Pardon?' said Annie.

'She says what she thinks, and she can be really brusque, but honestly I couldn't like her more.'

'Mmm,' Annie said. How lovely, she thought, to be entirely liked by Josie. She sat comfortably at the kitchen table, Finn on one side of her chair and Betty on the other. The little collie had rested her chin on Annie's blue patent foot, and it seemed like such a compliment that she was loath to shift position. She wiggled her toes inside her shoe to ward off cramp, and studied her curious surroundings. The room was bigger than she'd imagined. Without all the clutter of Josie's stock, it would be really quite spacious. Only one room per floor, though, each one placed on top of the other in ever decreasing circles. The bathroom was directly above, accessed by a narrow flight of wooden stairs, which disappeared through a round hole in the kitchen ceiling. Annie hadn't dared use the lavatory, for fear of the acoustics. Josie's bedroom, Annie presumed, must be upstairs again. What an odd way to live, she thought, all the rooms piled up like hatboxes.

'I've always wondered what this place looked like inside,' she said. 'I never imagined you could buy curved furniture.'

Josie turned and smiled.

'You can't really. Not very easily anyway. I had to have all these pieces made specially.'

Annie regarded the room silently: two long pine cupboards and a dresser, following the contours of the space they occupied, and an old butler's sink set into the curved top of another honey-coloured pine cupboard, the plumbing concealed behind two wooden doors. On the dove-grey walls were deep curved shelves, also painted grey but a shade or two darker, bearing gaudy, unmatched crockery, a collection of photographs and a line of small pewter tankards filled with bunches of dried herbs; sage, rosemary, mint and thyme. Of the furniture around the room's perimeter, only the range didn't stand flush to the walls, but sat proud and square on a low brick plinth.

Josie poured boiling water into the teapot and brought it to the table.

'It's very ...' Annie said, '... very circular.'

Josie laughed and poured the tea.

'You're not local, are you?' Annie said.

'No, I grew up in Donegal, in Ireland.'

'When did you come here?'

'Oh, eleven years ago, no, twelve. I was following my heart, but it didn't work out.'

'Oh dear,' Annie said, a little flatly because she was unused to the sharing of confidences. She had no idea what to say, so she just sighed and said, for the second time, 'It's been lovely.'

'Well, do pop in any time. I'm always here. Except when I'm not, and then I'm *really* gone.'

'On your travels I expect?'

'Buying trips, but I stick to one a year now.'

'I've never even been on a plane.'

'I prefer to drive, actually, but the red tape's put a stop to that for the time being.'

Annie's eyes were wide. Drive? To the land of camels and woven silks? 'Well I never,' she said. 'How ever do you find your way?' She thought about the difficulties she encountered on her rare shopping outings to Meadowhall – slip roads, traffic lights, multi-storey parking, green, pink and blue zones – and she felt at a loss as to how Josie could lock the door of this quaint little home then set off blithely for – where was it?

'Where is it you go again?'

Josie added a splash of milk to the tea. 'Central Asia,' she said. 'All the 'stans, basically. Or most of them.'

Really, she might have been speaking a foreign language. Annie watched Josie push a cup and the sugar bowl across the table.

'Well wherever it is, I think you must be very brave,' Annie said.

Josie placed her elbows on the table and laced her fingers, making a little hammock for her chin. 'Reckless, more like, and clueless – at least when I first went. I was only twenty, and I tried to drive one of the old silk routes

86

from Switzerland to Kazakhstan in a clapped-out Land Rover.'

'Tried to?' Annie's voice came out quavery and anxious, as if she'd been asked to make the same trip.

'Mmm. Broke down near Istanbul, then hitched as far as Ashgabat. Took weeks and weeks.'

'Alone?' Annie could think only of Josie's mother – whoever and wherever she might be. Bad enough waving Andrew off at Heathrow when he flew to Brisbane, but at least she could find it on a map.

'Well, you meet people along the way, don't you?'

'Do you?'

'Stacks. Anyway, I got the bug, and went back a year or two later in a decent vehicle, a van this time, and I filled it with stuff, then drove back home only to have the whole lot confiscated by customs at Dover.' She laughed gaily at her carelessness. 'Finally got it back after six months, and started Silk Road Textiles, and here I am, still at it.'

Annie took a sip of tea. She was shocked by the taste, bright and bitter and quite unlike her usual brew, but in the spirit of adventure that had brought her here in the first place, she sipped again, stoically. The kitchen was warm, heated by the range. Annie's wool dress made her armpits itch, but apart from this small discomfort, she felt surprisingly at ease. She cast her gaze around the kitchen again, at the rails and piles and higgledy-piggledy boxes, and she thought about her own pristine little house, where Michael went mad if his banana tree was at the wrong angle on the worktop.

'So do you have a shop?'

'Not any more,' Josie said. 'It's all internet sales now. I

used to have a shop, in Islington. Well, I had a stall when I first started.' Yes, Annie thought; I could see all this tat on a market.

'It was nice, the stall, the market,' Josie said. She looked dreamy, nostalgic. 'I mean, these online sales are all very well, but I never get to meet anyone.' She looked so content though, so comfortable with life, that Annie couldn't really believe she had any regrets.

'I worked in a shop once,' Annie said.

'Did you? What did you sell?'

'It was a haberdashers. Ribbons and buttons and wool and whatnot.' It was after Vince left, she remembered, and before he came back. Vince! She was so startled at the thought of her husband that she jumped immediately to her feet, and Betty, shaken from slumber, looked up at her with hurt eyes.

'Annie! Whatever's the matter?'

'I have a meeting with Vince's doctor at four and it's nearly quarter to now and there's no way on earth I can be at Glebe Hall in fifteen minutes.'

'Yes you can, if I drive you.' Josie was up, reaching for her car keys from a hook on the wall. 'Leave Finn with Betty here; Mr Dinmoor can let them out if need be, and I'll drop you off and wait. Come on.'

And she was off, out of the door, calling the plan across the garden to Mr Dinmoor – who didn't turn, but raised an arm to show he'd heard – and bustling Annie into the passenger seat of the Citroën.

'Glebe Hall,' Josie said. 'Now then, I once knew a lady there, an old neighbour. I know exactly where it is.'

She reversed out of her short drive and into the lane without due caution for what might have been coming, but Annie barely registered this. Instead, she sat in mute gratitude and confusion at a turn of events in which Vince's home for the demented was all of a sudden out in the open and a perfectly ordinary place for him to be. Josie hadn't even *blinked* when Annie blurted it out, even though it must have occurred to her by now that while Annie hadn't exactly lied about Vince's condition, neither had she been completely truthful.

Oh, it must be lovely to be like Josie, to live life with an open spirit and a happy countenance. Josie, thought Annie, was the sort of person who only had to step out of the house to make a new friend. Look at Mr Dinmoor! Calloused hands and earthy fingernails, and his hair so closely shaved that the exact contours of his skull were on display to the world. Never in a month of Sundays would Annie have befriended an old man like that. No, but then, when it came down to it, she would never have befriended Josie either. Annie went through life with cautious steps, looking away when someone new approached, averting her eyes. It was partly mistrust and partly a dyed-in-the-wool humility; a conviction, formed in childhood and borne out by experience, that everyone else was busier, bolder and more interesting than she was. But now here was Josie, a woman who lived in a windmill; a woman who had driven alone across continents to cities that Annie had never even heard of, and still she had a warm smile for most and a special warmth for some, among whom Annie – unless she was mistaken – could now count herself. She sneaked a look, and saw Josie's sweet face in profile, intent on the road ahead, her whole being committed to getting Annie to Glebe Hall. She wasn't hunched though, or tense; she was just humming a tune and driving swiftly towards Barnsley, as if this was just as pleasant as it had been to sit in that quaint round kitchen eating lunch. Junctions seemed magically clear of traffic and even the lights in Hoyland that were always red were green for Josie. By the time she swung into the Glebe Hall car park it was seven minutes past four.

'Fashionably late,' she said, turning to Annie with a grin. 'Off you pop; I'll just wait here.'

And Annie crossed the car park with a lighter, happier tread, because Josie would be there when she came out.

10

At Ecclesall Woods there were three mossy stones bearing Neolithic cup-and-ring carvings, and Josie knew their precise location. It was Dog Day Wednesday again, a cold, cold early November morning, and she'd led them from their parked cars, picking a careful trail through the trees.

'Okay, turn right here at this stump,' she said, 'and we need to keep that big old oak within view, two hundred yards straight ahead.'

'Right-ho, Pocahontas,' Sandra said, and Annie laughed. Look at me Michael, she thought: here, with my friends. She was cautious though, not carefree. She followed Josie and Sandra carefully, watching her feet, wary of roots and rabbit holes and the treachery of dew-soaked grass.

The woods were lovely, a dappled, verdant, bosky swathe of ancient Yorkshire, and before she'd met Josie and Sandra, Annie hadn't even known it existed. There were paths and bridleways and wooden steps for conquering the steeper parts, but today Josie had taken them well off the beaten tracks and into the depths, to find the stones. Their location had never been made public, she said. 'It's a secret, otherwise some hooligan would spray-paint them, or worse.'

'A secret,' said Annie wonderingly.

'Beats me how you can find them,' Sandra said. 'One big old oak's much like another, as far as I can tell.'

'Who showed you?' Annie asked.

'Mr Dinmoor. He drew me a map once, but I don't need it anymore.'

'Ah,' said Sandra. 'Mr Dinmoor.'

Josie stopped walking, and Betty bumped into her legs. 'What?' she asked Sandra.

'Nothing.'

They'd all stopped now, except for Finn, who continued on in an ecstasy of space and freedom, bounding after squirrels in a harmless, hopeless, exuberant fashion. They shot up tree trunks and mocked him from the highest boughs.

'No,' said Josie. 'What? Whenever I mention Mr Dinmoor, you do this.'

Sandra shrugged and smiled, but she looked uneasy.

'Don't you like him?'

'I don't *not* like him,' Sandra said. 'But I don't love him.'

'You don't need to love him,' Josie said.

'I just think ...'

'What?'

'I just think he's a bit of a know-all,' Sandra said. 'That's all.'

Annie watched, agog, holding her breath, the beginnings of distress forming at the back of her throat. Was there to be a row, a fallout, over that wiry old man with the daffodil bulbs and the dirty nails? If Josie stormed off, then where would they be? Lost in Ecclesall Woods, that was where. But Annie was reckoning without Josie's sunny spirit, because though she was trying her level best to be stern, she slowly broke into a smile, and then a laugh, and then she flapped a hand at Sandra.

'Ah whatever,' she said, turning and continuing to walk. 'I suppose he *is* a bit of a know-all.'

'Yeah,' said Sandra, following, the relief evident in her voice.

'In the nicest possible way, mind you,' Josie added, tossing the words over her shoulder, and Betty glanced backwards too, as if to be sure that Sandra understood that Mr Dinmoor was friend, not foe.

On they went, moving quietly through the woods, and for half an hour now they hadn't seen another soul. Annie felt rather intrepid: an entirely novel sensation. She felt as she imagined an explorer might, charting a new route through uninhabited lands, except that Josie evidently knew exactly where they were heading.

'All right at the back?' she called now, craning round to smile at Annie.

'Fine, thank you,' Annie said, and she was. She was perfectly used to the company of her own thoughts, and today she had plenty to think about. Andrew had phoned last night with details of his flight, and he wasn't coming this week, but next. A week on Friday, he'd said, which was quite a long time for Vince to hang on in the land of the living. But Bailey, who worked in a pre-school nursery, couldn't just drop everything, and Riley was a possum in a play, so *that* couldn't be missed.

And anyway, thought Annie, it's not as if Andrew and Vince were ever close, Vince not being the sort of man who encouraged closeness, at least not with his family. He'd somehow managed to keep his distance even when he came back to them for good. No, Andrew must do what was convenient for him and his family, and in any case, Vince wouldn't know who he was.

When she broke the news to Michael that Andrew was definitely coming he'd sniffed and said, 'Really? And what's the point, Mother? You might as well send the bloody milkman to the old bastard's bedside; he'd know no different.'

Oh, he had a foul mouth on the subject of Vince. Annie had long ago stopped trying to correct it; not that she'd ever had much influence over her obstreperous elder son. Nor could she blame him either, in all honesty.

She said none of this aloud, in the woods. She didn't tell them, either, that today – and in fact almost to the minute – it was fifty-one years since she'd married Vince. *Fifty-one years*. She didn't call it an anniversary, since that conferred a significance to the day that, in truth, it had never deserved.

Not once, in all that time together, had Vince bothered with a card. Not once; not even when he'd possessed the capacity to go out and buy one. Of course, right from the off she'd had many more – and bigger – causes of concern than a lack of anniversary good wishes from her husband. Oh dear, yes; and she'd wished, over the years, that she could simply forget the date, so that it held no more weight or import than any other chill November morning. But up it popped, every year, the date that wouldn't be forgotten.

Did she rue the day? Not entirely, because there would have been no Michael – mixed blessing though he was – and no Andrew. But Vince hadn't been a happy choice. Well, he'd done the choosing, not her.

So no, she didn't mention any of this to the others. She tucked her miserable memories away, kept them to herself, as was her custom: a custom begun in childhood and honed through the years until the instinct of privacy was second nature, as easy and natural as breathing.

'Here we are,' Josie said. 'Ta da!'

With a showman's flourish she indicated a mossy boulder, which, from even a short distance, looked unremarkable. But the closer she got, the better Annie could see the rings and lines and shallow grooves connecting each shape to the next. She stooped as low as her stiff knees allowed and traced her finger around the ancient markings in the stone. She thought about a wild-eyed, bearded man squatting on the dried leaves and beechnuts in a rough bearskin, chipping away, rock on rock, making near-perfect circles with meticulous care in this very spot, where she had now planted her own sturdy shoes. Finn pushed his big head into her hand, wanting the same attention as the rock, and she used his bulk to brace against as she brought herself upright again.

'How old are they?'

'Neolithic,' Josie said.

'Neolithic?' said Annie, not knowing at all when that was.

'Or maybe Bronze Age.'

'It must've taken bloody ages to do that without a hammer and chisel.'

This was Sandra. She flopped down onto the forest floor and waited for Fritz, who was walking stiffly and stoically towards her, swaying his hips and using the momentum to propel himself – slowly, slowly – across the leaves. Now and again his legs gave way altogether and then he would sit down for a moment with an expression of weary recognition: oh, this again, his eyes seemed to say. Sandra held open her arms and he walked into them with a suffering sigh. 'Poor old boy,' she said.

'Dear Fritzy,' Josie said, sitting down close to Sandra. 'Remember when you got him, San?'

'I know,' Sandra said, turning to Josie and smiling. 'He was crazy, wasn't he?'

'So boisterous!'

'That day by the Dove ...'

'... when he cleared the river in one leap, I know.'

'Yes, straight over, and we weren't going that way.'

'Then he stood waiting for us on the wrong side as if we were slackers.'

'That fisherman fetched him back, didn't he?'

'Biggest catch he had that day.'

They smiled together at the familiar story and Fritz, lying now between the two of them, seemed to bask in the memories of his youth. Annie, still standing, regarded the scene. A shaft of pale winter sun filtered through the leaves onto the heads of the two women, anointing the cameo with a kind of special, excluding glow. It was wrong, Annie knew, to begrudge them their shared history, but she felt peripheral, all of a sudden: on the outside, looking in. It was ever thus, she thought; she should know better than to hope for more. She turned to Finn, but he'd loped a few feet away and was poking at acorns with his nose, like a truffling pig.

'Annie? Are you okay?'

Josie was watching her, with concern in her kind eyes. 'You look lonely there; come on, sit down.' She patted the ground next to her and Annie eyed it doubtfully. The last time she'd sat on the ground was a good three decades ago, and even then there'd been a tartan rug.

'If I sit down there I might never get up again,' she said, and Josie and Sandra laughed, although she wasn't joking. But Sandra was unzipping the rucksack she'd brought, and lifting out a flask, so it was evident that this was the coffee break whether Annie liked it or not.

'Come on,' Josie said, patting the floor again. 'I promise we won't leave you here for all eternity.'

'It's my knees,' Annie said.

'This'll loosen them up,' Sandra said, and she started to pour something that wasn't coffee into three enamel mugs. The crisp air smelled suddenly of cinnamon and cloves.

'Sandra!' Josie said. 'You wicked, wicked woman.'

Annie gasped. 'Is it wine?' she said.

'*Mulled* wine, harbinger of the festive season,' Sandra said.

'We've not even had Bonfire Night yet,' Josie said, but she was holding a hand out for her mug, Annie lowered herself gingerly to the ground and sat with her legs straight out in front of her.

'Ouch,' she said. 'Ooof.' There were beechnuts and twigs digging into her buttocks, and she couldn't remember ever feeling so uncomfortable. Finn, suddenly alert to this unusual development, abandoned his foraging and joined her, and she was grateful because he was something to lean on. Like this, their heads were the same height; his breath was hot against her cheek. Sandra passed another cup of mulled wine to Josie and she passed it along to Annie.

'Oh no, I'm not sure,' Annie said, taking it.

'It won't make you drunk,' Sandra said. 'All the alcohol gets cooked off in the pan.'

Annie sniffed the deep red liquid cautiously. She was fairly certain Sandra was wrong about that. There were pieces of orange bobbing on the surface, and a heady, honeyed, gentle steam rose up to seduce her.

'Go on, live dangerously,' Sandra said, so Annie took a small sip.

'Oh!' she said. 'This is *very* nice.' Her lips felt syrupy, and she licked them clean, and then took another larger sip.

A comfortable, contemplative silence bloomed and the dogs stayed still, and close. Fritz, sprawled out beside Sandra, made great wheezing sighs into the dead leaves. Betty watched the squirrels with a sort of detached gravity. Finn closed his eyes in the sunshine but he didn't lie down. Instead he remained just where Annie needed him: her pillar, her support. She drank her mulled wine and marvelled at its layers of flavour, its plummy depths. Sandra drained her own mug, topped it up, then leaned back on one elbow and squinted up through the tree canopy.

'I wish I had a fag,' she said. No one answered.

Josie was cross-legged, straight-backed, happy as a clam. She wore fingerless gloves and an old Aran sweater instead of a coat, and her hair looped and curled down her back and shoulders, glossy black against the cream wool. Annie thought she'd never known anyone as beautiful as Josie Jones, and when Josie grinned at her, she realised she'd been staring.

'Sorry,' Annie said. 'I was admiring your hair. It's a

lovely colour against that sweater.' Her boldness surprised her; she glanced down at the mulled wine suspiciously.

'Why thank you, ma'am,' Josie said.

'She's a Celt,' Sandra said. 'Black hair, pale skin.'

'Isn't Celtic hair ginger like yours?' Annie said.

'I like to say red,' Sandra said. 'And yes, it can be, but not in my case.'

'Sandra's from Dudley,' Josie said, and she laughed.

'Yes, that famous line of Black Country redheads.' Sandra grinned. 'Cross us at your peril.' She proffered the flask and Annie and Josie both held out their mugs for more. Annie took a hearty draught; she felt warm and peaceful.

'Look at Finn,' Josie said. 'What a brick.'

Annie smiled. 'He has his uses,' she said.

'What I like about dogs,' said Sandra, 'is that they don't expect anything in return for their devotion.'

'Mmm,' Josie said.

'Unlike men,' Sandra went on, 'who see love as more of a trading position. Here's a wedding ring, now *this* is what you owe me.'

'Oh San,' Josie said.

'Don't oh San me,' said Sandra, but not snappily. 'You've never been wed, so you're not entitled to an opinion.'

'Well anyway, I *like* Trevor,' Josie said.

'That's because you're not divorced from him.'

'I can't think why someone like you *isn't* married, Josie,' Annie said, blurting out the words then blushing at her rashness, but Josie only sighed and said, 'Oh well, I fell in love with the wrong man.'

'Married with four children, the absolute bounder,' Sandra said.

'Actually Sandra didn't know him, Annie. She's right – he was married, and he had children, but he wasn't a bounder or I never would've fallen for him. It was a long time ago.'

Annie was quiet for a moment then said, 'My husband was certainly a bounder,' and Sandra sat up in a trice, sploshing wine from her mug. 'Ooh, dirty linen, do hang it out,' she said.

'Sandra!' said Josie.

'What? Let her spill the beans.'

'No,' Annie said, shaking her head emphatically. 'No, no, I should never have spoken. It's this wine,' she said. 'It's making my tongue loose, not my knees.' The others began to laugh and in spite of herself Annie laughed too. Next to her, Finn smiled and braced himself to stop her falling over.

Later, when there was no putting off their departure, Annie had to be hoisted up and off the ground by Josie and Sandra, taking one arm each, and it was no mean feat.

'Bloody Nora, Annie,' Sandra said. 'It's like lifting cement.'

'Charming,' Annie said. She stood a little unsteadily, adjusting to her upright position. 'My head's swimming,' she said, to Sandra. 'I'm not fit to drive.'

'Don't be daft,' Sandra said.

'It's probably a touch of vertigo, after all that time sitting down,' Josie said. 'Come on, there's a kiosk before the car park; we can have a cup of tea.'

'Give me a minute,' Annie said, so they stood there in the glade and waited, and the dogs assembled at their feet.

'Look,' Sandra said. 'I think Fritz is having the same trouble.'

He was up, but only just; his rear legs were semi-buckled and he swayed gently from side to side. They all looked down at him and Fritz looked at the floor. His coat was drab and sparse and the whiskers round his muzzle were grey. He looked as old as time.

'Poor old boy,' Annie said.

'Sometimes I wish he wouldn't wake up,' Sandra said, and they both knew what she meant. She said, 'I just don't want to ring the vet.'

'I could do it for you, if that helps,' Josie said.

Sandra shook her head fiercely. 'No, I'll do it, but I mean I don't want to *have* to.'

'Maybe it won't come to that,' Annie said. 'Maybe he'll slip away, in his sleep.'

'Maybe maybe maybe,' Sandra said. She sounded snippy, and at once Josie said, 'Let's go,' so they did: a more melancholy bunch now, the pleasant effects of the mulled wine receding, and Fritz's slow, painful gait setting their pace. They made it to the kiosk and had strong, fortifying tea from polystyrene cups, and small, dense squares of flapjack, and the dogs were offered a bowl of water, which Betty spurned, being too much of a lady to share with the slobbering boys. She turned her pretty face to the east and surveyed the view, the very image of gracious forbearance.

II

Vincent Doyle and Annie Platt were married on 2 November 1963; only three months after his proposal was confidently made and timidly accepted. Everyone who knew them was surprised at his choice, but no one more so than Annie. She wore her late mother's 1930s wedding gown, which for all the passing years had been stored in the dark in a shroud of tissue paper to keep it from turning yellow. When Annie fetched it from the trunk in the attic and peeled away the wrapping, the white silk crêpe unfurled like a butterfly from its cocoon, and Annie cried sentimental tears for a mother she remembered only patchily, and not always with fondness.

The gown was too small at the waist and across the back, so Annie let out the seams and gave up potatoes until after the wedding. It'd taken days and days of pressing and airing to eliminate the creases and the persistent smell of camphor from the delicate fabric. But all of this was worth it for the satisfaction of seeing her father blanch when she stepped from her bedroom in Lillian's dress, with her hair curled and pinned just as Lillian's had been twenty-five years earlier.

She knew, though, that she didn't really resemble her

mother. And if she hadn't known, there was certainly someone willing to tell her.

'You look just like that Doreen woman,' Mrs Binley said, when the young bride emerged. 'Doesn't she, Harold?'

Annie's father didn't follow her meaning and looked at his second wife with his eyebrows knitted.

'Doreen?'

'The sister. The plain one in the wedding album.'

'Oh, *that* Doreen.'

'She has the same nose,' Mrs Binley said. 'And the same pudgy chops.'

'Well now,' Harold said, dimly conscious that a bride on the morning of her wedding should not, perhaps, be subjected to such unkind scrutiny. 'I wouldn't necessarily say so.'

'Oh wouldn't you?' said Mrs Binley.

'Lillian was a great beauty of course,' Harold said, with misguided pride.

'Yes, well, much good it did her,' Mrs Binley said. 'All fur coat and no knickers.' And she stomped away, preparing to make her husband suffer for his folly. Harold and Annie regarded each other for a moment.

'Agnes can be a little thoughtless,' he said.

Annie nodded. She had, after all, been forced to live with Agnes Binley's particular brand of thoughtlessness for ten years now. From the day they heard of Lillian's death, Mrs Binley – she was always that to Annie; never Mrs Platt, never Agnes and certainly never Mother – had presided over their Coventry home like the cat that got the cream. Annie's mother had suffered a terrible, lonely fate, choking in the London smog, asphyxiated by the smoke and fumes that had rolled softly over London like a deadly eiderdown. A policeman had found her, stone cold and slumped in a heap on Regent Street. He'd lifted her from the pavement and carried her to a Red Cross van, where she was pronounced dead. For a day or two, nobody knew who she was: just a lady in fur, with red shoes. They held the funeral in Peckham, and Annie wasn't allowed to go. Instead she stayed at home with the curtains drawn and watched Laurence Olivier in *Rebecca* while Mrs Binley shared a pound of grapes with her parrot, Mr Christian. He was a blue and gold macaw, and could say, among other things, 'cowardly rascal' and 'pieces of eight', but Annie hated him, almost as much as she hated Mrs Binley. When Harold was out of the house, Mr Christian was let out of his cage to hop around the furniture and preen his feathers on the ormolu mantel clock, and his beady black eyes followed Annie around the room. When the parrot fell sick, Mrs Binley cried on and off for a month, until he regained his glossy good health and swung from his perch again, keeping a malevolent eye on Annie.

'But, you know, your mother could be thoughtless too,' Harold continued. 'So don't judge Agnes too harshly. At least she's still here, with us.'

'Has the car arrived, Father?' Annie said. She simply couldn't wait to be married. Afterwards, she planned never to see either of them again.

Vincent Doyle was a great novelty, a great hit, at the National Provincial. He was a bit old – at twenty-eight – to still be a lowly clerk, but he didn't seem to mind so no one else did. He'd come to Coventry all the way from

Newcastle: a Geordie lad, cheeky with the women, pally with the men, and when the manager passed through the back office, Vincent made comical suffering faces to make everyone snigger behind their hands. Harold Platt didn't bother much with the clerks, so he never noticed Vincent's dark, rangy good looks or the insolent light in his eyes. Vincent, on the other hand, noticed everything. That was why he knew there was a boss's daughter, an only child, apple of her daddy's eye. Well, that was what Vincent assumed, and she certainly looked plumply pampered when he saw her at the bank, trotting self-consciously through the staff corridors on an errand for her father. When she trotted back out again, Vincent jumped up from his desk without bothering with his jacket, and followed her out into the spring sunshine on Broadgate. When he fell into step beside her Annie gave a little squeal of fright, but his laugh was so warm and kind that her alarm was instantly replaced by a deep, blushing, swooning sensation which made her wish she could sit down.

'Miss Platt?' he said with carefully hesitant charm, although he knew full well who she was. 'May I introduce myself? Vincent Doyle.'

He held out a hand, and although she wanted to flee, good manners compelled her to stop walking and take it. Once he had her in his grasp he didn't let go, so they stood for a while, hands clasped, a still point in the busy street, him looking down, her looking up. Nothing in Annie's life so far had equipped her for such a moment. Her heart pounded in her chest and that silly expression 'weak at the knees', which she'd read in romances and never believed, suddenly seemed an entirely accurate physical symptom.

'I'm sorry to act so impetuously, Miss Platt,' Vincent said, 'but I need to speak to you most urgently.'

'Oh!' Annie said. She was raspberry pink under his gaze and he studied her with interest. Her cheeks looked softly pliable, as if with a prod and a squeeze of his long fingers he might rearrange her face, leave dimples in the dough. Her eyebrows and lashes were of the white-blonde variety, the type that at first glance seemed not to be there at all. Her nose was small but blunt, her eyes were as round as a china doll's and underneath her chin were the beginnings of a second one. She was not, thought Vincent, a looker, but she had a sweet naivety about her that wasn't unappealing.

'My word, you're lovely,' he said. He was putting on a bit of a voice; his Noël Coward special, the one he used on girls he thought would fall for it. He wasn't sure yet exactly where this little bird fitted in his mental catalogue of the species, but anyway Noël Coward seemed to be doing the trick. Spellbound, Annie blinked her blue eyes.

'Far too pretty for the likes of me, but even so will you do me the honour of letting me take you dancing on Saturday night?'

Annie stared. Vincent waited.

'Cat got your tongue?' he said, in his normal voice. She was an odd one and no mistake, he thought. She was behaving as if this was the first time she'd been asked out, and of course, it was, but Vincent didn't know that. In his world, the precious only daughters of bank managers were there to be preyed upon, and the streets were full of hunters.

'I'll pick you up at seven. Cocktails at the Leofric then on to the Locarno.'

The question mark was missing, Annie noted; the deal seemed to be done. She nodded her head, and he reached out and took an experimental pinch of her cheek between finger and thumb, before smiling a swift farewell and jogging back to the bank. Annie had to stay put and catch her breath before she could continue on down the street. Her cheek, where he had squeezed it, felt a little hot, a little sore, but she took this as proof she wasn't dreaming.

Annie sat quietly, waiting for her date, but her outward calm belied an interior that was all a-flutter with anxiety. She had conquered a number of self-inflicted obstacles – doubt, indecision, mortification – to reach this point of relative stillness on the arm of the sofa in the drawing room; but the greatest hurdle had been the practical necessity of asking her father's permission. This, by rights, should have been Vincent's job, but it was only later that she learned he always took what he wanted without asking.

She'd tried very hard to get Harold on his own, choosing a moment when she knew he'd be in his study, the only room in which he was allowed to smoke his pipe. But Mrs Binley had a sixth sense for intrigue.

'What's that?' she'd said, bursting through the door of Harold's den like the Gestapo.

Harold took the pipe from his mouth. 'The girl has been asked out.'

Mrs Binley laughed in disbelief and Annie's spirits sank further still.

'Has she now? Who by?' *By whom*, thought Annie.

Harold nodded at Annie, inviting her to speak. She cleared her throat.

'Vincent Doyle,' she said.

Mrs Binley screwed up her face. 'Vincent Doyle, Vincent Doyle, no – not the first idea who he is.'

'He works at Father's bank,' Annie said.

'The blazes he does!' said Harold.

'A clerk,' Annie added.

'Ah,' said Harold. 'Well then, I can't be expected to know every minion in the back office.'

'No,' Annie said. 'But anyway, I'd like to go to the dance with him.' *And I shall*, she added privately.

'I'm sure you would,' said Mrs Binley. 'But your father doesn't know him so that's that. You can't be seen walking out with any old jack-the-lad, y'know.' She'd long ago forgotten how far she herself had risen, although Annie hadn't.

'Father didn't mind that you were a char lady,' she said. 'So I don't see why he should mind that Vincent is a bank clerk.'

Mrs Binley set her mouth into a tight line of fury. Swift as a cobra she slapped Annie across the cheek.

'Take that back,' she shouted. 'Harold, make her take that back.'

But it was only the truth, and while Harold very often chose the path of least resistance, he was also a pedant, irredeemably literal, and therefore was simply unable to demand a retraction from his daughter. However, he stood up, the better to assert his scant authority.

'Annabelle, go to your room,' he said.

'I will, but may I go out on Saturday with Vincent?' she said. Mrs Binley's fingerprints were burning red on her face, but Annie hadn't allowed a single tear to form, or raised her own hand to the wounded cheek. She was buoyed up by hatred; it was her solace and her support.

'You may,' said Harold. 'Now go to your room.'

And Annie left, sending a shallow, sardonic smile to Mrs Binley as she passed.

Now, here she was, waiting, in a pale yellow brocade dress, sleeveless, with a wide cowl neck and a tulip-shaped skirt that narrowed just below the knees, and therefore hid them, which was her intention. There were plenty of clothes in her wardrobe, because Harold gave her a small allowance and she had little else to spend it on, but still she had been in agonies of indecision over what to wear. Hopeless, unhappy hours were spent considering her reflection in the cheval mirror, weeping tears of frustration that her soft, ample belly refused to be subjugated, or that her pale blonde hair curled in a haphazard way that was not, and could never be, chic.

She wondered how it would feel to confide her insecurities to a girlfriend: to seek advice, to share beauty tips, to swap dresses. But Annie's lonely childhood had continued on into lonely adolescence, and now here she was, twenty-two and still quite solitary. She believed she had no talent for friendship – she didn't know why – and anyway where were friends to be found, now that she was an adult, cloistered in her father's house and seeing no one but him and Mrs Binley?

But now there was Vincent Doyle. She listened to the clock, and her own steady breathing, and she waited for the doorbell to ring. She would answer it swiftly and leave the house before Mrs Binley could swoop down upon them.

Vincent Doyle. She said his name aloud, very softly,

and she wondered; was he her first real hope? Her best hope? Her last?

At the Leofric Hotel, she perched on a bar stool and looked for somebody famous. Everybody knew this was where the stars stayed when they were in Coventry and for a moment she thought she'd spotted Pearl Carr at a corner table, until the woman in question waved right across the room at Vincent, who winked and waved back. 'Call me Vince,' he'd said to Annie on the walk here, but she hadn't called him anything yet, because there hadn't been any reason to use his name. He'd parked her at the bar then gone to talk to the woman who wasn't Pearl Carr, while Annie sat alone and tried not to see her own reflection in the glass behind a dizzying wall of liqueurs.

'You choose,' she'd said, when he came back and asked her what she wanted, and he ordered a Blue Hawaiian, which came in a tall glass with a slice of pineapple, a maraschino cherry and a palm-fringed straw.

'It's mostly pineapple juice,' Vince said, when she widened her eyes in alarm.

'Then why is it blue?'

'Curacao,' he said. 'Just for the effect.'

'It's exactly the same colour as Mrs Binley's parrot,' Annie said.

'Come again?'

'Her parrot, Mr Christian. He was a blue macaw. He's horrible,' she said.

Vince laughed, but he was distracted again, this time by a man, who called out, 'Vincey boy!' and pointed at the door before exiting the hotel.

'Okay, sup up,' Vince said then. He hadn't taken a

stool, preferring to stand with his back to the bar, looking out across the busy room. He had a patently restless air, and was drinking his pint of bitter with efficient speed. She was fascinated by his Adam's apple, which bobbed vigorously as he swallowed, although she tried not to stare. She couldn't think of a single thing to say now, and she deeply regretted mentioning the parrot. Vince's eyes scoped the room, sweeping left and right across the flushed and chattering faces. Annie, trying to follow the direction of his gaze, found it barely settled before moving on.

He certainly wasn't what she could call attentive, or even particularly gentlemanly, although he'd smiled right at her when she'd opened the front door, he'd been kind about her dress, and now and again he called her Blue Eyes, which she liked. But now, at the bar, it was almost as if he'd forgotten she was there.

'Do you like working at the National Provincial?' she said at last, making a tremendous effort to end a few long minutes of silence.

He looked at her, and seemed to take a moment to focus.

'It's all right, for now,' he said. 'What do you do?'

'Do?'

'For a job.'

'Oh! Nothing,' she said, and blushed. Around them the bar had filled up with couples who laughed and canoodled and tried each other's drinks. She sipped at her blue cocktail.

'Nothing?' he said.

She nodded. 'I suppose you think that's feeble?'

'Nope. I'd do nothing like a shot, if somebody'd pay

me for it.' He laughed as if this was a great joke. 'Nice work if you can get it,' he said, and roared again. She was pleased he was amused, even though he was laughing at his own wit, not hers.

'Well,' she said, 'Father gives me an allowance and I can easily manage on that.'

'I'll bet.' He studied her with a frank, assessing stare, so that she had to look away. 'So there's only you, at home?'

'Well, and Father and Mrs Binley, his wife,' she said.

Yes, yes, obviously, but no brother, no sister?'

'Oh!' she said. 'Sorry, no, only me I'm afraid.'

'Well, aren't I the lucky one for finding you?' he said. She smiled, pinkly.

'Finish that pop, Blue Eyes, and we'll see what's what at the Locarno.'

Obediently she drank up, and when she hopped down off the stool, he steadied her then slung an arm across her shoulders, so that when they walked out of the Leofric everyone could see they were together: a couple. Annie cast her modest gaze downwards, but her heart sang.

Vincent and Annie Doyle moved into an end-of-terrace on Sydney Road; he thought it a little palace, she knew it was a comedown, but it was the best Harold Platt would do for them, and far more than Mrs Binley thought them entitled to. If she had had her way – and she usually did – then the young couple would have managed on their own, just as she had had to do when Ray Binley married her after the Blitz and there was nowhere to rent and no money to rent with. But Harold was a fusspot for how things looked and he wouldn't countenance a daughter in lodgings. So he bought the little house outright and put it through the bank before his wife properly knew what was happening. He also paid for the modest wedding and for a week in the Lake District, sending them up to Keswick on first-class train tickets to a discreetly plush hotel where mousy little Annie, to Vince's surprise, showed wonderfully willing in the bedroom.

So Vince had come back to Coventry content, thinking all this was just the beginning of Harold's largesse, when in fact it turned out to be the end. Vince had thought he might leave his clerking; start up his own little business – a real ale brewery, an independent bookmakers – backed by an affluent father-in-law and further supported by the monthly allowance that came to Annie. But as the first weeks of marriage ground on he began to fully understand how things stood. Annie hated Mr Platt's second wife with a surprising passion and for her father she appeared to feel nothing at all. Meanwhile Harold, having provided a respectable home for his married daughter in a different part of Coventry from himself, had shut up shop, drawn the purse strings, all but washed his hands of her. A woman with a working husband needed no handouts from her father, Mrs Binley told him, and Harold – who after all couldn't possibly be accused of miserliness – was inclined to agree. Meanwhile, at the bank, there was no special treatment, no rise in pay, no small privileges to lift Vince above the strictly ordinary. Harold Platt, in fact, barely looked his son-in-law in the eye.

'Your father's a stuck-up old fucker,' Vince said to Annie one evening, his tongue loosened by beer. It was two months into married life and he was giving vent to his disappointment, trying to shock her with profanities.

'Oh, he is,' Annie said, with conviction.

Vince, momentarily wrong-footed, gave a burst of laughter. But he was cross as hell that he'd allowed himself to be misled by assumptions, not guided by facts. He was cross, too, that when he suggested she build bridges between themselves and the Platts, Annie wouldn't budge.

'I don't want them here,' she said. 'Mrs Binley with her nasty jibes and Father looking at me like he doesn't remember who I am.'

'He's worth a bob or two, though.'

'That's of no account.'

'Might not be to you, but it is to me.'

Annie looked at Vince, long and hard. 'You're after his money,' she said, in the flat voice of a woman on whom a hard truth had just dawned.

'Well who's he going to give it to, if not you?'

'I don't know. A rest home for elderly parrots, perhaps.'

'What the bloody hell are you going on about?'

'Don't shout, there's no need.'

'There's every need, you silly cow. I'm not slaving in his bank for the pittance he pays while he's sitting on a small fucking fortune. Why do you think I married you? For your show-stopping looks? I don't think so.'

Vince took some small pleasure in finally making Annie cry, but it didn't alter the fact that he was stuck with a wife he barely knew and didn't much fancy unless the lights were out or his eyes were closed. He felt a wash of panic, followed swiftly by the more familiar sensation of steely resolve. Annie was weeping in the way a small child would cry, screwing her fists into her eyes and sniffing.

She'd been baking when he stalked into the house. She had a floral pinny on and flour on her hands and now it was all over her face, too.

'You're just as horrid as everyone else,' she said, through her sobs. 'I was making you a sponge cake. I was being nice.'

'Oh shove it,' Vince said, and he walked back out of the house.

His voice these days was coarse and harsh and Noël Coward was gone for ever from Annie's life. All she had was Vincent Doyle, and she didn't really have him, either.

Vince was gone for almost two weeks, and Annie didn't tell a soul. She didn't know where he was or even if he was still in Coventry, although she knew he wasn't going into work because every morning she left the house to lurk near the National Provincial with the hood of her mac pulled low over her brow, watching the employees arrive and pass, chatting and laughing, through the Doric columns of the bank's imposing entrance. She saw her father too, of course. He arrived by car, although he no longer drove it himself. Instead, a chauffeur in a peaked cap drew up in the Rover then got out and walked around to hold open the passenger door for Harold Platt, who climbed out onto the pavement and walked into the bank without a word of thanks or a backwards glance.

'Stuck-up old fucker,' Annie murmured under her breath and then wondered what was becoming of her. It didn't cross her mind to follow Harold and ask for help. Instead, she went home and waited for Vince, believing that he'd come back because the alternative was too dreadful to contemplate.

And he did return, coming through the house with his playboy swagger, whistling a jaunty tune as if all he'd done was nip out for a packet of Benson and Hedges. Annie didn't ask him where he'd been, but instead blurted out the astonishing news that she was expecting their first child. A honeymoon baby, she said, feeling suddenly shy. Due next August.

'Right,' he said, without much interest. 'Well, I've news too. I've left the bank, got a job as regional sales rep for Whitbread.'

'The brewery?'

'The very same. Better money, better prospects, and well out of range of your poisonous old man.'

'Oh,' Annie said. She felt pleased, actually: excited. A handsome husband, a baby to love, a new job.

'It's in the north-east,' Vince said.

'What is?'

'The job. Regional rep, north-east.'

'North-east Coventry?'

'North-east *England*,' he said, as if explaining to a simpleton. 'Newcastle and thereabouts. You can stay here, though. No need to uproot. I'll come back now and again. Send you money, that kind of thing.'

Annie's face was stricken.

'What?' Vince said, as if he was truly baffled: as if he was offering her paradise and still she wasn't happy.

12

Finn had disappeared. They were crunching happily along gravel paths in the grounds of the old stately home in Josie's village, and he'd been there, dashing about at choppy angles, lunging this way and that as if his tail was on fire. And then, without anyone seeing the direction of flight, he'd vanished.

Annie, rooted to the spot, turned a slow full circle, and the colour drained from her face.

'He won't be far, Annie,' Josie said.

'He can't be, we've only been out of the cars for ten minutes,' said Sandra. 'And he was with us for eight of them.'

But Annie was quiet because she was concentrating; willing Finn to appear; bringing him back through the power of thought.

'Shall we try those trees?' Josie said. 'See? That coppice over ...'

'Shush,' Annie said. She closed her eyes and Sandra grimaced at Josie, who shrugged. Fritz thought the walk was over already and lay down gratefully, but Betty, who'd been sitting on Josie's feet, suddenly stood, her lithe little body tense with coiled energy, her ears up, her eyes bright. She gave three shrill barks, which bounced back at them from the hills as if another little collie was out there answering.

'Betty?' said Josie.

'Good grief,' Sandra said. 'She can bark.'

'Look,' Annie said with a satisfied smile. She pointed at Finn. He was streaming towards them from the distant fields, further away than any of them had expected, except he wasn't alone. A small grey terrier came too, matching him for speed even with his short legs. Together they hurtled towards Annie and she grabbed Josie's arm, for fear of being skittled off her feet, but then the dogs made a sharp right turn, circled them twice, then ran off again in the direction they'd just come from. Annie, stunned, watched them go in stricken silence.

'Okay,' Josie said. 'Let's go that way, shall we?'

Years ago, when Annie had taken Finn to puppy school, the trainer – a former policeman, big on canine psychology – had told the class that an owner should never follow an errant dog. 'Walk the other way,' he'd said. 'Show the dog that you decide the route, not him.'

Like all the other advice she'd been given at the time, Annie had forgotten it. And anyway, Finn's precipitous departure just now seemed distinctly purposeful. They set off after him.

'He should really be on a lead,' Sandra said. 'There's signs everywhere. There's a gamekeeper here, y'know, and he'd take a dim view. Dogs like that, loose on the land.'

Annie's eyes threatened tears and Josie said, 'Oh Sandra, hush. He's fine.'

'Well, it's only the truth.'

Josie ignored her and picked up the pace. Finn and the

grey dog were still visible, but only just: a golden streak, a grey smudge. Annie had pulled a whistle from the depths of her fleece but it hung useless from the corner of her mouth like an unlit cigarette; she was out of puff trying to keep up with Josie, and it made feeble wheezing noises with every outward breath. Sandra, walking at Fritz speed, fell behind, but she followed the same route as the others, off the path and onto the wide grassy expanse of the great house's stately grounds.

'They're headed for the fields,' Josie said, over her shoulder. 'He's not in the coppice – he ran that way.'

There was no sign of the dogs now. Annie stopped for a breather and scanned the landscape with terrified eyes. Never, for all his boundless energy and high spirits, had Finn actually run off like this. What he did was gallop back and forth, not gallop away and disappear.

Josie strode on with Betty, who was on red alert, fully aware that a search was on, although for what, she had no idea. At the coppice Josie took a left, just as she'd seen Finn do. Annie trotted behind on wobbly legs and Sandra, remarkably, wasn't too far behind. She pulled on Fritz's lead and even he seemed to be responding to the whiff of drama, pushing himself onwards and upwards with a stiff, effortful gait.

Ahead, there was a sagging metal fence topped off with a nasty spiral of barbed wire. Puffs of dirty white wool clung in clumps to the spikes. The field sloped sharply downhill and from where they stood there was still no sign of Finn. Josie and Betty stopped and let Annie catch up.

'I think he's out there somewhere,' Josie said. She cupped her hands round her mouth and called his name, once, twice, three times, but her voice sailed unanswered into the autumn sky. Annie gave a plaintive blast on her whistle. Then they listened. Somewhere far off, a shot rang out and Annie screamed.

'Crow scarer,' said Josie, and Annie was fairly – but not entirely – certain she was right. 'Just listen, there'll be another in a few seconds.' They waited, holding each other's gaze, until, just as Josie had said, a second gun crack split the silence. 'It's only a farmer's gadget,' Josie said and Annie nodded. 'I'll have to climb over, Annie,' Josie said. 'Do you want to hold Betty and wait here?'

Annie's fence-vaulting days were long past, if they'd ever existed at all. She nodded dumbly and took the lead.

Josie clambered over the wire and into the field and walked forwards, wondering bleakly why, if there was evidence of sheep on the fence, there were none to be seen in the field.

Then there they were, packed in a huddle at the bottom corner of the lower field, invisible from Annie's vantage point but perfectly evident to Josie, who stopped walking, horrified and mesmerised by the scene she beheld.

The strange amber eyes of the flock were fixed on the two dogs, which were a few feet away from them, standing over the prone body of a solitary sheep. Finn had it pinned, although the possibility of its escape had long passed. There was blood on his muzzle, but his head was raised and turned away, as though he couldn't bear to watch his accomplice, busy at the rear, pulling entrails from the lifeless animal with casual savagery. The flock, like Josie, watched in rigid shock, but then at some silent primal signal they suddenly scattered in a dozen directions and the terrier was off, abandoning his dead quarry for the thrill of a new chase. Finn stepped back and stared about him, as if uncertain where he was, or why, and Josie screamed his name, but the dog was deaf to everything but the call of the sheep; their toneless bleating filled the air and they blundered stupidly across the coarse grass on spindly legs that hadn't evolved for flight from danger.

Easy enough, then, for Finn to suddenly launch himself at another one and bring it immediately to its knees. The terrier, quick as mercury, surged across the field to where Finn now held the new victim. The sheep bucked and rolled its eyes but Finn was a strong and steady captor; his gentle giant paws were sunk deep into its woolly haunch.

The thin, piping, ludicrous note of a dog whistle drifted on the breeze and Josie, remembering Annie, dimly wondered how all this would end, while still doing nothing, nothing at all, to bring it to a conclusion. Then behind her she heard the thud of hooves, felt the turf under her feet vibrate, and it seemed perfectly plausible in this waking nightmare that a horse was coming at her, intent on mowing her down, but it was only Sandra, who ran past her into the melee and put Josie to shame.

Sandra was wielding a stout stick, brandishing it like a cave woman with a club. She hurled herself at Finn, kicking and cursing, and the dog drew away from the sheep at once and stared at Sandra with wide white eyes. She brought the stick down across his back and he sprang away further still, then she turned on the terrier, kicking its soft underbelly with the toe of her boot to bring it off the sheep and flailing wildly with her stick, matching its savagery with her own. The sheep, bleeding from its hind quarters, staggered to its feet and barrelled off to the flock and the little dog spun away with a shrill, unnatural scream, then turned back to face his assailant with bared teeth and narrow, wicked eyes. His face dripped blood and though he was only small he seemed in this moment more wolf than dog. His hackles were high and he inched towards Sandra with evil intent.

'Don't you even fucking think about it,' she said, showing her own teeth, and snarling too. She lunged and whacked him again with a great roar of fury, and this time he bolted, tearing up the field, far away from Sandra's reach, making his escape. Just once he stopped and turned, meeting Sandra's wild eyes with an insolent stare, then glancing at Finn with a sort of disappointed canine contempt. And then he was off: wiry, wily, and fuelled by bloodlust, lost from sight in mere seconds. Sandra turned back to Finn, who shrank from her in terror. He flattened his body on the grass, and his eyes seemed suddenly to fill with abject sorrow. Sandra, looking exhausted, dropped the stick.

One dead sheep, one injured, and the stink so strong that Josie could feel it on her skin. Fear, blood and sheep shit. When Sandra turned away to walk up the hill, Finn slunk along behind without being told and without once looking back.

Annie, her face screwed up in concern, was waiting behind the fence with Betty and Fritz, but when she saw the others approaching she beamed. That was before she spotted the blood on Finn.

'He's hurt,' she said. 'Where's he bleeding? Was it this barbed wire?'

Sandra said nothing. She felt nauseous, that was the truth of it: shaken by the sight and the smell of fresh death down the hill. She climbed over the fence with scant regard for the barbs and then flung herself onto the floor next to Fritz, who was fast asleep. Annie stared at them. Josie, still in the field, said, 'Annie, they killed a sheep.' How else to say it? There was only this way: swift and to the point. Annie looked at her, stupefied.

'Has he done anything like that before?' Josie asked. 'Because he seemed to know exactly what he was at.'

Finn was sitting, bedraggled but otherwise nice as pie, waiting to be helped through the fence, and now Annie stooped to pull at a loose lower bar, so that the dog could squeeze under.

'You managed to get through this fence before, young feller-my-lad,' she said. 'So why can't you manage it now? Now then, where's all this blood coming from?'

Josie and Sandra exchanged a look.

'He's not bleeding,' Sandra said. 'He went for the sheep, like Josie said. Well, that terrier did, but Finn joined in.'

Finn slumped to the floor, in much the same way as Sandra. The smell of traumatised sheep was potent and pervasive and there was no disregarding it; Annie had to allow the truth to filter through the mists of her denial. 'Oh dear,' she said. 'Oh dear oh dear oh dear oh dear.' She shook her head, hid her face in her hands. Sandra had no patience with it. She was determined that facts would be faced.

'Who farms this flock then?' she said, to Josie.

Josie shrugged. 'It's estate land, I think,' she said, 'so probably the man at Home Farm. Mr Wright.'

'Well you'll need to see him, Annie,' Sandra said.

'Oh no, I can't do that,' Annie said, through her fingers.

'Really?' said Sandra coldly. 'Why not?'

Annie moved her hands from her face and she looked so woebegone that Sandra's heart almost went out to her. 'Because he'll shoot Finn,' Annie said shakily and then broke into a wail so pitiful that Josie, who was still in the field, vaulted smartly over the fence and tucked her into the protective curl of her arm.

'Hush,' Josie said. 'Of course he won't shoot Finn. That's not how it works, is it, Sandra?'

Sandra said nothing. She found she couldn't look at Annie so she inspected her hands, which were flecked here and there with dark blood. She wiped them on her jeans.

'If I were you,' Sandra said, still staring at her hands, 'I'd go right away and find the farmer. In fact I couldn't live with myself if I didn't.'

'How about if I came with you?' This was Josie; she'd released Annie, and had clipped Finn onto his lead, although he was flat out on the grass now, going nowhere. Annie seemed rooted where she stood, incapable of motion, but she answered Josie briskly enough.

'No,' she said. She shook her head emphatically.

'But you *will* go?' Sandra said. 'Because if you won't, I will. That second sheep's injured and there's a little bastard terrier still on the loose that needs catching.'

'I'm taking Finn home,' Annie said. She reached out for the lead, and Josie passed it to her.

Sandra felt a rush of frustrated anger. She heaved herself to her feet, looming over Annie as she fussed and fretted over Finn. 'That sickens me,' Sandra said, with cold fury. She flung an arm out, pointing at the field beyond. 'There's a dead sheep down there and another one trailing blood, and all you want to do is pretend it never happened. Well, I call that cruel and selfish and almost certainly illegal and—'

'Oh shut your bloody mouth!'

Sandra and Josie both stared at Annie, who stood there, shaking from the impact of her own outburst.

'Annie!' Josie said.

'I'm taking Finn home,' she said again, and she jerked at the lead so that Finn stood up at once and began to walk beside her. He hung his head though, and his smile was gone.

Twice on the drive home Annie had to stop to be sick. It was the smell of sheep: the smell, and the shock of it all. The first time, she managed to get out and scuttle round the car onto the verge, so that she could vomit tidily into the grass while screening herself with the car. But the second time came upon her too quickly, so that she only managed to open the door and lean out over the road. A boy on a bike said 'Rank!' and pedalled away laughing, and a woman in a green Range Rover slowed down and stared, but didn't stop.

Finn hunkered down in the boot, his bloodied snout an abomination. There was sheep's wool snagged on his teeth. Annie could barely bring herself to look at him and certainly she had nothing to say. The dog, sensing his disgrace, just watched and waited.

She parked outside her house on Beech Street and sat for a while, worrying about the vigilance of the local Neighbourhood Watch, usually such a fount of comfort and reassurance. Not today though: not now. Oh, what a band of nosy parkers they were! Peering round their curtains, taking notes, running to the community police-man with their unusual sightings. Were they watching her now? thought Annie. Could they tell she was har-bouring a fugitive? The incriminating evidence – the blood, the wool, the cloying stink – was abundant, but she couldn't sit here until after dark so she picked a quiet moment and made a dash for it, chivvying Finn up the path, into the house, and all the way through to the back patio.

Finn tried to oblige her in every way possible. He held his mouth open when she pulled the wool from his teeth; he even stood motionless when she turned the pressure hose on him, soaking him through in a matter of mo-ments with a pitiless blast of cold water that could have shifted barnacles from a rock. Blood dripped from his sodden fur, pooling around his paws, and Annie chased it away towards the drain with further bursts from her power nozzle.

Finn – placid, stoical, dignified – began to win back her affection with this unresisting acceptance of his fate; the more patiently he withstood the icy torrent, the more her heart swelled with love. By the time he and the patio were clean again and Annie stood back to let him shake, all was restored between them. Let that farmer do his worst. Let him just try. She would place herself squarely between the barrel of his gun and her beloved dog, if that was what it came to.

Finn wasn't coming in the house yet though, not until she could be sure her carpets were safe from his big wet paws.

13

Yesterday, Finn had killed the sheep. Tomorrow, Andrew and his family were coming. Today, Glebe Hall rang to say Vince had suffered another episode overnight, but was conscious and reasonably lucid.

'Well, I say lucid,' the duty nurse, Brenda, added. 'I mean lucid in a rambling sort of way.'

'Yes,' Annie said. Her chest was tight with anxiety, not for Vince but for herself and for Finn, and for Andrew on that jumbo jet. She found it difficult to concentrate on the conversation.

'Oh well,' she said, 'I shall leave him be today, then come tomorrow with Andrew, all being well.'

'All right, Mrs Doyle.'

Annie imagined she could hear disapproval in Brenda's voice; a tinge of disappointment at responsibilities shirked. Of all the staff at the home, Brenda was the only one who made her feel this way. Something in her tone suggested that while a laissez-faire approach might suit the likes of Annie Doyle, it would never do for her.

'Michael might be able to come, though.'

'Michael?'

'My other son, the older one.' Annie knew her voice had a defensive edge. She knew, too, that pigs would fly before Michael went to Glebe Hall on a Thursday. Well, any day really, but on Thursdays he had classes nearly back-to-back and then chamber choir in the evening.

'Well, we shall look forward to seeing Michael later then,' said the nurse doubtfully.

Annie cracked under the pressure. 'Oh well, I suppose I could come on my way to Morrisons,' she said, and there was no mistaking the resentment in her voice. How heartless she sounded! She winced at the impression she must be making. She just felt so ... well, she didn't really know what she felt, but she knew she'd better make amends. 'I mean, if he's awake I'd like to come and say hello,' she said.

'Up to you, Mrs Doyle, but better safe than sorry.'

'Yes.'

'He's very poorly.'

'Yes, but he'll hang on for Andrew, won't he?'

Until she'd asked Andrew to come, Annie hadn't minded when Vince died: sooner the better, in her view. His tenacity in clinging to life was plain irritating; *just let go, you horrid old man*, she wanted to shout; *nobody wants you!* Now, though, she had a vested interest in Vince's condition. It must remain critical, but stable. She didn't want Andrew to feel guilt at missing the last goodbye yet neither did she want him thinking she'd fetched him here on a fool's errand. In an ideal world, Vince would die this weekend; next Monday at the latest, then Andrew could still be here for the funeral. She realised these matters couldn't be organised to suit flight times though; it was only wishful thinking.

'I expect he will,' Brenda said. 'On the other hand, one bad turn ...'

'Deserves another,' Annie said recklessly, and Brenda chuckled, so they ended their conversation quite jovially considering that there was a human soul at stake.

Annie replaced the receiver and looked at the phone warily. Last night it had rung and rung and she'd known it would be Josie; felt it in her bones. She'd ignored it and worked on a jigsaw puzzle but then Michael had come in and of course he picked up.

'Ye-es?' he had said in his telephone voice, which conveyed boredom and irritation with the caller even before they'd spoken, and in the living room, Annie had frozen. She'd heard him say, 'I expect so, hang on,' and then shout, 'Mother!' so she'd peeped round the door with desperate eyes and had vigorously shaken her head. Michael, smirking, had returned the receiver to his ear. 'Apparently she isn't here,' he said in an amused, ironical tone so that Josie – because it must be her – would know he was fibbing, and Annie felt foolish. 'Who was it?' she asked nervously, when he put the phone down. 'What do you care?' Michael had said. 'You're not even in.'

Now the phone sat peacefully on its table. Annie looked at her watch. Five past nine. Finn was shut in the living room but she could sense his watchful bulk on the other side of the closed door. Yesterday's crime seemed distant and illusory on this crisp new morning, something she'd dreamed in the restless small hours of the night. She'd told no one; not even Michael. Well, especially not Michael. But now she was about to leave the house to do the right thing, which was to see the farmer and offer him recompense for the loss of his live-stock. She was proud of that line: she'd rehearsed it and liked its tone of practical professionalism. *Recompense for the loss of his livestock*. She'd keep Finn out of it entirely. Finn was nobody's business but her own. It was purely a financial transaction, and no one need know anything about it, other than herself and the farmer. There was nothing at all to worry about.

Still though, there was a cold clod of fear in her chest as she left the house, and she had to endure the sorrowful gaze of her dog, who had his front paws on the inside ledge of the living-room window and was watching her leave without him.

Back in Wentford she found the farm a little too easily. It seemed no time at all before she was parking on the uneven, frosty flags of a yard, which was occupied on two sides by low outbuildings and on a third by a square farmhouse of blackened stone. There was a general ramshackle air; rusting machinery parts were piled in a heap, and an old livestock trailer, filthy with splattered mud and missing a wheel, listed sadly against the wall of a barn. And the smell! A bitter, potent mix of sheep, rotting grass and creosote assailed Annie as she picked her way tentatively towards a drab front door. If she hadn't been so afraid of slipping she would have held her nose, but she needed both arms for balance. Her stout dog-walking shoes would've been the thing but instead she had on her shopping shoes, and they had no grip. She found herself edging sideways to the door like a cautious crab and then it opened before she reached it, and a bony woman with a beaky nose and two hard black eyes challenged her with a stare. Annie panicked and her mind emptied of anything useful. The farmer's name? Gone. Her own? No idea. The two women considered each other without speaking. Annie's face glowed red.

'Now then, tha'll be 'ere about them sheep.'

This was a man's voice, and it came from behind her. 'Oh!' she said, and turned, and this small action caused her right foot to slip an inch or so on the frost. She teetered like a woman on a tightrope.

'Steady,' said the man. The peak of his tweed cap put his eyes in shadow, so Annie couldn't properly judge his expression. She hadn't expected him to know about the sheep yet, but she supposed farmers must check on their stock periodically. She cleared her throat to deliver her speech, but he said, 'Big lass beat thi to it.'

'Pardon?'

'Big lass, came yes'di. Carrot top.'

'I'm not with you,' Annie said. She wanted to offer recompense for the loss of his livestock, and instead she was listening to riddles.

'Copper knob,' said the woman at the door. 'Big red 'ed.'

'Sandra,' Annie said, suddenly understanding. She felt a stab of sharp indignation.

'Aye, that's it. Left 'er name and number yes'di morning.'

'Well, she had no business to,' Annie said. 'It's nothing to do with her.' She edged close enough to the door to be able to reach an arm out and support herself against the wall. The farmer took off his cap and gave his sandy hair a rub, so that it stuck out at odd angles. He eyed Annie with curiosity. She could see that he was a lot younger than the woman on the doorstep, who Annie now realised was quite ancient: tiny and stooped. Odd couple, she thought. The woman's hostile black eyes were

132

riveted on Annie's face, but the farmer's expression was mild, his tone phlegmatic.

'It were your dog, were it?'

'Well and another one, a little one, a stray, but it was, yes, and I'd like to offer you recom—'

'Poor do. Them ewes were in lamb.'

'Oh! Oh dear. Well I insist on offering you—'

'Bad business,' the farmer said. 'What dog is it?'

Annie steeled herself, mustered all her courage. 'That's neither here nor there,' she said. 'But if you'll let me know the—'

'See, some breeds are more prone 'n others to savaging.'

'I'm sure that's right but—'

'Pit bulls, mastiffs, they've a killer instinct. Yours a mastiff, is it?'

'No it is not. *He* is not,' Annie said indignantly. 'My Finn's a pedigree golden retriever and has never hurt a fly.'

'Until yes'di.'

Annie was silent at this incontrovertible truth, and anyway she'd already said more than she meant to. She'd resolved to keep Finn out of it and now at the least provocation she'd uttered his name! Next she'd be fetching out the photograph she kept in her handbag. The crone at the door said, 'Aye, an' 'e'll do it again,' and the farmer nodded.

'Aye,' he said. 'They get a taste for blood. A golden, eh? Well I'm surprised, but they're big buggers, reight enough. That little 'un couldn't 'ave managed wi'out yours. They work in packs, dogs. Now then, let's 'ave a brew, Mother.'

His mother: of course!

He made for the door and Annie wondered if that was

that. Surely not? She cleared her throat again. 'Erm, please can I offer you recompense for the loss of your livestock?' she said, finally managing to relay her rehearsed message, albeit to the back of his head. The old lady had retreated inside and now Annie could see into the porch through the open door. There were two dead rabbits hanging from a peg, and yellowing newspaper on the floor where there should have been lino.

'Aye, tha mun pay up,' the farmer said, pulling off his filthy wellies and leaving them where they fell. 'But not before we've 'ad a brew.'

Annie realised with panic that she was expected to follow him into the farmhouse. Should she take off her shoes too? No, she decided; they were as clean as a whistle, and judging by the state of the porch she'd need them to keep her socks clean. Still, the newspaper seemed to crackle reproachfully as she stepped inside.

In fact the kitchen wasn't half as bad as the porch suggested; old-fashioned, but there was nothing wrong with that. The tiles on the floor were cleanish, the sink was empty of pots, and apart from a crowded fly strip in the window, there was nothing dead that Annie could see. The old lady was sprightly in spite of her stoop; she bustled about making tea and slicing teacakes while the farmer, pleasantly courteous, offered Annie a chair before sitting down himself. They were at the table, facing each other. Wright, thought Annie, suddenly remembering his name with utter relief.

'Mr Wright,' she said at once, 'I can't tell you what a shock it was. I've had Finn for three years and he's soft as a brush.'

The farmer looked sceptical.

'No, really!' Annie said. 'He's never so much as looked at a sheep before.'

'Makes no odds to me,' he said. 'Fact is, 'e killed mine.'

'Well, yes.'

'One dog, no problem. Two dogs, trouble.'

'I see.'

'Bonnie and Clyde,' his mother said and cackled, without turning round from her post at the worktop.

'Right,' Annie said.

'I'll 'ave to charge market rate, you understand? Two ewes, four lambs, plus shiftin' them bodies from that top field. It all costs.'

'Four lambs—?'

'One ewe dead, one shot, an' both were carrying two apiece.'

'One shot?' Annie said.

'Aye, else it would 'ave bled to death.'

'Oh I see.' She felt chastened and, suddenly, profoundly sad. Those unborn babies, those slaughtered mothers.

'So I'll tot it all up and let you know.' Mr Wright appeared infinitely less affected than Annie. His mother had put a plate of large, flat toasted teacakes on the table, thickly spread with yellow butter. He pushed the plate towards Annie and she shook her head. 'No, thank you,' she said, believing herself too agitated to even think of food, but her mouth watered when she watched him take a bite. The old lady poured two mugs of dark brown tea and sloshed milk straight from the bottle into each one with no delicacy or finesse, yet when she brought the sugar to the table it was in cubes, in a china bowl, with silver tongs. She didn't sit with them, but instead fetched the rabbits from the porch and laid them out on a board by the sink.

'Now,' said the farmer. 'About that dog.'

Annie, alert to danger, sat up straighter in her chair.

'Where is 'e? Now, I mean?'

'Mr Wright,' Annie said, trying hard to sound implacable. 'I've apologised and I've said I'll pay whatever you ask, but I will not – I *will not* – surrender my dog to you.'

He laughed. 'Keep thi 'air on,' he said. 'I only asked where 'e is.'

Annie's heart pattered. She pictured Finn at home: contrite, lovable, loyal as the long day, and tears of compassion sprang to her eyes. Mr Wright's expression turned from amusement to concern.

'Ey, now, dunt take on,' he said, and he pushed the teacakes at her again as the only gesture of sympathy available to him and this time she took one.

'All I meant was, keep 'im out of 'arm's way, until you've decided what to do.'

'Do?' Her voice was muffled on account of the teacake, which was perhaps the most comforting thing she'd ever tasted.

'Aye, and int meantime you mun keep 'im away from sheep.'

'Your sheep?'

There was another cackle of amusement from his mother and Annie glanced round at her uneasily. The old lady was pulling the skin off a rabbit all of a piece, like a long furry sock. Hastily, Annie looked away.

'Nay, lass, any bugger's sheep. Yon dog'll not be fussy where 'is next mouthful comes from.'

Annie swallowed. 'So you don't want him shot?'

He shrugged. 'If I'd caught 'im at it, and I'd 'ad mi gun ... but nay, not in cold blood. Weren't 'is fault, were it?'

By which he means, thought Annie, that it was mine. She looked down at her hands. It struck her that she hadn't yet said sorry, and this in turn made her think of Sandra, who would have rolled her chilly green eyes and said 'typical'.

'Mr Wright, I really am very sorry,' Annie said now. 'I probably should've come yesterday.'

He nodded in agreement, but made no remark.

'It won't happen again, I promise you that.'

'If I were you,' he said, 'I'd mek sure o' that by givin' 'im away.'

'Oh, but I can't do that!' Annie said at once. 'He's family.'

'Kindest thing. Else, what will you do? Keep 'im tied up? Goldens need to run. Nowt worse for a big dog than a life on a lead.'

He was looking directly at her, but Annie was looking around the room. She wasn't seeing the green walls or the Formica units or even the old woman hacking a naked rabbit into pot-sized pieces. All she could see was Finn, pulling her arm almost out of its socket as she took him time and again down Beech Street to the rec. Even there she'd be fearful of letting him run free because who knew where sheep might be lurking to lure him to murder again? But give him away! The mere thought made her want to lay her head on the farmhouse table and sob.

Instead, she wrote down her address for Mr Wright and took her leave. He walked her to the car, even offered his arm so she wouldn't slip, and when she drove away he stood and watched her out of the yard as if he was sorry to see her go.

14

It was a squash in the car. Andrew was in the front seat with two suitcases on his lap, Bailey, Blake and Riley were in a row along the back, and in the boot the rest of their luggage was crammed untidily, so that it'd taken an almighty effort for Andrew to force shut the hatchback door. It was ten in the morning, but in Byron Bay it would be nine at night, and the flight had taken twenty-three hours, not including a one-hour stop in Dubai. Annie had given up trying to work out how any of that was even possible, let alone how it might make a person feel. Riley, the little one, was in a deep, deep sleep, immovably wedged in place – much like the suitcases – between his brother and his mother. Bailey rested her head on the small triangle of rear window and shut her eyes. 'I'm zoning out?' she said. 'I'm zonked?' Blake, though, was preternaturally alert. All the way from the railway station he fired little bullet questions at Andrew, each one quite unrelated to the last, and Andrew answered in a level, patient voice that he certainly hadn't got from Vince, who could never be doing with childish prattle. 'Ask your mother,' he would always say, or 'Button it,' if he was feeling ratty.

Blake wanted to know why the houses were so close

together, why the moon was out when it was morning, how many miles they were from Byron Bay, what was Andrew's favourite food in England, why the cattle here were black and white, what did the hob mean in hob-goblin; on and on he ploughed, coming up – it seemed to Annie – with any old question rather than allow a minute's silence to settle. Andrew listened and supplied a steady stream of thoughtful answers. Nobody mentioned Vince.

'What a chatterbox!' Annie said, when Blake drew breath. He hadn't yet addressed one word to her.

'Talks for Oz,' Andrew said. 'Don't you, buddy? We're in training for the next talking Olympics.' He still had traces of an English accent, but Annie only noticed because she was listening hard for them. He had been so young when he went to Australia, it was no wonder he'd gone native. But at least he didn't turn every statement into a question, thought Annie. They were turning into her road now and she said, 'Here we are, Beech Street.' Blake peered through his window doubtfully.

'Dad, where's the ocean?' he asked.

'Not that kinda beach, buddy,' Andrew said. 'Beech with two "e"s. It's a kinda tree.'

'So where're the trees?'

Andrew laughed. 'Good point, buddy, but if you look around at the other roads, you'll see they all have tree names too, see? Elm Street across the way, Ash and Oak further down. They're just nice names, see?'

'Bit dumb,' Blake said. 'Should be No Beech Street, No Elm Street.'

Annie looked at Andrew, waiting for some mild judicious reprimand, but none came. 'I guess so,' was all he said. 'Strictly speaking.' He yawned widely. 'So, let's haul these bags into the house, show Gram how strong you are.'

Annie wanted to be Grandma not Gram, but anyway she said, 'You've certainly grown, Blake – you're going to be a very tall young man,' but it was a statement, not a question, so she supposed she shouldn't expect an answer. A smile would have been nice, though. As it was, the boy simply clambered out of the car and said, 'These houses are *tiny*,' in a voice high with incredulity. Bailey opened her eyes.

'Jeez,' she said, squinting out dozily past Riley, through the door that Blake had opened. 'Is that a bear at your window?'

She meant Finn, who had his paws up on the ledge inside the house and was watching their arrival with mounting interest.

'Oh,' Annie said, 'that's just Finn.' She gave him a wave and he grinned.

'Finn?' Bailey said.

'Hon, don't freak,' Andrew said. 'Mum, you didn't say you had a dog.'

'Oh, well, I do,' Annie said. 'But he's ever so friendly.' She thought of the sheep. 'He *loves* people,' she added.

'It's just, I'm allergic?' Bailey said.

'Hon, it's cats that set you off.'

'It's pet hair?' Bailey said, turning her sleepy eyes on Andrew.

'Well, let's see how it goes,' Andrew said. 'You might be fine.' How *reasonable* he is, thought Annie: how *easy*. They'd been together for years, Andrew and Bailey, just kids when they met, but Andrew was as nice when he spoke to her now as he ever was. Annie wondered if Bailey knew the extent of her luck, being able to lay claim to Andrew: handsome, kind, capable. He had the boot open now, and was hauling luggage onto the pavement while Bailey grappled Riley out of the car, a dead weight in her arms. His head lolled backwards and his two skinny legs swung like plumb lines. Blake had his nose pressed against the living-room window and was pulling faces at Finn. Annie hurried up the path to unlock the front door.

'Michael home?' Andrew asked.

'No, no, not on a Friday morning; he has classes till one.' She worried what he'd say when he saw all these bags; perhaps, she thought, they could be quickly carried upstairs and unpacked, then stacked on the back patio out of the way, under a plastic sheet.

'We'll just dump these here for now,' Andrew said, following her through the small porch and into the hall. He dropped two holdalls on the floor, then went out for more. 'No need to unpack anything yet,' he said over his shoulder, and then, 'How about a cuppa, Mum? Blake! Quit scaring the hound and pick up a bag.'

Bailey crossed him on the path, bearing Riley before her like a sacrificial offering. Inside, she made straight for the stairs. 'I'll just dump him anywhere?' she said, already partway up.

'No!' said Annie, a little too forcefully, so that Bailey stopped and widened her brown eyes. 'Sorry, but not Michael's bed,' Annie said. 'Not the front one, the room with a music stand in it. Not that one, I mean.'

Bailey laughed.

'Well it's just—'

'It's cool?' Bailey said. 'I get the picture?' and she continued on upstairs with her load. Annie watched her for a moment, just to be sure, and then bustled off to the kitchen. She felt lightheaded, remote, dizzy with unresolved anxieties. The boys were so much *bigger* now; even Riley, whom she hadn't yet seen upright, seemed all legs and arms. Bailey had struggled under his weight. And then Bailey! Walking straight upstairs like that without so much as a by-your-leave. Yes, she was Andrew's wife, but still; niceties should be observed, permissions asked, or else their visit might take on the qualities of an invasion. Annie put the kettle on and ventured back to the hallway. The two front doors were wide open still. Blake was now cartwheeling up and down the front path and Andrew was filling the house with bags; there were six pieces of luggage so far, two of them directly blocking the foot of the stairs. Michael would come home to chaos, and then they'd all know about it.

Behind the closed living-room door, Finn crooned and whined, longing to be released into the fray, but Annie turned a deaf ear to his lamentations. The very last thing she needed right now was him turning giddy circles through the melee to express his delight.

When Andrew was a little boy, he'd loved Annie with a fierce and urgent heat; he would hug her as if he was trying to claim the ground she stood on. Michael always kept a distance, needing only the material fundamentals of mothering – clothes, food, clean sheets – to sustain him. Andrew though: he needed all of her, heart and soul. School came as a terrible wrench for both of them. For the least of reasons she would let him stay at home, where the two of them would sit contentedly at the kitchen table dunking custard creams in milky tea and listening to the wireless. If she'd been asked to predict which of her sons would stay with her, and which one would move across the globe ... well.

'Custard cream?' she asked Andrew now, wondering if he remembered, but he only shook his head and gave her a neutral smile. He stood across from her in the small kitchen, nursing a mug of tea in both hands. She let her gaze rove all over his face, feasting her eyes, taking him in, and he blew across the top of his tea and watched her.

'What?' he said.

'You haven't changed a bit.'

Andrew laughed. 'It's only been six years, Mum.'

'No, I mean I can still see the little boy in you.' She really could; she could see him now at that Formica table in their Coventry kitchen, blowing on his tea to cool it, regarding her with his calm grey eyes. His hair was darker now than it had been then, but he still had as much of it, and it was still prone to unruliness. And there was that fragile white line of a scar running from his temple to the corner of his right eye. When he smiled, it puckered.

'Have you ever thought about a loft conversion?' he said, bringing her back to the present. 'You could have another floor, easy-peasy.' This was one of the ways he made a living in Australia, putting extra rooms in people's roof spaces. There wasn't much Annie would change about Andrew, but she did wish he wasn't a builder: wished he'd taken more exams instead of loafing off to France on a train and falling in step with Bailey, years and years ago, when they were still in their teens. But anyway.

'Oh,' she said, 'no, not really. It'd be a lot of disruption and there's only two people.'

'Yeah but one of them's Michael,' he said.

'Oh, Andrew.'

'Seriously, he could have a whole floor to himself, his own bathroom too, maybe. You wouldn't be worrying you'd left a hair in the sink or a sock on the floor.'

Actually that sounded nice, Annie thought, but all she said was, 'It's full of clutter.'

'Yeah, that's 'cause it's a loft, but you clear it out before they start, y'see. Most of it can probably be binned anyway.'

'Oh, I don't know, maybe. I'll see.'

Michael would hate it, she was thinking. Michael would be impossible to live with through building work.

'I'll check it out for you,' Andrew said. 'Stick my head through the hatch and have a look. Now, how about we visit the old bastard?'

'Andrew!'

'Shall we?'

'I thought it could wait till tomorrow,' she said. 'I thought you'd be too tired, or too busy, you know, unpacking.'

'I reckon Bailey can manage that when she surfaces.'

Bailey hadn't reappeared after taking Riley upstairs. She was discovered fast asleep, stretched out alongside Riley on Annie's bed. They were both on their backs with their heads turned towards each other, as if in conversation.

'Well, we can't just leave, with them asleep upstairs!' Annie didn't want to go to Glebe Hall, that was the truth of it. She wanted Andrew to herself for a while, without having to include Vince.

'Sure we can. We'll take Blake with us and leave a note.'

'Blake?' Annie said. 'Oh I don't think ...' But Andrew was already emptying his mug, swilling it out with water from the tap.

'Well, he won't know you,' Annie said. 'Last time Michael went he took him for an intruder and threw a beaker at him.' Three years ago now, she thought, and Michael hadn't been since.

Andrew grinned happily. 'Sounds reasonable,' he said.

'He's in a world of his own half the time, so don't be expecting a big reunion.'

'Mum,' Andrew said. 'I came to England to see Dad, so why're you trying to talk me out of it?'

Oh anyway, Annie thought, what difference did it actually make who went to see Vince, or when? Chances were he'd be fast asleep, and if he was awake you'd hardly know it. So she let Finn out into the back garden to cock his leg while Andrew wrote a note for Bailey, then they shut the dog away again, and off they went.

At Glebe Hall Blake held his nose the moment they stepped inside and said, 'Gross!' so Andrew had to step straight out again and have a quiet chat with him. Annie waited in the stuffy front reception. There was no one at the desk, but a hum of muted conversation drifted across from the staff room and from the row of ground-floor bedrooms came the sounds of competing televisions, showing their daytime chat shows and antique hunts. Annie peered down the corridor. The door to Vince's room was propped open, and from this angle she could just see the very end of his metal bed, the white top sheet tucked tight at the corners, undisturbed by his feeble, motionless legs. Her spirits sagged at the thought of Vince's emaciated limbs and slack features, but then Moira the Irish nurse appeared from a different room and Andrew came in with Blake, and suddenly the thick, still air of the foyer was full of introductions and laughter and Annie felt heady with pride at being able to lay claim to this handsome man and his tousle-headed boy.

'Well now, this is an event right enough,' Moira said, clapping her hands, and directing her words downwards at Blake. 'It's a red letter day when I have visitors all the way from Australia!'

'We came to see Gramps, not you,' Blake said.

'Blake,' said Andrew, sounding a warning note, but Moira was hooting with laughter as if she'd never heard anything funnier. She set off down the corridor, speaking to them over her shoulder. 'He's awake, you're in luck,' she said perkily, and Annie's heart sank. They trooped single file into Vince's room, Annie last behind Andrew and Blake, who followed the nurse. The television was on but the sound had been turned right down. A slick, silver-haired man waggled his head at a studio audience; they laughed uproariously, in silence.

'Now then, Vince,' Moira said, too loudly, leaning across the bed so that she looked down directly into his eyes, which gazed up at the ceiling. 'Some special people to see you.'

Vince turned his head at the sound of her voice and Moira moved out of the way and left the room. Blake took a cautious step backwards, nearer the door, but Vince only seemed to see Annie; he let his hooded eyes, red-rimmed and damp, settle on her, and he tutted as if to say, 'Not you again?' although likely as not he meant no such thing. His everyday responses were jumbled these days, hard to interpret; a shake of the head might not mean no, a nod could mean anything.

'Look, Vince, Andrew's here,' Annie said. 'All the way from Australia – isn't that nice?' She was trying to sound bright but in fact she sounded, to her own ear at least, like a second-rate actress delivering implausible lines. She had no idea whether Vince understood, but anyway his eyes slid from Annie and onto Andrew.

'Hey, Dad,' Andrew said. 'How're you doing?' He perched on the edge of the bed. Vince stared, suddenly transfixed, his dull eyes unmistakably brightened by a light of recognition. Andrew was encouraged. He tried to draw Blake a little closer, but the boy held his ground, so that Andrew had to stretch his arm backwards to reach him. 'This is Blake, remember? My eldest boy?'

Vince ignored the question but lifted a crêpey hand from the bedcover and pointed a quivering finger.

'Where've you been?' he said. His voice was thick, as if he had a mouthful of porridge, but his words were still audible and his tone clearly accusatory. Andrew laughed, trying to be cheerful, though Vince's expression had turned grim.

'At home, in Byron Bay,' Andrew said. 'It's a long way away.'

'You only went out for a loaf.'

'Come again?' Andrew leaned forwards, releasing Blake, who immediately stepped away out of reach and stood in front of the noiseless television, arms folded, watching the screen.

'You went out for a loaf, that was all.' Vince looked

now at Annie, appealing to her for sympathy. 'She never came back,' he said. Horrifyingly, his voice cracked and tears began to stream down his cheeks.

'Oh come on,' Annie said. 'Let's go.' But Andrew said, 'Hey, Dad,' and placed a gentle hand on the old man's head. Vince just turned his face to the wall. He made guttural, staccato sounds of grief.

'Leave him,' Annie said. Her voice sounded too harsh, so she added, more softly, 'It'll do him no good, getting worked up.' She tugged at Andrew's sleeve. 'Come on,' she said again. 'We can come back tomorrow.'

Andrew ignored her altogether.

'Dad?' he said, and he took Vince's hand, folding it in his own and stroking it with his thumb. The gesture was so tender, so natural, that Annie, watching, felt at first a pang of pure jealousy and then a swift rush of dislike for Vince, the old conman, up to his tricks again. So like him to rouse himself just enough to cause trouble.

'I said leave him.'

This time she didn't bother to hide her feelings and Andrew shot her a startled glance. Even Blake paid attention, slowly turning his head from the screen and regarding her dispassionately, like a cool little owl.

'It's all show,' Annie said, unrepentant. 'They're crocodile tears.'

Everyone looked at Vince. Under the covers, his fragile body made barely an impression, as if he had only two dimensions, front and back. With what seemed a gargantuan effort he shifted position so that he was looking directly at Annie, and then he snarled, drawing back his top lip and showing sharp yellow teeth. Very cautiously, Andrew slid his hand away from Vince's.

'See?' Annie said.

Blake laughed. 'He's growling,' he said. 'Awesome.'

'You,' said Vince, glowering at Annie and speaking through gritted teeth, 'make me sick.'

'Dad!' Andrew said. He stood up, sat down again, then looked at Annie, who was white as the sheets on his father's bed. She took a few hesitant steps backwards, towards the open door.

'And you, Martha.' This was Vince again, looking at Andrew with a softer expression, though not a loving one; rather, he seemed weighed down with disappointment. 'Never thought you'd do that. Never in this world.'

Andrew gave a small, desperate laugh of relief. 'Dad, it's me, Andrew. I'm not Martha. Mum, who's Martha?'

He turned to Annie for the answer, but she was gone.

15

All the way home it was Martha this, Martha that, as Andrew and Blake speculated who Vince might have had in mind. Blake found it hilarious that his grandfather had taken his dad for a woman. Andrew took the matter more seriously, searching the past for a lost Martha who may have drifted into Vince's fractured mind. Annie, put out by the episode, said she knew nothing that could shed light on the matter, and anyway she couldn't care less. Pointless to speculate, she said. Why, only two weeks ago he'd introduced her to Moira as the tooth fairy.

'Well, that's diffcrent,' Andrew said. 'That's just non-sense.'

'Yes, and so's this,' Annie said. She would be drawn no more on the subject, and drove them back in a tight-lippcd silence which neither Andrew nor Blake seemed to notice.

At home there was a mud-caked Land Rover parked exactly where Annie's car had been.

'Who the dickens ...?' Annie said. She huffed and tutted as she edged her little Nissan into a different space behind the towering Defender, which looked entirely out of place in the tidy, regular proportions of Beech Street. So rude, thought Annie, to plonk a great filthy beast like this outside the wrong house: outside *her* house. She felt tired and a little tearful, and Michael's padlocked bike was leaning against the side of the house, which only meant there was more trouble in store. She found, as she walked up her own garden path, that she was dreading going in, but then the door flew open and Riley stood there, with a smile on his face that acted on Annie like a ray of sunshine.

'You're my grandma,' he said, in an informative manner. 'I'm Riley.'

He had a sweetly piping voice. Two of his front teeth were missing and his hair was blonde and thick, just like Andrew's had been when he was six. He had Andrew's soft grey eyes, too; the likeness filled Annie's heart with a strange sorrow, a hopeless longing for something she'd lost. He reached up to her with both arms for a hug, and she was smitten, captivated.

'I know exactly who you are,' she said, bending down to receive his clumsy embrace. 'Did you have a good sleep?' He smelled of yeast and sugar, like a newly baked teacake. She wanted to gather him to her and inhale his little-boy essence but she was afraid she might alarm him, so instead she stood upright again, and only left a hand on his narrow shoulder.

'There's a man here,' he said, ignoring her question.

'Uncle Michael?' Annie said. Oh, she hoped Michael was being amenable.

'No, he's upstairs, but there's another man. He's with Mummy. Hi, Daddy!'

He edged around Annie and ran to Andrew, who swooped him up and swung him round so that his skinny legs trailed out like streamers, and Blake started clamouring for a turn. Annie went into the house, tentatively now that she knew there was a visitor. No one ever came to call, apart from canvassers in gaudy rosettes on polling day and, occasionally, Jehovah's Witnesses selling *The Watchtower*. But there wasn't an election, and who would invite a Jehovah's Witness into the living room? She could hear Michael playing a feverish violin solo in his room upstairs. She could also hear the rising lilt of Bailey's voice through the living-room door, so she pushed it open and saw Mr Dinmoor settled comfortably on the sofa, and Bailey cross-legged on the floor with Finn prostrate at her side, his head in her lap, eyes closed. Annie's mouth dropped open. Bailey looked up at her and registered her arrival with a lazy smile.

'Hey, Annie?' Bailey said. 'Alf here's been telling me about his travels in Australia? Quite a guy.'

Mr Dinmoor flapped a dismissive hand and beamed. He said, 'Good to see you again, Annie,' as if it was a perfectly natural occurrence for him to be sitting here in her front room: as if they were friends, when in fact she barely knew him. He glanced down at Finn, whose eyes were still closed in perfect bliss as Bailey scratched the top of his head. 'He looks all right anyway,' Mr Dinmoor said. 'Forgotten all about it, I expect. How about you, though? What a shock for you.'

Bailey looked puzzled. 'What's happened?' she said.

'I thought you were allergic,' Annie said. She couldn't look at Mr Dinmoor, so instead she glared at Bailey. 'You've dog hairs all over your clothes.'

'He's such a sweetheart? And I guess Andy's right, it's just cats?'

'I rang last night, no, Wednesday night,' Mr Dinmoor

said. 'Talked to a fella, your son, I think. Said I'd try to pop round. Didn't he say?'

'So what's happened?' Bailey asked again.

Annie found she couldn't speak. How could she say that her sweet Finn was now a savager of sheep? Just like that perhaps: straight out with it, bold and brutal. But she wasn't in the habit of outright honesty so she didn't answer and instead allowed the silence to grow as she refused to meet Mr Dinmoor's friendly gaze or Bailey's curious one, then behind her Andrew saved the day by sticking his head round the door.

'Hey, guys,' he said chirpily.

'Alf Dinmoor,' Mr Dinmoor said with evident relief, standing up and offering a hand.

Andrew came into the room to greet him. 'Andy Doyle,' he said.

With four of them in there, and Finn stretched out like a living hearthrug, it was beginning to feel crowded and hot. Annie swayed slightly where she stood, and pulled the woollen turtle neck of her sweater away from her throat. She felt distinctly queer: wondered, in fact, if she might be hallucinating.

Bailey uncrossed her legs and Finn shifted position too, pulling away momentarily then lolling heavily against her when she settled again. Annie caught his eye and at once he stood up and walked to her side, where he panted up at her with an anxious, love-struck expression, although she didn't fuss him, only folded her arms and regarded him coolly.

'Alf knows Byron Bay?' Bailey said, to Andrew. 'And Brunswick Heads?'

'Is that right?' Andrew said, with a lively interest that Annie found irritating.

'Ah, now,' said Mr Dinmoor, sitting down again. 'I wouldn't say I know them exactly.'

Bailey shot him a puzzled look.

'I mean, it was a long time ago ...' He trailed off, seeming uncertain how to proceed, and at last Annie turned to look at him, but he was staring down at the carpet between his sturdy brown brogues. He looked a good deal smarter than he had at Josie's last week; he had on a pair of grey trousers, a discreetly checked flannel shirt and a navy V-neck sweater, all of which were quality garments, meticulously pressed as if he meant to make a favourable impression. Still though, she hoped he was sorry he'd come; his intentions were undoubtedly kind, but if he thought she was going to discuss Finn's misdemeanour with him, and in front of everyone, he was sorely mistaken. Perhaps he aired his business to all and sundry, but it didn't mean she had to. She cleared her throat to speak.

'Mr Dinmoor, Andrew and Bailey haven't been here long, and we've some catching up to do.'

He leaped to his feet as though he'd been stung.

'Yes, right, well, I'm sorry, I can see it's not a good time.'

'Ah no, it's cool,' Andrew said. He smiled, managing to include everyone in the warmth of it, and said he was making a pot of tea, and why didn't Alf stay for that? But Mr Dinmoor had edged towards the door, and Annie was pretending Andrew hadn't spoken.

'Cheerio then,' she said firmly, and she led him out into the hall. Upstairs the violin reached the summit of a violent crescendo then ceased dramatically, and Annie hurried Mr Dinmoor towards the exit with renewed urgency. The two doors gaped open, and a sharp winter wind disturbed the pages of Michael's music magazine, which waited for his attention on the plant stand. Blake and Riley were leapfrogging each other down the path, their faces red with cold and exertion.

'Grand lads,' Mr Dinmoor said.

'Come inside, you two,' Annie said. 'You've no coats on, you'll catch your deaths.' Riley looked at her wide-eyed and Blake scowled, but they filed obediently up the path.

'Dunt feel the cold at this age,' Mr Dinmoor said, 'do you, lads?'

They didn't answer, but squeezed past him into the hallway. Blake mooched sulkily into the living room, but Riley stood by Annie and stared at Mr Dinmoor.

'Bye then,' Annie said. She stepped forwards, forcing him into the porch.

'Look,' he said. 'I was concerned about you, Annie, that's all, and I—'

'Yes,' she said. 'I know you're being kind, but there's really no need. Everything's fine.'

She was all but pushing him out onto the step because behind her she could hear the soft creak of stairs, which was the sound of Michael descending in his slippers.

'Right. It's just, Josie was concerned and I said—'

She closed the door on his sentence, feeling terrible and triumphant at the same time. For a brief moment they stared at each other through the panes, their faces oddly distorted by the whorls and swirls of the patterned glass. 'Sorry,' she mouthed, but she didn't know if he'd understood because he just turned and walked away.

'Don't you like him, Grandma?' Riley asked.

'Oh well, I barely know him,' she said. Together they watched Mr Dinmoor's retreating shape.

Michael, who had paused at the foot of the stairs, said, 'Shut that damned porch, it's arctic in here.'

She picked up the magazine and stepped into the hall, followed by Riley, who closed the door. Annie could tell that the little boy already knew to be wary of Michael. His slight frame was poised for a hasty escape to his parents in the living room, but curiosity kept him by Annie's side.

'Do you want this *Strad*?' she asked, holding the magazine out to Michael like a pre-emptive peace offering. He ignored her and walked to the kitchen and her heart sank. His displeasure filled the hallway and soured the air they breathed. Beside her, Riley slipped a little hand into hers in a small gesture of solidarity.

The kitchen table wasn't big enough to seat everyone – and anyway there were only two chairs – so the evening meal had to be taken in the living room, with plates on laps. Finn was banished to the back garden out of temptation's way; he sat upright and noble on the patio like a stone lion. Annie busied herself with pans and plates, and Michael loomed, putting her on edge. She'd roasted six strips of salmon fillet, which she was serving with boiled potatoes and broccoli.

'Only you would give us a summer luncheon for dinner on a night like this,' Michael said as she plated up. She looked at him, appalled.

'I didn't think,' she said.

'Clearly.'

'Bailey doesn't eat meat, though.'

'Or fish either?' Bailey's voice preceded her, but then suddenly there she was in the kitchen, pushing her thick blonde fringe away from her eyes and peering at the plates. Annie was confused.

'You don't eat meat and you don't eat fish?'

Bailey shook her head ruefully.

'Then what do you eat?'

'Veggies, pasta, rice, pulses?'

'Pulses?'

Michael snorted. 'Edible seeds, Mother,' he said. 'Lentils. Chickpeas. Beans.' He picked up his plate. 'I'll take mine in my room, by the way.' He left the kitchen and carried his salmon carefully upstairs. Bailey watched him go then wrinkled her sweetly upturned nose at Annie in comradely collusion. 'He's cross as a frog in a sock, isn't he?' she said, sotto voce, and Annie was forced to laugh.

'Is he often like this?' Bailey whispered.

'I'm afraid so, yes,' Annie said, in the same hushed tones.

'He's not like Andrew, is he?'

'Not at all, no. Quite a lot like Vince, though.' Annie was speaking normally now, suddenly seized by a devil-may-care defiance. 'Irritable,' she said, in a voice he might overhear. 'Unreasonable.' She slid a salmon fillet off one of the plates. 'It's a funny sort of meal, Bailey, broccoli and potatoes.'

'Ah, no worries, Annie.' Bailey's open countenance was entirely cheerful and Annie found she was almost smiling too.

'Should I fry you an egg?'

'Genius idea,' Bailey said. 'But I'll do it, you go sit.'

So Annie carried plates through to the others while Bailey fried an egg for herself and sang in a clear, strong voice that filtered from the kitchen, sweetening the air, lightening the atmosphere. Annie couldn't remember the last time anyone had sung in this house but Bailey belted out the lyrics in an unconscious, uninhibited way, and she obviously did it often, because neither Andrew nor the boys so much as batted an eyelid.

'This is great, Mum,' Andrew said, although it was on the dull side of ordinary and Annie knew it.

'I don't like it,' Blake said at once. 'I want an egg too.'

'Oh, well ...' Annie began to rise from the armchair she'd just lowered herself into.

'No you don't,' Andrew said, waving a fork at her. 'Stay where you are, Mum. Blake buddy, eat your fish.'

The boy's face took on a glowering, mutinous expression, which his father ignored.

'You okay, Mum?' Andrew asked Annie. The skin around her eyes felt tight and drawn, but Annie just said, 'Right as rain,' and gave him a quick smile that invited no further inquiry. Bailey joined them in the living room, drifting in with her plate balanced on one hand. She dropped fluidly into a cross-legged position on the floor. Blake eyed her fried egg covetously. Riley speared a new potato with his knife and licked it like a lollipop. The room was still too warm and smelled of salmon, and upstairs would be fishy too now, Annie thought. She pictured Michael eating at his desk, directly above them in his bedroom. She felt ashamed of his behaviour yet grateful that he'd absented himself, then she jumped as

Riley appeared to read her mind.

'Does Uncle Michael always eat upstairs?'

The question was innocently asked, Riley being too little to judge a grown man for cold-shouldering his only brother and rejecting his family in favour of a solitary meal.

'No, love,' Annie said. 'Only sometimes.'

'Can I see Grandpa tomorrow?'

'He's crazy,' Blake said, perking up. 'He snarled like a dingo and he thought Dad was a woman.'

'He's confused, buddy, not crazy,' Andrew said. 'Mind you,' he added, talking now to Annie, 'he seemed pretty insistent.'

Annie didn't answer. Vince could die now, she thought. Tonight would be perfect. It'd be one less thing to worry about.

16

By the time Michael was three years old, Annie's life in Coventry felt almost normal, even though most of the time it was just the two of them and he wasn't much company for her either. He was an odd little boy, a paradoxical mix of independent spirit and needy reliance, so that in spite of an unwavering seam of cool and distant competence, he expected his mother to be always on hand. It was curious and unsettling, and most unexpected in a child so young. Annie couldn't work him out; couldn't fathom why he insisted on a story, many times a day, but would never sit on Annie's lap to listen, choosing instead to place himself alongside her, with a small gap between, of precisely the width of his hand span. From time to time he checked this gap, and if it appeared to have closed, even fractionally, he edged away until his hand could once more spread out between them, unobstructed. From this distance he concentrated furiously on the book, glaring at the pictures and nodding curtly when he wished Annie to turn the page.

Almost from birth, he hated to be touched, except on the rare occasions that he was hurt, when he might endure a swift hug. He especially hated to be held – most especially when he was unclothed – and he shrank from the warmth of human contact like a feral kitten born in a hay barn. When he was older he wouldn't take her hand even to cross a road, although he submitted to reins, which was a relief to Annie, who was unequal to his wilful ways and could never persuade him to do anything he didn't want to do. The child seemed to have come into the world with a lifetime of dislikes already in place: a comprehensive list of rules and requirements with which his mother must comply if they were to get along. She didn't understand him, not at all, but as time passed his oddness became routine, and it was only when Vince paid them a visit that Michael's behaviour came back into sharp relief.

But then, Vince was so rarely there, and when he left again, it was for weeks at a time – months, sometimes. He was vague about his exact whereabouts, but when people asked, Annie always said his job obliged him to live in Sunderland. This was where he went when he first left, in February 1964, but she knew he'd moved around a lot since then, and that he wasn't even working for the same company any more. He hadn't entirely forsaken her, though. Every month he sent a generous sum – guilt money, Annie called it – in small buff-coloured envelopes, and the postmarks on them told her more than Vince did: Newcastle, Sunderland, Hartlepool, Durham: places in the north-east that Annie was never invited to visit. She pictured them as grey and inhospitable, gritty and industrial; she wouldn't want to go to such places even if he did ask.

She didn't socialise with her father and Mrs Binley. They never asked her round or called in at the Sydney Road house, and Annie never invited them. When

Michael was born Vince let Harold Platt know, sharpish, in case the arrival of a grandson might unlock the coffers, but all they sent was a basket of fruit, wrapped in cellophane and tied with an oversized bow. Vince wouldn't let Annie eat any of it and left it outside by the dustbin, still beribboned: a shocking waste, but she wanted it no more than he did. Then Vince went again and Annie and Michael were alone together for weeks and weeks.

Those were difficult days. At the clinic they said they'd seen some miserable infants in their time but never one like Michael Doyle: a newborn with the personality of a grumpy old man. The nurses laughed at the baby's impotent fury as each week Annie handed him over, burning with shame, believing wholeheartedly in her own inadequacy because her baby hated to be undressed, hated to be weighed, hated to be dressed again. He balled his hands into miniature fists and screamed at a high, hysterical pitch that set everyone's nerves on edge. Inside the damp cavern of his open mouth, his little tongue quivered like the string of a bow, lending to each outward wail a warbling quality that tore at Annie's heart, but the nurses showed no pity. They were extra brisk when they dealt with him; they rushed, Annie knew they did. At home his rage filled the house, and he wouldn't be pacified with milk or a dummy or cuddles. When he deigned to settle to a feed, he either slid his dark eyes away from her with blank indifference or glowered at her over the bottle. Generally, when he slept, it wasn't because he was content but because he'd worn himself out. Annie was worn out, too. Once, in despair, she laid him tenderly on a blanket on the hard pantry floor then closed the door and left him there among the tinned peaches and

Carnation milk, while she shut herself in the bedroom – upstairs and at the opposite end of the house – and tried in vain to sleep.

But he was her baby so she gritted her teeth and loved him, and whether he liked it or not, he couldn't manage without her. She was sure of that, at least; his dependency was complete. Sometimes she wondered if he understood this, and hotly resented it. Might the nurses at the baby clinic have been right? Might he actually *be* an old soul trapped in a new body: an ancient Chinese despot, fetching up in Coventry in 1964?

They spent a lot of time outside because Michael was more settled when on the move, and Annie herself felt less worn down out of the house, bouncing Michael along in the splendidly sprung baby carriage that Auntie Doreen had sent up from Peckham. She walked for miles, just as she always had done, just as she did as a little girl; she took her baby all the way to the river, on the outskirts of the city, and together they watched the water dance innocently into the mouth of the culvert to be gobbled up by roads and buildings. She lifted him out of the pram to show him and he fought to be put back. She walked a long figure of eight through the city, from the edges to the centre, in and out, looping round to parts of Coventry that she barely knew, and it was on one such outing, when Michael was approaching six months old, that Annie stopped at the window of a haberdasher, remembering that she needed pearlised buttons for a knitted matinee jacket. When the pram came to a halt, Michael frowned even before he opened his eyes, and then, when Annie reached in to lift him out, he arched his back and stiffened his legs and began the rapid, hiccoughing protest that always preceded his outbursts of rage. If she was quick, Annie thought, she could be in and out before he reached full throttle, but it was an unrealistic ambition. She pulled a pack of buttons from the display and raced to the counter, but he was already scarlet-faced and square-mouthed, rearing away from her and bellowing his displeasure.

'I had one of them,' the woman behind the counter said, taking the buttons and slipping them into a paper bag.

Annie looked at her. She was quite elderly, but with a spry and playful air that was apparent even in this brief transaction; her smile worked like balm on Annie's spirits.

'Yes, right little devil my Peter was,' the woman said. Her eyes twinkled merrily at the memory. 'Unhappy in his own skin.'

'That's it,' Annie said. 'That's exactly it.' She felt a wave of excited gratitude at the diagnosis.

'Your first, is he?' The woman had to raise her voice above the racket.

'He is, yes,' Annie said. 'Probably my last, too,' she added, which was meant to be wry but came out sad, and the woman clucked at her sympathetically.

'Here,' she said. 'Pass him over, m'duck.' She reached out, and Annie gave him to her without a pause. It was simply wonderful to have someone take him.

'Now then, my Peter could never resist a ball of wool.'

'Wool!'

'Wool. He was the only one o' mine I used to bring to the shop, because he was never more content than here.' By now she'd plonked the squally little infant on the counter and was busy unbuttoning him, releasing him from his layers. She pulled off his hat then blew in his soft black hair, and when he looked up at her in shocked surprise she blew in his face too. He blinked and fell utterly silent. Annie watched in a sort of trance, awed by the other woman's deft competence. She wanted to say, don't undress him, he hates to be undressed, and yet there he sat, down to his vest, and the frilled plastic pants that covered and contained his bulky nappy, and all he was doing was staring.

'Now then,' the lady said. 'That's better, little man.' She picked him up, sitting him on her hip, and carried him to a large round wicker basket on the floor. It was three-quarters full of balls of wool: a mish-mash of colours and sizes. *ODDS and ENDS* said a sign attached to the front.

'Worth a try,' she said, and she sat Michael in the midst of it all, then picked up a ball of yellow wool and gave it to him, poking his little fingers into the strands so that he didn't immediately drop it. He'd been quiet now for approaching five minutes.

'Won't he spoil it?' Annie said. She meant the balls of wool, some of which were already flattened underneath his bottom.

'Nothing to spoil, m'duck,' said the woman. 'They're all ends or seconds. See now?'

Michael had extracted his fingers from the yellow wool and was now concentrating hard on getting them back in. He still looked fierce, thought Annie, but it was a calm fierceness, if such a thing was possible; he made small effortful noises as he worked.

'Now,' said the woman. 'I'm Barbara and you're ...?'

'Annie Doyle,' Annie said, looking at her saviour in wonder. 'And that there's Michael.'

'Well, Michael can stay put. You come this side o' my counter in case another body comes in, and I'll make you a cup of tea in my back room. I expect you could do with a bit o' peace.'

'Oh!' Annie said feelingly. 'Oh, I could,' and Barbara laughed. She left Annie at the till where all by herself she sold a packet of crochet hooks and a dress pattern, and watched Michael in his pool of wool. Then Barbara came back with the tea, and it was two hours later when Annie left the shop, by which time she had a part-time job as Barbara's assistant, on the understanding that baby Michael would come along too.

'Good for business,' Barbara said. 'Nothing sells wool like a real live baby.'

Michael hadn't cried once. He was allowed to keep the yellow wool and as Annie wheeled him out he held it aloft like a trophy.

Barbara's haberdashery was called Sew and Sew's: jaunty name, jaunty owner. She was the friendliest, most cheerful person Annie had ever known. Sometimes women came into her shop just to chat, but Barbara didn't mind at all. 'Oh, they'll buy next time,' she told Annie. 'Or the time after that.'

Annie hadn't noticed the shop before, for all that she'd paced miles along Coventry's pavements over the years. Part of her believed that it had sprung up by magic, to rescue her from the pit of despair. This wasn't the sort of nonsense she'd ever voice, but nevertheless she couldn't entirely shed the fear that one day she'd find it gone, without a trace. 'How long have you been here?' she asked Barbara, more than once, and Barbara always said, 'Oh for ever and a day, that's what it feels like anyway,' or 'Since Noah built his ark, dear,' and this jocular evasiveness only added to Annie's suspicion that Barbara and her shop were enchanted: the work of fairies, or benevolent gods.

For three years, Annie worked on Thursdays and Fridays; Barbara fetched in a second stool and they perched together behind the counter while Michael sat on the shop floor taking balls of wool from the basket, then putting them back again. Barbara told customers he was stocktaking. The shop was no busier on Annie's days than any other, but she made herself as useful as possible; dusting the fittings when there were no customers, tidying the stockroom so that everything down to the tiniest press stud could be found in a trice, lining the bay windows with new yellow cellophane to keep the light off the knitted clothes and bolts of cloth. She kept the books for Barbara too, and totted up the week's takings in a ledger, offsetting income – in black ink – against outgoings – in red – with net profit marked in green at the end of each page. She found she had a talent for it; she was, after all, a banker's daughter. Her wages were paid in cash from the till, and were little more than pin money, but she would've worked for nothing. No, she would've *paid* to work. And in all this time, Vince didn't ever know she had a job, which only added to the pleasure she took from it. His own life was full of secrets so now she had one of her own; that was how Annie looked at it. Tit for tat. It gave her confidence and a new defiant air around Vince that puzzled him, although he never really tried to get to the bottom of it, never did know anything about Sew and Sew's even though now and again Michael talked about Barbara and her wool shop right in front of his father, making Annie's heart skip in alarm. In time though she learned not to worry; Vince paid even less attention to Michael than he did to Annie. Still, it was Vince, in the end, who scuppered everything.

They were at home; Annie was peeling potatoes and Michael was hunkered down under the kitchen table, running a toy truck on the floor, back and forth, back and forth, back and forth, until Annie feared he'd make grooves in the green lino. All the time, through the legs of the chairs, he flicked his eyes between her and the truck, as if he couldn't be absolutely certain of either of them. The wireless was on, so nobody heard the front door open and shut, and anyway it was a Wednesday and Vince, when he came, only came at weekends. There he was though, out of the blue, striding into the room with a fat blonde baby boy tucked under one arm like a rolled-up towel.

'There,' he said, and put the baby on the floor, on his tummy. 'Bloody hell, he's heavy.'

The baby pushed himself up by the arms and took in his surroundings; his level gaze settled on Michael, who scowled and edged away, reversing further under the table, so that his back was against the wall.

'Who's this?' Annie said.

The baby heard her speak and turned his eyes away from Michael's stony profile and up to Annie, who was looking at Vince. Vince was filling the kettle as if nothing unusual had happened, but he looked shifty, Annie thought: shifty and possibly even nervous.

'Vince?'

'Right, don't blow your top,' he said.

'Do I have reason to?'

She'd thought nothing Vince said or did could shock her, but still she almost lost her footing when he said, 'He's called Robert, and he's mine.'

The potato peeler was still in her hand but now she began to shake and it fell to the floor. The baby made a valiant dash for it, half-crawling, half-sliding across the lino, and instinctively Annie bent down to stop his soft hands closing around the blade. They looked at each other and he smiled at her, a wholehearted, generous smile as if he couldn't be more pleased that she had won the race for the peeler, fair and square.

'Yours and whose?' Annie said. She was crouching on the floor now, leaning against a cupboard door; she didn't think she had the strength in her legs to get upright, and anyway she was half-mesmerised by the baby. He raised a plump hand to her knee and patted it in a friendly way. Michael, alarmed, shuffled forwards again.

'That's neither here nor there,' Vince said, with an attempt at bravado that Annie sensed was only skin deep. 'Fact is, he's staying here for the time being.'

Annie reached for the baby, who was irresistible. She perched him on her knees and he studied her face as if he was trying to memorise it. Annie felt her pulse quicken. She forced herself to look away from his beguiling eyes.

'You've had a baby with another woman, and it's neither here nor there?'

'Not your business,' Vince said, but he had the good grace to blush and his voice lacked conviction.

Annie gave a disbelieving laugh and the baby laughed too.

'Tell me everything,' Annie said. 'Or you can pick him up and take him away and never come back.'

She didn't mean to let the baby go; in fact she was already picturing him in Michael's old high chair, already looking forward to his next smile, but Vince didn't know that and the steel in her voice startled him. Michael, scuttling out sideways from under the table, pointed and said, 'Put that down,' but no one paid him any attention.

Vince cleared his throat and began to speak.

She was called Martha Hancock, and she was only sixteen, he said: fifteen, in fact, when he first met her, but she'd looked older, otherwise he never would have got involved. It was a devil of a business, he said, because when she fell pregnant they'd only done it once or twice.

'Which?' Annie asked. 'Once, or twice?'

'Six times.' He was startled by his own truthfulness.

'Right. Go on,' she said.

Vince cleared his throat and swallowed dryly, like a man in the dock. They'd got chatting in a café, he said. She worked behind the counter in the place he used for breakfast.

'Breakfast?' Annie said. 'You have breakfast in a cafeteria?' She was shocked at his extravagance: more shocked at this than at his infidelity, which she now realised had been a given. He looked at her helplessly.

'Go on,' she said again, and he took up the narrative in a flat voice. She'd been determined to have the baby, he said. He'd found a clinic where she could have been seen to, but she wouldn't hear of it.

'I should think not,' said Annie. 'But now she doesn't want him?'

He shrugged.

'So where is she, this Martha Hancock?'

'Beats me,' he said. 'Vanished. Upped and left.'

'But she dumped him on you before she went?'

Vince hesitated, and Annie knew at once that there was more to this: knew that if he wasn't exactly lying, neither was he disclosing the full truth.

'Were you together? Were you actually a couple?'

He stared at her dumbly, and to her horror and fury, tears welled in his eyes. If anyone should be crying, it was her.

'Well?' she said. 'Were you?'

'She'd moved in with me.'

'At sixteen! Living in sin!'

'It didn't feel sinful,' Vince said. His face was a mask now, shuttered and closed, but his voice shook with emotion and Annie found it hard to bear. She'd coached herself to feel nothing for him, but still, she wished he had once loved her the way he now loved Martha Hancock.

'She went out for a loaf a fortnight ago,' he said, and now his voice rose a little with bewildered hurt. 'She went out for a loaf, and she didn't come back.'

17

B ailey and Andrew were washing up together in the kitchen, and as Annie moved about upstairs she could hear their murmur of conversation and the gentle crash of crockery being stacked in the cupboards. They'd be putting everything away in the wrong places again. Annie cared less about this than she might have expected, but not Michael. This morning his mouth was a thin line as he opened the cupboard doors and slammed them shut, looking for the right bowl, the right glass, the right spoon.

He'd gone out now, off to one of his schools, his face a picture of fragile suffering, as if these present travails might be the end of him, but everyone just ignored him, and even Annie was learning to take no notice. She thought she might be picking up some of Bailey's insouciance; she found herself thinking, 'Oh, stuff him,' when Michael left the house without saying goodbye.

She still didn't know what to do about Finn, though. He hadn't been further than the back garden since last Wednesday, and because she hadn't told Andrew – or anyone, really – about the dead sheep when he first arrived, she found she hadn't been able to tell him at all. The words just wouldn't form, she didn't know why. Instinct, she supposed; a reflex desire to protect Finn's reputation, or perhaps her own. She'd got an invoice today from the farmer; it was sitting on the doormat when she came down, and it gave her quite a start, because although she certainly hadn't forgotten what Finn had done, she'd managed to somehow shelve it behind the greater problem of Vince and his last-ditch attempt at mischief-making. Anyway, the farmer had tried to be kind, billing her in the form of a polite note, apologetic in tone but clumsily put. *Dear Mrs Doyle*, it said, *begging your pardon but for the loss of livestock it'll have to be two hundred and forty pounds.* He'd written the numbers out like that; it gave the letter a look of antiquity, like the old church tithe records at St Peter's. *I'm sorry for the amount, which more than likely seems a bit steep, but it's because them ewes were in lamb. Cash would be much appreciated. Yours sincerely, Edward Wright.*

He'd dropped the letter round by hand first thing, before any of them had even stirred. There was a big dirty thumbprint on the back of the envelope, which was smeared as if he'd tried to wipe it clean. Annie was deeply grateful that he came so early. Bad enough having Mr Dinmoor pop in unannounced without having to explain away a visit from a sheep farmer.

His note was in the pocket of her trousers; it crinkled when she sat down, reminding her of her duty. She planned to call at the farmhouse later, when she'd withdrawn the money from the Halifax. Now, though, she was trying to get the house straight without anyone noticing what she was up to. She'd been sliding suitcases – again – under beds upstairs, and wiping around the sink where rogue blobs of toothpaste seemed to spring up each morning and evening like fungi. In the shower tray, six large rubber dinosaurs were now lined up against the tiled wall in height order, and a fat blue squeaky lobster hung by his claws from the soap basket. Blake and Riley took showers together; they sat either side of the plughole and re-enacted some great tumultuous dinosaur battle during which Riley inevitably ended up in tears. Why they couldn't just have a lick and a promise at the sink, Annie didn't know.

In the spare bedroom she found Blake, sitting on the floor, playing a game on his gadget. He didn't budge or look up when Annie bustled through, hiding suitcases wherever there was a gap large enough. Blake wanted to go home; she'd heard him telling Bailey earlier. It was boring here, he'd said, and when Bailey reminded him that it was important to visit Gram, he'd said, 'Says who?' and Annie wished she hadn't been listening at the door.

Now, she put the cases down and said, 'Hello, Blake love, what're you up to there?'

'Candy Crush,' he said, his eyes on the screen.

She watched him for a moment and thought that if these little hand-held computer doobrics had been around when Michael was eight, he'd have used one with the same introverted intensity as Blake.

'Do you think you could look at me when you speak?' she said.

There was a silent pause.

'Blake?'

'Yeah?' he said, all his attention on the game.

'Could you look at me, please?'

He sighed deeply and finished what he was doing before he looked up and said, 'What?' But now she had his attention she didn't know what to do with it so she just said, 'Where's Riley?'

He shrugged to show he hadn't a clue then immediately returned to crushing candy. She regarded him with narrow eyes, but his expression was rapt as he stared at the little screen, so she just left him to it.

She went downstairs and because Andrew and Bailey were busy in the kitchen, she took herself into the living room. There she found Riley, on the sofa, balancing a bowl of cornflakes on his lap. He smiled at her and waggled his spoon.

'Hello, Grandma,' he said. 'I'm eating cornflakes.'

'So I see. Don't spill milk on my settee.'

'What's your settee?' he said.

'The thing you're sitting on. Shall I open the curtains?'

'Will it be sunny?'

She laughed. 'I doubt it, pet, but let's see.' She pulled the cord and the curtains swept open to reveal Sandra and Josie, sitting in Sandra's car on Beech Street, directly outside Annie's house. She saw them before they saw her and she briefly entertained the thought of drawing the curtains again, or bobbing down below the sill and crawling out of the room on all fours.

'What's wrong, Grandma? Who's there?'

Really, thought Annie, was the child a mind reader? Josie waved and Annie gave her a wan smile. She turned round to look at Riley.

'It's my friends,' she said. 'We walk the dogs together.'

'Oh, your friends. I have friends too, at home. What do they want?'

'Not sure. A walk, I expect.' She glanced back through the window. 'I shan't go, though.'

But she did, because Andrew urged her to – he might make a start on the loft, he said, while she was out – and anyway as usual there was no resisting Josie's insistent warmth, even though Annie assumed Finn was for ever barred from the society of Betty and Fritz: even though it wasn't even a Wednesday. Riley came, too. Josie and Sandra waited in the car while Riley scrambled out of his pyjamas and into jeans and a jumper and Annie, feeling simultaneously terribly anxious and wildly impetuous, changed her shoes and put on her fleece. Finn, fetched from exile on the back patio, went crazy with excitement, knocking the telephone clean off its table in the hall and filling the small space with great resonant woofs. What with that, and Bailey and Andrew hooting with laughter at the pandemonium, it was a relief to get the dog in the car and set off. Riley, who was deemed too slight to be safe on the front seat, sat in the back and Finn, squashed into the boot, panted wetly into his ear. Blake was asked but wouldn't come and Annie wasn't sorry. It was wrong, she knew, to make a favourite of one grandson over another but actually, how could it be helped? She looked at Riley through the rear-view mirror and smiled at his innocent profile. He was watching the world go by through the car window, waving with touching optimism at everyone they passed and adding up his conquests, the ones who waved back.

They followed Josie and Sandra to the reservoir and when Annie came to a careful halt in the car park Riley sprang forward and managed to let himself out of the car before she'd even unclipped her own seat belt. By the time she'd swung her legs out, planted both feet on the ground and unfolded herself in the crisp morning air, Riley was already chatting to Josie about Byron Bay. Sandra stood next to them, checking her phone for messages and only half listening.

'No, I can already do it,' he said. 'Daddy taught me.'

'Amazing!' Josie said. 'Standing up, and everything?'

'Sometimes. It's quite hard though, so it's okay to ride on your belly.'

'Well that sounds fun, too.'

'What's that?' Annie left Finn in the car for the time being; he watched her humbly, taking nothing for granted.

'Surfing,' Riley said, and he bobbed about, arms out, riding an imaginary wave. 'Daddy's awesome.'

This was news to Annie. 'Really?' she said. 'He never had much balance as a boy.'

'He can balance now,' said Riley, with pride. 'We all can in our family.'

Annie laughed. 'I hope you're not including me, pet. You won't catch me on a surfboard.'

'No, you live too far from the ocean,' said Riley.

'That'll be why,' Josie said. 'Now let's get poor old Fritzy out of the car. He can't manage on his own anymore.'

Riley peered with interest through the dusty back window of Sandra's Volvo estate. 'There are two dogs in there,' he said.

'Well thank you, Sherlock,' said Sandra, because she spared no one, not even children.

'I'm not Sherlock,' he said, 'I'm Riley.' Then he

stepped back to allow her to swing the boot open. In a trice Betty sprang to the ground, precise and feather light, to sit politely at Josie's feet. Fritz heaved a sigh, and closed his eyes.

'Doesn't he want a walk?' Riley said. He reached in and patted Fritz on the head.

'He always thinks he doesn't,' said Sandra. 'But he likes it once he's out.' She shovelled her arms underneath the dog's belly and braced herself against the car, then heaved him up and out. 'Good God,' she said, and she blew out through puffed cheeks like a weightlifter while Fritz dangled limp and passive in her arms. Sandra lowered him to the ground. He looked incapable of supporting his own weight but after a small stagger he locked his joints and stood blinking in the breeze, swaybacked and grey-faced.

'He looks like an old, old man,' Riley said.

'If he was human, he'd be nearly ninety-eight,' said Sandra.

'Whoah!' He spun round to Annie. 'Even older than you!' Then he blushed red, afraid that he'd been rude.

'Only by a whisker,' Annie said, and everyone laughed. Riley grinned and nudged against Annie in a comfortable, proprietorial way, and she felt herself grow an inch or two taller. She turned to her car and opened the boot for Finn, and then they all crunched across the car park to the footpath, Finn pulling and pulling on his lead, trying to get to the water.

Sandra walked slightly ahead, Josie linked an arm through Annie's and asked all about Andrew; Riley held on tight to Finn's lead with two clenched hands and got his trainers wet at the water's edge while Finn, happy to have his paws in water, slowed temporarily to a manageable pace. Betty danced along beside Josie, and Fritz, poor old thing, was taking his time at the back. Everything was almost perfect; and yet, thought Annie, there was something hanging in the air, something waiting to be said. After all, it was Monday, not Wednesday. This was not meant to be a Dog Day. And Finn had killed the sheep, and Mr Dinmoor had been all but thrown out of her house, and she was as sure as she could be that all this cosy chat about Andrew was merely a prelude to some awkward questions from Josie.

So Annie filled every small silence with conversation. Oh, she could be crafty when she needed to be! On every dangerous in-breath, when Josie seemed poised on the very edge of the dread topic, Annie was ready with questions and comments of her own, and when all else failed, there was Riley to talk about. She felt dizzy with the effort, though; it was a strain, warding off the inevitable. Because it *was* inevitable, she realised that. It was inevitable, too, that it was Sandra, not Josie, who suddenly and brutally, and within earshot of Riley, said, 'What's the deal with Finn then?' She stopped walking to speak, and because she was ahead of everyone, they all stopped too. Annie didn't answer, only glanced evasively at the water, where a mallard drake and his harem were eyeing her back, trying to assess the possibility of bread.

'Have you had to pay up?'

Annie turned to her. 'It's two hundred and forty pounds,' she said quietly, trying to be discreet, and Sandra whistled through her teeth.

'Jesus,' she said. 'That was an expensive dog walk. So what next?'

'Why did we stop?' Riley said, to Annie. His cheeks were a vivid, mottled pink from the cold. He stood on one leg like a stork and looked up at her, and his eyes were as bright and dark as a robin's. Annie marvelled that he was hers alone in this small group; that if he needed a hand to hold, he'd choose hers; that when he wondered something, he spoke directly to her, in full confidence that she'd know the answer. His faith warmed and emboldened her.

'We stopped,' she said, 'because Sandra here wanted to know if I've paid the farmer. I owe him some money, because Finn attacked his sheep and two of them died, you see.' There. It was out. The first time she'd said it aloud. She took a deep, fortifying breath of fresh air and swallowed hard.

'Oh,' Riley said. He looked sideways at Sandra. 'But why did you stop? Can't you walk and talk at the same time?'

He didn't mean to be rude; innocent curiosity shone from his face.

Sandra regarded him. 'I can,' she said, 'but I sometimes stop walking to say something that I think is important.'

'Oh,' Riley said again. He showed not the remotest interest in the news about Finn, but instead dropped onto his haunches and clucked encouragingly at Fritz, who was still catching up. Riley held out his arms to the old dog, who trod a slow, meandering path to the boy then sat down stiffly in front of him. Riley leaned in and hugged him then touched his nose against Fritz's, and for a short while they stared at each other, cross-eyed.

'Shall we stop here anyway?' Josie said. She slung the rucksack from her shoulder and patted it. 'I have coffee.'

So they sat on a fallen tree and Annie had to submit finally to Josie's gentle interrogation about Finn, the farmer, the future, but mostly about Mr Dinmoor, who had gone back to Wentford hurt by his hasty dismissal. He had come to Annie with a suggestion, Josie said: a practical solution. He was a lovely person, big-hearted and wise. Why hadn't she been able to let him speak?

'Because,' Sandra said, guessing correctly, 'she hadn't told anyone.' She spoke as if Annie wasn't right there on the tree trunk with them.

'Well, I'd told the farmer,' Annie said, quite hotly, all at once rattled by Sandra's tone and her own predicament. 'Although not before you'd stuck your nose in.'

Sandra was unruffled. 'Well, somebody had to,' she said. 'You can't let these things lie for a day or two, Annie. He could've set the cops on the case. Thought I'd spare you that at least.'

'Mr Wright wouldn't be so hasty. He's a very nice man, as it turns out.'

'Yeah, he was all right. A fellow of few words, mind you.'

'He was chatty enough when I went.' Annie thought about the farmhouse kitchen and the toasted teacakes. He *hadn't* been chatty, exactly, but he had been kind.

'Well anyway,' Josie said. 'Mr Dinmoor has a sister; she lives on the coast in Formby.'

Annie looked at her. 'Formby?' she said, faintly. Why ever, she thought, might she be interested in Mr Dinmoor's family members?

'She takes in dogs,' Josie said.

'Rescues 'em,' Sandra added. 'Saves them from themselves.'

Josie shot her a look and Sandra held up a hand and mouthed 'sorry', although she smirked.

'Grandma?' Riley shouted, from the water. 'Can I let Finn off the leash?'

Annie hesitated and looked towards the distant fields beyond, dotted – for all she knew - with grazing sheep, but Josie said, 'Oh surely? Just for five minutes?' and it was true that right here, by this flat man-made expanse of water, there were only birds and fishermen, no sheep. 'Go on then,' Annie said. 'But stay right there, no running. And don't take your eyes off him.'

'Her name's Dora,' said Josie, 'and she has a big house near the pinewoods in Formby, up near Liverpool. She takes in dogs, as I said. Provides a permanent home when they can't stay with their owner for whatever reason.'

Annie stared, then the penny dropped. 'And Mr Dinmoor thinks I should give Finn to his sister?'

'Exactly,' Josie said.

'I see.'

Annie hadn't seen this coming: not at all. She gazed ahead bleakly and waited for her scattered thoughts to settle. Finn was playing with Riley, and this gave her something to look at, the two of them making a fast, crazy circle on the narrow path. The farmer had said something similar, she remembered now: send Finn away, to a place without sheep. But Finn! However would she go on without him?

Josie was unwrapping china cups from a tea towel. 'So,' she said. 'What do you think?'

Annie hardly knew what she thought. 'Oh, well ...' she said, 'I mean ...'

'Think about it, at least.'

'Formby,' Annie said.

'Yes. Pine trees, sweeping dunes, big skies.'

'And no sheep?'

'It's a coastal town, Annie,' Sandra said. 'There are red squirrels, mind you, but unless he can climb trees ...'

'I expect you think I'm silly,' Annie said – there was a moment's quiet while no one disagreed – 'but,' she went on, 'I don't think I can let him go.' She knew, as they didn't, precisely what her life was: precisely how narrow, precisely how limited. Yes, all right, so once every blue moon Andrew brought his family to visit and her days were briefly filled with noise and activity and purpose, but otherwise it was simply her and Finn, versus Michael and Vince. She knew – had always known – that it didn't do to depend only on a dog for happiness, but nevertheless, there it was. 'I don't think,' she said now, 'you can possibly understand how hard it would be for me to say goodbye.'

'Actually,' Sandra said, 'I might be able to.'

There was a beat of silence, then Josie said, 'Oh.'

Sandra nodded. 'It's just a matter of when, the vet says. We get to decide. Well me, I do, because Fritz is mine.' She glanced down at the dog, then away again, then all three of them looked at the old Alsatian, who was prostrate on the path, resting his bones. For once his eyes were open, and he stared back at them over his front paws with glazed indifference. He looked entirely compliant with his fate: quite resigned, thought Annie. But still she found her cheeks were suddenly wet with tears.

184

Oh dear, the world could be a strange, sad place! So little to rejoice in, so much to lament. Then from the reservoir's edge, where the water lapped the muddied path, there came the unmistakable sound of happiness. Annie let her damp eyes move away from Fritz and across to Finn. Magnificently alive, lit by a bolt of winter sun, he stood in the shallows shaking water from his golden coat while Riley danced in the shower of droplets, squealing with laughter.

18

Later, driving to Barnsley with Riley, Annie found that something had cleared in her mind, and not gradually but all of a sudden, like the screen used to do on their old television set in Coventry, when she thumped the top with the side of her balled-up fist. Now, she could see Finn racing through the waves on Formby sands: could picture him tearing up and down the hollows of the dunes. If he stayed here, with her, he would be always on a lead, with the occasional meagre five minutes' freedom in the shallows of the reservoir. His life would be all constraint and frustrated longing. It wouldn't do, she thought: it wasn't fair. Yes, she loved him completely. But might it also be an act of love to let him go? And might it not be so bad, to say goodbye if she knew who had him and where he was? She could visit, even. Walk with him on the sands, maybe. Whereas poor old Fritz ...

'Grandma?'

Riley had negotiated his way into the front seat. He only wanted Finn's head on his shoulder when the dog was dry, he told Annie. 'He smells gross when he's wet, like Blake's old joggers,' he said, so Annie took pity on the child and let him clamber forwards and settle next to her in the front. Personally she couldn't see the problem with it anyway – it was Bailey's rule, not her own – and it was nice to have him beside her: more companionable. But she knew Bailey wouldn't like it so he was tightly strapped in and she flung her left arm across him each time she braked. Her anxiety was infectious so Riley had his hands on either side of the seat, gripping on for dear life. He looked as if he was mid-ride on a roller coaster.

'Grandma?' he said again, because Annie, lost in Finn's new life on Formby sands, hadn't answered.

'Yes, pet?'

'Where are we going now?'

'To the Halifax.'

'For lunch?'

'No, it's a building society, a kind of bank. Are you hungry though?'

'No.'

'Well that's a pity, because next to the bank, there's a baker's called Fletcher's, where they sell the best cakes in the world.'

She felt Riley look at her so she glanced across and nodded at him. 'It's true. So we can get you something there. You don't need to be hungry to eat a cake.'

'Okay,' he said, then, 'Grandma?'

'Yes?'

'Were you sad when Finn ate the sheep?'

'He *didn't* eat them,' she said, a little sharply, although Riley didn't seem to notice.

'Wasn't he hungry?'

'He *attacked* the sheep. He didn't eat them.'

'Yeah, but *why* didn't he eat them?'

'Because ... oh, I don't know,' Annie said. 'Maybe he didn't get the chance. Sandra fetched him off, you see.'

The image of Sandra, bloodied and furious, rose briefly before her eyes. Annie blinked, and it was gone.

'Oh,' Riley said. 'I bet Finn was cross.'

Annie chuckled. 'I bet he was, too.'

It wasn't funny, of course, but the child's frank acceptance of the facts, his unruffled curiosity for more detail, had helped to heal her tormented soul by somehow relocating the incident to a more manageable realm in her mind. Well, what was so calamitous about it anyway? Wasn't it really quite ordinary for a dog to set upon sheep? Wasn't it almost humdrum? In this new spirit of cheerful defiance she withdrew the cash from her building-society savings account and then, having wedged the bundle of notes into the very bottom of her handbag, she took Riley into Fletcher's where, to her undisguised disappointment, he chose a gingerbread man over a vanilla slice or an éclair.

'But it's so plain!' she said to him. 'Have something with cream.'

'I like his face,' Riley said. 'And his buttons.'

So Annie had no choice but to buy it for him, and they sat in the car to eat with a modicum of privacy. It was cosy, side by side in the Nissan, the windows steamed up by Finn's damp fur and hot breath, so that they remained unobserved by passing shoppers. Riley nibbled with delicate respect on one of the gingerbread feet while Annie battled valiantly with a custard slice.

'Yours is really big, Grandma,' Riley said, watching her over his biscuit.

'Not really, not when you think about it,' she said. 'It's only a bit of pastry with a filling.' Her voice was clotted with custard, which made both of them laugh.

'What are you going to buy now?' Riley asked. He'd eaten the foot, and was sliding the gingerbread man back into his paper bag. Annie looked at him quizzically. 'Buy?' she said.

'With all those dollars.' Riley nodded down at the handbag, which sat in the footwell of the passenger seat with the shoulder strap hooked twice round the gearstick to foil a snatch-and-grab attempt.

'They're English pounds,' Annie said. 'Two hundred and forty of them. They're for a man called Mr Wright.'

'Mr Wright,' Riley said, trying out the name. 'It's a heck of a lot of money.'

She laughed. 'It is. He's the farmer, y'see, the one whose sheep died.' She heard her own words and felt as if she was slipping back into her old evasive ways so she added, 'Were killed, I mean.'

Riley thought for a moment then said, 'Can I come too, to pay the farmer?'

'Oh, well ...' Annie said. She certainly intended to visit Mr Wright today but it didn't seem quite proper, somehow, to take the child.

'Ple-ease,' Riley said. 'I want to see the farm.'

'It isn't very interesting. Just buildings and a muddy yard.'

'I'd like that. I like buildings and mud.'

She considered him for a moment. 'Well ...' she said again.

'Thanks, Grandma,' he said, and he gave her a cheeky grin, which reminded her so powerfully of the infant Andrew that she gasped and laid a hand on her heart, as if to steady its wild beating.

*

Instead of driving into the farmyard as she had last time, Annie parked in the lane. Finn was still in the car, after all: it wouldn't do to flaunt him under the farmer's nose. She tucked in so close to the hedgerow that spindly fingers of hawthorn pressed against the windows and Riley had to get out of the car on her side. Then they walked hand in hand up into the yard where the sounds from an outbuilding – bleating and quite audible cursing – hinted at the whereabouts of Mr Wright. Riley's face lit with excitement and he shucked off Annie's hand and barrelled off towards the noise, sploshing through thick brown puddles, sending a trail of who-knew-what up his trouser legs. Annie opened her mouth to protest, but then simply followed in his wake, grateful for her sturdy walking boots.

The barn into which Riley had now vanished was long and low, and patently lopsided; the roof had slumped at one end, as if from fatigue or disappointment. The open doors hung askew too, listing away from their moorings where the old hinges clung on to softly splintering timber. Annie peered into the gloaming of the interior. There was a fetid stink, as thick in the air as a solid wall. The farmer seemed to be straddling a sheep, which bucked and tossed between his legs. She stepped further inside and saw that Riley was already positioned on the edge of the action, his arms folded as he watched with cool concentration. Annie couldn't tell from here whether Mr Wright – wrapped up as he was in the task in hand – had seen the boy so she ventured further still and coughed, but no one seemed to hear. The sheep, mad with panic, tossed and thrashed then let forth a stream of urine, which gushed around the farmer's leather boots and splashed into the matted straw of the barn floor.

'Foot rot,' Mr Wright said, and he seemed to be answering a question. 'Spreads through a bloody flock like bastard wildfire.'

'Mr Wright!' Annie trotted closer to Riley, gravely alarmed.

The farmer shot her the briefest glance but the sheep, sensing a chance, struggled with new violence inside the brace of his legs, which only made the farmer swear again, a base, barrack-room curse that sent a jolt of shock down Annie's spine. She wanted to seize Riley and run away, but she was immobilised by the grotesque novelty of this situation and anyway, the little boy – whose face registered no distress, only lively interest – had stepped sideways, out of reach.

'Op'n that gate, lad,' Mr Wright said, nodding at a metal pen ahead of him.

Riley sprang into action and slung open the gate. The farmer hauled the sheep out from between his legs, one hand gripping its neck, the other clutching a woolly rump. He launched it with all his grim strength so that the momentum left the afflicted creature with little option but to bundle forwards into the pen, whereupon Riley swung the gate shut, smart as a regular farm hand, and with a mighty two-handed effort slid the metal bolt across to secure it. The sheep lowered itself tenderly onto its front knees and glowered at him through slitted eyes.

'Grand job, lad,' Mr Wright said, in the pleasant tone of voice that Annie remembered from their previous encounter. 'Nah then, who are you?'

'Riley Doyle,' Riley said. 'Pleased to meet you.' He held out his hand and the farmer shook it.

'Grand job,' he said again. 'Shut that gate like

lightning.' He ruffled Riley's hair with a large, grimy hand and smiled at Annie, who wasn't remotely ready to smile back. Instead she stood in a stupor and stared at him. She couldn't bear bad language, had no defence against its strange and sinister power. She thought of the thug in the white van, days and days ago. She thought of Vince, in a temper. Mr Wright, oblivious to his offence, studied Riley and wagged a finger at him thoughtfully. 'Nah then,' he said, 'that's nivver a Barnsley accent, so wheer's tha from, lad?'

Riley looked at Annie, and for his sake she managed to say, 'Australia.'

The farmer whistled through his teeth and Riley, understanding through his grandma's answer the question that'd been asked, dived in with details of exactly where in that vast and far-away land he came from. 'And I'm staying at Grandma's because Grandpa's nearly dead so we needed to see him,' concluded the boy, with piping cheerfulness. 'But today we took Finn for a walk and now we've come to pay you for the killed sheep.'

'Oh Riley, shush,' Annie said, stung into speech by the boy's carefree indiscretion, and the farmer, meaning to reassure, gave her an understanding wink, which made her purse her lips in annoyance. 'You want to mind your language,' she said. 'The words you used in front of this child!'

'Beg pardon,' he said, unabashed. He shoved his hands deep into the pockets of his brown corduroys and grinned at Riley. 'Lad can't foller what am sayin' anyroad.'

'Well, I can,' Annie said. 'It wasn't nice. It wasn't right.' The smell inside the barn was oppressive and she wondered if it would cling to her clothes, like cigarette smoke.

'Aye well, beg pardon,' he said again. 'Not used to comp'ny except for sheep, an' they dunt mind a bit o' swearin'.' This made him laugh, so Riley laughed too, although at what he had no idea. Mr Wright took a shapeless tweed jacket from a hook in a beam and shrugged himself into it. 'Nah then, follow me, I've summat to show you.' He set off out of the barn and Riley skipped after him. Annie said, 'No, no, we can't stay,' but only the sheep in its pen remained to hear her, so she followed her grandson and the farmer out of the gloom and into the cleaner, colder air of the yard.

They ended up, to Annie's agitation, in the farmhouse kitchen but there was no sign of the rabbit-skinning crone, only a litter of brand-new Jack Russell puppies to look at, six of them in a companionable heap, blunt-nosed and blind in their basket. The mother, a weary-looking white-and-tan terrier, sprawled in their midst and regarded Riley with a sort of resigned mistrust when he knelt on the floor and hung over her brood.

'Don't touch,' Annie said, because she'd always thought this was an absolute and unbending rule, but Mr Wright said, 'Nay, it's all reight,' and he scooped up a pup in his big hand so that it lay upside down in his palm, then tipped it onto Riley's lap. Only the boy's quick reaction stopped it from rolling clear onto the stone floor.

'Oh!' Annie said. 'Be careful!' but the farmer only chuckled. Tenderly, Riley lifted the little creature, cupping it in two hands. He sniffed its head and nuzzled his nose into its yeasty warm fur then laid it down again with infinite care among its tangle of siblings.

'Pick up another one, lad,' Mr Wright said. 'She'll

not mind. She's not keeping 'em, anyroad.' The terrier matriarch, surrounded by her young, looked away from them with steady indifference, as if to prove his point.

'Cool,' Riley said, lifting another warm body from the basket. It lay on its back in the hammock of his hand. 'They're so cool, aren't they, Grandma?'

'If you say so,' Annie said tightly, but then she gave a little laugh, because her heart was thoroughly melted at the sight. It cast her back three years, when she'd driven all the way to Huddersfield to view a litter of retriever puppies. She'd imagined going home with a little female, whom she planned to call Lottie, but in the event she'd asked the breeder for help; left to herself, she'd have taken all of them, just to avoid having to pick only one. The breeder, a brisk, sharp-nosed woman named Mrs Purley, had immediately hauled out Finn from the confines of an open-topped metal cage, picking him up by the loose skin of his neck so that he hung there, as slack and unformed as a string bag of groceries. Annie snatched him to safety and held him tight to her breast. He looked much like the rest, she thought, but Mrs Purley told her she'd seen something in this one; a loyal heart, she said; he'd love her till the end of his days. As well, she pointed out his broad head and fine, pale colouring, and showed her his parents' excellent hip scores, which Annie didn't care about, although she'd nodded her approval. He came with a Kennel Club certificate and a long family tree of dams and sires, and his pedigree name was Finnberg Myttendale Moorquest, but from the moment Annie held him, he was simply her own dear Finn. Thinking of him now, with the beginnings of fond tears in her eyes, she remembered the twenty-pound notes at the bottom of her handbag and the purpose of their visit.

'Oh!' she said, and she rifled through the contents of her bag until her fingers settled on the wad of money. 'Here!' She thrust it at Mr Wright, who looked startled, and then acutely embarrassed as he realised what it was. He pushed the notes into the pocket of his trousers with bungling haste and looked everywhere but at her as he did so. Well, good, thought Annie. Nice to know she wasn't the only one prone to the blushes.

When they got home, Andrew opened the door before they were even halfway up the path. He looked different, Annie thought at once: a little serious, a little guarded. He looked like a man with something significant to say, something uncomfortable perhaps, something that had to be aired, whatever the consequences. He let Finn through into the house, and then Riley, waiting for the boy to pass before speaking, and Annie knew then that Vince had died; she was certain of it. She prepared herself to receive the news soberly, appropriately, without betraying so much as a grain of relief.

'What is it, love?' she said, and her heart beat faster with rising hope. In response he held out a small, square black and white photograph, irreparably creased from a long-ago fold across its centre. It had been shot in sunshine and overexposed, and Annie had to squint at it to make out the image. A young woman smiled shyly at her from down the years, holding in her arms a baby, loosely wrapped in a trailing blanket.

'I started on the loft,' Andrew said. 'We need to talk.'

19

For a while after turning up with baby Robert, Vince hung about the house as if he was trying to live there, giving it a go. Annie knew that the unremarkable routines of family life were a privilege to which he was no longer entitled, but even so each time she saw him – on the stairs, in the bathroom, at the table – she felt a jolt of surprise, followed by an undeniable stirring of satisfaction that her husband was home. Anyone might have thought his flagrant and unapologetic infidelity would be too much to bear, but even at the very beginning, when they were first married – no, before then – she'd known he'd look elsewhere: identified his roving eye, his restless spirit, his selfish vanity and knew, too, from her own face in the mirror, that she was no match for him. Still though, she'd been able to peep shyly at his handsome features and take some pleasure and pride in his belonging, in some small way, to her.

It was the same now. He was older, of course, just as she was, but he was handsome still, in the right light, at the right angle, if those louche Lothario looks were to your taste. She didn't *like* him much, mind you. She treated him as coldly as she dared, punishing him for his sins. But she took secret pleasure in his maleness, the layered smells of aftershave, cigarettes and beer. She appreciated the space he took up in the house, his long legs folded awkwardly under the kitchen table, or stretched out too far across the hearth rug in the poky sitting room, which she wouldn't use if he was positioned there, recumbent on the sofa like a semi-domesticated old wolf.

For his part, Vince had no real intention of sticking around for long. He was biding his time, waiting for the next adventure to present itself. This little terraced house in Coventry, no longer his home in any meaningful sense, was a refuge, a place to lick his wounds and regroup. Of course, little Robert was his trump card; his wife had wanted another baby, so back he had come, carrying one. She could be as pious as she liked, but when he caught her with the baby in her arms, waltzing him through the narrow hallway, crooning a love song, Vince knew his own position was unassailable. Even so, he was truly wrong-footed when one day, perhaps two weeks into his uncomfortable residency in Sydney Road, he said, 'Morning, Robert,' to his younger child and Annie said, 'His name's Andrew.'

Vince gave a foolish laugh. 'It's not,' he said. 'It's Robert.'

'It *was* Robert,' Annie said, then she clamped her lips shut into a tight line, as if she'd already said too much, as if she regretted her weakness. The baby, in the high chair, smiled magnanimously at the adults, each in turn, and waved a rusk above his head before releasing his grip and letting it fall to the kitchen floor. Michael, at the table eating Weetabix, paused with his spoon in mid-air, and stared first at the baby and then at his mother.

'Wobert,' he said, and pointed at the beaming inter-loper, his rival, his amiable enemy.

Annie turned her gaze on Michael. 'No, pet, this is Andrew.'

'No that's Wobert,' Michael said firmly.

'Hear hear,' Vince said. 'Well said. You can't just change his name; it's not legal.'

'I can do what I please – he's mine,' Annie said.

'He's yours? Since when?'

'Since you gave him to me,' Annie said. 'Your fancy piece doesn't want him, so she doesn't get to name him. I suppose Robert was her idea? Yes, I thought as much,' she said, without pausing to hear his answer – knowing, anyway, that she was right. 'I'd always imagined two little boys, Michael and Andrew. Or Michael and Angela for a boy and a girl, or Angela and Julia if they turned out to both be girls. So he's Andrew, always was in my mind. Andrew Doyle. Andrew, Andrew, Andrew. Michael and Andrew Doyle.'

All the while she was wiping the baby tenderly with a damp flannel. He tilted his face and opened his hands obligingly, while she gently coaxed the sticky remnants of rusk from his darling face and the creases of his palms. She wiped in time with her words and Vince and Michael stared as if she were the last remaining member of an entirely different species.

'Andwew,' Michael murmured, trying out the difficult new word.

'That's it,' Annie said.

Vince snarled. He stalked out of the kitchen, then spun on his heel and jutted his head back into the room, poking a finger at her, stabbing the air. 'There'll be no girls, you mad cow,' he said. 'I'll not be coming anywhere near you, and who else would bother?'

And then he did leave, slamming the front door as he had so many times before.

'Eat up, Michael,' Annie said, nodding at the remains of his milk-sodden Weetabix.

He scowled at her and pushed the bowl away, meaning to provoke, but she only shrugged and picked it up, then spooned what was left into the baby's willing mouth.

'Mine!' Michael shouted, beating a cross little tattoo on the yellow Formica.

'No, *Andrew's*,' Annie said. 'So next time, think on.'

She sent a regretful note to Barbara at the haberdashery, apologising for her sudden disappearance. She wanted to say that she'd had another baby, but that would be ridiculous, obviously, although she did consider inventing a surprise pregnancy, even wrote it out in draft to see how it looked. But Barbara was the only other living soul who knew just how rarely Vince came home, and how things stood between them when he did, so instead she wrote that 'family matters' were keeping her away from work and would continue to do so for the foreseeable future. She thanked Barbara for taking her on in the first place, and for allowing Michael to go with her. She wished Barbara well for the future. It was all very nicely put, but later when she read the letter through before slipping it into an envelope she worried it sounded bland and distant, as if the time she'd spent at Sew and Sew's had been an insignificant thing, as if Barbara hadn't thrown her a lifeline at one of the loneliest periods Annie had ever known. To put all that in writing, though ...

well, it might have seemed theatrical, thought Annie: melodramatic, overblown. The truth was, of course, that Barbara would have taken Robert-now-Andrew's arrival entirely in her stride; she would've relished the details of Vince's hair-raising cheek; she would've doted on the baby – well, who in the world wouldn't love him, instantly? Barbara, unshockable and endlessly warm, would have helped mend the wrongness of Annie's situation by ignoring ... no, by *accepting* it. All this Annie knew. But pride, respectability, an inclination towards perfect privacy – all these characteristics rose to the fore and propelled her to the post box with her polite little resignation letter, which, in the end, irritated by her own ditherings, she quickly sealed, stamped, addressed and dispatched.

So Annie excised her only friend from her life, but it was bearable because she had Andrew. His arrival had granted her another chance, a reprieve, a blessed last opportunity to love and be loved. He submitted to her at once and wholeheartedly, and returned her devotion fiercely and fully, with unconstrained delight. It was a meeting of hearts; also, it was as if the child – so utterly accepting of this new source of warmth and affection – was being mothered for the first time. Since Martha Hancock was only just out of girlhood herself, Annie assumed that this must be true. She had only a sketchy idea of who or what Martha was – she wanted no details from Vince on the subject, and in any case he was soon absenting himself again for long periods – so she filled in the considerable gaps with her imagination and soon had her cast as either a feckless hussy with an eye for the main chance, or a hapless, soft-headed victim of Vince's predatory charm. Either of these incarnations allowed her to nurture a seam of contemptuous pity for poor runaway Martha, although, in the most private recesses of her mind, she acknowledged her personal debt to the girl, for leaving Andrew behind when she fled.

Michael hated him. At first, when he could logically hope that the baby might be taken away as suddenly and mysteriously as he had arrived, the little boy's hostility manifested itself harmlessly, in a kind of permanent passive scorn. He contemplated the baby from a safe distance, with the sort of withering disdain that a medieval monarch might have reserved for a scrofulous serf. But days, weeks and months passed and yet Michael still found that he was expected to share the world with Andrew. Worse, Michael discovered he was expected to sometimes play second fiddle: to wait for a story, to wait for his shoes and coat, to wait for his soft-boiled egg. His mother – his own mother! *His!* – spoke sharply to him often, and occasionally ignored him altogether. He didn't have the words to express it, but Michael came to understand that somehow this noisy, clumsy, dribbling addition to the family had usurped him in his mother's affections. He was no longer King Michael; the young pretender had seized the crown. What was worse, Andrew yearned to be friends, and he was unceasing in his efforts. As soon as he became properly mobile he followed Michael doggedly through the house, never fully grasping the depths of animosity of which the bigger boy was capable.

'Get off!' Michael would scream. 'Get out! Get lost!'

'Michael Doyle!' Annie always said. 'Be nice to your little brother!'

'But I hate him!' Michael yelled, with his face tipped up to the ceiling as if he was speaking to the gods, appealing for their intervention. Once – in a hot, blind temper, when his meticulous castle of Lego bricks had been scattered across the bedroom floor and two pages of his *Rupert* annual were ripped beyond repair – Michael screamed so hard and for so long that for a few moments he blacked out and Annie thought he'd died of rage. When he came to and opened his eyes she was hanging over him with a look on her face that he dimly remembered from earlier times, a look of desperate, fathomless devotion. For a fleeting second their eyes locked and he thought he had her back, but then Andrew staggered forth on uncertain legs and whimpered in confusion. Annie scooped him into her arms and shushed him and told Michael to be a big boy: to dry his eyes and sit up so she could read them both a story. This incident was seared on Michael's memory like a brand on a bullock. It replayed in his mind over and over again; it never really left him, remaining in his memory long after the time that childhood injustices should have been forgotten.

Annie fantasised about a cottage in a wood, in a part of the country where no one knew her. She'd live there with her boys and there'd be a brook and a vegetable patch and a swing in the garden. There were no prying neighbours in this imagined paradise, but in Sydney Road, of course, they suddenly seemed legion, and by their curious stares and bold enquiries they called Annie to account, wondering who this second little boy was, and why he'd come. Annie, when it simply couldn't be avoided, spoke evasively of a distant sister in dire health, a likely death, a probable adoption, before ending the conversation and racing away, Andrew bouncing about cheerily in Michael's old pushchair, Michael trailing behind, sucking his forefinger in that odd way he had, issuing dark, oblique looks from beneath his fringe. It was just as well she'd always kept these people, these inquisitors, at arm's length, Annie thought; just as well she'd protected herself from the forensic intimacy of female friendship. Always, always, it paid to keep your own counsel, and the less she shared, the less she was obliged to explain.

When Michael started school – outraged yet again at what was being asked of him, hanging limpet-like to the frame of the pushchair until his mother peeled him off and handed him over – life altered once more. Annie and Andrew spent uninterrupted hours pleasing themselves, pottering together in the house, or finding treasure along the canal path: pebbles, feathers, twigs. At two years old, little Andrew had a collector's eye; his choices, while perfectly ordinary in themselves, somehow revealed a certain everyday loveliness when they got them home – a whorl of blue-grey on a brown stone, unexpected speckles on a wing feather. At home they resided in a shoebox treasure chest and on wet days or wash days Andrew could while away an entire morning laying out the specimens, talking to them, changing their places then changing them back, then returning them carefully to their tissue-paper bed. They pressed wild flowers too, but this was more for Annie's benefit, since Andrew had no interest in a bluebell or a cowslip that must be left alone between the pages of a dictionary for long, uninterrupted weeks on end. Annie told him they'd keep for ever once they were properly pressed, but he didn't understand, and his expression, when she tucked the flowers out of sight and out of reach, was of puzzled pain.

Vince was working in Tamworth by this time, for a company that sold guttering and downpipes. He was in sales, at which he excelled. The money still came like clockwork, in envelopes that were a little fatter than before, and Annie was surprised by this, and mutely grateful. If this had remained her only contact with him she would have been perfectly content, but sometimes Vince came back too, so that his boys didn't forget their old man. They didn't much like his visits – or anyway Michael didn't – because everything changed when he walked into the house. The atmosphere shifted, became brittle with ill-feeling, and even though Vince sometimes brought little paper bags of bulls' eyes or slender bars of creamy Caramac, his hearty joviality hung badly on him, like a cheap suit. Domesticity made him irascible. His high spirits were not to be trusted; they could be replaced in a heartbeat by harsh words or, worse, the back of his hand. Andrew, being amenable and lovable, had nothing much to fear from his father, who swung him about to make him scream with laughter or hoicked him on his shoulders instead of using the pushchair. But Michael provoked Vince with his sullen looks and odd habits, and the small concessions his mother made at mealtimes in pursuit of a quiet life were all either mocked or banned altogether when his father came home. Any old plate must be used, not Michael's special one; a dropped spoon must be picked up and used at once, without washing the germs off it; milk must be poured onto cornflakes, not served in a glass on the side; beans must be on top of the toast; gravy must be allowed to run where it wished, not corralled in one corner of the plate by a mashed potato dam. In fact Vince's rules rendered a Sunday roast practically inedible to Michael.

But if the boy bucked and squirmed under the terrible scrutiny of his father, Annie dreaded the visits for exactly the opposite reason. Vince simply behaved as if she wasn't there. In his presence she was anonymous, hollowed out, insubstantial. He looked straight through her while keeping up a stream of ostentatious, one-sided banter with the children. He proposed boys-only outings, and although Michael would never go with him, Annie took no comfort from this. Andrew always went, sunny and chatty, taking his father's hand with a trustfulness that Annie feared was unfounded, because for her, the spectre of the mysterious, unmentionable Martha Hancock haunted these outings. A secret rendezvous, an assignation, an agreement. Until she heard the key in the lock again, Annie couldn't function. She sat on a hard kitchen chair, drawn and silent, listening to her own dark thoughts, and waited for him to bring Andrew back. Then in they would come, bundling through the house, bringing with them the smells of outside, the fresh wind, the cold rain, the cloying sweetness of candy floss, and Annie always rose from her seat and resumed her run-of-the-mill domestic tasks, as if she'd only just that minute sat down. If Vince had only known her fears and understood his power, he'd doubtless have kept Andrew out longer.

20

Annie took her time untying the laces of her walking shoes, stepping into her slippers, unzipping her fleece, hanging it on the coat-stand, but Andrew simply waited for her, standing in the hallway in silence, holding the little photograph, his ticket to the past. When it was simply no longer avoidable, she allowed him to lead her through to the kitchen, where the small table bore an old wooden box, a small chest scarred with age. It sat in the midst of its curled and yellowing contents, which were laid out carefully in an ordered display: a letter or two; a postcard; more photographs.

'I found all this,' Andrew said. 'In the loft.'

Together they stared at it.

'It's Dad's stuff.'

'Well then,' Annie said. 'We shouldn't pry.' Her heart pounded; she wondered that its beating wasn't audible in the desperate silence. She hadn't ever laid eyes on this box or its innards before, but she knew that they could only do harm.

'Mum, this is Martha.'

Andrew placed the photograph flat on the table, and tapped at the young woman with one finger. He turned the picture, showed her the faded scrawl: *Martha and Robert, July 1967*. Annie was silent and pale.

'And this one.' He picked up another photograph – the same young woman, no baby. She wore a girlish printed cotton dress and sandals. Her hands were on her hips, her head tilted coquettishly. She was laughing in the picture, and so palpable was her happiness that Annie had to look away. Again Andrew flipped the picture over. *Martha Hancock, Whitley Bay.* There was no date. Annie wondered where she herself was, when Vince and Martha were together at the seaside.

'So who exactly is she, Mum?' Andrew hung over the table, taking it all in. He was entranced by his find, fascinated by his father's secrets. 'And who's that baby? Who's Robert?'

'Ask your father,' Annie said sharply. Her mouth was dry but some reflex in her throat forced her to swallow hard, gulping at nothing.

'Well I can't, can I?' He looked at her, surprised.

'They're not my things,' she said. 'I've never seen them before.'

'Sit down, Mum.' He held out a chair for her but she hesitated and remained standing, looking anywhere but at him.

'See here,' Andrew said, trying to draw her along with him. 'This postcard was from her, to Dad.' He picked it up and started to read. '*Dear Vincent, you made me promise to send you a card so here—*'

'Stop!' Annie said. She held the edge of the table so he couldn't see her hands shaking.

'Mum, I'm sorry, but this stuff matters.'

She looked about her. 'Where is everybody?' she said,

hoping to create a distraction, find some room to breathe. Riley and Finn, she knew, had slipped into the sitting room and were watching cartoons but she hadn't seen Blake or Bailey since they'd come in. Andrew stared at her for a moment.

'They went out to the park,' he said, irritation now creeping into his voice.

'Park?' Annie said. 'There is no park!' She threw out her hands in startled confusion, as though whatever drama may have been about to unfold in the kitchen, it was utterly eclipsed by this new crisis.

'Jeez, Mum, down the road there, the grassy area.'

'That's a rec, not a park.'

'For God's sake, Mum, can we talk about this lot? Whatever Dad was up to, it was donkey's years ago, and it's not as if any of us thought he was a saint.'

Then Finn appeared, and he leaned against Annie's legs so she could feel the heat he'd absorbed by loafing about too close to the fire. 'Oh!' Annie said, realising all of a sudden that a most wonderful opportunity had presented itself. 'Oh Andrew!' She wailed the words and covered her face with her hands for fear that the cunning relief she suddenly felt might be visible in her features.

'It's awful, Andrew,' she said, through her fingers.

'Just tell me,' he said. Gently he prised her hands away with his own. 'It can't be that bad. We all knew what a rogue he was.'

'Who?'

'Well Dad, obviously.'

'Him! I'm not talking about him! It's Finn. He killed a sheep, Andrew, and another one had to be shot, and now I have to give him away.'

She looked at him cautiously, not yet certain that the other danger was past. It wasn't.

'Mum, why're you talking to me about the dog?' Andrew folded his arms now, and regarded her appraisingly. 'Finn's fine, it's me you should be worrying about. I'm struggling here. I might have discovered a half-brother we didn't know existed, and you want me to worry about the dog?'

Annie's vision swam and jumbled thoughts clamoured inside her head, though one pushed itself powerfully forwards. Martha Hancock was back. Martha Hancock had come to take her revenge. She turned from Andrew, who only watched in utter confusion as Annie bolted upstairs to the bathroom, locked the door, sat on the lavatory lid, and wept as quietly as her consuming grief would permit.

How did it come to her, to take her woes to Josie? And, having had the thought, how had she actually arrived here? In the car, obviously, since that was where she now sat, outside Josie's windmill, gripping the steering wheel as if she needed it for balance. But the period between crying on the lavatory seat and crying here, two miles away from home, was a blank, its shadowy details eluding her as if she'd driven to Wentford in her sleep. She shivered, although it wasn't cold in the familiar upholstered confines of her Nissan. But she felt exposed all the same: raw with horror, riddled with terror, sodden with self-pity. The flimsy certainties of her life, few enough though they were, hung in shreds now that Andrew – her boy, her lovely boy – had found that cursed trove of secrets. If only she'd known it was there! She wondered how Vince had contrived to bring it from Coventry when they moved, given his – by then – enfeebled state. Perhaps *she* had packed it in one of the trunks or cases, shoving that box in with all the other boxes in her haste to be gone, unwittingly laying a time bomb for her own destruction. Or perhaps it was Vince's doing after all; he would have liked to think of her finding the box and leafing through its contents with familiar dismay, reminded again of how little he had loved her when love was still a possibility. Now she pictured the box in flames, its pernicious contents curling and melting in the heat, Martha Hancock's winning smile gone for ever, as it should be, as she had thought it was.

There was a tap at the window, breaking her miserable reverie.

'Annie. Annie!'

Josie stood outside the car, peering in. She was wrapped up like a child in a big blue duffel coat and Betty was beside her. Josie smiled through the window; she expected Annie to wind it down, but she didn't.

'Sorry, did you try my door?' Josie said through the glass. 'It's open – you could've gone and waited for me inside. I just took Betty through the village for a change of scene.'

Her voice was muffled through the closed window, but Annie heard well enough the happy acceptance of this unexpected arrival, and she wished – another wish, to add to all the others – that she too owned some small quantity, a grain, just an atom, of Josie's perennial calm confidence. Annie couldn't speak. She couldn't smile either, but only stared helplessly at Josie, letting tears course down her cheeks unchecked. Josie opened the car door and asked no more questions. She guided Annie from the driver's seat, and held on tight to her arm like a nurse with an invalid as they inched up the path. Annie, gazing downwards, saw red brick herringbone edged with clipped lavender that waited for spring and its perfection made her think of her own plain grey flags so that she felt sadder still. Oh, anything and everything could wound an already wounded heart; this lovely garden path might have been placed there only to taunt her.

Inside, Josie sat her down on an armchair, not at the table where she'd sat before. It was tidy in here today, Annie noticed. There was no sign of ethnic bric-a-brac, except for Josie's possessions, which all had their place. The room glowed with copper pans, gaudy ceramics, burnished wood, and there was a spicy smell from a fat candle that guttered softly in its glass dish. Annie leaned back, let the chair support her. It was old; the green velvet that covered its cushions was torn in parts and faded, but its seat was deep and its arms were wide, and Annie felt embraced, enfolded. In moments there was a box of tissues on her lap and Josie was busy with a pan of milk on the stove. Tea wouldn't do, she was saying. Tea was too thin for comfort. At times such as this, Josie said, the very best thing was hot chocolate. Annie waited in the chair, saying nothing but feeling better, safer, in this circular room with walls as thick as a fortress.

Josie grated chocolate from a thick dark slab and kept one eye on the milk, which hissed in its shining pan. She talked as she worked, about inconsequential matters such as how too many foodstuffs with chocolate in their title tasted of anything but, and had Annie ever eaten chocolate custard in her school days? 'A case in point,' Josie said, 'a classic example of something bearing the chocolate name without earning the right.' Annie barely registered the words, and certainly didn't reply, but watched the chocolate shavings fall from the grater, piling up on the plate like a heap of tiny autumn leaves.

'This is the Spanish way,' Josie was saying. She was whipping up cornflour with a dash of cold milk. 'Lots of chocolate, not so much milk, cornflour to thicken. Really, when it's finished, you should be able to stand a spoon up in it.'

She lifted the pan from the stove, tipped in the chocolate, added the cornflour paste and whisked the mixture with concentrated vigour, and then glanced up to smile across the room at Annie.

'There,' she said, and she poured a dense, generous slick of molten hot chocolate into a wide sky-blue teacup. 'This'll soothe your spirits.'

She passed the beautiful cup to Annie, poured another, then sat down opposite her on an old wooden carver, which creaked contentedly. Annie took a sip and the unctuous, creamy sweetness ran into her like balm. It was astonishing.

'So now,' Josie said. 'Tell me everything.' She was expecting a sad tale of an old man's death compounded by grief at the imminent loss from her life of Finn, but Annie began to speak and revealed another story entirely, of pain and deception and long years of denial. She talked and talked and Josie listened, and if she was shocked, she hid it well.

'So Andrew is actually Robert, although he's always been Andrew to me, but now he thinks he has a half-brother, and I wish that was all it was,' Annie said. She was exhausted by her confession; she was running out of words. 'I don't know what to do,' she said. 'I don't know what to tell him.' And then abruptly, she stopped talking.

Josie drew a slow line through the thick chocolate inside her cup and licked her finger. 'You must tell him the truth,' she said carefully. 'You simply must.'

'I suppose so,' Annie said. 'But I don't know how.'

'Yes you do, you just told me.'

'Oh, but I can't tell Andrew what I've told you!'

Josie laughed kindly. 'Why not, Annie?'

'Because it's ... it's ...' She petered out uncertainly. Because it was different here, she wanted to say; it was safe and closed, as secret as a priest's confessional.

'You see, you can't *not* tell him,' Josie said. 'Not if you love him.'

'Well, I could just let sleeping dogs lie.' Annie's voice had a touch of sulky defiance. The hot chocolate was all gone now; its cathartic effect was starting to recede. 'Vince can't tell him anything, can he? He's not capable.'

'Vince *has* told him something, by leaving those pictures,' Josie said. 'Now Andrew needs your help to fill in the gaps.'

There was a silence.

'Try to see it as a good thing, Annie, like setting down a heavy bag you've carried for years. The relief of it!' Josie suddenly seemed to hear her own cajoling tone and she clamped shut her mouth and waited. Betty, curled in her basket, whimpered in her sleep. Finally Annie said, 'But what if Andrew can't forgive me?'

'What's to forgive? You took a young woman's unwanted child and loved him. That's no crime, that's a generous act. It's laudable.'

Annie shook her head.

'You don't understand,' she said.

'I understand this much,' Josie said. 'Andrew's a grown man, with children of his own. He'll know what you did for him and he'll see your predicament, Annie. He'll see why you've never told him this story before.'

Annie looked bleak. She was grateful to Josie, she was glad she'd come here, but still she knew she was alone. Josie believed she understood and yet, thought Annie, she didn't. She didn't. She didn't.

Back at Beech Street the house was empty except for Finn, whose greeting was muted, as though he knew she was bruised. Andrew and Bailey had gone who knew where with the boys, but they'd washed the dishes, tidied away the toys, plumped up the cushions in the sitting room, so that, downstairs at least, you might never know they were staying here. The red light blinked on the answerphone and when Annie pressed play, a man's voice startled her with talk of Finn until she realised that it was just Mr Dinmoor, so she let him speak but walked into the kitchen without listening. He ended his message with a bright cheerio and she stood in the silence for a moment, considering. The wooden box and its arsenal of mementoes was gone, and there wasn't a single thing out of place in here; all was as it should be, as it ever was, but the perfect order now seemed steeped in loneliness and Annie sat heavily on a chair, worn down by sorrow, spent and fearful. When the front door opened and closed she didn't so much as stir, and when Michael called her she didn't reply, so that he was instantly rattled when he found her in the kitchen.

'So you *are* here,' he said, in a huff. 'Don't know where you've been, but you've missed all the action.'

'What?' Annie said, although she barely registered interest.

'Oh, high drama.' He stood behind her, so she had to twist in the chair to look at him. She knew that expression; he was spinning out the moment. Well, let him. She turned away again. She wondered if he knew about the shoebox and decided he probably didn't, because it was years since Andrew had shared anything with his brother.

'Well? Do you want to know?'

'Not really,' Annie said, and she knew from the stunned silence that this was as shocking to Michael as a slap in the face. She knew, too, that something in her offhand manner had impressed him; he walked around the table and sat down opposite her.

'Father's on his deathbed,' he said.

'Again,' Annie said.

He conceded with a small laugh that they had indeed been here before. 'But really, this time,' he said. 'The home rang, spoke to Andrew. The old bastard had a massive seizure by all accounts. They want you in there pronto, to sign a DNR.'

She looked at him, puzzled.

'Do not resuscitate,' Michael said.

'I see.'

'I told Andrew I didn't think you'd have any moral objection to that.'

'None whatsoever,' she said, and they shared a rueful smile, a rare moment of understanding. 'So where's Andrew now?'

'Dashed off to Glebe Hall with Bailey and the sprogs in tow.'

'Oh. Oh dear.'

'Rang a taxi! I suggested they wait for you but—'

She stood up abruptly so that he stopped mid-sentence. 'Was he carrying a box?' Annie said. She was heading out of the kitchen as she spoke.

'What? A box?' Michael left the table too, followed his mother down the hall. She was shrugging on her coat and Finn thought it was for his benefit and stretched luxuriously, limbering up for a walk. Annie was oblivious; she ignored the dog entirely and Michael, noticing this, thought that of all his mother's present strangeness, this fact was the strangest. It pleased him to see the dog spurned, put him in a better frame of mind.

'Well was he?' Annie snapped, poised to leave the house.

'No. Oh well, maybe.'

He was perplexed at his mother's behaviour, her tone; nothing about her seemed quite as it should be. Michael tried to picture Andrew, leaving the house, carrying a box under one arm, and the image had a ring of credibility to it.

'Well actually ...' he said, but Annie was already dashing away, leaving the door open behind her, and he called out to her to wait, that he was coming too. She didn't even look round: extraordinary! He shut the door and jogged after her, without a coat.

When he slid into the car, she threw him a sceptical look. 'When did you last see your father?' she said. He laughed, thinking of the painting, but she wasn't amused; her profile was rigid with tension as they drove slowly along Beech Street.

'Yes, all right,' he said. 'Point taken.'

He was being facetious, but still, she was surprised, because Michael never admitted to being at fault. But then, she thought, when had she ever truly laid fault at his door? She glanced at him and seemed about to speak but he raised his eyebrows at her and flourished at the windscreen with his long fingers.

'Eyes on the road, Mother,' he said.

She turned away, and Michael reclined his seat, closed his eyes, and hummed snatches of Mendelssohn all the way to Glebe Hall.

21

Vince's eyes were open but he looked dead already, desiccated, empty of spirit or light, and with Andrew motionless on one side of the bed and Bailey on the other, the scene had the look of a morbid still life. The boys weren't here, but all Annie was looking for as she scanned the room was the wooden box, and there it was, on the floor on Andrew's side of the bed, its lid off but its contents still contained. She looked at it warily, then at Andrew, who smiled uncertainly at her, clearly unsure what to expect. The last time he'd seen her she was running from the house like a scalded cat.

'You okay?' he asked. She nodded, although she wasn't okay, not remotely, and her immediate concern was just how soon she could make a grab for the box.

Bailey stood up and stretched, and said, 'Hey, Annie, hey, Mike,' and Michael winced.

'Please don't call me Mike,' he said, but Bailey only laughed and left the room to find the boys, whose voices could now be heard in the corridor. Michael heaved a suffering sigh and wandered to the window.

'Have you seen the doctor, Mum?' Andrew asked. Preoccupied by the box, she forgot to speak, and he stared at her, waiting for an answer. He must be disappointed, she was thinking; he must have planned to spread the pictures and postcards across the bed, share them with Vince. She felt their malevolent, lurking presence. The air in the room was thick with dry, sterile heat and Michael pulled effortfully at the window but it didn't budge.

'They keep them fastened,' Annie said. 'Stops patients escaping. Will you find the doctor for me, Michael?' She wanted him out of the room.

'I'm sure he'll be along soon enough,' Michael said, more from the habit of being disobliging than from any real objection to the task. He turned from the window with a grimace. 'Imagine living and dying in a room with a view of the Doncaster Road,' he said.

'Dad doesn't mind,' Andrew said. 'He's long past caring what the view's like.'

'Yes, Andrew, thank you for that insight. How lucky we are you're here to speak for Father.'

'Oh, go fuck yourself, Michael,' Andrew said, flatly.

'Boys,' Annie said, but there was no heat in her reproof, no conviction. Andrew and Michael both looked at her, then at each other, and Michael seemed about to speak, then the door swung open and Moira the nurse glided in, with the young doctor following behind, holding a clipboard against his chest like a shield.

'Hello, Mrs Doyle,' he said, with a stab at compassion that sounded silly in one so young. Poor boy, thought Annie. Moira put an arm round Annie's shoulders and gave her a squeeze. 'How're you bearing up?' she whispered. 'Can I bring you a brew?'

'Some iced water would be nearer the mark,' Michael said. 'This room's an oven.'

'There's chilled water in the dispenser by reception,

Mr Doyle,' Moira said. She didn't like Michael. It'd been years since he'd visited, but she remembered him right enough.

'Splendid,' he said. 'Perhaps you could bring us some?'

'Could you come with me to the quiet room, Mrs Doyle?' the doctor said. Annie hesitated, wanted to refuse. Her place was here, with the box.

'Mrs Doyle?' The doctor looked puzzled. 'I'd like to explain the situation to you, and I'll need your signature, you see.'

'Yes,' Annie said. 'Yes, of course. But I'll just bring this.' She darted forwards and lunged madly for the open box at Andrew's feet, but it tilted, spilling half the contents onto the floor, and there was Martha Hancock again, smiling up at her from the vinyl tiles with vindictive glee. Michael was onto the photographs in a flash.

'A-ha, the mysterious box,' he said. 'Its secrets revealed,' and Annie knew then that this was the only reason he'd come. She bitterly regretted mentioning it to him; bitterly regretted, too, her bungled snatch-and-grab because now everyone in the room was looking at the pictures, even the doctor. Everyone except Vince, that is. He still lay on the bed, wired up to a heart monitor, gazing upwards at nothing. Annie was thankful for this, at least; she had imagined him sitting up, rosy-cheeked and revived by the call of the past, remembering Martha and everything she had meant to him.

'Well now,' Moira was saying. 'Is that the young Vince?' She smiled at Annie, utterly without malice, only with genuine interest. She saw too many bewildered old people here at Glebe Hall; it was grand to be reminded that once upon a time they were young and vital. She was holding a photograph of Vince in a sharp black suit and winkle pickers, his hair swept up in a rockabilly quiff.

'Would you look at that?' she said. 'What a heart-breaker!'

'Oh my God, this isn't you, Mother, so who is *she*?' Michael said, poring over the shot of Martha in the sunshine, adorable in her cotton frock. He flipped it over and read aloud, 'Martha Hancock, Whitley Bay. Martha Hancock, Martha, Martha.' He was thoughtful, tapping an index finger on the edge of the photograph. Annie, light-headed with the approach of the truth, wondered if the reach of Michael's memory could take him as far back as early boyhood.

'One of his conquests, no doubt, randy old goat.' He was studying the image now, not the writing. Annie, watching and waiting, felt almost liberated by her own helplessness.

Now Bailey swung into the room, a boy in each hand, and Blake immediately said, 'What's that?' so Michael absently passed the photograph down to him, already distracted by another. Blake scrutinised the image and Riley, craning his neck slightly to see it too, suddenly exploded with laughter and said, 'Daddy! Why are you wearing a dress?'

There was a potent silence. Michael immediately took the photograph back, held it up to the light. The likeness to Andrew was startling, now it'd been voiced. He had another one in his other hand, the picture of Martha with baby Robert, and now Michael compared the two.

'Well well well,' he said. 'Out of the mouths of babes.' He looked at Andrew, then back at the photographs. 'Uncanny resemblance.' Annie remained oddly passive;

she let the scene unfold, explaining nothing. Her life story was unravelling, and yet they still didn't know the half of it. She felt no panic, only a kind of relief, which she believed was due to the fact that Vince, her arch-persecutor, was incapable of speech. She looked at him, prone on the bed, his eyes open but somehow also closed, and she wondered if he could hear them all. Part of her hoped that he could, if it added to his suffering.

Moira and the doctor had taken a step back towards the door, aware that the small room was suddenly charged with an uncomfortable tension.

'I'll be in the quiet room, Mrs Doyle, when you feel ready,' the doctor said, and left with unprofessional haste, all but running through the door to freedom. However, Moira lingered; she felt invested in Vincent Doyle, and in Annie, his dutiful wife. She felt entitled, now, to witness this drama, although she held herself on the very edge of the action, hoping not to be noticed. The little boys, bored by the peculiar behaviour of the adults, were squirming around on their bellies under Vince's bed, and no one told them to come out.

Andrew stood and Annie noticed for the first time that he'd been holding Vince's hand, his fingers laced through his father's. He always did have more love to give, she thought, and he never did have to suffer the very worst of Vince. Bailey moved to be beside him, and Andrew encircled her waist with his other arm.

'Andy?' she said. 'What's happening here?'

He was shaking, and he didn't answer, but Michael did.

'I put it to the jury, your honour,' he said, 'that this young woman is, in fact, the defendant's mother.' He grinned the wolfish grin that he'd inherited from his father, and brandished the photographs triumphantly in Andrew's direction. 'I bloody well knew you were a cuckoo in the nest.'

Finally Annie was goaded into speech. 'That is quite enough!' she said, and her voice, which so often quailed and quaked in the face of conflict, was almost authoritative – enough, at any rate, to command the attention of the room. The children, believing themselves to be the objects of her sudden fury, slid out from under the bed and stared up at her from the floor, round-eyed. But she was glaring at their Uncle Michael, not at them.

'You've a nasty streak in you, Michael Doyle, but I will NOT allow you to taunt your brother,' she said steadily.

'Half-brother,' Michael ventured, although he mumbled like a sulky teenager and looked at the floor.

Annie seemed to growl, a low, threatening rumble of warning. She kept her eyes on Michael as if she couldn't trust him to behave, but then glanced at her daughter-in-law.

'Bailey, please take the children out of the room,' she said. 'I need to talk to my boys.'

'Sure thing, Annie.' Bailey clicked her fingers at Blake and Riley, who immediately began to haul themselves out of the room and into the corridor, sliding with ridiculous effort across the tiles like giant caterpillars. Bailey kissed Andrew on the cheek. She looked wary and worried, uncertain what any of this meant for her husband, but as she passed Annie, she paused briefly and touched her softly on the arm, an instinctive gesture of warmth and support, and Annie thought how lucky Andrew was, how lucky they *all* were, to have Bailey. She wondered why she hadn't seen this sooner.

So there they were: Mother, Father, Michael and Andrew, reunited. How long had it been since they were all in one room together? Fifteen years? Twenty? She had striven all her adult life to appear ordinary, Annie thought now, striven to present a normal face to the world. But the Doyles had never been able to cleave together, never managed to pull off, with any conviction, a united family front. Always there were betrayals and lies, divisions and sides being taken, small skirmishes, seismic battles, lengthy silences. Even so, they were and always would be bound together, the four of them. She wouldn't include Martha, and make it five.

Annie looked at her boys. Andrew sat, his head in his hands. Michael stood, his back to everyone, his arms folded. Vince, on his way out of this life and onto the next, dominated the room. His breathing had altered, so that although no one was speaking yet, the silence was filled by the rattle and wheeze of his inward and outward breaths. His cheeks had hollowed, and his eyes lay deep in their sockets: flesh returning to bone. He should be dead, thought Annie; he was supposed to have died years ago. He'd been in this home for too long, swearing like a navvy and soiling his bed. He wasn't even in his forties when he was diagnosed with dementia. Not even forty! Annie wouldn't have believed it possible if she hadn't seen his decline with her own eyes. Oh yes, and he was nasty to be with in those early days of the illness, though goodness knows he'd been nasty enough in the first place. Pick's disease, the consultant had called it. When he told her what to expect – a loss of interest in people, a loss of empathy and personal warmth, a tendency towards tactless or inappropriate remarks – Annie had wanted to laugh because he'd just described the husband she already knew. But in fact Vince did alter as the years passed; he did worsen. It was just that he didn't die, and she'd been banking on that because the doctor had told her he wouldn't last ten years. Well, she wished the same doctor could see her now, thirty-odd years later, still dancing to Vince's tune.

She felt ready to speak now and she cleared her throat. Andrew looked up, Michael turned, and Annie launched into the same story she'd told Josie, although it benefitted from the earlier rehearsal; there were no tears this time and, thinking only to spare Andrew any pain, she cast a rosy light over the whole tale, so that it seemed as if the arrival of baby Robert was the result of a perfectly harmonious arrangement between a husband and wife. The pill was thoroughly sugared but still, she felt that by and large the truth was out. When she stopped speaking she allowed herself a private moment of self-congratulation, but then Michael laughed and Andrew looked at her suspiciously.

'Hang on,' he said. 'You're saying you knew I was coming? You were expecting me, like a sort of surrogacy arrangement?'

Annie hadn't entirely meant to suggest this, but it seemed like a helpful interpretation. 'Well, yes! Yes, you might say that,' she said, with hideous brightness.

'Who called me Andrew then?'

'Well, I'd always liked it,' Annie said, 'and it suited you better than Robert.'

'Did it?' Andrew said.

'Well *I* thought so. We both thought so, me and your dad.'

'So you just changed my name?'

'You were only a baby – you didn't know what you were called.'

'Still though, Mum, jeez.' Andrew ran his hands through his hair, his brow furrowed as he tried to puzzle out exactly what was being said.

'Oh, Andrew, the main thing is that your arrival was like … like … oh, all our Christmases come at once.'

'I've never liked Christmas,' Michael said.

Andrew gave a grim laugh, and Annie said, 'No, Michael, we were all excited, all three of us.'

'I bet I wasn't. In fact I'd swear to it.'

'Oh, you can't possibly remember,' Annie said crossly, flapping her hand at him like she would at a wasp.

'Educated guess,' he said.

'No, no.' Annie screwed up her brow, pretending to think back, to remember. 'No, you were definitely pleased to have a little brother.'

This was plainly ridiculous, but she soldiered on.

'And in due course, when he was old enough to understand, Andrew was very happy to have a *big* brother.' She smiled at Andrew and added, 'You were such a lovely baby, such a beautiful little boy.' Michael scowled. He simply couldn't help himself.

'But Mum, what about Martha?' Andrew said.

'Oh, she was nothing, just a girl.' With a sharp little toss of her head, Annie tried to imply that more than enough time had been spent on Martha already.

'But did she keep in touch?'

'Of course not!' Annie seemed startled at the very idea. 'No,' she said again, less excitably. 'It wouldn't have been appropriate.'

'But if she was happy to give me away, if it was all amicably agreed, might she have, I don't know, followed my progress or something?'

'Well she might have, but she didn't.'

'Did you forbid it?'

Annie looked hurt. 'Why would you accuse me of that?' she said.

'I'm just trying to understand. Was Dad in touch with her?'

'Oh dear no,' said Annie, a little wildly now. 'He just moved on to the next conquest.'

'Well, this Martha girl obviously meant something to him, Mum. There's this box, and he's been mentioning her, hasn't he?'

She didn't answer.

'Are there papers? Am I adopted or what?'

'Andrew,' Annie said, 'you're like a dog with a bone.'

He stared at her, astonished.

'I'm just trying to understand,' he said again, but with less hope.

'Let me explain,' Michael said. 'You started out with one mother, but ended up with another.' He was grinning, as if all of this was a huge joke, and indeed he did find it amusing. He glanced across at Vince, who had been temporarily overlooked by them all as he laboured through each and every breath. 'Nicely done, Father,' Michael said. 'One last well-aimed hand grenade before you pop your clogs.'

Annie ignored Michael entirely. She went to Andrew and took his beloved face in her hands. 'You completed our family,' she said, and this much, at least, was true.

She held his gaze, so he could see how she'd loved him then, and loved him still.

Michael yawned and said, 'Touching cameo,' and then behind them, in his bed, Vince stole the show by taking a last, laboured, rattling breath, then ceasing to live. They knew he'd gone from the sudden utter silence.

'Oh,' Annie said, looking across at him. 'Well. That's that.'

'We should call the doctor,' Andrew said, moving to his father's side.

'Rather late for that,' Michael muttered.

The three of them stood there, at the end of Vince's bed, and bowed their heads. There was little outward sorrow at his passing and even Andrew, who had less reason to dislike him than Annie or Michael, remained dry-eyed. Instead, by their mutual silence, they acknowledged a kind of regret that, at this closing of a long, long chapter in their lives, there was barely a single happy memory of him between them.

22

The first letter came about eighteen months after Andrew's arrival, when he was two years old and utterly adorable, Annie's darling, her daily delight. The postman had dropped a flimsy envelope onto the door-mat, and when Annie picked it up she saw the address written in blue ink in an unfamiliar hand. She opened it and her eyes immediately sought the sender before she read the contents. Martha Hancock. Her rounded, loopy handwriting was barely contained by the narrow lines of the notepaper. Annie carried the letter through to the kitchen and sat down. She felt nauseous and filled with pounding fear, like a soldier about to face his first sortie in enemy territory. Martha wrote in a strange, direct, informal style and her opening salvo eschewed all niceties and cut to the chase with two brutal sentences.

> *Mrs Doyle, I got a letter from Vincent to say he longs to see me and he'll bring Robert back to me whenever I want him to. You can keep your husband, but I think I'll have my baby.*

Annie recoiled as if from a physical attack, as if Martha had walked into the kitchen and slapped her, and she gasped for air, drowning in distress, clutching the edge of the table for support. Of all the betrayals in her life, there had been no greater one than this: that Vince should give her Andrew to love as her very own, yet promise him back to Martha Hancock as a lure, a bait, in pursuit of his own wicked ends. It was as if the child was nothing more than a library book: a borrowed object, overdue for return.

Burn it, Annie thought, her heart hammering. Destroy it in the range. She twisted the notepaper into a tight skein and held it at arm's length, as if it were already on fire, but after a moment she placed it back on the table, flattened it out with the palm of her hand and made herself read on.

I'll come to Coventry to get him. I don't want to see Vincent, and I don't want him to know where I live. He wrote to me care of Father Patrick, my old parish priest, and that was the only thing he could do because he has no idea where to find me, so in case you're thinking Vincent and me are still in touch, we are not.

Annie stopped again and looked up. Andrew had come into the room pulling a wooden duck on a string. It quacked as it rolled along, and Andrew mimicked the sound, the two of them in unison as they did a circuit of the kitchen. She was immediately and gratefully fortified by the solidity of him; his sturdy presence made Martha's letter seem somehow less real and certainly less threatening. He plonked himself down on his bottom, and picked up the duck, taking an exploratory bite of its beak, then he looked at Annie, and released the duck from his mouth to beam at her.

'Mumma,' he said, holding out the toy. 'Quack quack.'

'It's a duck, sweetheart,' Annie said. 'Duck.'

'Quack,' Andrew said.

Annie read on, feeling calmer.

We had a bad start, me and the baby. Robert was born in mortal sin according to my mam, and she said I'd shamed her and shamed God by falling pregnant out of wedlock. She threw me out and Vincent took me in.

I'll bet he did, thought Annie.

But even though I sinned I don't think a child can be sinful and I think Mam will come round in time and also you already have your own boy, Mrs Doyle, Vincent told me that.

'Two boys,' Annie said, aloud. 'I have two boys, Michael and Andrew.' She thought of the girl's mother and her Catholic wrath; she thought of incense and eternal damnation, and she shuddered.

When Robert was born, I tried to look after him but I didn't know how to love him, so I left him with Vincent because I knew he would keep him safe.

Ha! thought Annie: safe my eye. All Vince had done was run straight back here. The only person Vince looked after was himself.

*Now I want him back. My mam doesn't know yet
so I won't give you my address and don't tell Vincent
I have written. I will write to you again to arrange
things.*
    Martha Hancock

That was it. Annie stared at the letter for a few moments. No, she thought, I won't tell Vince you've written. Sending love letters to a schoolgirl care of a Catholic priest – she was ashamed of him, and for him. But if Martha Hancock thought she could write to her, Annie, and demand she hand over Andrew, she could think again. She looked at him now, pottering about on the floor, rolling the duck through the chair legs in a state of simple, happy absorption.

'Andrew,' she said, and he immediately looked up at her. 'Come here, pet,' she said, and held out her arms. He came, and she pulled him up onto her lap and kissed his cheeks and smelled his sweet, milky skin. He squirmed and laughed as if this was just another game, but her arms held him tight and even as she made him squeal, blowing raspberries into the folds of his chubby neck, she made a silent, solemn vow to never, ever let him go. He was her own boy, her very own. Then she let him slide to the floor again so that she could stand up and open the door of the Rayburn, and watch its red-hot coals turn Martha's letter to ash.

After this the letters came sporadically: three, perhaps four, over a period of about a year, and then they stopped altogether. By some small mercy, and because he was so often away, all of them arrived when Vince was absent and

Annie destroyed them in the fire, every one unopened. She did this to protect herself from further agony, but it came, instead, at the price of perpetual anxiety because she gained no further insight into Martha Hancock's intentions, no understanding of her determination. Annie tried to believe that she could discourage the girl simply by ignoring her. She tried to believe that a girl of – what, eighteen years old? Nineteen? Certainly no older – would be quickly distracted and diverted from her purpose. And yet, and yet ... the girl's voice in that first letter had lodged itself at the very heart of Annie's insecurities. The pages were gone, but she could remember them almost word for word, and the Martha Hancock of that letter – gauche, blunt, forthright – gave no indication of feebleness, no suggestion she might simply give up the chase. So although Annie told herself one thing, she reluctantly believed another, and the first time the young woman appeared on the street in front of her, Annie felt no surprise, only recognition. In fact, she'd never seen this girl before, never even seen a photograph, but nevertheless she knew this could only be Martha. Something in the girl's steady grey-eyed gaze, the defiant tilt of her chin, the curve of her lips. She looked like Andrew.

Annie had him by the hand. They were walking to the primary school, to collect Michael. It was early March, but there was frost in the air, and although the sun hung low in a bright sky, there wasn't a scrap of warmth to be had from it. The child was wrapped under layers of wool: hat, scarf, coat, mittens. He was trotting along beside Annie, blowing puffs of smoke from his mouth, trying to make a doughnut in the air, the way his daddy did with cigarette smoke. He was curious when they came to a halt. He smiled up at the lady, and she smiled back at him, then turned to Annie.

'Mrs Doyle, you're very rude,' Martha said. 'You haven't answered even one of my letters.'

Her tone was sardonic, and it made her sound a lot like Vince: that, and the Geordie lilt. Annie tightened her hold on Andrew's hand. She didn't answer at once, but stalled for time and boldly considered the girl's appearance, looking her up and down: cheap kitten heels and a tightly belted navy gabardine coat, short in the cuffs, worn on the collar. Annie concentrated her mind on these imperfections, to stop herself from seeing the terrible youth and beauty of Martha's face.

'I didn't reply because I didn't read them,' Annie said at last. 'I saw the postmark and put them straight in the range.'

'The range? You burned them?' Martha was smiling, as if this was funny, a twist in the game, and it unnerved Annie, who had meant only to wound. So she didn't answer, she just walked away, pulling Andrew with her in a fierce grip. Martha stayed where she was, but said, 'That's my boy you have there, Mrs Doyle.'

Andrew looked back at her, over his shoulder, but Annie, still holding his hand, stepped up her pace so that he had to gallop alongside her to keep from falling. Being Andrew this made him laugh, not cry. They arrived at the school too early and Annie was on pins as they waited, then, when the bell rang and children streamed out into the playground, the teacher asked for a word, and kept her there at the gate while she talked at some length about Michael's latest catalogue of misdemeanours. Michael held himself aloof from the little group and listened impassively to the details of his crimes.

'... and then, after all that, Mrs Doyle, he's completely incapable of saying sorry. Mrs Doyle?'

The teacher looked at Annie for affirmation, or sympathy, or some recognition at least of the problem, but Annie's eyes were darting up and down the street; she was barely listening.

'Perhaps if his behaviour was managed better at home?' said the teacher, turning hostile in the face of Annie's apparent unconcern. 'Perhaps if you and Mr Doyle could—' but Annie just said, 'I really have to go now,' and she seized Michael by the coat sleeve and marched the boys away down the pavement, in completely the wrong direction for home. She was deaf to Michael's protestations as they weaved their way back to Sydney Road via a strange, circuitous route that forced them to walk part of the way in single file beside the railway tracks and make a terrifying bolt across the Ringway. Only when they were safely inside the house, with the bolts drawn top and bottom across the back door and the key turned in the lock at the front, did Annie allow herself to drop her guard, and even then for the rest of the evening she found her heart was skittering and her breathing came fast and shallow.

After that, Annie saw her everywhere; that is, she *thought* she did – a flash of blonde hair, a swift turn of a slim ankle, a steady gaze across a busy street – and the torment lay in not knowing when the girl was real or imagined. The streets of Coventry were suddenly filled with menace; the walk to school, a trip to the library, the butcher, the greengrocer: all of these ordinary destinations took on a newly threatening aspect and Annie walked everywhere with darting eyes and her hand firmly clasped around Andrew's. She knew she was being watched: she knew it. And one day Martha confirmed it by boarding the same bus as Annie and Andrew but at a different stop, taking the seat behind them and speaking in a low, insistent voice into Annie's ear. *You're a thief and a fraud, and I'll have him off you, and you won't be able to do a thing about it.* Annie, trapped like a partridge in a copse, just let the words drop into her ear until she could free herself at the next stop and hurry on, turning her face away from Martha's knowing stare through the bus window. But she passed each day in watchful agony and became a benign jailor to Andrew, who was never free, never alone, even to play and potter in the small, enclosed back garden in Sydney Road. She told no one – well, there was no one to tell – but she found she missed Barbara, all over again, and longed to sit with her old friend in the cluttered cosiness of the haberdashery and spill the contents of her wounded heart. She could all but hear Barbara's voice, indignant on Annie's behalf, absolutely on her side. But Annie didn't go to Sew and Sew's: she kept her distance and held her misery close, and repeated to herself the pledge that, while ever she had breath in her body, she would never, never, never relinquish Andrew. She considered Michael, with his oddness, his white-hot fury, his darting eyes and private mind, and she understood that he could never be enough, could never compensate for the loss of the child whose existence had shown her how it felt to be loved. If she lost Andrew, she would lose everything.

One day, Martha changed tactic and knocked on the door and Annie, expecting the milkman, opened it wide. Before she understood what was happening, the girl had stepped clean inside the house, grim-faced and fleet-footed, so that Annie could only close the door and face her foe, although she nipped around Martha and stood in her pinny, arms folded across her chest, occupying the foot of the stairs like a sentry. Martha only smiled and gazed boldly, judgingly, around the little hallway. She was far, far prettier than Annie wished her to be; her long hair fell in loose waves, and her eyes were just like Andrew's, grey, wide, beautiful. But she wasn't a good person, Annie thought: oh no. She only had to look at her to see she was hard-edged, spiky, demanding. Her mouth was twisted in disdain, as if the wallpaper wasn't to her liking, or the carpet offended her. She was wearing flat red pumps today and a pair of flared jeans, and her short belted jacket was cinched in to show her waist and the curves on her aggravating, arrogant young body. She carried a bulging white shoulder bag made of the sort of cheap patent leather that cracked and peeled at the edges like dry skin. She seemed to fill all corners of the hallway with her presence: that and her scent, which was cheap and sugary. Woolworth's, thought Annie: trollop, she thought. With such silent insults she bolstered her courage, while at the same time keeping the peace so that Andrew might sleep on upstairs until she could get Martha back out onto the street.

'Right,' Martha said, bringing her unsettling eyes back to Annie. 'I'm bored with all this. I suppose he's upstairs. Bring him to me now.'

Annie staggered and groped for the bannister as if it was the deck rail of a lurching, storm-tossed ship. Martha laughed and stepped a little closer.

'Oh God, you're pathetic,' she said. 'Vincent was right about that.'

Her tone was as insulting as her words. She spoke without fear, as if Annie was beneath her, as if she, Martha, was the older woman.

'Thing is,' she said, 'I can just bloody well take him from you, and if you don't like it, hard cheese. I've tried asking nicely.'

'Have you?' Annie said, rallying with pure indignation. 'Whispering your threats in my ear, while the child sits beside me on the bus?'

Martha widened her eyes mockingly.

'You don't love him,' Annie said steadily. 'Look at you, playing foolish games over a child's future. You might think you want him now, but within a week you'd be bored with him and on to the next thing.'

Martha shrugged her narrow shoulders. 'Still,' she said. 'Robert's mine.' She looked past Annie, up the stairs, and Annie shifted her stance as if she was trying to fill the space between Andrew and Martha. She thought – no, she *knew* – she could thwart this chit of a girl. She just didn't, at this moment, know how.

'He'll be four next birthday,' she said to Martha, in an urgent whisper. 'He's not a baby who knows no better.'

Martha gave a short laugh. 'Yes, well he was two when I first wrote to you.' She pointed up the stairs. 'He's up there, isn't he?'

Annie nodded, because to deny it was absurd. 'And he's staying there,' she said. 'You're a stranger to him

– do you think he'd just take your hand and walk away with you?'

'Maybe,' Martha said. She stepped closer again, but Annie stood her ground, although she couldn't look directly at Martha: couldn't let her own eyes settle on the girl's calm, casual allure. Instead, she kept her gaze down, looking at Martha's feet, her scuffed red pumps, waiting for them to make one more move towards the beloved little boy upstairs.

One more move, thought Annie; but her heart was hammering, and then suddenly it came – a lunge forwards, sharp nails in the flesh of Annie's arm, a violent sideways shove. Annie spun as Martha gained the stairs, and she grabbed out wildly, but Martha was too quick. She reached the landing easily and then, by pure chance, she pushed open the right door, the door to Andrew's room, and she saw him there, sleeping in his cot, face down, bottom up in the air, a soft grey velvet rabbit squashed under one arm.

Martha seemed to hesitate now, on the threshold of his room, as if the reality of this sleeping infant hadn't entirely struck her until this moment, and the few seconds' pause gave Annie the time she needed to reach her.

'Get out of my house,' she said, in a low, threatening voice.

Martha turned to look at her, and then took her gaze back to Andrew.

Annie said, 'I'm warning you, if you touch my child—'

'*My* child,' Martha said, but miraculously she stepped backwards, away from the open door, and there was a grain of uncertainty in her expression, a small but crucial loss of self-belief.

Annie said, 'He's more mine now than he is yours.' She wanted to add, to beg, *Please leave us alone, please, please go away,* but it would have been too weak, too revealing, so she said no more, only reached for the handle and pulled the door shut, very, very softly.

Martha began to go downstairs and Annie followed. The constriction round her heart was beginning to loosen; the girl was leaving, Andrew remained safely upstairs, reason – it seemed – had prevailed. She allowed herself the faintest glimmer of hope and then Martha, at the foot of the stairs and with terrible contempt in her voice, said, 'I *will* have him, but I'll just get him from Vincent.'

And she walked to the front door as if she was leaving, then turned and laid a look on Annie of naked pity. 'He'll do *anything* for me,' she said. She tossed a hand in the air as if she was discarding an apple core. 'But you can have him. It's just the bairn I want.' Again she made as if to leave, but once more she seemed to think twice. 'Oh,' she said, bitterly cheerful. 'Nearly forgot.' She delved into the white shoulder bag and took out a piece of paper, the pale parchment colour of officialdom.

'Know what this is?' Martha asked, but got no reply. 'Robert's birth certificate,' she said. She unfolded the document and held it out, but Annie kept her arms folded and shook her head.

'No,' Annie said, and she was astonished at the steel in her voice, her outward calm. 'There is no Robert, there's only Andrew, and you lost all claim when you walked out of his life. This is where he belongs. This is what he knows. This is where he'll stay.'

Martha shrugged again, her gesture of infinite uncon-cern. 'That's what you think,' she said, and she folded the document and put it back. 'But I'll write to Vincent and tell him your game, then we'll see.'

'We shall,' Annie said, feeling none of the confidence she was feigning. She knew Vince too well. One sniff of Martha Hancock and he'd be out of this house like a rat up a drainpipe, dragging Andrew behind him.

Martha tossed her another cheerless smile and left the house, closing the door with quiet control, and Annie gazed at the space she'd vacated, wondering miserably what the girl's next move might be. She knew now that she had a formidable foe and that she herself must stay steadfast and strong, but for the time being she had to lower herself carefully onto the bottom stair to let the terror dissipate. She steadied her breathing and tried to think what she must do. Martha's lawful claim on Andrew had no meaning for Annie, who loved him more than any other being in the world, and yet the birth certificate had shaken her. She wished she had such a document, and wondered if they could be bought. Or stolen. Or forged. She leaned her head against the newel post and wondered bleakly if she'd ever be free from fear.

23

It was Wednesday morning, Dog Day again, but someone was up before Annie and the comforting, surprising smell of toast and bacon rose through the little house and woke her long before the alarm began to chirrup on her bedside table.

She rose, washed, dressed and trod softly down the stairs. Andrew was in the kitchen at the stove, his back to her, nudging bacon rashers around the frying pan. He was in yesterday's jeans and a clean white T-shirt. Barefoot. From behind he still looked like a teenager. The bacon spat in the hot fat and he cursed mildly and turned to the sink, then leapt in shock to see Annie standing in the open doorway watching him.

'Jeez, Mum, you frightened the life out of me!'

She was so happy to hear him say *Mum* that she smiled hugely, as if she was delighted to have startled him, and for a short while they just looked at each other, thinking their separate thoughts. She was remembering a dream from the depths of last night; in it, Andrew had called her Annabelle, shaken her hand and said how nice it was to meet her. That was all, but in the dream she'd cried and cried and Andrew had only walked away, indifferent to her distress.

'Mum? You okay?'

Yesterday, he had discovered that a young woman named Martha Hancock was his mother, not her. He'd discovered he was once an unwanted baby called Robert. He'd discovered that she, Annie, had kept these facts secret from him all his life. Then, while this extraordinary information was still in the first, shocking flush of infancy, his father's life had come to a shuddering halt, so that although Vince had seemed already lifeless, his shattered body took on a new degree of stillness, as if he was no longer a man, but a waxwork of a man. The only person who had cried was Moira, but then, she didn't really know him.

'Mum?'

He was so generous with his concern, and it astonished her. He would be justified in raging, making demands, crushing her with recriminations.

'I'm all right,' she said. 'Where's Finn?'

'I let him out for a pee.'

'Oh.'

'Will you have a bite of breakfast?'

'Andrew, I couldn't,' she said, but anyway she did, joining him at the little kitchen table, eating strips of bacon cooked the way he liked it: crozzled, he called it: burned, she said. The kitchen was a tip following his exertions. The hot frying pan fizzed in the sink, the bacon pack was still out and there was a trail of breadcrumbs scattered along the worktop. Annie put the bacon in the fridge but left the rest and sat down. Pot it, she thought. What did a bit of mess matter, anyway?

'I'm walking the dog this morning,' she said. 'On his lead, poor thing. Round the res, with Josie and Sandra.'

The bacon was crisp and salty, quite delicious. He was licking his fingers so she did too. There was a camping quality to this early-morning tryst; there seemed no cause to stand on ceremony.

'That's good,' he said. 'I'm glad you have friends.'

He meant he was glad she wouldn't be entirely alone when he went back to Byron Bay. This was unspoken, but entirely understood. She nodded.

'Come visit,' he said. 'What's to stop you? Riley'd love it. We all would.'

She couldn't fly to Australia; such a journey was beyond her imagination; he knew this as well as she did. She said, 'My friend Josie drove all the way to, erm, Pakistan was it? Or somewhere.'

'Well then.' Andrew rocked back on the rear legs of his chair and picked bacon from his teeth. Oh, the rules that had been broken since he arrived! 'What's stopping you?'

'Well, but she's one of these free spirits,' Annie said. 'She sells ethnic bric-a-brac in a shop on the internet.'

He smiled. 'She sounds interesting. I bet she'd tell you to visit us.'

'Oh, she would.'

But they left it there, each of them knowing the subject was closed. Outside, Finn looked in, his black nose touching the glass of the kitchen door. He was silent, as he always was when he wanted Annie's attention. He was *willing* her to let him in, his dark eyes fixed upon her, trusting that she'd oblige, and she was about to – she was getting up from her chair – when Andrew said, 'Look, about yesterday,' and her stomach somersaulted so she sat back down.

'I don't want to drag up the past,' he said, and she

thought, amen to that. 'I mean, I'd love to know a bit more about Martha, but I know who my mother is, and it's you, obviously.'

She was overwhelmed with gratitude, but all she could manage was a damp smile. He reached across the table and enclosed one of her hands in his.

'You're the one who wanted me. You're the one who loved me and raised me and sent me on my way,' he said.

'I never meant you to go as far as you did,' she said, and he laughed, although she was entirely serious.

'Well, anyway, I've told you now, and I want you to remember that, so that if I do a bit of digging, you won't feel hurt or angry.'

What could he mean, digging? Annie looked at him fondly, wondering why his face was all of a sudden so grave.

'I mean it's important, Mum. A whole different gene pool from the one I thought I had. I need to find out something about Martha Hancock – who she was, you know?'

'Oh!' Annie pulled her hand away from under his.

'Mum, don't be like that. My kids share their DNA with a stranger and it's freaking me out.'

'Well anyway, you won't find anything,' she said, and she stood up.

'Why? You can trace practically anyone on the internet these days. All those genealogy websites ...'

'People like her don't leave traces.'

She was up now, bustling about, letting in the dog, preparing to leave the house.

'People like what?' Andrew said, following her with his

eyes, trying to keep his voice level. 'See? You know more than you're letting on.'

She'd gone to the coat-stand now for her fleece, and she couldn't see him so it was easy to say, 'Well I never met her, but what kind of woman would abandon a baby?'

'Well, quite,' Andrew said. He was in the hallway too now, leaning against the wall, his hands in the pockets of his jeans. 'What kind of woman *would* leave a baby? That's what I want to find out.'

She sniffed, opened the two front doors, then patted her jacket pocket to check for the car keys, knowing full well they were there. 'It's ancient history,' she said airily, although actually she would have liked to scream and pound at his chest with her fists. 'Let bygones be bygones,' she said, and off she went down the path with Finn.

When she arrived at the reservoir Josie was already there, leaning against her car, watching Betty sniff about in the long grass, and then before Annie had finished squaring up the Nissan – back and forth she went, back and forth, making small adjustments to her angle – Sandra swept into the car park like a getaway driver, thudding to a halt, all skew-whiff. She seemed to leap out of the car in one seamless bound and Annie was wondering what the emergency was, but then she noticed Sandra's face, and it was stricken. Sandra went straight to Josie.

'It's today,' she said in a sort of stifled wail, and Josie said, 'Oh love, come here,' and wrapped Sandra in a tight embrace. Annie, watching, felt like an intruder. She was thinking she might just creep away unnoticed, when

Sandra pulled away from Josie's arms and gave a mighty sniff then noticed Annie for the first time, so Annie climbed out of her car and released Finn, who bounced over to greet Betty. Sandra looked at Annie bleakly.

'It's Fritz,' she said. 'He couldn't move at all this morning. The vet said it's time.'

Her voice cracked, and she was undone: hard-headed, sharp-tongued Sandra. Her distress was noisy and shocking, and Josie was crying too, although with more restraint. Annie swallowed hard and turned her head so that she could just see the old Alsatian lying in the boot of Sandra's car. She moved over to the rear window and peered in at him. He was staring at her, his eyes damp and glassy.

'Can I open the boot?' she asked, and Sandra nodded, so Annie clicked the latch and raised the door. Fritz looked ancient, the oldest dog in the world. Annie leaned in and placed her hand on his head, feeling the tired bone of his skull beneath the grey-brown hair. 'There there, Fritzy,' she said. 'Night night, darling dog,' and he closed his eyes as if all he needed was permission. Annie drew back and turned around and Sandra, quieter now, was staring at Annie as if she didn't know who she was.

'Well he's ready to go, bless his heart,' Annie said.

Sandra nodded dumbly.

'He knows how much you love him, you know, and really that's the main thing, the only thing.'

'Annie,' Sandra said. 'Thank you.' She was calmer now, but she still looked traumatised, her face so colourless it was almost translucent and her eyes teary pools of the palest green. 'I think maybe I'll go now,' she said.

'Should we come too?' Josie asked, but Sandra shook

her head and said she'd be okay now, and that they should walk without her, so Annie and Josie stood back and watched her reverse the big dusty Volvo. Josie blew a kiss and Annie held up a hand, half-wave, half-salute. Betty and Finn, scenting sorrow on the breeze, sat beside their owners with a solemn canine dignity and as the car moved away they watched it go as if they knew, and were sad, that poor old Fritz was leaving the car park for the last time.

Josie was too tactful to ask directly about Andrew, but Annie told her anyway about the moment when little Riley saw a picture of Martha Hancock and took her for his daddy in a dress. There was comedy in the retelling, although at the time she'd felt only horror. How extraordinary, thought Annie, that in the course of a day and a night, a family crisis could turn into something almost harmless. It was as if people discovered all the time that they weren't who they thought they were. So they talked for a while about Andrew but soon their conversation drifted back to Fritz, and from there to Finn. He was off the lead, but only so that he could paddle, and the two women stood watching him. Josie wanted Annie to talk to Mr Dinmoor about his sister, in Formby. He'd already mentioned Finn to Dora.

'She'll take him,' Josie said. 'She's happy to.'

Annie felt instantly queasy, but then she thought about the dead sheep, and Mr Wright's kindness in the matter, and even poor old Fritz, for whom all options were now closed, who was perhaps already gone, and she resolved to be strong, or at least as close to strong as she could manage. 'Well then,' she said. 'Should I give him a ring?'

'Sure, I'll let you have his number. Or if you like, drop in later. He's coming for tea.'

On balance this sounded like the lesser of two evils, so Annie agreed; three o'clock at Josie's. Then Finn chose just this moment to trot back towards her from the water with his generous smile and his feathery tail held high like the Royal Standard, and she rubbed his ears, feeling like Judas Iscariot bestowing the fateful kiss.

'Oh dear,' Annie said. 'I do feel awful.'

'Don't. He'll have a wonderful time on Formby sands.'

'This Dora lady, is she old?'

'No, I don't think so. She's younger than Mr Dinmoor, if that's what you're worrying about. He calls her his baby sister.'

'Where's Formby again?'

'Near Blackpool, up there by the sea, north-west coast,' Josie said. 'We could all go, when you take him. It'd be a road trip, like *Thelma and Louise*, but we won't shoot anyone or drive off the Grand Canyon.'

Annie had no idea what Josie was talking about and anyway was hardly listening. 'Whatever will I do without Finn,' she said, and it wasn't really a question so Josie didn't reply and for a while they walked silently in single file along the reservoir path. Then Josie said, 'You were so lovely back there, to Fritz.'

'Poor old thing,' Annie said.

'You helped Sandra a lot, you know, just by being kind.'

'Did I?'

Josie nodded. They walked on. There was nothing to see on the dark winter water, no birds or fishermen. Even on the brightest of summer days this reservoir never sparkled with turquoise light, but today it was black as treacle. Annie thought about the cormorant they had seen a few weeks ago, wondered if it was an omen of bad luck. She thought about the contents of the shoebox and how very much she'd like them back, but Andrew wanted them, he'd already told her, and what could she say but yes to such a reasonable request? Still though, if there were some way of setting those photographs alight, turning them to ash one by one, she would do it, wicked though it might be. Until that blasted box emerged from the loft, Martha Hancock had been eradicated from everything but Vince's addled memories. And just at this point, just as Vince entered her head for the very first time today, Josie said brightly, 'So, how's Vince doing?'

Annie stopped in her tracks so that Josie walked right into the back of her. 'Oh!' Annie said, turning to face her friend and knowing that what she had to say was going to appear absolutely unforgivable. 'Vince died. He's dead.'

To walk and chat for all this while and forget to mention – forget to even remember! – that Vince had passed away; well it was disgraceful, really. How must it look? Covered in shame she raised her eyes to Josie to gauge the depth of her disapproval, but saw she was trying not to laugh.

'Annie Doyle,' Josie said. 'You really are the limit.'

24

Michael had always told Annie that she ought to read more, by which he meant books, not magazines. Not any old books either, but difficult novels, the kind with stark monochrome covers and a foreword and a lengthy section of explanatory notes at the back. Annie didn't mind a bit of Dickens, but it turned out he didn't cut the mustard with Michael. Sentimental, florid and two-dimensional, apparently, so Annie supposed he must be right. She once tried *Tess of the d'Urbervilles* but didn't get far. She'd read everything by Agatha Christie, twice, and she loved trashy romances of the type sold by her local newsagent, but she didn't often read these either, usually choosing nothing at all over Michael's searing derision. But now here she was at Josie Jones's windmill, buttering a scone and listening anxiously to Mr Dinmoor, who'd seen a list of the nation's favourite books and thought it was rubbish. To prove it, he wanted to know what *her* favourite ever book was and oh, how she was wishing now that she'd paid attention to her son's challenging reading list. Josie had already said hers was *To Kill a Mockingbird* – which turned out to have been number six on the list – so Mr Dinmoor was looking expectantly at Annie to back up his theory and save his face.

'Well now, let me think,' she said, playing for time, her mind entirely blank of anything other than *The Disgraceful Duke* by Barbara Cartland and she couldn't, she wouldn't, say that. Before the silence became awkward, Mr Dinmoor said, 'For me it's *The Dogs of War* but you'll never find Frederick Forsyth on a favourite books list.'

Josie was enjoying herself. 'Because?' she asked.

'Because nob'dy tells the truth when you ask 'em,' he said. 'They think if it's going on a list, they'd best think up summat clever.'

Annie found herself nodding in agreement with Mr Dinmoor. She was encouraged, and being encouraged, she relaxed enough to remember *Death on the Nile,* which she blurted out triumphantly.

'Yes!' said Mr Dinmoor. 'Exactly. Marvellous book. Any of them Poirot stories, for that matter. But are they on that list? Are they heckers like. Instead, we've got *The Unbearable Lightness of Being* and *Madame Bovary,* because all folk do when they're asked is try to remember what they were forced to read at school.'

'Well I'm sticking with Harper Lee, and I make no apologies for it,' Josie said. She broke open a scone with her two thumbs, no knife, and paused for a moment to admire the soft interior, studded with sultanas. 'Aren't scones the best thing?' she said. 'But they have to have fruit in them, and never, ever cheese. Have another, Mr Dinmoor.'

'Alf,' he said, as he always did, although there was no expectation in his voice that she'd oblige him. He reached for the plate and helped himself.

Annie took a good bite of her scone, happy to have joined in. She found she actually liked Mr Dinmoor; he paid her attention, but gently, not in a forceful way; also his shirt, which was clean and pressed, smelled comfortingly of Persil. In spite of her rudeness to him at their last encounter – bundling him out of the door, denying him the chance to speak – he'd shown nothing but kindness to her since she arrived. She peeped shyly at him now and again; even his tattoo had taken on a sort of piratical, rakish charm. Did he say he was a mapmaker, last time they met? Herself, she felt like the opposite of a mapmaker, if such a thing were possible; her own orbit had been so very limited. Mind you, she could have drawn a map of Coventry from memory: every street, every ginnel, every dark dead end. Still could; its geography was drawn indelibly in her mind.

She rose from her reverie and was startled to find he was addressing her. Josie must have briefed him, because he already knew Vince was dead, but rather than piling sympathy upon her, he seemed to be saying that death was just as likely to bring relief as sorrow.

'My Alice passed away twenty years ago,' he said, 'and I loved her, but I couldn't stand to watch her suffer, do you follow me?'

Annie nodded her head, her mouth being too full to risk opening it.

'She once asked me to suffocate her, y'know, wi' a pillow.'

'Oh God, really?' Josie said.

'Aye, but I dint,' he said. 'She passed away natural, like. But not peaceful, no, nowt like peaceful. It were agony, for me and for her.'

Annie, free at last to speak, said, 'And there's Fritz, put quietly to sleep to end his suffering.'

'Yes,' Mr Dinmoor said, pointing at Annie across the table. 'Exactly, Annie. We accord more rights to a dog than we do to a human being.'

'Well, but hang on ...' said Josie.

'We do,' said Annie. 'Vince lived thirty years longer than he should have. Thirty years when he didn't know up from down.'

'Yes, but we can't go putting people down willy-nilly,' Josie said, but Annie and Mr Dinmoor weren't really paying attention to her.

'My Alice never lost her mind. She died too young for that.'

'My Vince lost his mind when he was still in his thirties,' Annie said. 'Started to, anyway.' Privately she wondered, *my* Vince: when was he ever that?

'In his thirties!' said Mr Dinmoor, and he whistled through his teeth. 'Well I never. I didn't think that were possible.'

'Oh yes,' said Annie. 'Dementia can strike at any age, although it's much more common in older folk, of course.' She felt like the resident expert and she was pleased with Vince for affording her this small moment of importance in Josie's kitchen. So on they went, sharing stories from the past, and Josie just watched and listened and topped up their tea until Betty trotted past the table and they remembered they were meant to be discussing Finn.

'She has four other dogs at the moment,' Mr Dinmoor said, 'and she's got room for six.' He was talking about his sister, Dora. 'She doesn't take strays, she leaves them to the corporation kennels. But she takes dogs from people she knows, or from people who know people she knows, are you with me?'

'Just about,' said Josie.

'Four other dogs, though!' Annie said. 'What are they?' In truth, she didn't really care; she was already thinking this wouldn't do at all.

'Little 'uns,' Mr Dinmoor said. 'Nice little Westie, a couple o' Jacks and a Yorkie. But she's pleased as punch about your Finn.'

'Is she?' Annie, bridling at Dora's presumption, tried to keep the edge out of her voice.

'Oh aye, she likes a golden retriever,' he said. 'We had one when we were bairns. Beautiful dogs.'

'Well yes, they are,' Annie said, susceptible, as always, to retriever flattery. 'He *is* handsome. Finn, I mean.'

'Best thing is if we take 'im up there, see what's what,' Mr Dinmoor said.

'You make it sound very easy, Mr Dinmoor,' Annie said.

He pinned her with his blue eyes. 'Alf,' he said. 'Alf.'

'Alf,' Annie said, and he grinned at her so warmly that she had to look anywhere but at him until her blush subsided.

The funeral took place at the crematorium, which was far too big for the purpose. There were a hundred pale oak chairs set in rows on either side of a central aisle, but only ten of them were filled today. Annie sat front left, flanked by Michael on one side and Andrew on the other, then Bailey, Blake and Riley next to him. Front right there was Moira and Brenda from Glebe Hall. Josie and Sandra had come, and were on the same side of the aisle as Annie, but three empty rows behind, because after all they'd never met Vince, and some unspoken protocol prevented them from putting themselves further forwards. Ten people, thought Annie, gazing ahead to what she could only think of as the stage, where Vince's coffin would be placed; ten people after a lifetime on earth. It wasn't much of a send-off, but then how many more would attend her own funeral? Mr Dinmoor might come, perhaps. Alf. That'd be eleven. But then, of course there'd be no Moira, no Brenda, unless – God forbid – Annie ended up in Glebe Hall herself. She shook her head at this dreadful thought and forced her mind to dwell on other things.

Next to her Andrew and Bailey were chatting quietly and the boys were playing an almost-silent game of jacks, which Annie didn't mind though she hoped they'd stop when the coffin came in. On her other side Michael was picking his nails. She'd suggested he might play something on the violin, but this was really for the sake of Marjorie Bevin, the unenviable funeral celebrant who'd come to the house to discuss the order of service. Marjorie was a youngish woman, plumply pretty, sweet smelling and soft voiced, and she'd utterly failed to hide her shock when Michael point-blank refused.

'Come off it,' he'd said, and snorted contemptuously. 'When did Father ever show an interest in my music?'

'Well he's dead anyway, isn't he?' Annie had said. 'But you could play for me, and for the other mourners.'

'There won't *be* any mourners,' Michael said, 'because none of us are that fussed he's gone. Unless Andrew's managed to track down the mysterious Martha.'

So Annie had dropped it and apologised to Marjorie, and Marjorie had managed to collect herself enough to suggest simply the standard order of service, with a few words from her about Vince's life. And now here they were, in the blandly tasteful chapel, listening to piano music chosen by Marjorie and waiting for Vince.

'Here he comes,' Michael muttered. He hadn't turned round, but he was right; the music had changed from piano to strings and the pall bearers supplied by the funeral director were slow-stepping in with an oak veneer coffin supported on their shoulders. Blake and Riley dropped the jacks and twisted in their seats to stare. Bailey and Andrew held hands, and Annie and Michael kept their gaze straight ahead as if they were waiting for a film to start. Nobody stood. Moira sniffed and dabbed at her nose with a paper tissue. Marjorie waited for Vince to be set down, and for the coffin bearers to retreat, then she stepped forwards and offered Annie a sad smile, which Annie politely returned.

'We are here to remember and celebrate the life of Vincent William Doyle,' said Marjorie and Michael said, 'William?' a little too loudly. Annie dug him sharply with her elbow. Marjorie continued.

'Vince, husband to Annie, father to Michael and Andrew and grandfather to little Blake and Riley here, passed away last week in the Glebe Hall nursing home. But in many ways his family feel they lost him a long time ago to the dementia that afflicted him at such a terribly young age. So I understand that it's with relief as well as sorrow that we say farewell to him today.'

'You can say that again,' muttered Michael.

'Relief, that is, at a long-awaited end to his suffering,' Marjorie intoned. 'But we must remember, too, the life he lived before his cruel illness took hold; a life that was filled with laughter and love.'

Michael cast a sideways glance at Annie. She narrowed her eyes at him and pursed her lips then looked steadfastly ahead again. She was dreading the next ten minutes. She'd made up a pack of lies for Marjorie, who knew no better, and she was just hoping they could complete the service and commit the body to the flames without anyone laughing out loud.

'Vincent loved nothing more than to be in the bosom of his family,' Marjorie said. 'He was proud of Michael and Andrew, and although his work as a salesman kept him away from Coventry for long periods at a time, he always stayed in touch, sending gifts and sweets through the post, and writing long letters to the boys describing where he was and what he was up to.'

Annie could feel Andrew's eyes on her, and she knew that Michael's eyebrows were rising up, up, up in disbelief.

'He was a doting father, and a loving husband; a family man in every sense of that well-used term. He was no angel, though ...' Marjorie paused, a twinkle in her eyes.

'Here we go,' said Andrew, very, very softly.

'... No, he liked a pint or two of stout with a whisky chaser, and he spent longer in the bookie's than his wife was always happy with ...'

Another compassionate smile. Annie looked down at her shoes.

'But,' Marjorie continued, 'Vince knew that home is where the heart is, and until he became ill, that was where he was always glad to return after long weeks on the road.'

'What utter bollocks,' Michael said, in a voice that was entirely audible, but valiant Marjorie soldiered on.

'And so at this point in our service, I'm offering you

all the opportunity to step forward, if you feel you'd like to, to share with everyone your happy memories about Vince.'

She waited, and the silence was awful. No one moved. Andrew looked as though he might be about to, out of sheer embarrassment, but Annie clutched at his arm and kept him beside her.

'No, we wouldn't like to, thank you all the same,' she said, looking directly into Marjorie's empathetic eyes and very firmly handing back the awkwardness to the person who'd created it. In a matter of seconds Marjorie registered her faux pas, fleetingly lost her composure, then recovered with admirable speed and good grace.

'Can I ask you all now to simply take a few moments for quiet reflection?' she said, as if her previous request had never been uttered. 'Think privately about what Vince meant to you, perhaps give thanks for the time you had together, and take comfort from the knowledge that his death came as a release from suffering.'

Marjorie bowed her head. Michael had his arms folded and he was staring balefully at the coffin but everyone else dutifully hung their heads, even if it was more out of relief than respect. Annie could hear Michael breathing hard through his nostrils like a bull. She felt an icy chill around her ankles, a sudden bitter draught, and she wondered if it was Vince on his way down, nipping at her heels, taking his final leave of her with one last moment of spitefulness. She closed her eyes and tried to pray, but found she had nothing to say, even to herself, so she let her mind drift instead to a moment in time, long, long ago, when Vincent Doyle smiled upon her on a sunny day in a busy Coventry street and asked her to go dancing at the Locarno.

25

So Martha was as good as her word. She wrote a letter to Vince, and posted it by hand through the letterbox, on the second morning of his next visit home. He found it on the doormat and immediately rushed outside; worse, he rushed down the street, first one way and then the other, barefoot, in his vest and trousers, with the braces dangling in two long loops at either side. Annie had never seen him so distressed. He was driven half-mad by the knowledge that Martha had been here, outside his own front door. But anyway, she'd gone again, and Vince took out his frustration on Annie, waving the letter in her face and pelting her with ugly words. Annie was as certain as she could be that Vince already had another woman – he never brought dirty laundry home and his clothes smelled of something other than Omo; this was her proof. But it was still Martha he wanted, the one woman that he apparently couldn't have. Oh, the desirability of the unobtainable! Annie knew all about that. She bowed her head in the face of his fury and waited for it to subside. There was no return address on the letter and Martha made it plain she wanted nothing to do with Vincent; all she wanted was Robert. She said she'd be in touch regarding the handover: that there'd be further instructions.

Annie laughed wildly and said Martha was crazy. 'She sounds like she's talking about a briefcase full of money, not a living, breathing boy,' she said. She was desperate that Vince, for once, should take her side. Hadn't she been a devoted mother to Andrew? Wasn't it obvious how much she loved him, and he her?

But no, apparently it was not; Vince thought Martha should have him.

'It's cruel, what you're doing,' he said. 'Standing between a mother and her child.'

He was smiling, that curl of the lip he called a smile. Annie, who knew him so well, was newly shocked by his villainy. 'Cruel!' she said, 'I'll tell you what's cruel – wrenching me and that child apart now, after all this time.'

'Oh, spare me the melodrama. He was on loan, you knew that.'

He didn't care a jot about Andrew, thought Annie. Or rather, he believed he'd have Andrew anyway, because he'd win back Martha. *That* was what he thought.

'You'd use him, a three-year-old child,' she said, hissing the words, mindful that the boy was only upstairs, and the bedroom door was always open. 'You'd use him to get back to her.'

He smiled a private smile; he was full of secrets.

'She doesn't want you, Vince. She couldn't be plainer about that.'

'Ah, but she'll not be able to resist me,' he said, and Annie wanted to tear with her nails at his complacent face, but instead she turned away and ran upstairs to Andrew's room to be within reach of him. He was playing with all the cogs and wheels of Michael's Spirograph, which he'd taken from the landing cupboard and tipped out of the box onto the floor. Andrew couldn't manage the pins and the pens and the paper; what he was doing was running the serrated edges of the wheels up and down through the deep pile of the carpet, leaving tracks that zigzagged and criss-crossed around him. Michael wouldn't like it, thought Annie at once; it was in everyone's interests to pack it all away again before the little tyrant discovered the desecration. Andrew looked up at her.

'It's roads, Mummy, roads for worms, but I need some worms now.'

Just hearing his voice was fortifying; his solidity, the incontrovertible reality of him, reassured her that under no circumstances could he leave this life for a new one with Martha Hancock. It wouldn't happen, because Annie wouldn't let it. If necessary, she'd vanish with him, to a distant town: another country, if need be. The practicalities of such a plan when she depended entirely on Vince for money and when she couldn't drive a car didn't trouble her at the moment; nor what she'd do with Michael, whom she didn't see when she pictured the getaway. Not that she would ever leave him at the mercy of Vince, who, when he didn't ignore the child altogether, met his odd ways with angry impatience.

'We make roads for worms in the garden, pet,' she said. 'Not in the house.'

His face fell.

'Remember?' she said. 'We were playing in the soil outside, weren't we? That's why we had worms. They don't like it inside.'

'Oh,' Andrew said. He looked down at the tracks and trails he'd made on the dark red carpet and sighed in that accepting way he had, so different from his brother. Annie felt almost calm again, although she knew this was only temporary. She could hear Vince stalking about downstairs as if he was caged, and Annie knew – hoped, anyway – that he'd go out, to the pub or to the bookie's, seeking the company of men. There was no problem in Vince's world that couldn't be alleviated by a nicotine fug or a pint of Guinness. Michael was keeping a low profile in his bedroom, as he always did when Vince was about, and Annie crouched down to Andrew's height and said, 'Shall we tidy this up quickly, before Michael sees it?'

Her voice was hushed and conspiratorial, and Andrew recognised it at once, from many a time before. It signalled a game that had to be taken very seriously.

'Yes,' he whispered, and he handed her the wheel that he was holding, then twisted round onto all fours to reach the others, which were scattered about.

'Watch you don't kneel on anything,' Annie said.

It was skilled work, re-packing the Spirograph into its box in such a way that Michael wouldn't know it'd been disturbed. There were separate sections for the wheels, cogs and pens, and the ridged cardboard into which Michael pinned his paper must be stacked neatly back too, with the special pins stashed underneath. It had to be done swiftly, but it couldn't be rushed.

Downstairs, the front door slammed, which meant Vince had gone out.

So, thought Annie; time was short now. Andrew handed her three more cogs, and she aligned them with the others and slotted them in the box.

'Chop chop,' she said, trying to keep her voice light. 'Double-quick time.'

Andrew grinned at her, but there was anxiety in his smile because he sensed it in her. He pushed himself up into a standing position, the better to check for rogue bits and pieces, and a small cog dropped off his knee, leaving a hard red circle on his skin. He peered at the mark, fascinated.

'Look, see there, I said *don't* kneel on the pieces,' Annie said, but the cog was intact, not even cracked, so she brightened her tone to make up for the reprimand.

'Nearly done!' she said, and they really nearly were, they'd made excellent progress, but were not alas quite finished when Michael's bedroom door creaked open and he tiptoed down the landing to look in on them. He stepped with infinite caution into Andrew's room, toe then heel, as if the carpet might be wet, or muddy, or charged with electricity. His unreadable eyes swivelled across the room, taking in everything at a glance. Annie followed his gaze, tried to see what he saw. Nothing was cracked, nothing was torn, but there were still a few papers strewn on the floor, blank sheets as well as treasured designs of fabulous intricacy in red, green and black biro, and – and this was unfortunate – Andrew had chosen just this moment to press a wheel hard against his face so that his little nose and part of his mouth were squished through the centre.

'Hello, Michael,' Andrew said, through the porthole.

Michael's expression blackened.

'Now, Michael,' Annie said, as softly as if she was coaxing a fawn to come and eat from her hand. 'Don't worry, it's nearly back in, look.' She offered the open box, showed him its near-perfect orderliness. 'Take a deep breath, love, like I showed you.'

He glowered at her, but he did take a breath, although it was only to fuel a roar at Andrew.

'Get off my stuff!' he screamed, in a voice so loud it must have hurt his throat. Andrew dropped the Spirograph wheel and clapped his hands over his ears. He looked round at Annie in panic, because he knew from past experience that he wasn't safe. She reached for him, and if he'd moved towards her at the same time she would have hauled him to safety, but he was rooted to the spot with fright and she just couldn't snatch him up in time. Michael had picked up a glass-domed snow globe, a miniature magical kingdom of dancing penguins and top-hatted snowmen. Upside down it felt hard and cold, perfect in the curve of his palm, and he allowed himself a fraction of a second to shiver with pleasure at its beautiful weight before hurling it directly at his little brother, striking him with a splintering thud on the side of his head. Andrew dropped to the floor like a puppet with cut strings. The globe had split into small, lethal shards around him and there were flakes of artificial snow in his hair and plastered to his cheek. Annie lunged at Michael but he was quicker than her. He jumped backwards and she missed, lunged again, missed again. His eyes never left her face, and they were wide with interest at what he'd unleashed in his mother. At the third lunge she caught him, digging her nails into his skinny arm and bringing him down to his knees onto broken glass. She slapped him twice around the face, and the imprint of her palm bloomed white and red on his cheek. Behind her Andrew said, 'Mummy, I blooding,' and his voice shook with heart-rending fear.

Annie, shocked at her own red-hot fury, tried to speak

levelly to Michael as she turned to attend to Andrew, but her voice sounded jagged and sharp. 'Go,' she said. 'Go to your room.' But when she turned away to lift Andrew into her arms, Michael poked out his tongue and stayed in the room, pushing himself backwards on his bottom until he reached the wall, from where he could watch his mother croon over Andrew and dab at the gash on his temple with a clean white handkerchief. There was a cut on Michael's right knee too, just a small one, but he worked at it with his fingers, trying to widen it, trying to make it hurt.

She should probably have taken Andrew to the hospital for stitches, but her instinct was to stay away from authority figures who pressed her for answers, so in the green first-aid tin she found a packet of sterile strips, which she used to pull together the two sides of the cleaned wound. It started just above his temple and continued in a jagged line to the corner of his left eye. Imagine, she thought, if one of those glass shards had pierced ... oh God! She shuddered, and held him to her while he sucked his thumb and basked in her love.

Michael was sloping about on the fringes. He'd been asked to apologise to Andrew, but he couldn't. Sorry was one of the things he didn't say and, over time, the word had become simply impossible to utter. It didn't always mean that he *wasn't* sorry – although right now, he really wasn't – but rather that he didn't like the word, just couldn't bring himself to form the syllables. Other things he didn't say were porridge, needle and bless you, but his mother hadn't noticed the absence of these; sorry was the only one that grown-ups seemed to care about.

Michael had a plaster on his knee now, but he'd had to put it on himself. His mother wouldn't look at him, although Andrew did, gazing over the top of his thumb, which he sucked and sucked like a baby with a bottle. Michael concentrated hard on telling Andrew, silently, how much he hated him and perhaps the younger boy understood, because he blinked and looked away.

The lock on the front door rattled with Vince's key, and all three of them were in the kitchen, with no means of escape. His heavy footfall crossed the hallway, then he pushed open the kitchen door and propelled himself in, belligerent with beer. Andrew, still fairly impervious to the knife-edge ups and downs of Vince's moods, took out his thumb and sat forwards on Annie's lap.

'Mine head,' he said. 'Look, Dad.'

He twisted his neck, presenting Vince with the injury.

'Huh?' Vince grunted. He stooped to peer more closely. The strips across the gash were close together, but there was blood seeping through, and the visible skin around the wound was scarlet. 'What the devil happened?' Vince said. He looked at Annie.

'Accident,' she said.

'That'll leave a scar, that will.' He leaned closer still; the smell of the taproom was pungent and Annie drew back, pulling Andrew away from the fumes. 'What kind of accident?' Vince asked. Michael watched from under his thatch of black hair, waiting for developments. His father would be angry with him, but he wasn't scared, or even apprehensive. In fact he welcomed the sensation of steady coolness he felt in the face of another person's hot anger. It made him feel strong, heightened his sense of separateness. But this time his mother chose to protect him.

'He fell against the sideboard,' she said. 'It's not as bad as it looks.'

Michael darted a triumphant smile at Andrew, who smiled back guilelessly. There was a heavy silence while Vince decided whether he wanted to make something of it, but then he straightened up and belched, and patted his stomach with both hands.

'What's for dinner?' he said. So, Annie wondered, are we forgetting about Andrew's head then, and all that Martha business? She stole a look at her husband's expression, and it was patently unconcerned. It was as if none of it had ever happened.

'Fish and chips,' she said, which was the first thing that popped into her head. But it was a good idea, because Vince seemed pleased and the atmosphere in the kitchen lightened. 'I'll pop out with the boys,' she said. She felt desperate, suddenly, to get some air. She'd like to go on her own, but that was out of the question. She might come back with the wrapped fish suppers to find Andrew gone. She didn't trust Vince an inch.

'I'll have a haddock,' Vince said, 'and some peas.' Then he ambled through to the living room to watch television, and sleep off the beer. Annie settled Andrew into his pushchair and waited for Michael to fasten his shoes and every toggle of his duffel coat, then off they set for the chip shop.

26

Sandra had Fritz in her handbag, she said. She meant his ashes, of course, collected this morning from the vet. They were in a plastic Ziploc bag, which in turn was stuffed into a Tupperware food saver. She wouldn't have mentioned it on the day of Vince's cremation, but she was encouraged to speak up by Annie's carefree demeanour. The post-funeral tea and sandwiches at her little house in Beech Street had been positively festive; really quite noisy, with the two little Australian boys leaping off the stairs into the hallway from ever more daring heights and shouting 'Geronimo!' with every go, and Andrew regaling Marjorie Bevin and the Glebe Hall nurses with tales of his father's scurrilous past. Andrew was being wonderful – had been since the day began. He was so sociable and charming, Annie thought; so *debonair*. He was handsome too, in his dark blue suit and white shirt, although he wore these formal clothes as casually as he possibly could: no tie, shirt flap untucked on one side, jacket loose on his shoulders as though he'd got distracted part way through putting it on. The impression was one of boyish charm; Moira and Brenda were lapping him up. Now and again, Annie couldn't help noticing, Bailey gave his backside a proprietorial pat and he winked at her and smiled. Bailey called him 'hon' and Andrew called her 'babe'. They reached for each other from time to time, clasping hands or circling each other's waist, and once, very swiftly, they sneaked a kiss. Annie marvelled at their open, easy affection, and when Bailey caught her staring, Annie beamed at her daughter-in-law to show she didn't disapprove.

And she didn't disapprove; she didn't at all. She felt energised and optimistic, as thoroughly alive as Vince was thoroughly dead. Her face was flushed and bright and nothing – not the noise, not the mess, not the dirt the boys had fetched in on their shoes – bothered her a jot. She'd made six fresh pots of tea so far, and her tinned salmon sandwiches had been a roaring success.

'I thought we could take him on one last walk,' Sandra said. She patted her bulging shoulder bag in which her dog's ashes resided alongside her purse, a chequebook, an unpaid parking fine in its yellow plastic wrapper, a packet of paper tissues and a motley collection of money-off vouchers that she'd clipped from newspapers. 'Scatter him somewhere nice.'

'Now?' Annie asked.

'Oh, well, no,' said Sandra. She waved an arm to indicate the room: the tea things, the people. 'You've other things going on,' she said. 'I thought perhaps tomorrow.'

'I'm hot,' Annie said, flapping a hand in front of her face. 'I wouldn't mind a little walk.' She sounded hopeful. Josie and Sandra looked at each other and Sandra shrugged.

'Up to you, I suppose,' she said to Annie.

'Well, there are no more sandwiches, and I'm sure it'll all be finishing soon,' Annie said. 'Michael's gone out, hasn't he? Nobody minds that.'

This was true, but even Josie and Sandra, who'd only met him for the first time today, could see that Michael was hardly a barometer for acceptable behaviour. He'd gone off on his bike somewhere, still in the black funeral suit but now with clips round the trouser legs and a startling yellow helmet rammed on his head. Apart from the occasional surly heckle at the crematorium, he hadn't spoken a word to anyone.

'He reminds me of Billy,' Sandra had said to Josie, as he shouldered his way past them in his cycling gear.

'Yes,' Josie said, 'but Billy's—'

'Fifteen,' said Sandra, cutting in. 'I know. That's my point.'

They'd smirked at each other, so that when Annie suddenly loomed at them from behind they'd jumped a little guiltily. But Annie had only smiled and asked Sandra how she was feeling, now that poor old Fritz was gone. Which was when Sandra patted her bag and suggested a memorial walk.

'Andrew,' Annie said now, trying to make her voice carry. The guests – the *mourners*, Annie kept having to remind herself – were not very great in number, but in the confines of this house they seemed quite a throng. Andrew turned his head at once, even though he was mid-sentence, and he threw her a sweet smile. Moira and Brenda, who'd been hanging on his every word, carried on staring at his profile, as if he was a television programme on pause.

'You don't mind if I step out for a while with Josie and Sandra, do you?' Annie said.

'Go for it,' he said. 'We can clear up here.'

Bailey shimmied through the room towards them.

Her dress was matt black silk, cut on the bias, and it clung appealingly to her lovely figure.

'You do look beautiful,' Josie said, and Bailey tipped her head and laughed. She had white, white teeth, even and straight, and at this close range the pale brown freckles that peppered her nose and upper cheeks looked carefully applied, dotted on with the finest of fine-tipped brushes.

'You'll be leaving for Australia soon, I suppose?' Josie sounded almost wistful, and in some small way she was. She liked Bailey, on first acquaintance. She knew they would be friends, given half a chance.

'Yup,' Bailey said. 'Back to the real world? *Our* real world?' she added hastily, in case anyone had taken offence.

Sandra said, 'Surf, sun and sand sounds pretty *un*real to me.'

'We-ell, there's work too?' Bailey said. 'And school, and shopping for groceries, and cleaning. It's not wall-to-wall fun, is it, guys?' She was talking to Blake and Riley, who'd wrung every last drop of entertainment from the staircase and were now hanging around her, one on each arm. Blake ignored the question but Riley said, 'It *is* fun, but I really like it here,' and Annie's eyes suddenly swam and her mouth softened, at the prospect of him leaving. Bailey said, 'Hey, the world's a village these days?' which was no comfort, because Annie had no idea what she meant by it. All Annie could think was, another six years and he'd be twelve. She pulled out a clean hankie from the sleeve of her blouse and blew her nose loudly. Blake rolled his eyes at Riley, who crossed his eyes at Blake, and they both laughed.

'We're popping out,' Josie said to Bailey, giving Annie time to collect herself. 'To say goodbye to Fritz.'

'Two funerals in one day?' Bailey said.

'Oh,' Riley said to Sandra. 'Did your dog die?'

'He was put down by the vet.'

'Oh. I liked him.'

'Me too,' Sandra said.

'Can I come with you?'

Sandra raised her eyebrows at Bailey, who said, 'Fine by me.'

'Cool!' Riley danced a little jig. 'We can take Finn, right?'

Sandra didn't want to leave Fritz at the reservoir and Annie didn't want to take Finn anywhere near the Wentford estate, and Ecclesall Woods seemed too far to drive, so instead they headed for the outcrop, a swathe of open land on the edge of Hoyland, parking their cars on Hawshaw Lane where Annie had once lived with Harold and Lillian. The house that had been theirs was long gone, demolished in the early seventies and replaced with a large L-shaped bungalow in pale stone with huge windows, front and back, although there was no view to speak of. Perhaps they were for looking into rather than out of, Annie thought, and certainly she found it difficult, as they passed, not to stare in and notice the low cream leather sofas and cherry wood dining furniture. In her mind's eye, Annie saw fragments of the past: a fan-light of coloured glass over the door, casting yellow and green patterns onto the floor: fireplaces disgorging soot into the chimney sweep's sack; wet washing on a wooden clothes horse and herself alone inside the V, breathing in the smell of wet wool. Long ago. A lifetime ago.

'Annie?'

'Mmm?'

'You're staring straight into that house.'

'Oh!' Annie shook herself from the reverie and trotted up to the others. 'I was daydreaming,' she said. 'I used to live there.'

They all stared now, imagining Annie in the chic blonde bungalow.

'Well I say there, but it was a different house then.'

'When you were younger, Grandma?' Riley said.

'As little as you are now,' she said.

He laughed at this implausible idea. They were walking through the old disused graveyard now, opposite the church, heading for the footpath beyond. Finn was on his lead but behaving badly, lurching and lunging ahead so that whoever was holding him – Josie now, to spare Annie's shoulder – was forced into a permanent tug-of-war.

'Did my dad live there too?' Riley asked.

'No, he was born in Coventry.' She blushed at the lie, which had slipped easily and automatically from her tongue, still truer to her than the truth. Josie glanced at her, but said nothing.

'And then you came back here?'

'Well, to Beech Street, yes.'

'Why did you move back?'

This was Sandra, and it was probably only her usual brusque manner, but the question had a hint of interrogation about it. Annie swallowed and thought about her answer. She considered, only for a second, being wholly truthful about all the reasons she had for leaving Coventry, but what she said was 'Because I like it here.'

'Me too,' Riley said. He was holding her hand and swinging her arm to and fro. His little palm against hers was warm and dry.

'Shall I let Finn loose?' Josie said. 'I can't see any sheep.'

'We couldn't see them before,' Sandra said. 'But they were there.'

'But if he just sits here, by us?'

Annie shook her head, no. True, this wasn't farm land, just a few hundred acres of grassed-over slopes that had once belonged to a colliery. But she couldn't – wouldn't – risk a mishap. There was a date now for the trip to Formby, where Dora Dinmoor was preparing to receive Finn, and having taken the plunge by agreeing to the plan, Annie felt keenly responsible for its smooth running. She felt she had Finn's future happiness in her hands. 'Keep him safe,' Mr Dinmoor had said last time he rang, 'and I give you my word it'll all be fine.' They were going together, Alf and Annie, in the Land Rover. Just the two of them. 'Who would've thought it?' Josie had said, when she told Sandra the news, and Sandra had said, 'Aye aye,' and winked, so that Josie had had to make her promise *never* to take that tone with Annie, or the whole scheme would founder.

So Finn remained tethered, close at heel, but they'd stopped walking now, so he didn't seem to mind. He narrowed his eyes and scanned the view, then dropped into a sitting position and Riley did the same, as close to the dog as he could be, with one arm draped around his wide, soft shoulders. Annie, watching the two of them, sighed.

'There'll only be Betty soon,' she said. 'Isn't that sad?'

'You'll get another dog, though?' Josie said to her. Annie looked doubtful. There'd only ever been Finn.

'Get back in the saddle, girl,' said Sandra. 'I know I will, else who'll bother to look up when I walk into the house?' She was standing, legs akimbo, arms folded, casting a critical eye over the bland vista of local authority landscaping. 'It's not exactly scenic, is it?'

'It's okay,' Annie said. 'It's green, anyway, and it's nice and close to us all.' When she was a girl, and even for a while after she came back, there had been a pit yard and winding gear directly ahead, and wet black slag heaps.

'I've always thought I'd bury Betty when her time's up,' Josie said. 'Under a cherry blossom tree, or something.'

'Hmm, well I never had that in mind,' Sandra said. 'But this's just a bit boring, these new trees and the grass so sparse.'

'Shall we leave him in his Tupperware?' Annie asked. 'Take him somewhere else, another day?' She was feeling a little guilty. If it weren't for her scruples about Wentford's unhappy associations, that was probably where they'd be now, among centuries-old oaks and Capability Brown parkland.

'Nah,' Sandra said. 'What does it matter, really? Fritz's certainly past caring.' She delved into her shoulder bag for the tub, and Riley craned his neck, curious to see the actual remains of an Alsatian.

'On your feet,' Sandra said to him. 'You can be in charge.'

Riley leaped up, all eagerness, and Sandra handed him Fritz's ashes. The little boy rearranged his expression into one of studied solemnity. Sandra placed a hand on the crown of his head.

'On behalf of Fritz, because you liked him and he liked you, I nominate Riley Doyle as funeral celebrant.'

'Well! Isn't that nice, Riley?' Annie said. Sandra shushed her.

'Lick your finger,' Sandra said, 'then hold it up in the air.'

He looked at her curiously. 'Why?'

'Whichever is the coldest side of your wet finger, that's the direction the wind's blowing.'

He furrowed his brow, none the wiser.

'You mustn't be downwind of the ashes,' Josie said. 'They'll blow all over you.'

'They'd get everywhere,' Annie added. 'In your mouth, your eyes, up your nose ...'

'Ew, gross,' said Riley, lapsing momentarily from the dignity of his funereal responsibilities. He sucked an index finger then held it up, considering the evidence.

'So,' he said finally, 'this bit, where my fingernail is, feels the coldest.' They all obediently made a ninety-degree turn and Riley flushed with proud importance. Annie gave him a secret smile, which, being in charge of the funeral, he could only allow himself to return fleetingly, like the switching on and off of a light.

'Okay,' said Sandra. 'Lid off.'

'Are you going to say anything?' Josie said. 'A eulogy?'

Sandra laughed. 'I was going to say something like "there you go, Fritz".'

'No!' said Annie, quite vehemently. 'Say a poem or something. We need a sense of occasion.' There had been none at Vince's funeral, unless you counted Marjorie Bevin's cobbled-together tribute, but Annie felt no guilt, nor any irony either, at this heightened swell of emotion for a deceased dog. She knew where her heartfelt sympathy lay, and it was with Fritz.

'A poem?' Sandra said. 'I only know limericks, and a bit of Spike Milligan.'

Riley, standing with the Tupperware aloft but still lidded, said, 'I know a part of a poem.'

'Do you?' Josie said. 'Do you think it's one Fritz would've liked?'

Riley nodded. 'It's about a dog,' he said. 'I only remember a bit of it though.'

'A bit of it is fine,' Sandra said. 'So, say your poem, then fling the ashes as far away from us as you can manage.'

'Right.'

He lowered his arm and prised off the lid, spilling a little ash as he did so, but they all pretended they hadn't noticed. Then he took a deep breath and yelled out his words to the sky, in a slowed-down, sing-song style.

'HE WAS VE-RY POOR AND HUM-BLE
AND CONTENT WITH WHAT HE GOT
SO WE FED HIM BONES AND BIS-CUITS
TILL HE HEARTENED UP A LOT.'

He heaved the ashes from their plastic pot and they spun and tumbled through the air in a dusty arc, tiny particles of Fritz, catching on the breeze. There was a small, stunned silence and then Sandra said, 'Awesome, just awesome.' There were tears in her eyes.

'Oh Riley, that was perfect,' Josie said. 'I *love* that poem.'

Riley was pleased, but apologetic. 'It's really longer,' he said. 'But I only know the bones and biscuits bit.'

'But I bet that's the best part,' Sandra said. 'Definitely that's the bit Fritz would've liked. Thank you, Riley. I'll always remember what you just did for me and my dog.'

Annie was lost for words, so she just bent down and hugged him.

27

It was a relief to leave the house and Annie walked briskly along the pavements of Coventry with her two boys, paying no particular attention to where they were heading. Michael held the frame of Andrew's pushchair and managed to keep step with his mother by jogging now and again, although for once he didn't complain. Andrew closed his eyes the moment they were on the move and now he was sleeping, his thumb jammed in his mouth and his head turned to the right, so that the nasty wound and its makeshift dressing was on display. Annie glanced down at it from time to time. She was worrying about infection, although she'd swabbed it clean as best she could with TCP and cotton wool. Andrew was peaceful, though, and she took heart from this. It was only a cut, after all; children were always in the wars.

They were supposed to be fetching fish and chips, but first she needed to clear her mind and get some air. The further away she was from Vince and Sydney Road, the better she felt. Lately she'd found herself mentally arranging a move back to her childhood home, in Yorkshire. She remembered the house in Hawshaw Lane with exaggerated fondness; the intervening years had wreathed her memories in a flattering, misty light. The unhappier she had become as an adult, the happier her childhood seemed, until those first ten years of life in Hoyland became, in her mind, an exalted decade of perfect order and cosseted joy. If her father, Harold, grew remote and cold and her mother, Lillian, grew selfish and neglectful, these were things that happened here, in Coventry, after they moved house. This was what Annie believed, and in this way she protected this small, distant part of her life from blight.

She allowed her thoughts to slip into the past now, as she walked the children blindly through the town. She thought about her mother's death – so strange and so far away from home that it hardly seemed real, either at the time or even now. She blamed this on her father, who left her at home with Mrs Binley and the blasted parrot when she should have been allowed to mourn her mother's passing. It was folly, she thought, to shelter children from the passing of a parent; it was cruel. They needed the nailed-down finality of a coffin and the solemn rituals of a funeral service, otherwise the death became just another fact they'd been told by adults and were simply expected to believe. When her mother left and never came home, Annie used to wonder if her fatal accident was only a malicious lie, a fabrication by Mrs Binley operating in cahoots with Harold to erase Lillian from their lives. Even now Annie sometimes imagined Lillian, vital and beautiful, living a whole other life somewhere distant and glamorous, like the French Riviera or Martinique: places Annie had read about, places she could picture her mother, frozen in time, in an open-topped car or a speedboat, swathed in a Grace Kelly chiffon scarf, her lips a vibrant crimson, her nails painted to match, her face raised to the warm blue sky, laughing and laughing at the great joke she'd played on them all.

'I'm hungry.'

This was Michael, and Annie was startled by his voice, so lost was she in the past. She had to stop walking and look around to get her bearings, letting the familiar Coventry landmarks reveal themselves through the fog of the past. They were on Priory Street, not far from the cathedral, and she was shocked by how far they'd come. She thought of Vince, waiting for his haddock.

'You said we were getting fish and chips,' Michael said.

'And we are. I just needed to stretch my legs.'

He looked her up and down in his odd, assessing way. 'Stretch your legs,' he said carefully.

Oh, here we go, she thought. 'Yes, it's what we say when we need some exercise.' She wasn't going to rise to his pedantry.

'Stretch them so they're longer?' he asked.

'No, Michael, don't be silly.'

'So, not stretch them then?'

'Michael ...'

'So, not stretch them?'

They were racing towards Bayley Lane now, and the pushchair bumped on the cobbles so Annie had to slow down. The little boy had begun to stir, shifting in the seat and grumbling sleepily although he was barely awake. His head must hurt, Annie thought: poor little mite. She glanced at Michael, erstwhile villain of the piece, who despite the gallop had managed to keep up. Now they were on the cobbles he couldn't avoid stepping on lines, but still he tried, trotting in tiny steps, on tiptoe. Annie knew he'd expect an answer to the leg-stretching issue in due course. He never forgot an unanswered question, especially when he knew the answer to it already.

Ahead was Hay Lane and Annie swung a sharp left. The pavements were quiet, and the few other pedestrians they'd encountered stepped diplomatically out of the way. A double-decker bus rumbled across the junction with Broadgate, and Andrew, who'd developed a sixth sense for large vehicles, especially red ones, sat up from his restless slumber and pointed.

'Bus!' he said, as if he'd spotted exactly what they'd been searching for all this time. 'Bus, Mummy!'

'It *is* a bus, yes,' Annie said, and she surged onwards to give him a better view. It pulled up at a stop a few yards ahead of them and Andrew bounced in his seat, a little gingerly because of his head. Three people stepped down from it: an elderly man with a stick and a flat cap, a thin girl clad entirely in denim, and Martha Hancock. Annie jerked to a halt and swivelled round so that the bus was behind them, and Andrew wailed in protest. In a flash Annie leaned over the top of the pushchair and clamped a hand over his mouth, and his eyes looked up at her in bewildered alarm. For a few seconds she and Andrew were frozen in this strange attitude while Michael looked shiftily between his mother and his brother, trying to process this new development.

No one approached.

Cautiously, covertly, Annie looked back. Martha was sauntering down the street away from them. The fear that had gripped Annie's heart and squeezed her lungs now eased in a mighty pulse of relief as she comprehended the shift from being observed to being the observer: from suspect to spy, quarry to hunter. She turned. Andrew, free now to protest, was nevertheless utterly silent. The bus had gone. He sat back in the pushchair and plugged in his thumb.

'So if your legs stay the same length, they're not actually stretched?' Michael said.

Annie started to move forwards. She'd follow Martha Hancock, and find out where she lived, and then she'd ... well, she didn't know what she'd do, but at least she'd know something about her tormentor, and knowledge was power, wasn't that so?

'Are they?'

'No, Michael, my legs are not actually stretched.'

'Then what you said was wrong.'

Annie kept her eyes on the back of Martha Hancock's head. Her long hair was scraped into a ponytail and she looked like one of the grammar-school girls, except that Annie had seen her worldliness, the hard-headed confidence at her core.

'What you said was wrong, wasn't it?'

'Yes, Michael, except you're the only person in the world who wouldn't understand what I meant by it.'

He thought for a moment. 'Then the whole world is wrong and I'm the only right person. Are we following that lady?'

Annie was shocked at his acuity, though it was entirely typical. 'Of course not,' she said, although they patently were. They weren't heading for the fish and chip shop, or even for home. Martha had walked past the Godiva statue and into Ironmonger Row, so they had too, creeping along at an unnatural pace to keep the distance between them safe and wide.

'Why are we following that lady?'

'Dat lady,' Andrew said, although he wasn't looking at Martha, only mimicking his brother.

Annie kept her voice light and said, 'If you're both completely quiet for five whole minutes we'll ...' She cast about for a treat, any treat. Nothing much presented itself at this grey time of day, when the shop fronts were shuttered and people were closing their curtains against the encroaching evening. 'We'll get an ice-cream.'

Andrew unplugged his thumb and said, 'I-cream?'

'Ssshh. Only if you're quiet.'

'An ice-cream?' Michael asked, his voice full of scorn.

'In five minutes, and only if you've been quiet.'

'But it's cold. We only have ice-cream when it's warm.'

This was true, and even if it were summer it would already be too late in the day to find such a treat. But Annie's strategy was only to distract Michael's forensic mind into questioning something other than her motives in trailing Martha Hancock. She'd become skilled at diversion, and did it again now.

'Watch those lines,' she said, pointing down at the pavement and speaking quietly, although Martha was too far ahead to hear. 'Be ever so careful where you put your feet.'

He glanced down in spite of himself. 'I will but it's not because of the bears,' he said. 'There aren't any bears. It's because of the pattern.'

'Mmm?' Down the Cross Cheaping they wandered, towards the Burges, treading the path trodden by Martha. Annie wondered how far they were going, and where.

'If I tread on the lines it spoils the pattern.'

Oh! Annie thought; she's going to the river! And as if Annie had willed it, Martha turned immediately right, heading towards that strange, brief, degraded stretch of the Sherbourne behind the Burges; the only place in the city centre where the buried river came up for air. Annie knew it so well she almost called out to Martha to tell her. She was just a girl herself when she first found it; a low, slow, surly stretch of water, so dark it seemed unrelated to the sparkling little river on the outskirts of the city. Ah, thought Annie, the river, the river; her childhood companion, her secret solace. Even now she preferred the sloping banks of the Sherbourne on the fringes of the city to any of the parks and open spaces provided by the corporation, but back then, in her solitary childhood, she'd believed she was the only person in Coventry who knew about its underground journey. This section of it, dragging along beside the bins and back doors of shops in the Burges and Cross Cheaping, smelled of rank, rotten vegetation: murky and unwholesome. There were railings, and a steep drop to the water down vertical banks, cladded and over-hung with tenacious ivy and sad, plucky buddleia. It was accessible to anyone, though no one ever came, and even the surrounding buildings had turned their backs to look the other way. It was a place for unhappy people, Annie thought: a limbo, between the sky and the earth's bowels. It was a dead end.

Annie glanced down at Michael. He was sucking a finger from the corner of his mouth as if it was a pipe. Andrew was heavy-lidded again, peaceful and slack limbed. They turned into Palmer Lane. Martha couldn't be seen, but Annie knew where she would find her.

'Michael,' Annie said. 'See the bricks on this wall?'

He followed the line of her hand and nodded.

'Can you count them all?'

She knew he could, and he knew she knew. He nodded again disdainfully.

'Then let's park Andrew here by you where he's safe, and you count every single brick, and by the time you've finished I'll be back.'

He pulled out his finger with a wet pop. 'Where are you going?'

'Just round the corner,' she said. 'Count loudly so I can hear you.'

'But why?' he said, and it wasn't an unreasonable question, but she didn't have an answer, and anyway she was already walking away from him. She just said, 'Every single one, mind,' without looking round, and because Michael found numbers impossible to resist, he began to count.

Martha was leaning against the railings, staring down into the murk of the water, and Annie was almost upon her by the time she turned, but instead of jumping in alarm, Martha only smiled knowingly.

'Hello,' she said, perfectly calm. 'Did you think I didn't know you were behind me?'

Annie, who moments ago had felt stealthy and powerful, was crushed, but she didn't reveal this. She felt at home here, by the river; she had that at least, and it gave her the strength to appear as calmly cold as Martha. She didn't answer the question, so Martha spoke again.

'Where's Robert? You had him with you when I got off the bus.'

'There is no Robert,' Annie said.

Martha laughed that pitying laugh of hers, and shook her head slowly as if she had never in her life encountered anyone so wilfully blind as Annie Doyle. Annie, watching her, felt a kind of gear shift in her head, as if she'd slipped into a fourth dimension so that she was as remote as she was present: an observer and a participant at one and the same time. She could see that Martha was speaking, but she could no longer fully hear her because of the insistent sound of her own heartbeat, the pulse and thud of blood against her eardrums. More than anything, standing here by the brackish water of the Sherbourne, she felt the great weight of this encounter, its pivotal significance to her own history; herself and Martha Hancock, face to face in a shadowy place where they were unobserved except by the wordless river. Martha's voice swam back into audible focus, but it was echoing and distorted like a voice in a dream. She'd waited long enough, she was saying; she was going back north and she'd take Robert now and there wasn't a damned thing Annie could do to stop her. She adjusted her stance, hoicked her bag further across her shoulder, and Annie knew that any moment now Martha would push past her to the lane, where she'd find the child sleeping in the pushchair, and away she'd go, sweeping him out of Annie's life and into her own. Annie looked into Martha's scornful eyes, and knew she had to act, not merely resist. She knew she couldn't stand this any more. She wouldn't – couldn't – live her life without her beloved little boy, nor could she live with the constant fear of losing him.

So while Martha was still berating her, Annie dropped like a hawk onto the footpath, where she'd already seen a sharp, pockmarked lump of stone, as grey as iron. It fitted her palm as if it belonged there. Martha's brow creased and she regarded Annie with curiosity, puzzled as to her intentions. Annie stood, and cut straight through Martha's confident litany of her rights.

'You brought me here to trap me,' Annie said. 'But you made a trap for yourself.'

Martha looked sceptical, amused even: certainly she wasn't afraid. Annie tightened her grip around its cratered surface.

'Nobody ever thinks I'll *do* anything,' she said, in wondering tones, as if even she was surprised to find herself here, forcing her nemesis with a weapon in her right hand, ready to strike. 'But I'm stronger than you think, and you'll never, ever have my boy.'

Now her voice shook with vehement emotion but Martha just laughed, and said, 'Oh, give it a sodding rest.' She moved; a lazy, casual, sidestep, as if Annie wasn't dangerous, or threatening, merely tiresome, and it was this nonchalance, this blithe disregard, that pushed Annie into action. She lashed out blindly with a full, desperate, wide-armed blow and the rock in her hand connected with Martha's temple. Now, at last, the younger woman's eyes registered fear, but Annie felt only a rush of unusual power. Once again she swung her arm, bringing the rock across the side of Martha's jaw. Martha gave a shout of pain and staggered against the low railing, then jack-knifed over it so that her legs were on the foot-path and her body hung over the riverbank. She was limp and loose and her bag slid casually to the ground as if she was just putting it down, only for a moment.

Annie stared. She dropped the rock and, for a brief while, she looked wonderingly between it and the inert body, as if each object was a puzzle to her, and entirely unconnected to her own actions. But then the memory of Martha – an intruder in her home, standing over Andrew's bed – came into Annie's mind and she sprang forward, heaving Martha's legs up and over the railing until her body lay prone on the narrow bank, her face tilted up to the evening sky. Annie clambered over too, and she peered down into Martha's eyes, but they were closed. Blood matted her hair and the skin at her temple was split, and the horror of what she'd done was suddenly evident to Annie, although it wasn't regret that she felt, only a kind of grief, and anyway it wasn't enough to stop her pushing desperately at Martha's body until it rolled in a twisted, haphazard fashion through the mud of the bank and down into the dark and brackish water.

Now there was no triumph: only cold, and fear, and a deep sinister silence. Annie leaned as far as she dared over the edge of the bank; there was Martha, face up in the water, defeated, unresisting, and slowly, slowly, inch by inch, being carried on the sluggish current out of plain view and into the dark interior of the tunnel. Annie blessed the Sherbourne, her stalwart friend, then she closed her mind to Martha, turned her back on the river, and climbed back over the railings, and there was Michael, staring at her through narrowed eyes. She was panting and her coat was torn and muddied.

'What are you doing?' he asked.

'Where's Andrew?'

'What are you doing?'

She darted past him, into the lane. There was Andrew, where she'd left him, but there was an elderly woman too, clucking over the little boy and she tutted when Annie rushed up.

It's a poor do,' she said, 'leaving a little dot like this on his own.'

'He isn't on his own.' Annie said. Her breathing was ragged and her face was a livid white, but the woman only had eyes for Andrew.

'That cut looks nasty,' she said.

Annie ignored her and grabbed the handles of the pushchair. Now the woman looked at her and narrowed her eyes. Annie thanked God for the darkness.

'That's quite a rip you've got there, m'duck,' she said, nodding at Annie's coat front where a long V-shaped tear in the wool revealed the teal-blue lining. 'It's a shame, a rip like that in a good coat.'

'What were you doing?' Michael said, appearing from the alleyway into the lane. He was like Mrs Binley's parrot, thought Annie: same phrases, over and over and over. The old lady hung about, waiting to hear the answer, but Annie just said, 'Good evening then,' in a genteel but pointed way, so she harrumphed a little and went on her way. Annie watched her for a while then shut her eyes. She was utterly exhausted, tired beyond tiredness; she could have lain down on this hard pavement and slept.

'What were you doing?'

'Nothing,' Annie said.

'Where's Martha Hancock?'

Oh God. Oh good God. Annie snapped open her eyes. Michael had Martha's handbag over one shoulder and a book in his hand.

'She dropped this,' he said, holding up the white bag, and then he held up the book. 'And this was in it,' he said. 'She wrote her name inside here, look.' Carefully he opened the cover and pointed.

Annie held her hand out, but Michael clasped the book to his chest and took a stride backwards.

'Fine,' Annie said, feigning indifference. She gripped the pushchair to hide the shaking and started to walk away from him down the Burges. Michael followed slowly, a few feet behind.

'Give me the bag and the book,' Annie said casually, without looking round. She marvelled at the controlled authority of her voice, but she wouldn't let the child see her eyes, which she knew were desperate.

'No,' said Michael, always quick to sense an advantage.

'Okay.' Annie stalked away, as if she didn't give a jot about anything; didn't even care whether or not he followed her. He galloped along behind and said, again, 'What were you doing?'

'Give me the things and I'll tell you,' she said. She wondered what he'd seen. Not much, she was sure, or else he'd have been parroting that, too.

'Do you promise?'

'No,' she said. 'I don't promise.'

This puzzled him; not *what* she said, which was easy to understand, but how she said it. He hadn't heard this voice before. It didn't sound like his mother. He trotted along beside her for a while, thinking, and then he held out the book. Annie stopped walking and took it, pushing it into the folds of the pushchair's hood without revealing any sign of interest in it.

'Bag,' she said.

He slipped it from his little shoulder and handed it over. She opened it and took out a purse, a hairbrush and the birth certificate Martha had once waved at Annie. These things went into the pockets of Annie's coat, then she flattened the bag and stuffed it deep into a litter bin. Michael watched.

'Right. Fish, battered sausage or pie?' she said. She felt strong, suddenly: invincible. Certainly she felt a match for this strange boy of hers. All that remained was to get the boys home, as naturally and normally as possible.

'What were you doing?' he said, but he knew she wouldn't answer. He could tell, by the new look in her eyes.

'What were *you* doing?' Annie said. 'You were meant to be counting the bricks.'

'Where's Martha Hancock?' he said again.

'Gone,' said Annie. And then she said nothing else, no matter how hard he tried to make her, until they got to the fish and chip shop and she ordered their supper in a light, bright voice, so that no one seemed to notice her damp hair and ruined coat, and all the while Michael stared at her, brimming with unanswered questions.

When they eventually got home it was late and all the lights were off in their house, although the television was on in the parlour. Annie peeped cautiously round the door and saw Vince spread out across the sofa in his string vest and trousers, fast asleep. His feet were bare; they looked bony and oddly vulnerable.

She turned on a light in the hallway then bent down in front of Andrew and unbuckled the strap that held him safe. He smiled dozily at her.

'Mummy,' he said, and held out his arms. 'Chish and fips.'

'Coming up,' she said. She kissed his warm cheek, then carried him and the hot, damp parcel of food through to the kitchen. She put him on the floor and put the supper on the table then went to the sink and ran the hot tap over her hands, sluicing away the memory of the weight and the feel of the rock she'd held, and how she'd used it. Vince, woken by the light and the voices, loomed in the doorway and she braced herself, but he just said, 'Who are you?'

'Who am I?' she said, amazed.

'No,' Vince said impatiently. 'I know who you are.' He scratched his head, rubbed his face. He looked older, suddenly.

'Your haddock's there,' she said, nodding at the table. This odd conversation felt like the first they'd had for a long, long time.

He looked at the wrapped parcel, looked at her, looked at the parcel again. He seemed to be trying to work out what it could contain. Annie watched him, but neither of them spoke. Then Michael came in, holding Martha's book, which he handed to Annie.

'What's that then?' Vince said. He seemed somehow out of his depth, thought Annie.

'Dat den,' said Andrew. 'Dat den dat den dat.'

She looked at the cover for the first time. *Tess of the d'Urbervilles*. Annie swallowed her shock that Martha Hancock should have possessed such a book, then, 'Thomas Hardy,' she said, with steady nonchalance. 'I thought I'd give it a go.' She gave Michael a hard stare, and he stared back. They understood each other perfectly.

28

Alf had made a picnic, which worried Annie because she wanted to be sure there'd be a lavatory stop en route, and a Welcome Break lunch would have made certain of it. He whistled as he drove: whistled as if he was playing a clarinet or a saxophone. It was 'Fly Me to the Moon' and he phrased it like Sinatra, with all the same jazzy, carefree savoir-faire. In the passenger seat of his Land Rover Annie felt ludicrously high; she could see over hedges and into houses. It took her mind off the purpose of the drive. Finn had the rear all to himself, although his bed, blanket, bowls, lead and sack of kibble were packed in a crate next to him. Michael, who would be alone in the house overnight for the first time, had watched from the front porch as they drove away, but refused to say goodbye to Finn.

'He's a dog, Mother,' he'd said, as if she didn't know.

'Yes,' she'd replied. 'And you won't see him again, Michael.'

At this he had arched his brows and twisted his lips into a little moue, as if to say, thank goodness for small mercies.

'You have a heart of stone,' she had said, and this was the last thing she uttered to him before she let Alf help her up into the Defender and shut Finn in the back. She didn't even turn to wave as they left.

Truth was, she was angry with Michael for so much more than his indifference to the dog. His behaviour was intolerable. Not that it was any worse now than before. It was just that over the years there'd been so few people in their orbit, she'd fallen out of the habit of comparing him. His disdain, his demands, his peculiar way of being had run on unchallenged for so long that it had seemed quite ordinary. Then along came Josie's friendship, and Sandra, and Alf here, not to mention Andrew and his family, especially dear little Riley. Well, it was as if these past few weeks had been just stuffed with people behaving kindly, reasonably, lovingly, *normally*, and all of them had thrown Michael into sharp, unflattering contrast. For all her anxieties surrounding this extraordinary trip to Formby, Annie had felt only defiant relief when Alf steered down Beech Street away from her son, who, although she wouldn't look, she knew would be wearing a sardonic half smile, if he was bothering to smile at all.

'I feel as if I'm running away,' she said to Alf.

He grinned at her. 'Aye well, we all need to escape sometimes,' he said. He was too much of a gentleman to voice his own feelings about Michael, but Annie felt sure he must be the rudest person Alf had ever met.

'I am *so* sorry,' she said. 'About Michael, I mean.'

He glanced at her again. 'You don't need to apologise for anything,' he said.

'Yes, but I haven't helped,' she said. She cringed when she thought about Michael refusing to shake Alf's offered hand, recoiling from the contact, crossing his arms across his chest and tucking his own hands under his armpits where they were safe. 'I've never really stood up to him. Even when he was a little boy, I let him get away with all sorts of nonsense for a quiet life.'

'Well it's not easy,' Alf said. 'It's just a question of managing, int it? Getting by.'

'What's not easy?'

'Autism.'

'Autism?'

Alf shot her a puzzled look. 'Am I wrong?' he said. 'Beg pardon, but I thought Michael were a cut and dried case. Has it never been diagnosed?'

Annie looked at him. 'Diagnosed?' She gave a short, disbelieving laugh. 'Are you saying Michael's not just awkward?'

Alf was silent for a while as he negotiated the turn onto the A616, then he said, 'I'm fairly sure your lad's autistic, but that dunt mean he's not awkward as well.'

'What's the difference, though?'

'Well, we can all be awkward, like, but if you're autistic, you can't help it.'

There was a silence while Annie digested this. Autistic; nobody had ever said that to her in the sixties.

'So, it were never mentioned at school?'

'Oh he was forever in trouble when he was little, but we all just thought he was rude. Well, and naughty. He was clever, mind you. *Is* clever.' She thought of his bookshelf, and the foreign language titles on it: thought of him taking O-level maths at eleven, A-level at fourteen: thought of the violin, which came to him as easily and naturally as talking.

'Often the case,' Mr Dinmoor said. 'Maths wizard, I

expect?'

'Yes!' She stared at him, astonished.

'Aye well, that's it, and it explains that violin, too. Maths and music aren't far apart to lads like your Michael.'

'Well I'll be blowed,' Annie said. Her mind was working feverishly now, remembering episodes down the years where Michael's singular behaviour, his fiercely held likes and dislikes, had made her feel a failure, a crashingly inadequate mother. He had been such hard work! She said as much to Alf, and he tutted and shook his head. A disgrace, he said, that she was never offered any help. But it was a different time, she said. And anyway for someone to offer help, thought Annie, she would have had to seek it, and she had never willingly sought the attention of health professionals after ... oh, well, it was all years ago.

'You rub along all right though, don't you?' Alf said, encouragingly.

'I suppose.'

She sighed deeply and thought about returning to her little house with only Michael in it, not even Finn. Andrew and his family had flown home two days ago and she still felt scarred by the farewell, truth be told. She had driven them to Sheffield railway station and they'd all been quiet except for Blake, who was longing to get home, and talked nineteen to the dozen, just as he had on the day they'd arrived. At the station, while they waited for the train, Andrew had asked the boys for their high points of the trip, and Blake had said it was now, heading for the airport. Riley said he couldn't choose only one because there were three, and they were equal: being in Mr Wright's barn, with Grandma and the sheep with foot rot; eating his first gingerbread man in Grandma's steamed-up car; saying a goodbye poem for Fritz, the dead dog. Annie had begun to cry, and she hadn't been able to properly stop until long after they'd gone. Bailey's shoulder had been wet through with Annie's tears. Andrew had held Annie's hand, and said they could Skype if she got herself a laptop, but Annie had looked so blank that he'd changed tack and talked instead about a visit to Australia.

'Please come, Mum,' he'd said. 'Come and see why we love it out there.'

She'd told him she might, just to ease the pain of parting, and he'd hugged her so tightly that she felt completely wrapped in love. But then she'd spoiled the mood a bit; asked him not to dig up the past; asked him – begged him, actually – not to look for Martha. And Andrew had withdrawn, become solemn and subdued, so that when the train came rushing in to the station there was still an awkwardness between them, and then when they were settled at a table and the train began to move away, only Riley and Bailey had given her a proper, hearty wave. Blake was already eyes down, switching on his Nintendo, and Andrew had simply raised one hand and watched her with a look in his eyes that was ... oh, she hated to think about it! He'd looked disappointed, that was it; he'd looked at her as if they'd had an arrangement, and she'd broken it. Now, of course, she wished she hadn't even mentioned Martha Hancock. Maybe by doing so, she thought miserably, she'd only firmed his resolve.

She sighed again, and Alf said, 'Let's put the wireless on,' which he did, and there was a Cambridge professor discussing the Ming dynasty with Melvyn Bragg. Annie closed her eyes and tried her best to listen for a while, but instead she found herself being lulled into a strange, light sleep, in which she seemed to float above the steady rumble of the road and the erudite conversation on the radio, hearing it but not hearing it, and the next thing she was fully aware of was the unusual green pagoda of Burtonwood Services, where Alf had stopped the car so they could both spend a penny.

Formby seemed pleasant, thought Annie as they negotiated the wide, leafy avenues looking for Dora. Alf hadn't been for a while and he couldn't find the road, let alone the house. Annie considered making a joke about a mapmaker getting lost, but she couldn't think how to phrase it. Meanwhile Alf covered his embarrassment by saying it'd all changed, although to Annie these streets and houses looked timeless, too substantially distinguished ever to have been troubled by the disruption of modern planners or new one-way systems.

'Here we are,' he announced suddenly, with evident relief. 'Number twelve.' The Defender came to rest at the kerb outside a grand Victorian villa, detached and set well back from the road. Annie gazed at it from her elevated position inside the car. The front garden looked like a small park, planted with glossy box hedging and abundant shrubs and trees.

'Down there's the sands,' Alf said, pointing straight ahead, although there was absolutely no sign of a beach, only trees and houses. Annie thought of Blake, looking for the sea on Beech Street. 'Formby Point,' Alf said. 'We'll have a walk down there with Dora.' He opened his door and jumped down nimbly, then scooted round the vehicle to open Annie's door and help her down onto the pavement. She liked the feel of his strong grip, her hand in his, and the way he watched where she was putting her feet. She thought how little it took for a person to feel valued by another; by these small gestures we show our humanity, she thought, and then wondered where she read that, or was it on the radio earlier, somewhere on the M62? Anyway, she didn't think they could be *her* words.

Alf was swinging open the big rear door and releasing Finn, who bounded out unassisted. He came to Annie immediately and shoved his dry black nose into her hand, pushing at her palm for some attention, so she scratched his head and fondled his ears and fought back tears.

'Took no time to get 'ere,' Alf said, because he could see how she was feeling. 'Any time you want to visit, just say the word.'

She smiled at him and he smiled back, and handed her the lead, which she looped over Finn's head, and then someone called, 'Yoo-hoo!' and a small, doughty-looking woman swung into view, not from the garden of number twelve but from down the avenue, the way they'd just driven. She had a collection of little dogs on leads, ranged around her feet and looking up at the sound of her voice, like tiny hairy acolytes.

Annie knew this was Dora because Alf shouted, 'Our kid!' and he was clearly pleased as punch to see her. He stood with his hands on his hips watching her approach, then, when she reached him, he took her in a bear hug and rocked her from side to side. She grinned at Annie over Alf's shoulder.

'And you two are Annie and Finn?' she said, so Alf

released her and Dora handed him the terriers' tangle of leads then shook hands with Annie and bent down so close to Finn that he went cross-eyed looking at her.

'My oh my, you're a handsome fellow,' she said. 'Welcome to the seaside.' Finn smiled and lolled his tongue. 'Come on,' Dora said, standing up. 'Let's go and get acquainted.' She took Finn's lead as if he was already hers, and Annie followed her through the gate and round the circuitous garden path feeling a complicated mixture of relief and sadness and – she couldn't deny it – a shade of jealousy at Dora's easy rapport with her own, dear Finn.

It was a fine house, but it was given over to the dogs really, so the smell of hound hung in the air and there was canine paraphernalia everywhere: baskets, bowls, blankets and bones. The terriers and Finn skittered around each other on the wooden floors in a frenzy of excitement and Dora seemed neither to notice nor care, then suddenly she snapped her fingers and shouted, 'Baskets!' and the little dogs immediately bounced into their wicker beds leaving Finn looking foolish in the middle of the room. He sat down and watched Dora, not Annie.

Annie watched Dora too, but more covertly, trying to gauge her age but finding it hard to tell: much younger than Alf, anyway. She had a lot more hair than him as well; a wild hairdo of wiry curls in brindled shades of grey and brown, but her bright blue eyes were exactly the same shade as her brother's. She'd shucked off her anorak to reveal a red checked flannel shirt, and with it she wore jeans and a pair of tan cowboy boots. Annie wondered if there was a Stetson somewhere, to complete the look.

They had tea and fruit cake, and Annie listened to Alf and Dora catch up with each other's news. The little dogs rested their heads on their paws and observed from their baskets while Finn mooched about licking up crumbs. Annie wondered how quickly he'd learn all the new rules here. She wondered where he'd sleep, and where he'd be fed, and whether he'd look for her after she'd gone. These thoughts bombarded her mind and she put down her cup and her cake, too upset to swallow properly. She felt heartless, like a devious mother leaving a small boy at boarding school without his knowledge.

'He has a Bonio at bedtime,' she suddenly blurted out, apropos of absolutely nothing. 'I've packed some with his other things.'

'Right-ho,' Dora said smoothly, as if she hadn't just been interrupted mid-sentence on another matter entirely.

'And at home he sleeps indoors, not in a kennel.'

'Well, he will here too,' said Dora. She smiled. 'Would you like to see where?'

Annie nodded, and they made a small tour of the ground floor. It was huge by comparison with her own house, and there were no carpets, only wooden floor-boards, so Dora's Cuban heels made a hollow clopping noise as they progressed through the rooms. At the back of the house, in a room of elegant proportions where French windows revealed a long garden of lawns and herbaceous borders, there were more dog beds and water bowls scattered around the floor.

'Ta da!' Dora said. 'The dormitory. We'll put Finn's bed in here and they can stay up late and have a midnight feast.'

Alf laughed but then stopped when he saw Annie's face. 'Tell you what,' he said. 'Let's walk down to that beach. We've been a long time sitting.'

It was ideal, Annie could see that. The expanse of sand and the flat, distant sea felt like the ends of the earth and Finn streamed about as if he'd never before been free. Dora had taken him and the terriers all the way to the water, which was too far away for Annie, so Alf stayed with her by the dunes.

They'd reached Formby Point by following a long sandy track through a pine forest and Dora had immediately taken charge of Finn, winning his heart with a bag of boiled chopped pig's liver. He was on his lead, but he hadn't once yanked Dora's arm, only walked politely alongside her, fixing her with an obsequious upwards gaze, waiting to be rewarded. Even the red squirrels that danced boldly through the pines went unobserved by Finn, who only had eyes for his new, liver-scented guru. Now, from her vantage point on a windy dune, Annie could see him running to Dora whenever she called him, which she did by whistling through her fingers in a competent manner. The terriers seemed to know that this liver training was for Finn alone, because when Dora whistled they only glanced at her then looked away. They were self-contained, scrupulously well behaved. They pottered contentedly through the dried seaweed and driftwood, a tight little unit. Annie hoped they'd let Finn join their gang.

Alf, chatty and cheerful in the bracing sideways wind, pointed out the dim silhouette of Blackpool Tower and, in the other direction, a vague mist-shrouded suggestion of Liverpool. Annie looked, but didn't much care. She could see this vast arc of sand was a kind of heaven for Finn but personally she was finding Formby Point a melancholy place, lonely and remote. She couldn't look at the sea: the reach of it, the impossible distance to the horizon. She liked to be landlocked, not teetering on the margins of terra firma. Also the sand on the dunes was dry and fine and the wind whipped it up into their faces so they had to turn their backs on the sea and look towards the car park.

'I wouldn't mind making a move,' Annie said.

'Off the beach?'

'No, out of Formby altogether.'

They'd planned to stay at Dora's for the night. There were two rooms prepared for them upstairs and Alf's bag was already deposited in one of them. But Annie knew now that she didn't want to linger. Finn would be happy here; she could see that, just as clearly as she could see her heartbroken self in the days ahead. But if there was to be pain, she'd rather meet it halfway than wait placidly for its arrival.

'I'm sorry,' she said. 'I just don't want to hang about. But you stay with your sister, like we planned. Just drop me at a station or something.' She said this casually, as if she was always jumping on trains in strange towns, although in fact the prospect made her feel sick with anxiety. But anyway, she should have known better because Alf harrumphed with friendly indignation.

'Not on your nelly,' he said. 'I've a much better idea than that.'

29

Vince was waiting for another visit from Martha. He hardly left the house and when the flap of the letterbox swung open and shut he was at the door like a whippet out of the gate.

'What about work?' Annie asked. He was meant to be in Tamworth, selling drainpipes.

'Sick leave,' he said. He was lying on the single bed in the spare room, which was now his room really, as it was where he chose to sleep. He was reading the *Coventry Telegraph* and he spoke to her from behind it, so she couldn't see his face.

'Sick? *Are* you sick?'

He lowered the paper. 'I'm certainly sick of you,' he said and laughed, so Annie left the room, which was always her only recourse. Sometimes this was how he was: sharp and hurtful, just as he'd been for years. Other times, he stared at her through a fog of incomprehension, and only answered her questions with others of his own. Annie had no idea what was wrong with him, although she knew there was something. He slipped between nastiness and befuddlement, and sometimes he was nasty *and* befuddled.

This had all happened since Annie had left Martha

Hancock for dead in the river then come home with fish and chips, although there couldn't be a connection between those events and Vince's state of mind, Annie knew that. Still, since that night – when Vince didn't recognise Annie or the haddock he'd asked for – he'd been strange and unpredictable. He hadn't returned to work and instead he either lay on his bed or lay on the sitting-room sofa, waiting, waiting, waiting. They all crept about the little house like the three Billy Goats Gruff trying not to goad the troll, but none of them knew what the next trigger might be and each day held new disasters: tea the wrong shade of brown, a missing newspaper, a smell of fried onions when there were none cooking, sunlight slanting through the nets and into his eyes, an imaginary swarm of wasps in the outside lavatory. Annie took the worst of his wrath, but none of them were safe from his irrational fury, and the boys learned to hide from him, retreating under their beds and breathing very, very quietly until he forgot his purpose and gave up the rampage. His forgetfulness was his saving grace.

But Martha Hancock's days were done and this was Annie's sustaining strength. She had returned to the river only once, in the early hours of the next day, and although she'd found one of Martha's shoes snagged on a tangle of ivy, there was no trace of the body, even when she craned her head into the tunnel. Annie had uttered a small, fervent prayer of thanks to the river for hiding the evidence beneath the city and then had walked home in the dawn light, holding Martha's shoe under her coat. And while she knew she must live, now, in a permanent state of guilt and with full knowledge of her own wickedness, she found these burdens more bearable than the constant fear during those dark days when Martha had roamed the streets of Coventry.

Annie had burned the shoe, the purse, the brush and the birth certificate, just as she'd burned Martha's letters, but for some reason that she couldn't have articulated even to herself, she'd kept the book for a while, and tried to read it, surreptitiously, when Vince was asleep or out or absorbed by the television. But she soon found that Tess Durbeyfield rose from the early pages with startling clarity, a beautiful, potent mix of womanliness and childishness, and it was as if Martha Hancock herself were in the story, as if *she* were Hardy's tragic heroine, catching the eye of the wrong kind of man. Annie had thrown the book across the bedroom with shaking hands and then at once retrieved it to send it the way of everything else: into the range, to be burned down to a collapsing heap of pale grey ash.

So Annie felt no regret, only a kind of guilty release. Her world, already small and under-populated, shrank still more, and she never ventured further than she absolutely had to. The school, the butcher, the grocer, the post office: these four essential points formed the outer reaches of her daily universe. Certainly she never again trod the streets with the children in that blind and careless way of the evening she found Martha stepping off the bus. Perhaps, she reasoned, someone would see them who'd seen them before, on that terrible night; perhaps the old lady who'd fussed over Andrew would see her again and recall the bloodied neck, the brutal rent to her coat, the wet footprints leading from the river to the lane. No, thought Annie: stay in, stay close. Keep the boys close too, away from strangers, away from the water.

She wished to be as quiet, as good, as self-sufficient as it was possible to be. She wished to be invisibly ordinary; which, after all, wasn't too much to ask and was really the only thing she'd ever wanted.

There was a heady atmosphere on the day, six months later, that Vince eventually stopped waiting for Martha and got back outside into the world of work and women. He picked up where he'd left off in Tamworth, leaving behind him a basketful of dirty laundry and a lingering smell of fags, so Annie baked a cake to dispel him entirely. It was a two-tiered sponge filled with lemon curd and she let Andrew slap thick white icing all over the top, any old how. They had finger rolls filled with egg and salad cream and Michael was allowed to have his hard-boiled egg unsliced, and his sauce and his bread roll served independently of each other and on separate plates. When he'd finished he asked to get down from the table instead of just sliding off his chair and sloping away. Annie and Andrew stayed where they were, playing I spy and singing nursery rhymes. The boy's face shone and now, when he smiled, the livid scar left by the snow globe puckered at its edges like a pulled seam. Annie called it his war wound. She felt battle-hardened herself, too: a survivor.

She wondered if Vince could hold his job down, now that he sometimes forgot names, faces, places. She wondered, too, if he'd be able to curb his anger and frustration when it welled up in the face of a customer or a colleague rather than herself or one of the boys. But days passed, and then weeks, and still he didn't come home, which was no bad thing except that neither did he send money. This made her feel abandoned, not liberated; the brown envelopes had been proof to the world that she was a wife. Now she had to eke out the contents of her housekeeping tin, shopping frugally, as if they were on rations. She thought about Sew and Sew's, and wondered if Barbara might have her back when little Andrew started school. She wondered if she was brave enough to ask.

Then one day a letter fell on to the doormat. It was in a stiff brown envelope, larger than average, and her name was typed on the front, not handwritten. Her heart seemed to stop when she first picked it up, although it wasn't a letter from beyond the grave or a summons from the police, but a very formal communication from a solicitor; her *father's* solicitor, acting on behalf of Harold. She read the words many times over in order to fathom their meaning, though she wasn't completely certain she grasped it. It was definitely to do with her father though, and his wife, Mrs Binley. Unless Annie was entirely mistaken, it seemed they might both be dead.

She read the words aloud, the better to understand.

We are writing to you in accordance with Mr Harold E.G. Platt's last will and testament, which states that if his wife pre-deceases him or if his gift to her should fail for any other reason, then, following payment of funeral expenses and administration costs, all his estate, both real and personal, should go to you, his only child, Annabelle Doyle, nee Platt.

'I'll be blowed,' Annie said. It sounded very much as though she'd been left something by her father, now deceased. Or was he? Perhaps this letter was simply to notify her of her father's intentions *should* he die. She lowered the document and tried to conjure her father in her mind's eye but all she could see was a bowler hat and a waxed moustache. Mrs Binley loomed large though: that shelf of a bosom, those calculating eyes, that self-satisfied smile. What the devil could have become of her? Annie felt quite certain that Mrs Binley was too determinedly fleshy and substantial to have done anything so feeble as die. But the next morning, in the unexpectedly dowdy office of Harper, Madely and Prince, she sat on a grey plastic chair, Andrew on the floor at her feet with crayons and a colouring book, and heard that Agnes Platt had in fact died alongside her husband in a fatal car accident in Norfolk.

'A motoring holiday, last month,' Mr Prince said, darting a glance at Annie over the top of his tortoiseshell spectacles. He was elderly, small and trim, with the keen, beady appearance of a clever little mouse, but there was dust on his desk and the diary, open in front of him, looked lamentably blank; Annie could see her own name in there, but no other. Business was hardly brisk here. She wondered what had happened to Harper and Madely: there was certainly no room for them in this drab little office if they happened to turn up.

'Collision with a stationary tractor on a lane outside Burnham Market,' Mr Prince continued. 'They must have been driving at quite a lick.'

He seemed cheerfully unfazed that she was receiving this news for the first time. Annie thought it was just as well that she didn't happen to mind very much. Still, though: last month! She attempted indignation.

'Shouldn't I have been informed earlier?'

'This is why you're here now, Mrs Doyle.'

'At the time, I mean. What about the police? Don't they tell next of kin?'

'Ordinarily, I suppose they do, yes, although sometimes people can slip through the net, as it were.'

'I see.'

'I believe your relationship with your father was rather distant?'

Annie thought this impertinent so she ignored it. 'And the funeral?' she asked.

'Yes,' said Mr Prince. 'Ten days ago, a double ceremony, followed by a double cremation. It was all organised, I gather, by the sons of Mrs Platt.'

'Mrs Binley,' Annie said.

'Excuse me?'

'Never mind. Do they get anything?'

'They?'

'Her sons.'

'Erm, I don't believe they—'

'Do you happen to know if there's a parrot?'

Mr Prince's eyes flicked nervously towards the door. Annie said, 'She used to have a parrot called Mr Christian.'

'I see.' He studied the paperwork on his desk. 'No,' he said, looking up. 'No mention of a parrot.'

'So what exactly has he left me then?'

'Everything, Mrs Doyle, except, it would appear, Mr Christian, although there's every chance he may have pre-deceased them.'

'When you say everything …?'

Mr Prince nodded. 'I do mean everything. A substantial property and all its contents, monies accumulated in savings, bonds and investments, plus a valuable life insurance policy which, according to the terms of the arrangement, now pays out to you.'

'Why?' Annie asked, suspicious that at the heart of this sudden good fortune might lie a cruel joke. 'I mean, I haven't seen or spoken to my father for years.'

'The fact remains you're his only issue,' Mr Prince said.

'Mrs Binley thought her sons would inherit.'

'If you mean Mrs Platt, then I do believe she exerted some pressure on your father to alter his will. I believe she may have *believed* it was, in fact, altered, although your father never had any intention of benefitting his second wife's extended family.'

'Really?' Annie said. She felt a little sad, now, for the first time. She wished she could have said thank you to her father, but then, he did seem to have intended her to discover his generosity only after his death. After all, he knew where she lived. He could have called in any time.

'Did you know my father well?' she asked.

He took off his spectacles, as if he couldn't answer a personal question while he was wearing them.

'I handled all his business,' he said. 'Did so for many years. But I can't in all honesty say we became friends.'

'No,' Annie said. 'I can imagine.'

'But our professional relationship was always cordial.'

'He didn't much like me,' Annie said. 'That's why I'm surprised at this will.'

Mr Prince cleaned the lenses of his glasses with a soft brown cloth. 'I've been administering people's dying wishes for many years, Mrs Doyle,' he said, and he popped the spectacles back on, although he still regarded her not through them but over the upper rim. 'And if the experience has taught me anything, it's the truth of that old adage: blood is thicker than water.'

'Speaking of that ...' Annie said, and then faltered. It had slowly been dawning on her that here, in the moral limbo of a solicitor's office, she might resolve a nagging loose end that, alone, she felt powerless to address. Mr Prince waited, and kept his bright dark eyes upon her, inviting her to speak.

'Well, that is, I wonder, as I'm here,' she went on, 'whether you can help me with another matter?'

'Certainly,' he said. 'If we can.'

'Oh,' said Annie. 'We?'

Mr Prince blushed an endearing pink, for he knew for a fact what Annie had surmised: that Harper, Madely and Prince was in fact a one-man band, and a rather under-employed one at that. He coughed, and continued.

'Figure of speech, Mrs Doyle: the royal we. It goes without saying that what passes between us here is entirely between you and me.'

'Thank you,' she said, with ingratiating meekness. 'It's just ...' She glanced down at Andrew, good as gold on the floor, his tongue poking out in concentration as he coloured in all the animals of a zoo in outrageous techni-colour. 'I need a birth certificate for this little chap.'

'I see, and have you spoken to the city registrar?'

'No!' Annie said, and then again, 'No,' in a more reasonable tone of voice. She considered for a moment then said, 'I hoped perhaps you could see to it for me?'

'I believe it's perfectly straightforward, Mrs Doyle. Perhaps Mr Doyle—?'

'He's never at home,' Annie said quickly. 'And he's not a nice person.'

Mr Prince was silent.

'I worry,' Annie said in a stage whisper, 'that I have no proof he's mine.' She was aware of the danger of exposure, of the potential risk to her carefully constructed story, but here she was with a brand-new fortune and the willing ear of a distinctly shabby solicitor, and after all, every man had his price. 'It's complicated,' she said. 'I'd like some documentation, without ... without necessarily going through the usual channels.'

She was practically holding her breath, waiting to see if she'd misjudged the situation, but Mr Prince only made a steeple with his fingers, to rest his chin. He looked thoughtful, amenable. He didn't look scandalised.

'Well,' Annie said. 'And if such a thing might be possible, then I'm able to pay for it, aren't I?'

'Well yes,' he said, 'after probate, naturally. These matters must run their course, but yes, yes.'

'*Whatever* the cost,' she said, and she raised her eyebrows at him.

'Ah, I see,' Mr Prince said. 'Yes, yes.'

'So, I wondered, then, if you'd handle this for me,' she said, appealing now to his professionalism as well as his greed.

'I believe I may be able to, yes,' he said. He glanced at the closed door, as if it might be listening and couldn't be trusted. 'Expensive business, mind you.'

'Well, and do my father's investments run to it?'

She honestly didn't know what a skilled forger might charge for a fake birth certificate: hundreds, thousands? Anyway, she'd pay it, if she had it.

'Oh yes, yes, you're most definitely a woman of means, Mrs Doyle.'

Andrew looked up from his labours and said, 'Mummy, what did he say?'

Annie reached down and ruffled the hair on top of his head. 'I think he said we're rich.'

'Oh,' said Andrew, and turned his attention back to the purple monkey, the blue bear, the orange crocodile.

So Mr Prince promised to be in touch, then handed over the keys, along with the paperwork pertaining to all Harold Platt's prudent investments, bonds and savings, and Annie returned to visit the house she had once shared with Harold and Lillian, the house she had thought she would never see again, the house that now belonged to her. Michael and Andrew were with her on the day she opened the solid oak front door and stepped back in time. The three of them stood on the large chequered tiles of the front hall and stared up and all around at the high ceiling, the heavy glass chandelier, the ornate plaster cornicing and the wide wooden staircase, which started in the middle of the floor and curved round to the first-floor landing.

'Big,' Andrew said.

'Mmm,' said Annie, 'and very empty.'

Somebody had plundered the place, stripped the walls of paintings and mirrors and carted away the furniture. The Binley sons, no doubt, thwarted in the end by Harold and determined to gain some small advantage for themselves. Daylight robbery, but Annie didn't really care. They could have it all; she'd buy new, and anyway the emptier the house, the fewer the memories. She'd have the locks changed, though, by nightfall.

Andrew started to tear about, excited by the space and

the echoing, empty rooms. Michael, always wary in new places, stayed close to Annie and accompanied her on a methodical tour, room by room. This took some time; you could fit their entire Sydney Road home into half of the ground floor, thought Annie. She was reminded of her father's grandiosity, his preening ambition. But then, what could he have meant by marrying Agnes Binley, with her rough hands and her brassy, knowing laughter? What wiles had she used to raise herself in his eyes from char to mistress to wife? Annie could think only of the bedroom, and she shuddered.

'What?' Michael asked.

'Oh, nothing.'

They wandered around and Michael was silent, though she could almost see his mind whirring and working, taking everything in, missing nothing. There was dust on the dado rails, old bills and newspapers on the floor, but other than that the house was a shell. Those Binleys, thought Annie. She could understand them taking the big-bellied mahogany chests, the solid walnut bedsteads, the gleaming rosewood nests of tables with their thin, bandy legs; but why would they want the socks and pants, the toothpaste and the lavatory brush, the salt, pepper, Bisto and beans? They must have been driven by the belief that this was their very last chance to get something for nothing.

'This was mine,' she said to Michael, when they were upstairs. It was a small, square room, with a window overlooking the street. At some stage in its history, Mrs Binley had had it redecorated, so the rose-sprigged paper that Annie remembered was gone and instead there was heavy flock in thick stripes of burgundy and gold.

'Like a tart's boudoir,' Annie murmured.

She could see that Michael liked the stripes, though. He admired their uniformity, their impeccable straightness. While Annie gazed at her old view – unaltered, except there were more cars parked on the road now, and the cherry trees were bigger – Michael began a tally, burgundy stripes first. He counted out loud, but in a whisper.

Annie let her mind slip back to when she had been a child in this room; she was always alone, and while she hadn't always been precisely *un*happy, she had no recollection of happiness either. She remembered, suddenly and vividly, a Christmas pantomime she never saw: the promise of fun, a longed-for treat that dissipated in the mysterious London smog along with her mother. She looked at Michael; his face was a scowl of concentration.

'What would you say to living here, Michael?' Annie asked.

'Fifty-five, fifty-six, fifty-seven, fifty-eight, fifty-nine, sixty.' He stopped counting and left his finger on the sixty-first stripe. 'I might like that, if I had this room all to myself and Andrew didn't live here with us. Sixty-one, sixty-two ...' Off he went again, her odd-bod boy. She watched him for a while. He was almost content these days, happier without the unforgiving daily scrutiny of Vince. If Andrew could possibly be removed from his life, she was quite certain Michael would even start to smile now and again.

'You must learn to love Andrew,' she said, pointlessly.

He ignored her, absorbed by his stripes and numbers. He had a new schoolteacher, a young man, who told Annie that Michael's extraordinary affinity with patterns and numbers could be turned into a good thing. Michael liked him. Or at least he didn't *dislike* him. 'Try him with the piano,' the teacher said, last time Annie had seen him at the school gate, 'or a violin. You'll find he flourishes.'

Annie didn't know. She hadn't a musical bone in her body, although Vince could hold a tune. Well, he could once upon a time. It was a long while since she'd heard him sing.

Andrew was clomping up the stairs, just for the joy of the racket he was making. She left the room to meet him, so that Michael could complete his inventory in peace. Andrew said, 'Hello, Mummy,' and Annie said, 'Hello, pet,' and they clattered back down the stairs together and started a game of hopscotch on the black and white tiles. She *could* buy a piano now, Annie thought. A piano *and* a violin: why not? She pictured a glossy black baby grand in the bay window of the drawing room, and, secure on their stand, a violin of polished maple and a horsehair bow. Outside, in the garden, she'd have a swing and a slide for Andrew, and a wooden climbing frame, or a treehouse in the big old lime.

What about Vince, though? His growling demeanour forced itself into her daydream and made her forget the game she was playing with Andrew. She looked up, as if he might be outside, about to come in. He'd always wanted her father's money, she thought. Perhaps this house could be the new start they needed; perhaps here, where Martha Hancock had never darkened the doorstep, she could make Vince love her. For a few foolish seconds she let herself believe this, but then her shoulders sagged as she remembered who she was: just Annie Doyle, who had to claim another woman's child in order to be loved.

Oh Vince would come back all right, of course he would, lured by the house and the money, and she'd regain the respectability of a resident husband. Then he'd hate her all the more because of his own weakness, and she'd allow and endure it because Vince was her price, her cross to bear. She knew this now. There could be no happiness, beyond the happiness she took from Andrew. But that was enough. That would do.

'Your turn,' Andrew said. He wasn't really grasping the game, but he did know that he wasn't meant to be the only one hopping. He studied her face silently for a while then said, 'Are you sad, Mummy?'

'No, I'm not!' she said brightly. She sniffed, and wiped her nose quite recklessly on the sleeve of her blouse. 'It's only the dust.'

30

The years passed, the boys grew. Vince's illness was given a name and from that very day he deteriorated, as if the diagnosis was a curse. He was foul-mouthed, lusty, offensively helpless. In their big, beautiful house Michael and Andrew watched their mother become Vince's round-the-clock carer, his nurse, his nanny. Michael hated his father for the demands he made and despised his mother for endlessly meeting them. Andrew, cut from different cloth, pitied Vince and admired Annie, but these days he loathed Michael, and Michael loathed him right back: always had. They were an unhappy quartet, on the whole, although Michael's music gave him pleasure and Andrew ... well, Andrew's natural disposition was for sunshine, not cloud, and rare was the day that Annie didn't thank God for him: God, and her own iron will, that kept him for herself.

Martha was gone, of course, but not forgotten, at least not by Annie. For his part, Vince hadn't mentioned her since he left the house in 1970 to sell plastic downpipes in Tamworth, and Annie sometimes wondered what his strangely diminished brain had done with her name, her face, the memory of their grand passion. Knowing what she knew, Annie could think about Martha without pain; the longer she was gone, the more reasonable Annie felt towards her. She felt a sort of detached, impersonal sorrow that Martha Hancock hadn't been able to lead a harmless, anonymous life up in, oh, where was it? Annie couldn't remember exactly where her foe came from, although she knew it was in the north east, Vince's old stamping ground, back in his heyday.

But when human remains were discovered in the Sherbourne and reported on the national evening news, all pity evaporated and Annie's heart once again beat fast with terror. The girl was reduced to a collection of bones, dragged from the water after nine years of lonely decay, but there she was in Annie's mind, glowing with good health, lit by the bright internal flame of that maddening, casual beauty and the insolent certainty of youth. There were no photographs on screen, because nobody knew who she was; *the remains of a body believed to be a young female*, said the newscaster. But Annie could see her, clear as day. 'So you thought you were rid of me?' Martha said, through the medium of the television. 'Well, think again.' Her grey eyes were full of steel.

Now then, thought Annie, clutching the arms of the chair, trying to breathe. Now then.

The Doyles were in Cornwall when this happened, at the end of a short, doomed attempt at a family holiday. Vince had been given new medication, which had tamped down his wildness so that now he was mostly just quietly malevolent. So Annie tried to seize the day; they were a family, she told herself, and they deserved a family holiday, and anyway, there was all Harold's money in her bank account and nothing much to spend it on. So that was why they found themselves in Padstow, staying at the Metropole, a hotel that had once been grand enough for Edward VII, before he was king. Michael and Andrew had a single room each, and Annie and Vince shared a twin. Annie would have liked a room to herself, but Vince couldn't be trusted alone. Left to himself he'd put on his clothes in the wrong order, or entirely forget to clothe his lower half, and there was no saying what he might do in the middle of the night: whom he might accost, where he might end up. He needed watching, and even so, in spite of the vigilance of Annie and the boys, he'd become a well-known public nuisance by the end of their first full day.

They should just have stayed away from the beach; Annie, seeing the sea for the first time in her life, found the swell made her feel dizzy and sick, so she had to sit with her back to it while still trying to keep an eye on Vince, whose new pills couldn't adequately subdue his interest in scantily clad women. Like a little boy spoiled for choice in the sweet shop, he ogled the young female sunbathers and not discreetly, not even silently. Then, just at the moment that Annie turned away from him to unpack the sandwiches, he managed to lunge at a girl as she walked past him to the sea. The fuss that ensued! Andrew wrestled his father down and pinned him to the sand, but the girl screamed and her father and brothers were at the scene in a trice, demanding retribution. In the end the Doyles packed up the towels and the folding chairs and the picnic, and left the cove before Vince was lynched. A crowd had gathered, the young woman at its centre, and there were catcalls as the Doyles made their exit. It was a good ten-minute walk along the estuary from Harbour Cove back into the town and all the while Vince grumbled and swore, while Annie nudged him onwards, trotting behind and beside him like a diligent sheepdog, and the boys, burdened by all the paraphernalia of a day on the sand, hung far enough back to seem unrelated to their parents.

Now, four days later, they were in the hotel in that deathly late-afternoon hiatus before dinner in the hotel's hushed and upholstered dining room. The weather had turned, and although it was May it could have been February; the sky was leaden and the rain pelted the windows like persistent handfuls of fine gravel. The forecast promised no improvement, but anyway tomorrow was their last day and it was a relief all round. Today they'd endured a visit to a tin mine near Penzance, and Annie was still feeling the strain of maintaining a chirpy interest in the face of relentless rain, Michael's vicious boredom and Vince's vacillating moods. Andrew made heroic efforts to enjoy himself, but it was never easy in this family of misfits, and now the boys had loped gratefully back into their rooms and closed the doors. Vince, for the time being depleted, was slumped on a wing chair, facing the television; he stared at the screen in a state of gloomy torpor. Alongside, in a matching chair, sat Annie, because the news was full of Mrs Thatcher's election victory, and she found herself drawn to the screen to witness the unfolding events.

'Look at that,' she said to Vince. 'A lady prime minister, would you credit it?'

Vince heard her but chose not to show it. She never really knew if it was his illness she was dealing with, or merely his habitual ill humour; the dementia had long been an excuse for all kinds of cruelties of which he had actually always been entirely capable. When his neurologist first identified the cause of his memory lapses and foul-mouthed outbursts, Vince had only grinned and said, 'Licence to please myself, then.' The consultant had been shocked; he'd expected sorrow or fear from his patient, not this grimly humorous defiance. But that was Vince for you, Annie had said at the time, trying to cover her own embarrassment as well as the consultant's, then Vince had said, 'Oh fuck off the pair of you,' and left the office.

So she didn't press him now, didn't repeat her comment, because if he answered at all it'd only be nastily. Andrew, always her ally, said she was saintly to put up with it, but of course Annie knew what she was, and it wasn't a saint. Putting up with Vince was her lot in life: a kind of atonement.

She didn't bother with the news as a rule but this evening she couldn't take her eyes off it. She was riveted by the pious composure of Mrs Thatcher, quoting Francis of Assisi over the melee of the press pack and the baying crowds. Annie had never voted in a General Election: in any election, come to that. She didn't feel qualified to take a view. But she thought, now, that she might have voted for Mrs Thatcher, just because it was one in the eye for all those men.

'What a hubbub,' Annie said. Vince said nothing.

'There's as many folk jeering as cheering,' she said.

They sat in silence and watched. Mrs Thatcher was a bit like Vince, thought Annie; she answered the questions she liked, ignored the ones she didn't.

'Look, they're going in now,' Annie said. 'I'd love to see inside. I wonder if they're putting the kettle on.'

She did this a lot: talked to Vince as if there was nothing wrong between them. It was for her own benefit really, because the silence, if it continued too long, mutated into menace. This evening though, Vince seemed only passive. She looked at him side on for a long moment, studying him quite openly as if he was an exhibit in a museum. Over the past few months he'd deteriorated physically as well as mentally; he'd lost weight and his face had become lean and angular, more like it had been when he was young, except it had an indoor pallor and there were deep lines from his nose to the corners of his mouth. The stubble on his chin and jaws was grey, his sharp nose was slightly hooked, his eyes were hooded: like a predator, a raptor, Annie thought now. And then, just as she was about to look away, he cut her a glance of such pure and withering dislike that she had to hug herself to ward off the chill. He'd forgotten so many names and faces over the years, he'd forgotten what was and wasn't appropriate behaviour, but he never forgot how much he hated her. He turned away again, satisfied.

And then, as if Vince himself had cued up the item, Mrs Thatcher was gone and Martha Hancock was on the news. *The remains of a body believed to be a young female.* Annie was horror struck. Her fingers tightened on the arms of the chair and she forgot to breathe for so long that when she remembered, it came in a gasping rush, as if it were she that'd just been dragged from the water. Vince was watching too, but he registered no particular interest, so there was that to be grateful for. Annie wanted to lean forward and turn off the television but instead she watched helplessly as the images rolled out on the screen: a senior police officer reading a statement, the steep mud-brown slope of the Sherbourne's banks, the yellow and black crime-scene tape cutting off access to the public, the corporation dogsbody who chanced upon the remains. Everyone was very sombre, very serious, and Annie sat, in a red plush wing chair in a Padstow hotel, the only person in the entire world to know who it was they had there. She knew her name, the colour of her hair, the particular grey of her eyes, the shape of her lips, the confident swing of her young hips, the slenderness of her ankles, the perfect pink of her complexion, all zipped up now – what little was left of it – in a plastic body bag. The screen switched back to the studio newscaster and Annie, rigid in her chair, watched his lips move. Beside her, Vince was lightly snoring.

'Mum?'

She leapt in her chair and turned around, clutching her heart. Andrew had come into the room, dressed for outside in an anorak and a woolly hat. His face wore its usual uncomplicated smile. Annie tried to smile back, but she was consumed by dread, steeped in it, as though Martha's ghost was right here in the room, waiting to reveal herself.

'I thought I might go for a walk,' Andrew said.

'In this?' Her voice sounded tight and strained, and she coughed to disguise it. She looked at the rain-lashed window, then back at Andrew.

'Yes, in this.' He was a fresh-air boy, always preferring outside to in. He glanced at the television screen, showing images of Margaret Thatcher again. 'Did you see Coventry on the news just now?' he said.

'I didn't notice,' she said. 'I think I dozed off.'

'Dad?'

Vince stirred and looked round at his son. He rarely ignored Andrew. 'What?'

'You okay? Did you see Coventry on the news?'

Annie forced herself to be calm. 'It was all Mrs Thatcher on our telly.'

'No,' Andrew said. 'They've found human remains in the river.' He widened his eyes. 'Grisly.'

Vince furrowed his brow, puzzled, and Annie blessed the fog that often clouded his ability to process new information. She looked at Andrew and shook her head fractionally, which meant he wasn't to bother his father. Her breathing had steadied and she'd released her iron grip on the chair arms. This too shall pass, she told herself. She could already sense Martha retreating, and anyway, Andrew only had to appear before her to remind her that she never really had a choice.

From down the corridor the halting strains of a new piece percolated from Michael's bedroom. Out of the question to come away without his violin: you might just as well have asked him to leave a limb behind. Annie hoped he wasn't disturbing anyone. He wasn't a considerate person; he would never think about his fellow guests, never imagine that Stravinsky wasn't everyone's cup of tea.

'Did you ask Michael if he wants to go?'

Andrew rolled his eyes. 'As if,' he said.

'Oh Andrew,' Annie said.

'Do you want to come, though?'

His generosity swelled her heart and she treasured him anew, her gift of a boy. How lovely it would be to walk out of the hotel with him and through the seaside town with its shops and boats and wet, dark harbour walls. How proud she felt, that this charming boy was her own.

'I can't, pet,' she said. She indicated Vince with her head.

'I'll sit with him if you want to get out.'

She smiled. 'No, you go, pet.'

'Righty ho,' he said.

'Be back in time for our evening meal, won't you?'

'Wouldn't miss it for the world.'

She raised her eyebrows at him. 'Cheeky,' she said.

He grimaced. 'Well,' he said, pulling a face. He found the dining room stuffy and over-dressed, and conversation round their table was strange and unstable. 'We should have fish and chips on a bench outside, looking at the boats.'

'Oh, should we?'

'You could make an exception, now we're by the sea.'

'No,' she said. 'Not tonight,' and she looked away, back at the television, so Andrew just sighed and left. Fish and chips, thought Annie; whoever decided they were a treat? Greasy and heavy, they sat in the pit of your stomach like a dead weight. Herself, she hadn't touched them for years.

Next day they left for home. In Annie's fantasy family holiday she had imagined a last-day picnic on the grassy cliff top overlooking Hawkers Cove, but rain still filled the sky and anyway, even Annie no longer had the heart for the fight. So in spite of the fact that they'd paid for one more night half-board at the Metropole, they loaded up the Austin and left Padstow in the insipid light of a watery dawn, creeping away unnoticed, leaving their keys on the reception desk along with a note saying thank you. Annie navigated and Vince drove, because – oddly – the actions required to handle a car remained intact in his memory so that when he was behind the wheel he was at his most lucid, rising manfully from the marshy depths of his dementia to the responsibility of the task in hand. In any case, Annie couldn't drive. Well, she could, but she couldn't pass her test. She'd taken it five times so far, and on each occasion her nerves had let her down. 'There is such a thing,' the examiner had told her last time, as he failed her again, 'as being *too* cautious.' So Annie must practise incaution, a quality she didn't understand, and meanwhile Vince remained in charge of the family car, although without Annie as the conscientious co-pilot, they could end up anywhere.

She half expected to find the police at their door when they finally reached home, seven hours after setting off. It was impossible that they could be, impossible that any link had been established between the ruined corpse and Annie Doyle, but still she squinted anxiously up the road towards their house as Vince made the turn into the wide, leafy avenue. All she could see were the usual cars, the usual trees, the usual well-maintained front gardens and glossy dark green privet hedges. Vince, recognising his surroundings, was evidently pleased to be very far from Padstow. He was silent, but he continued to behave in a civilised manner and helped Annie and Andrew carry the suitcases into the house. Michael only carried his violin in its rigid black case, and so well-established were the family's habits that no one expected him to do otherwise.

Inside, the house smelled of temporary neglect: stuffy, and vaguely vegetal. Vince dropped the case he was holding and bolted upstairs, his long legs taking two steps at a time, heading for the lavatory.

'Hope he remembers to come out,' Michael said. He was a tall, thin boy, with a face that would be handsome if he were happier, and if his acne would abate. He'd allowed his black hair to grow down past the collar of his shirt and Annie thought no music school would look twice at him because of this. His contempt for her opinion was infinite.

'He seems quite good though, doesn't he?' Annie said. 'Nearly normal.'

Michael made a sceptical grimace. 'I suppose we must enjoy it while it lasts,' he said. He talked, these days, with an affected drawl, as if he was speaking through a perpetual yawn.

'Okay, Mum, that's everything.'

This was Andrew, backing in with the last of the bags and kicking the front door shut behind him. Michael winced at the noise. He sat on the bottom stair and untied his shoes. 'You're not just leaving the bags there, are you?' he said.

'I'm leaving yours,' Andrew said flatly.

'Oh now, don't start,' Annie said. 'Anyway, I'll empty them downstairs. Most of it needs washing.'

'What an upheaval,' Michael said.

'Yes, well, never again,' Annie said.

'Four days of sheer hell,' Michael said.

Andrew said, 'Pity you didn't stay behind,' and then, before Michael could respond, he turned to Annie. 'I got you something,' he said. He delved into his canvas rucksack and produced a flat, square paper bag, striped pink and white, and handed it to his mother.

'Oh!' she said, immeasurably touched, even before she looked inside.

'It's a bit boring,' Andrew said. 'But the colours are nice.'

It was a crisp cotton tea towel printed in gaudy seaside colours with a recipe on it for Cornish pasties. 'I saw it last night on my walk,' Andrew said. He shrugged apologetically. 'It's not much but ...'

'Thank you, pet,' Annie said. She was thrilled with her gift and the thought behind it but she was also aware of Michael, glowering at the foot of the stairs, so she played down her gratitude; tried not to draw a comparison by her thanks between the son who gave and the son who only took. Still though, Michael's expression had darkened and he stared at Andrew with naked dislike.

'You're such an arse licker,' he said with a curl of his top lip.

'Michael!' Annie said. Andrew just returned Michael's stare but didn't speak and Michael stood, turned, and padded up the stairs in his stockinged feet. Andrew and Annie looked at each other.

'Are you sure he's yours?' Andrew said. 'Are you sure we're actually related to him?'

Annie gave a tight smile then swung away and climbed the stairs. For a while Andrew stared at the space she'd left behind, then he picked up his own and Michael's suitcases and carried them through to the washing machine in the back kitchen, to save his mother the trouble.

31

So they left Formby sands and walked back to Dora's house where Finn and the terriers gobbled bowls of biscuits then slumped in their baskets, utterly spent. Annie had the jitters. She waited in the hall for Alf to come downstairs with his overnight bag and was only able to make short, one-word replies to his sister's attempts at conversation, so that Dora grew discouraged and got on instead with rinsing out the tea cups. And then, with the hallway between them, she began to throw words of advice from the kitchen, as if the difficult matter of leaving Finn could more easily be raised when neither woman could see the other.

'I know this is hard,' Dora called, 'but if I were you I'd go without saying goodbye.'

Annie blinked and looked at her shoes. They were rimed with sand and there were sandy prints on the tiles: her own, Dora's, Alf's and a peppering of paw prints.

'Honestly, trust me,' Dora shouted. 'Dogs don't understand goodbye and he'll be right as rain here with me. You'll only upset yourself.'

But Annie knew better: knew Finn would look for her after she'd gone: knew he'd pad to the front door where her particular smell would still be in the air and on the floor, and he'd wait and wonder and fret when she didn't come back. She wouldn't dream of leaving him without a goodbye. It was just that she didn't know how to accomplish it without releasing the well of tears that she knew was waiting to spill and flow.

A creak on the stairs told her Alf was descending. When she looked up at him he smiled with careful kindness.

'All set?' he said. She nodded, but said, quietly, 'Dora thinks we should just leave, but I ...'

'No, you want to tell him you're off,' he said, and she nodded again.

'Pop in there now then and tell him you'll see him soon.'

'Will I, though?'

Alf said, 'Sure as eggs is eggs.' He smiled again. 'Go on,' he said gently, and because there really was no point procrastinating, Annie turned and pushed open the door to the big, light back room where the dogs were curled on their beds. The terriers regarded her with blank indifference but Finn sat up at once when Annie entered the room and his tail thudded a rhythmical greeting. She eased herself down onto her knees so they were eye to eye and he smiled.

'Finn,' she said. He moved his nose fractionally forwards as if to say, 'Yes?'

'Finn, you're the best dog in the world and I love you.'

No, she thought; this was the wrong tack. Her face was wet with tears already, because she was speaking of love: speaking with her heart, not her head. But after all, what else could she do? She *did* love Finn. He was her friend, her ally, her comfort.

'I have to leave you here with Dora,' she said, and her

voice was unsteady. 'You'll be better off here, and you'll have all the freedom you need. But I'll come back and visit you, I promise.'

His tail pounded the base of his basket and he ducked a little so she could lay the side of her face against the warm, flat pane of his head. He sighed contentedly and she let her tears run freely into his golden fur. On the other side of the door Alf coughed discreetly.

'Goodbye,' Annie whispered. 'Be happy.'

'Annie?'

Alf was in the room now; she could hear him crossing the wooden floor.

'Annie?'

He reached down and touched her shoulder and she lifted her face and sat back on her heels. She was ashamed of the tears; she didn't know where to look. But Alf only said, 'That's the hardest part done with,' and he reached out a hand to help her up.

'I feel a fool,' she said, standing stiffly, sniffing violently and patting her empty pockets, looking for a hankie. He produced one himself, washed, ironed, clean as a whistle, and she blew her nose heartily and gave a shuddering sigh.

'There's nowt foolish about being sad,' he said.

Finn rested his head on his front paws but kept his eyes on Annie.

'Be a good lad,' Alf told him, but still Finn only held Annie in his steady gaze. Annie looked at him and her heart filled with love and the awful necessity of turning her back and leaving, and in the end she only managed to move at all because Alf took her arm and moved her gently to the door.

'He'll be fine,' he said. 'He'll be more than fine.'

'Mmm,' she said uncertainly, not trusting herself to speak. On the very point of leaving the room she looked back and saw that Finn was settling comfortably onto his bed, laying his head on his paws, closing his eyes. He'd be out on the sands again later, and that was how it would be from now on – a walk in the morning, a walk in the evening: two long, wild seashore gallops, every day of the week, because here at Dora's, every day was a Dog Day.

Two hours later Alf and Annie faced each other across a large brown teapot and a plate of Eccles cakes in a Blackpool tearoom. The elderly waitress had an indifferent manner and a mouth like a glum goldfish but the tea was hot and the cakes looked tempting. Being a tearoom, it shouldn't have smelled of hot fat, and yet it did. Annie said, 'Do you suppose there's anywhere in Blackpool that doesn't sell fried food?' and then she regretted her remark, because it made her sound a snob. 'Sorry,' she said.

'If you say sorry one more time …' Alf said, with an unspecified warning in his voice and a smile on his face. It was true, she'd been apologising ever since they left Formby. She was sorry to drag him away so soon from Dora, sorry to put him to the expense of a B&B, sorry to be such a sad sack, silent and brooding in the passenger seat, no company for him at all.

'No, I know, I'm sorry,' she said, and they both laughed. She blew across her tea and sipped it. There was chatter all around them, so it hardly mattered that she couldn't think of much to say. Blackpool was so busy! She'd thought seaside resorts were summer places, but the Promenade was thronging with people, and even though it was only five o'clock, there was an air of drunken abandonment, as if she and Alf had stumbled into a giant party. She thought about Finn – as she had every five minutes since leaving him – and then, because she didn't want to be maudlin, she forced him from her mind and gazed out of the steamy window at the carnival atmosphere on the pavement outside.

'Is it always like this?' she asked.

Alf nodded. 'Pretty much.'

'You'd think, being November ...'

'Turkey and tinsel,' he said.

She looked at him.

'Turkey and tinsel,' Alf said again. 'It's for folk who can't wait for Christmas. They come to Blackpool and get the whole works a month early, for next to nowt.'

'Well I'll be blowed,' Annie said. 'Do they really?' She laughed at the thought. 'Trees and fairy lights?'

'The lot.'

'It's bad enough doing it once,' she said. She thought of herself and Michael and a rolled and boned turkey crown. No crackers; they hadn't had them for years because Michael said they were infantile, so who would bother, after such discouragement? Finn had always loved a bit of turkey, but this year ... well it might just not be worth the bother at all. Annie toyed with her Eccles cake and teetered on the brink of melancholy.

'Eat up, lass,' Alf said, sensing a bout of the blues and heading them off. She broke the cake in half and took a bite. It was densely packed with currants, sweetly delicious.

'I can't believe you've never been to Blackpool,' Alf said.

She swallowed. 'It's true. I went to Padstow once, and that was it.'

'That was what?'

'That was me finished with the seaside.'

'Blimey, what happened in Padstow?'

She considered her reply, considered what she *could* say, then only said, 'It rained.'

Alf laughed. 'Well, if that's your criteria for a failed holiday, there can't be anywhere in Britain that's safe.'

'It wasn't just the rain,' she said. 'It was all sorts of things. Vince was poorly by then and the boys didn't get on, but also I didn't like being on the edge of things. Do you know what I mean?'

He didn't, really.

'What I mean is, standing where the ground meets the sea. It made me feel dizzy, and a bit lonely, don't ask me why. It happened again today at Formby Point.'

Alf studied her. His eyes were so blue they seemed strange on an old man; shouldn't the colour have faded, like his hair? 'My Alice used to cry when she watched the sun set,' he said.

'Did she?'

He nodded. 'Aye, I'd forgotten that until now. She thought it were sad, like, seeing it drop below the horizon.'

'Well, it always comes back up the other side,' Annie said.

'It does. Are you done?'

'Pardon?'

'Wi' that Eccles cake? If you've finished we can move on to stage two of Alf and Annie's Big Adventure.'

'What on earth are you talking about?' She popped the

last piece of sugared pastry into her mouth and dabbed at the crumbs on her plate.

'That's for me to know and you to find out,' he said and he winked at her across the table, which made her blush.

'Pleasant Beach?' Annie said, repeating what she thought she'd heard. She glanced to their right at the flat, dark expanse of sand and the long, long arm of the South Pier. The noise, lights and competing smells were disorientating; they made her head spin.

'No, *Pleasure* Beach, Annie.'

'Pleasure?' There was alarm and mystification in her voice, as if pleasure was an unheard-of concept, or he'd just made an indecent proposal. He chuckled.

'Your face,' he said. 'You might have just landed from Mars. Blackpool Pleasure Beach is a funfair.'

'Oh I see,' she said, only relieved that they were going nowhere near that glassy, distant sea, and then, as the fact filtered through, she stopped short and said, 'What do you mean, funfair?' He nodded. He had a twinkle about him, an air of mischief. She felt a wave of irritation.

'If you think I'm going anywhere near those rides ...' she said.

'Oh come on, live life, why not?'

She was horrified that her hunch was right. 'I'm seventy-three!'

'And I'm nearly eighty,' he said placidly, as if the only thing under discussion was their respective ages.

'It's just not ... not ... fitting,' she said and he exploded into laughter, pressing a big white hankie into his eyes.

'Ah dear,' he said, 'they don't make 'em like you anymore. You're a one off, Annie Doyle.'

'No I'm not,' she said, tartly. 'I'm perfectly ordinary and sensible. Those rides are for youngsters.'

'We'll see,' he said. 'We'll see.'

She was huffy with him, although he appeared not to notice and just sauntered along the Promenade towards the noise of the Pleasure Beach; she stuck with him, too uncertain of herself to do otherwise, and at the entrance he bought wristbands at a kiosk without further consultation, then took her arm and attached a yellow neon strip, as tenderly as if he was helping her on with a piece of jewellery.

'I'd as soon go back,' she said. It was the first time she'd spoken in five minutes.

'You'll like it,' he said authoritatively.

'I shan't.'

'You'll never know if you never have a go,' he said. There was something compelling about his confidence and his smile but Annie was still in rebellion against the tawdry, raucous spirit of the place: the lights, the cloying mingled smells of hot dogs, honeyed peanuts, candy floss. A bass thrum of pop music seemed to enter her body through her feet and shake her bones. A pearly king on the Kentucky Derby whipped up business in a booming comedy Cockney voice, cajoling, coaxing, bullying to fill up his seats. Screams of self-inflicted fear, howls of laughter, a menacing back note of drunken cursing. Annie felt she'd walked into a gathering of nightmares, assaulting her senses and her standards of propriety and caution. Alf hooked an arm through hers and had to shout to be heard.

'Y'see, the thing is, everybody should ride one roller coaster in their lifetime.' He was perky and sure of himself, steering her over to a ride, pointing out its 1930s integrity, blinding and befuddling her with facts, as if she could possibly care when it was built or by whom. It was all a ruse, she thought, to bundle her forwards onto the roller coaster; she could see right through him.

'Twin track,' he was saying. 'Best wooden coaster in the world, classic Art Deco fairground architecture, a proper period piece.' Annie, following his sweeping hand, saw monstrous wooden scaffolding carving dangerous heights and depths out of the Blackpool sky. She recoiled, but anyway he guided her into the crowded approach to the ride and she let him, because she didn't quite know what else to do, and besides he was so firm, so assured, that some small part of her had begun to trust his judgement.

'It's called the Grand National,' he was shouting, 'like the steeplechase at Aintree. You're in a race with the other train.'

They were moving inexorably forwards and there was no way out unless a crane happened along to winch her up and away from the crush of people. She could hear the trains rattling above and beyond, and a cacophony of screaming. Was the structure actually *shaking*? Whose idea of fun was this? Annie felt a wild impulse to raise herself up on the bodies of the people near her, to squirm victoriously out of the line and over the barrier, back to freedom and sanity. Alf was smiling encouragingly but firmly, like a parent ushering a child into the dentist's chair, and then the two trains lurched into the station and disgorged their riders so that the tight queue that held Annie and Alf surged forwards and in short order she found herself installed on a wooden seat, in a wooden carriage, pinned into place by a wooden bar across her lap.

Too much wood, she thought; didn't it famously splinter under pressure? Alf laughed at nothing and clapped his hands and Annie turned to him to say how very much she'd like to get off, but then the train lunged forwards and she did too, slamming her midriff against the safety bar then flinging immediately backwards so that her neck seemed to crack. Everyone was laughing, and on the inside seats of each train, people were stretching out their arms, trying to hold hands. Annie kept her own tightly gripped on the safety bar and concentrated on being still and safe. Alf leaned over to speak in her ear.

'There's a climb first, then a dip,' he said, and as he spoke the trains were hauling up the tracks so that Annie could see the drab rooftops of Blackpool laid out below, the moving figures of miniature people walking securely on solid ground. She longed to be among them. The noise and upward grind of the train was relentless and she knew, from the angle of the rise, that they must surely be about to crest the summit; but still the first plunge, when it came, was an ambush. They hurtled pell-mell downwards, then up, then down again.

'Double dip!' Alf shouted. 'Woo hoo!' His arms were aloft; everyone's were, except for Annie's. She gripped the rail with utter dedication and gasped at the astonishing rush of cold night air, the effrontery of it, the ruthless heave and plunge. Alf was shouting something but she couldn't make out the words now, and she wouldn't risk turning her head to look at him. But as the carriage careered around the track and the blur of the Blackpool night streamed through her peripheral vision, the sensations that at first had seemed so intolerable began subtly to shift into something closer to ... well, not enjoyment, certainly not that; rather, a kind of liberation, as though her objections and inhibitions were being whipped away, one at a time, by the forces of time and space and speed. When the wooden trains finally slid into dock at the end of the ride and the passengers began to clamber out, Annie said, 'I'll give that another go,' and stayed exactly where she was.

Alf gawped at her.

'What?' she said.

'We're staying on?'

'Well I am,' she said. 'You can get off and wait if it's too much for you.'

Alf roared with laughter. 'Annie Doyle,' he said, shaking his head.

'What?' she said again.

'You're a dark horse, you are.'

'Well, I think I liked it, and I just need to check.'

'Right you are. Arms up on the drops though,' he said. 'It's more fun like that.'

'No thank you,' she said. 'You can have too much of a good thing. I shall hold on to the rail like last time.'

Later, in the stillness of her Blackpool bedroom, Annie lay as flat as she could make herself, pressing her spine down onto the blue candlewick bedspread. Three turns on the Grand National two hours ago, and she could still hear the rattle of wheels on wood inside her head. She smiled at the memory. Alf had handed her out of the train – talked her off it, actually: refused to let her stay on for a fourth ride – and she'd felt loose limbed and light-headed, but more than that, she'd felt exultant. She was surprised no one burst into applause when she alighted: surprised no one pinned a medal on her chest. She hadn't been able to explain to Alf what transformation had taken place during that first cacophonous rush around the tracks, but had only said it was the wind on her face, the sensation of flying. 'I felt like I'd never moved that fast before,' she'd said to him as they wove through the crowds, back to their lodgings.

'You should trade in that Nissan for a Harley-Davidson,' he'd said.

'It was so ... so ... *new*,' she said. 'So different from anything I've ever done before. Makes me wonder what else I've missed.'

But she'd needed a rest, a lie down. Her legs felt like jelly and as the euphoria ebbed, fatigue flowed.

'I'll knock in an hour,' Alf had said, and he'd seen her settled on the bed with a cup of tea beside her before he left the room, closing the door softly, as you might on an invalid, or a sleeping child. She hadn't slept though, only dozed, and now she was fully awake, listening to the roller coaster in her head and hearing, also, a deep rumble in her stomach which reminded her that she hadn't eaten a thing since the Eccles cake.

She sat up, her legs straight out in front of her, her back against the old wooden headboard of her single bed. When she'd first seen this bedroom earlier today she'd been charmed by its old-fashioned 1970s trappings: the teak starburst clock, the pink shag-pile carpet, the macramé wall hanging. Now though, she began to understand why they seemed familiar, because together they called to mind Coventry, that little house in Sydney Road, the spare room with its single bed, colonised by Vince. The candlewick cover had been yellow in there:

canary yellow to cheer things up, as if a splash of colour could have made any difference at all.

So she didn't wait for the tap-tap-tap of Alf at the door. Instead she swung herself off the bed, splashed her face with cold water at the vanity basin and ran a comb through her hair. Then she surprised him by knocking on *his* door and suggesting egg and chips on the Promenade.

32

They left Blackpool early the next morning: early enough to see the sunrise and too early for breakfast at the boarding house, which anyway hadn't been an appealing proposition.

'Sorry,' Alf said, as the Defender rumbled through empty streets. 'It wasn't the Ritz, was it?'

Annie said, 'Actually I slept very well. Mind you, I can sleep on a washing line if I'm tired enough. Anyway,' she went on, 'there's no point being in the lap of luxury in a town as tacky as Blackpool.'

Alf laughed and said, 'Blimey, nobody could accuse you of not speaking your mind.'

There was a pause before she said, 'They could, you know. I never used to speak my mind, didn't do it for years, really.'

'Right. So when did you start?'

'Just now,' she said, and he laughed, but she only gave him a half smile then turned a serious face to the passenger window and watched Blackpool thinning out by small degrees until soon they were on the wide blandness of the motorway and could have been anywhere.

She thought she might have a cold coming; her eyes felt hot, her eyelids heavy, and when she swallowed, her throat protested. Alf turned on the radio and Annie sat silently beside him, turning inwards, missing Finn, picturing him waking up in a strange house, and herself getting back to a home that would no longer contain him.

She thought about the Pleasure Beach, and now, in this mood of increasingly despondent self-pity, she began to cast the episode in a thoroughly different light: a silly diversion, a ploy by Alf to make her forget poor, dear Finn. Then she thought that if it weren't for Alf Dinmoor, she'd be waking up in Beech Street this morning to be greeted by her dog's ready smile and his constant, amiable affection, and before long she'd managed to make herself downright cross with Alf, who had no idea that he'd landed in the soup without even trying. She knew it was unreasonable, irrational, but even so, she sat there beside him, her emotions in a knot, blaming him for the way she felt. The motorway ground on beneath the wheels of the Land Rover and when a vast blue sign flagged up the number of miles to the next service station he said, 'I don't know about you but I could eat a horse.' She stayed quiet.

'Annie?' he said. 'Are you hungry?'

'Not really,' she said, although she was.

'There's a Welcome Break in sixteen miles,' he said. 'You'll feel better with some tea and toast inside you.'

'Tea and toast can't cure everything,' she said.

'No, but it's a start.' He was being determinedly kind, refusing to take offence. He was perhaps the kindest man Annie had ever known, and her eyes filled with tears as she tussled with her own, stubborn and complicated heart.

After a pause he smiled at her with unmistakable fondness and turned off the radio, and she felt a flutter of alarm. It was raining hard and the sturdy vehicle felt as intimate as a cocoon: the warmth, the hypnotic splash of the wipers, the soft sheen of the worn leather seats, the proximity to her hand of his own on the gear stick.

'Can I just say, Annie ...' He paused, as if he was waiting to be denied permission, but she just waited, her heart skittering. She hoped he wasn't about to declare undying love. He wasn't.

'I do understand, y'know, about Finn,' he said. 'I do know it's hard for you, leaving him behind like this. I've not been talking much about it because I thought, well ... I suppose I thought least said, soonest mended. But I hope I haven't come across as unfeeling.'

She dipped her eyes and shook her head and said, 'No, you haven't,' but that was all the reward he got for his graciousness because she couldn't manage anything more. She felt hot and increasingly miserable, and when she lifted a hand to her temple it burned against her cold fingers.

'I think I'm ill,' she said in a murmur, and when Alf said, 'Say again?' she didn't answer but only stayed quiet, lulled by the sounds of the road – tyres on tarmac, rain on the roof – until eventually she drifted into a kind of slumber, a half-sleep, drifting and feverish. Disparate images ran through her mind, pictures from the far and the recent past flickering behind her closed lids like a cine film with no regard for chronology. Herself in her mother's wedding dress; Finn in a field with a bloodied muzzle; Vince in winkle pickers at the Locarno; baby Andrew plump and lovable on her kitchen floor;

Vince growling at her from his hospital bed; her father leaving the house for work in pinstripes and a bowler hat; Michael scowling in concentration as he counted the paving slabs on the way to school; Martha Hancock smiling in a sun dress at Whitley Bay, and then again, on the seat of a bus in Coventry, and yet again, in the narrow hallway of Sydney Road. On and on the images spun and Annie watched them loom and fade with a strange, sleepy detachment until outside the car someone in another lane blasted their horn and she snapped open her eyes and sat up. Ahead, the low-slung contours of a silver sports car were streaking away from them.

'Blithering idiot,' Alf said, and then glanced at Annie. 'Sorry, were you asleep?'

'I'm not sure,' she said. 'I don't think so.' She felt dazed.

'Two miles to a cup of tea,' he said. 'What were you thinking about?'

'Pardon?'

'Just then, when you might or might not have been asleep?'

'Oh,' she said. 'Jumbled thoughts.'

'When I'm behind the wheel of my car I always get nostalgic,' Alf said. 'On a long journey, like. My thoughts always run backwards, not forwards.'

'Mmm,' she said. Her throat was beginning to hurt now whether she swallowed or not and inside her head a dull heat seemed to throb in time with the windscreen wipers, one-two, one-two, one-two. She imagined the virus barrelling through her system, growing in size and strength like a snowball rolling down a hill.

'Tell me one thing about your past, and I'll tell you one thing about mine.'

She stared at him, appalled, and he shot her a jaunty grin.

'You start,' he said. His eyes were back on the road again now, and he'd begun to indicate, ready to leave the motorway. She thought about the things she might say, and how utterly shocked he would be to hear them. 'Come on,' Alf said. 'One salient fact about Annie Doyle's past.'

Back and forth like a metronome went the wipers and now it was as if they were urging her on to recklessness. Annie considered the night she'd plunged down the riverbank with Martha Hancock; should she tell Alf Dinmoor all about that? The fear, the fury, the desperation, the smell of rotting vegetation, the shock of the water, the extraordinary endurance of guilt and relief and shame.

'You just think I'm a harmless old lady,' she said, and he laughed.

'Not necessarily,' he said.

'You have no idea.'

They were on the slip road now, and the noise of the motorway was already receding. He glanced at her uncertainly, vaguely alarmed at her dark tone, but the wet road required his concentration and there was a roundabout ahead.

'You think you've got my number,' she said.

'Ah now, hang on ...'

'But really, nobody actually knows me.' Her eyes burned, her head pounded, and she listened in some surprise to her own voice and the things it seemed to want to say. 'I mean, the real me.'

He risked a laugh, but she wasn't smiling.

'Everyone thinks I'm harmless and a bit silly but I could shock you with what I've done.'

'Well, if we're talking about past misdemeanours, I've one or two skeletons in my closet, too.'

'You don't understand,' she said. Her voice was spiked with urgency suddenly, as if what she was saying was of the utmost importance, and indeed, it did seem that way to Annie; it was imperative that he listened.

'If you knew me,' she said, 'I mean *really* knew me, you more than likely wouldn't want me in your car.'

'Annie, Annie.' He was indicating left now, pulling into the lane that would lead them into the service station. 'I've seen it all, and I can promise you there's nothing you've done that I'd judge you for.'

'There you go,' she said, 'you think I'm just a harmless old biddy. Nobody ever thinks I'll *do* anything.' She was right back at the river's edge looking into Martha's sceptical grey eyes, and Alf was silent. He patrolled the car park for a while, looking for a space, then reversed into a bay and cut the engine.

'Look,' he said, 'more than likely you're lightheaded wi' hunger, but if there's summat you need to confess, tell a priest, because it's not my business. God knows, we both have a past behind us and I certainly wouldn't want anybody poking their nose into mine. All I know is, I like you, so can't we just be friends?'

She pursed her mouth and silently hoped they could. But she wasn't sure.

'Come on,' he said, 'I'm starving. My belly thinks my throat's been cut.'

He was out of the car now, shutting the door, and then he walked round to her side to hand her down from the car's lofty seat. He peered at her and said, 'Are you all right? You look clammy.'

'I don't know,' she said. 'I don't feel quite myself.'

Alf pressed a palm on her forehead and his cool hand felt so comforting she wished he'd leave it there but instead he said, 'Aye aye, you're running a temperature. Come on, let's get you inside,' and off he set. At first she just stood and watched him, then after a few moments she followed. The smell of grilled meat, charred and salty, wafted on the wind from a burger van in the car park. Feed a cold, she thought, or starve it? Feed a fever, starve a cold, which was it? She couldn't think straight. Alf waited for her to catch him up but before she could ask him he picked up where he'd left off.

'In my line of work,' he said as they fell into step, 'I met some right villains. Talk about nasty secrets, dear me.'

'Mapmaking?'

'Come again?'

'Your line of work. You said were a mapmaker.'

'Oh,' he said, 'no, Byron Bay and all that? No, that was just a hobby, a bit of amateur cartography. Expensive business, mind you, gave it up years ago.'

'So what was your line of work then?' She felt a little disillusioned, reassessing him in her head, letting go of the mapmaker, preparing to meet the mechanic, the banker, the salesman of double glazing.

'Copper,' he said, and she didn't immediately grasp his meaning so he clarified. 'Policeman. Detective inspector, to be accurate.' She was silent, staring, so he shrugged and grinned. 'CID. So I've met plenty of crooks in my time, believe you me, and every one of 'em could give you a run for your money, whatever it is you say you've done.'

'Where?' Annie stopped short. Her head swam and she reached out and placed a shaking hand on a concrete post, privately thanking God it was there. Alf looked worried.

'Beg pardon?' he said.

'Where? Which police? What part of the country?'

There was a ferocity to her line of questioning that he didn't quite understand. He hesitated, then said, 'Manchester at first, a stint in Warwickshire in the late seventies, South Yorkshire till retirement. Itinerant detective, me.'

He was trying to keep things light, but it wasn't easy and Annie just kept on staring. He waited and she studied him: considered the possibility that here she was, found out at last, her dark deception uncovered. In her present state of mind it didn't seem outlandish that all this might have been planned and the past two days had only been the lengthy preamble to an elaborate sting. And yet the moment when he must surely charge her, arrest her, crush her with the full force of the law came and went and still he was merely offering her a pleasant, unguarded smile. He didn't know a thing.

'You all right?' Alf said. 'You're white as a sheet.'

Annie looked at him and his face was all concern, and she wondered whether it might actually be a blessing to shed her burden of guilt to this kind man: to offer up her liberty in exchange for a different kind of freedom. She didn't know, but standing there in front of Alf she was tempted. The past seemed all of a sudden to be pressing down on the carapace of her conscience, finding its fault lines.

'In 1969 ...' she said, experimentally, then stopped. 'What?'

'No, it wasn't 1969, it was 1970.'

'What was?'

'The very worst thing I ever did.'

'Water under the bridge,' Alf said.

She winced. She'd stopped walking now, and he watched her with folded arms and a vexed expression.

'Where were you in 1979?' she asked, changing tack. He laughed.

'No,' she said. 'Tell me. Where were you?'

'What are you getting at?' he asked.

'Just what I say.'

'Well, all right, let me see.'

'Coventry,' Annie said. She'd seen him before, she realised: those clever blue eyes, that unwavering determination in the line of his mouth.

He looked at her, surprised. 'Yes,' he said. 'How the devil did you guess that?'

'I just knew. I was there too, then.' Coincidence wasn't the word, she thought; fate was nearer the mark, and while coincidence could be marvelled at then forgotten, fate might have to be obeyed. She wasn't sure.

'Get away,' Alf said. 'Small world.'

'The girl's remains, in the river,' she said gnomically, but he knew at once what she meant.

'Oh aye, that's right,' he said, remembering. 'A bad business.'

'Yes.'

'That case was cold from the start.'

'You never found the killer.' It was a statement of fact, not a question.

'Well,' he said, 'we didn't know the victim, either. We had nowt to go on, except a long list of missing girls. You remember it then? I suppose we were all over the local news for a while.'

'You were, yes,' she said. 'Hoping someone might know something, I expect.'

'Oh somebody would've done, of that I have no doubt,' he said. 'Somebody always knows something.' She could hear he'd been a policeman now; it was creeping back into his voice. 'But it's hard to make progress when you don't even know who you've found.'

Martha Hancock's young, forthright voice said, 'It was me,' so clearly in Annie's head that she was sure Alf must have heard but he just shook his head. 'Young female remains, many years dead, apparently missed by nob'dy.'

Vince missed her, thought Annie.

'Anyway,' Alf said. 'One day, you never know. New evidence comes along, and suddenly ...'

'What?'

'Justice is done, wrongs are righted.'

'Maybe a wrong *was* righted,' Annie said.

She knew that Alf had turned his head to stare at her, but she wouldn't look at him. 'Well,' she said, 'I'm just saying.'

They walked on, towards the glass doors of the service station, which slid open to admit them into the food court. It teemed with fellow travellers although Alf and Annie were only aware of each other. He was preparing to say something; Annie could tell this from the quality of his silence, which was full of consternation. She had an overwhelming desire to sit down and rest her head on a table.

'So, what about 1970?' he said.

'Pardon?'

'You said summat about 1970, the worst thing you ever did.'

She looked at him as if she was assessing his suitability as confidante.

'Did you know her, Annie?'

They were in the cafeteria now, both of them holding trays, and it seemed so incongruous, this possibility of grand confession set against the banal activity of queuing for food. She studied the menu to avoid his eyes and bide her time, but just beneath the surface of her unremarkable skin lay the rush and roll of the past, the headiness of knowing she might reveal her darkest truth and wrest from Alf his complacent certainties, show him the infinite forms that wickedness could take.

'Annie, did you know that person?' he asked again. 'You should tell me, if you did.'

She turned to him and she *was* about to say it, about to draw him into her past in an orgy of truth telling, but an obstruction, hard and hot, seemed to rise in her throat before the words formed and made her heave and gasp and clutch at Alf's arm as if she was choking. He whacked her on the back, but there was nothing stuck, only the confession that'd gone unsaid for too many years. She didn't know this could happen to words, that they could clump and clot together, mutate into something solid that crowded the throat so that they wouldn't be, couldn't be uttered.

He led her to a table and sat her down, and she pressed the heels of her hands into her eyes and gathered her wits. When Alf came back with a packet of paracetamol and a tray of food, she apologised again and again, took two capsules with a glass of water, then gratefully ate her breakfast: scrambled egg, grilled tomatoes, soft white toast, hot, strong tea. Slowly it restored her to the person they both recognised – tearful, a little fearful, tired, ordinary. Alf was patently relieved. He had a bacon sandwich, which dripped with brown sauce, and he talked for both of them. He'd tried Dora, just now on the way to Boots for the tablets, but she hadn't answered and he'd realised she'd be on the beach with the dogs now so best wait until later, when they were back. Annie listened, and nodded. He said he wasn't surprised she'd had a funny turn, she was poorly and on top of that she'd left Finn behind in Formby and some sort of delayed reaction was inevitable. No, she said, it wasn't only that, but when he asked what was it then that ailed her, she only said it's fine, it's fine, it doesn't matter any more. He let it rest, but when they were back on the road a strange silence settled between them: Alf, wondering what she'd told him; Annie, wondering what she'd said.

The body in the river was yet to be identified, but it was days now since it had been found and the story had slipped down the running order of even the local television news. It was on, though, in the Doyles' sitting room and in Coventry in 1979 Annie was watching it with her newfound vigilance. The police were extending their investigation beyond Coventry, trying to match their own scant evidence with young women reported missing by their families over the past decade. An officer appeared on camera, a Detective Inspector Dinmoor from the special investigations unit, and said he hoped someone might come forward; they had very little to go on, he said, but someone, somewhere, must have information about a daughter, a sister, a niece who'd slipped out of their lives, never to return. Annie took against him at once; his eyes were a piercing blue; they looked as if they might see the truth no matter where it was hidden. She wondered if he already knew more than he was letting on. She wondered, too, if she should move house, or would that instantly cast her in a suspicious light?

She didn't need to be in Coventry at all. Michael was going to the Guildhall next September, Andrew could change schools, Vince would live where he was put – he had no choice. But the palaver! She shook her head at her own nonsense. The television showed a shot of the river again, but there was nothing to see besides the police tape and the sluggish water. It wasn't the part of the river where she'd left Martha, by the looks of things: not even close. But then, it'd been nearly ten years; she'd be bound to drift.

'If I never came home, would you bother trying to find me?'

This was Michael, nearly seventeen years old, lank-haired and spotty, as uncomfortable in his own skin as he had been as a baby. He didn't seem to love anybody, and therefore didn't expect to *be* loved.

'Oh Michael,' Annie said. 'What a thing to ask.'

'I'd leave no stone unturned,' Andrew said flatly, without looking up from *Shoot*. His own face was un-blemished, rosy with youth and easy good health, and his blonde hair was like a mane, lustrous and abundant. He was letting it grow to look like Roger Daltry.

'Fuck off,' Michael said.

'Michael.' Annie's protests always lacked conviction, never meant anything, had no discernible effect. In any case she didn't want to goad him because he'd turn on her again, demanding to know why after decades of indifference she now put the news on every night and watched it with unwavering attention. Michael never missed a change in anyone's behaviour, however small, however harmless, and he was cross with her because she'd fobbed him off with nonsense. Michael always knew when he was being silenced with an untruth, just as he knew instantly when an answer had a ring of authenticity. She'd be glad when he went away to college. She blessed the day she'd bought him a violin because otherwise she doubted she would ever have any peace from his ceaseless questioning of every tiny discrepancy in her life.

Vince, occupying the whole of the sofa, opened his eyes and gazed around the room to establish his whereabouts.

'Evening, Mr Doyle, welcome to the seventh circle of hell,' Michael said. Vince blinked at him.

'Where's she gone?' he said.

'Who?' Annie glanced away from the television to look at him.

'She only went out for a loaf.'

Annie stood up, filled with fear. Michael laughed.

'What's he on about now?'

'She only went out for a loaf,' Vince said again. His eyes brimmed with tears. 'What's her name? Beautiful girl, classy girl.'

The boys gawped. Only Annie knew that he was thinking of Martha, searching the morass of his mind for a name. Unlikely though it was, she believed the BBC news might have filtered through the complex webbing of his dementia to make some connection between his lost love and the found bones. In a trice she'd reached over and switched off the television and this one small action was enough to distract her husband, who snarled at her and said, 'I was watching that,' although he wasn't. She ignored him. Michael watched her from under his hair. Andrew skimmed the pages of his football magazine. Annie sat and waited for her heartbeat to slow and thought this won't do, this won't do at all.

33

Annie and Alf managed to remain carefully neutral for the rest of their journey – easy enough, since Annie was quite legitimately able to take refuge in her developing cold, turning her face to the window and half-closing her aching eyes, keeping conversation to a minimum. He dropped her off with a get-well-soon and a jaunty goodbye that she knew disguised a certain amount of relief, then she hurried inside, grateful beyond measure to be back. She'd decided, in the thoughtful quiet of the car, that she wouldn't worry any further about Alf and their strange, dangerous conversation, so the minute she was inside she busied herself with mundanities, unpacking her meagre quantity of washing as the kettle boiled and the tea brewed. Then she took her mug into the living room, sank into an armchair, and reminded herself, as she shucked off her shoes and wriggled her stockinged toes in the pile of the rug, how very unwise it was ever to stray too far from hearth and home.

Now, at last, she let herself dwell on Finn, or rather, the lack of him. She'd braced herself for sadness, prepared herself for the impact of an empty house, even considered the flimsiest of flimsy silver linings: that no longer would Michael find tumbleweed drifts of golden hair in the corners of the rooms.

But she hadn't banked on the solid depth and breadth of the silence: hadn't fully understood how *dense* it could feel. Without Finn, the house was preternaturally still, with the strange and sterile quiet of a mausoleum. Well: there was the ticking of the wall clock, and the hidden gurgling of the water pipes. But aside from these domestic sound effects, there was nothing at all. And it wasn't as if Finn was a noisy dog; no, he rarely barked, preferring instead to communicate telepathically, willing Annie to meet his needs by the power of thought. Still though, she realised now that she'd lost a life force in Finn and she imagined her homecoming again, as it might have been: Finn's skittering welcome dance, his unbridled pleasure in her arrival, his smile, the way he would be barely able to contain his joy, his satisfied 'humph' as he dropped down beside her to warm her feet while she drank her tea.

'Oh,' Annie said, with a sort of bleak astonishment. Then she bowed her head and wept, and once she started she couldn't stop. Indeed, the tears brought some relief to her bruised soul and she cried and cried, abandoning herself to grief. She sobbed and streamed, and tilted her head to howl at the ceiling. I'm alone in the world, she thought, letting dramatic hyperbole fuel her distress: alone in the world, and Finn, my Finn, will learn to love Dora.

Then the telephone rang, and she abruptly stemmed the tears and stood up. Dora, she thought wildly; this'll be Dora, who's decided Finn is too big, too boisterous, and she, Annie, must fetch him back. She wiped her face on her sleeve as she went to the hallway to answer, although her voice wobbled when she picked up the receiver and said, 'Hello?'

'Annie?' a woman's voice said.

'Yes,' Annie said, shakily hopeful.

'Oh, it didn't sound like you.'

'Dora?' Annie said.

'No, Sandra.'

'Oh,' Annie said, and all hope evaporated.

'I wondered ... well, are you all right?'

This was so unlike Sandra that Annie didn't answer immediately, just held the receiver and looked blankly at the wall.

'Annie? Are you there?'

'Yes,' she said.

'Are you okay?'

Annie tried to speak, but faltered. Then she swallowed, and prepared to lie. 'I'm fine, thank you,' she said, as steadily as she could manage.

'It's just, I wasn't, when Fritz went,' Sandra said.

'Oh.'

'No, I cried so much in the car on the way home from the vet's that I had to pull over.'

'Did you?' Annie's voice quaked, and she held her breath, closed her eyes and pressed her lips together in a tight white line. Her head ached, her throat hurt, her nose dripped like a tap, and Finn was gone.

'Annie?'

It was no good. She began to sniff, then whimper, then, even as she registered horror at her own lack of restraint, the dam broke and the tears poured forth once more.

'I'm coming over,' Sandra said, and hung up.

She was there in ten minutes, and though she had none of Josie's tenderness, she knew just what it felt like to lose a dog.

'I know,' she said. 'I know. It's horribly quiet, like the world just stopped turning.'

Annie nodded fervently. She felt calmer now; Sandra had brought her back from the brink with her own brand of grief therapy: a sort of sardonic realism mixed with stern sympathy.

'But look, nobody's died,' she said. 'I bet he's on the sands right now having a blast.'

'I expect so,' Annie said.

'But he's not here, right? So it's hard on you?'

Annie nodded again.

'Still, there's no need to cry yourself into a coma, Annie. You have to get a grip and consider things from Finn's point of view. I bet you have a right old headache, don't you?'

'I do,' Annie said. 'But then, I already did, even before I started crying. I picked up a cold in Blackpool.'

Sandra pulled a face. 'You got off lightly I reckon. You can pick up worse things than a cold in Blackpool.'

'Mr Dinmoor likes it.'

'Nowt so queer as folk,' Sandra said, and Annie laughed feebly.

Sandra made her a Lemsip and then stood with her back to the kitchen sink and spent ten minutes asking practical questions about Dora and Formby, so that through her own answers Annie, who sat at the table looking at Sandra through the restorative steam of her hot, bitter drink, found she was growing reconciled once again to the very thing that only half an hour ago had seemed unbearable. She associated this blessedly peaceful feeling not with any inner strength of her own, but with Sandra's steady presence, so when the younger woman looked at her watch and said, 'Right-oh, better make tracks,' Annie wanted to say, 'No, don't go!'

'Oh,' she said instead. 'Of course, yes.' She stood up.

'No more waterworks,' Sandra said warningly. 'Chin up, onwards and upwards.'

Annie gave a non-committal nod and they walked to the front door, then just as they got there Michael's lanky frame loomed up the garden path, pushing his bicycle. Annie said, 'Oh dear,' and Sandra laughed. She opened the door but Michael didn't even glance in their direction. Instead he busied himself with his Raleigh, slotting it into the narrow wooden bike store and clipping shut the padlock. The two women watched him. When he could avoid it no longer he looked at his mother, not at Sandra.

'You're back then,' he said, as if her not returning had been a possibility.

'Of course I am,' Annie said.

There were a few beats of silence when Michael might have asked about the journey, or the dog, or her feelings, and then Sandra said, 'Right, bye, Annie,' and walked past Michael to her car. Annie dolefully watched her go.

Michael stepped inside the house, all arms and legs on account of the Lycra he favoured for his longer rides. He looked like a lanky black spider, Annie thought. His normal clothes, she knew, would be folded up snug inside his backpack along with music manuscripts, reading glasses and a fountain pen. She watched him unclip his yellow helmet and release his hair, which dropped around and about the edges of his face in limp, stringy curls.

'Has everything been okay?' she asked him, since he was showing no interest in her.

'It has,' he said.

He was peeling off an outer layer and she waited, but he only glanced at her as if he was surprised she was still there. 'What?' he said.

'Well, I've been away, and I left Finn at his new home, and it'd be nice to be asked how I got on.'

He widened his eyes at the rebuke. Usually she allowed him to be as indifferent as he liked.

'How did you get on, Mother?'

His voice was wreathed in sarcasm, so Annie just sighed and Michael started to unpack his bag, sliding out the corduroy trousers and white cotton shirt on the palm of his hand. Crisply folded with corners sharp as an envelope, they could have been new out of the box.

'You were very rude just then,' she said. He looked at her.

'To Sandra,' Annie said. 'It's usual to say hello in that sort of situation.'

'I don't know her,' Michael said. 'She has nothing to do with me.'

He shook out his shirt and draped it fastidiously on the bannister but to Annie his absorption seemed affected, self-conscious.

'Alf Dinmoor thinks you're autistic,' she said.

He looked up, and his pale face had an unusual dash of colour, like a dab of rouge, high on each sharp cheek-bone.

'Why did you talk about me with him?' he said.

'I had to apologise to him for your rudeness, and he said you weren't being rude, or at least, you weren't being *intentionally* rude, because you're almost certainly autistic.'

He glowered at her for a moment, then said, 'Is this because I didn't ask about the bloody dog?'

'Is what?'

'This passive-aggressive pseudo-medical cod-diagnosis?'

Annie said, 'Can you say that again in English?' He curled his lip and looked away.

'I'm only telling you because it explains everything,' Annie said. 'It's not a word we knew when you were little.'

'Explains what, exactly?'

She shrugged. 'Everything. The way you were as a boy, the trouble we had with you at school, the way you took to the violin, the fact you couldn't leave for the Guildhall, when the time came—'

'Oh, the fucking Guildhall,' he spat. 'Back to that old chestnut.'

'And ... well ... just everything else, and the way you treat Andrew ... and me for that matter. It explains all that.'

'Might it simply be possible that I just don't like Andrew?'

'Or me?' Annie said. 'Do you not like me, either?'

Michael gave a bitter laugh. 'You're the one who made him Golden Boy,' he said. 'Andrew, the Chosen One.'

They held each other's gaze but Michael's expression was fierce and Annie was first to look away.

'Oh Michael, I don't know what to say,' she said,

utterly weary, utterly spent. In all their years together, she wondered, was this their first argument? She was always so ready to concede ground to Michael, always so wary of breaching the fragile peace of their small household.

'No,' he said. 'I dare say you don't.'

She sighed deeply and retreated to her default position. 'I'll put the kettle on,' she said.

A look of sly triumph passed swiftly over Michael's dark features, but he needed to be sure of his victory. 'Green tea,' he said as she made for the kitchen. 'Oh and Mother?'

She stopped and looked at him through bleary, cold-ridden eyes.

'Don't pass remarks,' he said. 'And I'd be obliged if your friend kept his opinions to himself as well.'

'He didn't mean any harm,' Annie said. 'Neither did I, although I suppose I did blurt it out a bit sharply just now.'

Michael waited a moment, as if he was collecting himself, mustering all his patience, then he said, 'It's not the manner of your delivery I object to, but the content of what you said.'

She knew what he was up to: backing her into a corner with his superior verbal skills.

'Look,' she said. 'I don't want to fall out with you, but might it not be nice to know there's a reason for the way you are?'

'*Nice?*'

'Reassuring, then.'

He tossed her a look of withering disdain, then turned to walk up the stairs.

'You could have studied at the *Guildhall*, Michael,'

Annie said. 'But you chose to stay here, in this little house, with your mother.' She spoke kindly now, not in anger or even irritation, but her words were laced with sorrow.

'And there's not a waking moment when I don't rue the day,' he said without looking round. He disappeared into his bedroom and slammed the door, and when she took him his tea, he wouldn't look at her.

Later, when she looked in his room and said goodnight, it was as if she wasn't there. But it was only what she expected; Michael hated many things and chief among them was to be reminded of his reliance on his mother.

In the bathroom she cleaned her teeth, washed her face and patted some cold cream into the pale soft flesh of her cheeks and neck. She stared at her reflection and recalled the despair it used to cause her when she was younger. She wondered, not for the first time, whether if she'd had the good fortune to inherit Lillian's looks instead of Doreen's, her life would have been happier. And then she thought – as she'd often thought before – that her pudgy, cheerful Auntie Doreen had seemed happy enough with all those children and a husband who never left her.

At Doreen's funeral there had been rows and rows of mourners, and the children – young adults by then – had wept and leaned in to each other for comfort, stricken with loss. Annie, sitting on the third pew from the front among a row of strangers, had cried too, but for herself, not for dead Doreen, and then soon after that she'd moved house, lock, stock and barrel, coming here, to this poky little place in Hoyland, where nobody knew them but where Annie felt safe. Safer, anyway: back where she'd started, when her life had been all ahead of her, an unwritten book. Vince went straight into Glebe Hall, so that had been a blessing, but oh, the boys had been livid, Annie remembered now; even Andrew, normally so placid and kind, had raged at moving from Coventry. He'd come along, of course; well, he was only fourteen so what choice did he have? Anyway, he'd made the best of things, done all right at the secondary school, collected a few O-levels ... except then he'd refused to stay on to do his A-levels. Instead he'd packed a rucksack and gone off on a train to Paris and met Bailey in a queue for the Eiffel Tower. Barely out of boyhood, and Annie lost him to a girl from Brisbane. He'd never really lived at home again, after that.

She'd still had Michael, of course. But that was only because he didn't know how to leave.

She found the paracetamol Alf had bought at the service station – was that really only today? – and took a couple more with a glass of water, swallowing painfully and tenderly prodding the glands in her throat to check for swelling. Sleep was what she needed more than any-thing but when she finally climbed into bed she found it wouldn't come and instead her overwrought mind whirred with anxious activity. She wondered about Alf: pictured him on the phone to some faceless Coventry de-tective, instructing him to re-open the case of the bones in the Sherbourne. He had a new prime suspect, Alf was saying; Annie Doyle: aged seventy-three, white hair, blue eyes, approximately five foot three inches tall, not believed to be any danger to the public but potentially a danger to herself.

What had she done? she wondered. What did she say?

Truly, she couldn't remember, though again and again she pictured herself speaking, pictured Alf listening, remembered the awkward silence that followed, but just couldn't recall the specifics. She tossed and twisted under the duvet and fell, eventually, into a patchy, exhausting sleep.

The next morning Josie rang the doorbell. She had a box in her arms, with holes punched in the side, and a smile on her face that immediately made Annie feel wary: a knowing smile, one that hid a secret.

'Welcome home,' Josie said. 'I brought you a gift,' then she looked closely into Annie's face. 'You look poorly,' she said.

'It's a cold,' Annie said. 'It's nothing.'

Josie clucked sympathetically. 'You're all bunged up,' she said.

Annie didn't answer but just stared at the box so Josie held it out. Annie didn't take it.

'Go on,' Josie said. 'Quibble-free return if you're not completely satisfied. Can I come in?'

She pushed the box at Annie, who accepted it, but only because Josie looked as though she might just let go. It was light, with a small, central point of heaviness that felt warm against Annie's hand. Whatever was in there was far too small for the box. 'Sorry,' Annie said. 'Come in.'

Josie followed her into the house. 'Don't shake it,' she said. 'Or drop it. Just open it.' She walked straight into the living room as if she was more at home there than Annie, then she sat down and looked expectant, so Annie placed the cardboard box on the floor and opened the flaps.

It was a puppy; white, black and tan, very small but with eyes as alert and knowing as an old sailor's. It saw Annie and promptly sat up, as if the boat it was waiting for had finally docked. Annie clasped her hands together, and stared at the little dog, which waited and watched, full of innate confidence in its own lovability.

'Mr Wright says she's all yours if you want her.'

'Mine?'

Josie laughed.

'The only girl in the litter, which just shows how much Mr Wright likes you, since he could have sold this one for twice as much as the boys.'

'Likes me?'

'Annie!' Josie said. 'Just pick her up!'

But Annie didn't want to, in case she couldn't put her down again.

'Look,' Josie said. She leaned down and lifted out the puppy between two hands, gently competent. She nuzzled her nose against its own then held it out to Annie. 'Mr Wright thought you'd miss Finn, and this is the puppy Riley liked. That's all.'

At the mention of Riley, Annie reached out and plucked the little dog out of Josie's hands. It squirmed and to make it safe she clutched it to her chest, where it tucked its tiny domed head under her chin and licked her throat. The warmth of its sleek body was a comfort, like the memory of one of her little grandson's hugs.

'I hadn't really reckoned on another dog,' Annie said, more to herself than to Josie.

'It's too easy to get used to not having one,' Josie said, 'and then there's always a gap in your day where the dog should be.'

Annie thought the last thing she needed was any more gaps in her day. She looked down at the puppy.

'So,' she said. 'I'll call her Lottie.'

Josie smiled. 'Nice. I'll tell Mr Wright she's staying, then.'

Annie thought of Michael and the new battles ahead, but they hovered hazy and manageable behind the greater sensation of creeping euphoria that this new little dog, this Lottie, could be hers. She was settling down, the puppy, curled tight as a nut in the soft hollow of Annie's hands and she wished Riley were here to see.

'So, how was the whole Finn thing?' Josie asked.

'Oh,' Annie said, and her face fell. 'He'll be fine with Dora but getting home yesterday ...' She tailed off and shook her head.

'Yes, I'll bet that was tough.'

'Sandra came.'

'I know. She's a brick in a crisis. And look, the hardest part's behind you now.'

'It is, yes. I should ring Dora. I meant to ring yesterday, but it all got a bit much.'

Josie looked directly into Annie's eyes. 'Mr Dinmoor's being a bit odd about your trip,' she said, lightly casual, as if she was trying to lure Annie by stealth into this conversational trap, but Annie only glanced at her and didn't speak.

'I said, "How was the trip?" and he said, "Very good, up to a point," and I said, "How do you mean?" and he said, "A bit mixed towards the end," and then he clammed up.'

There was a pause.

'I'll be needing that cage I used when Finn was little,'

Annie said. 'He slept in it for the first two weeks, just to get him used to being in one place overnight. Oh dear, he didn't half howl the first night.'

'I see,' Josie said. 'A conspiracy of silence.'

'Do you happen to know what food she's on?'

'Just tell me this: did you fall out?'

Annie looked at Josie, and did her level best to radiate unconcern. 'What a thing to say,' she said. 'Of course not.' She wouldn't, she absolutely wouldn't, tell Josie what she may or may not have told Alf Dinmoor. Even if Josie plied her with a gallon of hot chocolate, Annie would not even so much as hint at it. On that subject, her lips were sealed for ever.

34

Andrew Doyle had encountered few barriers in the search for his biological mother. Metaphorical doors swung open. Calls were answered and messages returned as if the authorities had merely been waiting for these very questions to be asked. And if global time zones proved problematic, there was still the World Wide Web, a teeming virtual market place of family histories, where hard facts were laid bare for the curious, the dogged, the displaced. He spent hours at his desk at home in Byron Bay, his face bathed in a pool of white light cast by the screen of his laptop. He'd meant to share with Annie what he found as he found it: to include her and thereby protect her from hurt. But the fact was, he didn't feel like speaking to her yet. A sort of delayed resentment was settling in his heart like silt in a dark pond.

Of course he already knew his birth mother's name and the name she'd chosen for him, and Andrew wondered now if his father had deliberately left these as clues in spidery ink on the back of the pictures, because he would hardly need to write those names for his own benefit. But as well he also knew, now, that he hadn't been born in Coventry, but in Durham. He knew that Martha Hancock's middle name was Catherine: that she was sixteen years and four months old when she gave birth to him: that Vince was nearly twice her age. There were birth records detailing all this information, and at first he was only relieved that for the past forty-six years he'd celebrated his birthday on the right day. But then he remembered his own birth certificate, which he dug out of the document box then stared at coldly, for a long time, reading and re-reading the lie that he was born to Annabelle Margaret Doyle, nee Platt. It was only a piece of paper, but it seemed to undermine his very existence, and what did it say about Annie? One thing to keep secrets, another thing entirely to go to criminal lengths to do so. He hung his head and Bailey stepped up behind him and kissed his neck, rubbed his shoulders. She understood Andrew's hunger for information; Martha's blood ran through their boys' veins and anyway, Bailey was intrigued by the photographs. Riley's eyes, Riley's smile.

Andrew hadn't yet discovered what became of Martha, but he was very far from giving up the search. Bailey suggested he go easy on himself by handing over the details to someone in the UK, a private detective perhaps, but Andrew didn't know. What he thought was, he might fly back to England and visit Durham. If someone found Martha, he said, it ought to be him.

He booked a flight. He didn't tell Annie a single thing.

Lottie was the new darling of Glebe Hall and Annie was welcome to take her to visit whenever she liked. It was Moira's idea. She rang and said that Annie mustn't feel she wasn't welcome, now that Vince was gone.

'Don't be a stranger,' she said. 'Bring that lovely big

dog of yours in with you – everybody loves a visit from a dog.'

'Oh,' Annie had said. 'Finn's gone.'

'Ah no,' Moira said, her words coming out on a sigh. She was picturing a double bereavement for poor Annie, until she heard that he was alive and well and living by the sea and that Lottie had taken his place in Beech Street. 'A Jack Russell puppy,' Annie said. 'Cute as a button.'

So Annie and Lottie dropped in two or three times a week. Puppy therapy, Moira called it, which made Annie feel official, like a social worker. It was a perfect arrangement, now that Vince wasn't there to snarl at her and remind her of the past. There was an old lady in Vince's room called Violet who believed she was sixteen and liked Annie to brush and plait her long grey hair. And across the hall was Trevor who had no visitors, only Annie. He held her hand when she let him, and his eyes welled with soft tears when she left. And Lottie wandered free-range around the home, visiting whom she pleased, getting a taste for garibaldi biscuits.

Sandra had a new dog too, a rescue greyhound called Beverley, lean and rangy and as dark and velvety as a mole.

'Beverley?' Annie said, when Josie told her the news.

'I know,' Josie said. 'It sounds like somebody you were at school with, doesn't it? But it's what she's called, so ...'

'Can't Sandra change her name now she's the owner?'

'No!' Josie said. 'It's bad luck, like renaming a boat.'

She'd phoned, on a late December afternoon, seeking out Annie, who, for the past three Wednesdays, hadn't joined Josie and Sandra for a walk. Lottie hadn't had all her jabs, Annie said, and Josie said, 'So? Carry her along in your pocket. Or let me carry her. But don't hole up there like a hermit.'

Annie demurred and Josie pressed, but it was impossible for Annie to articulate the precise reason she had for staying away, and truly, Lottie and her inoculations were the least of it. Rather, it was a reversion to old habits: a feeling that the merciless glare of friendly interest had somehow lit those dark parts of her past she longed to forget. That she alone had put herself in jeopardy – talking too much, dallying with confession – was beside the point. She couldn't even think about Alf Dinmoor without feeling a stab of alarm at what had almost happened. Her defences, painstakingly constructed over decades, were evidently easier to breach than she'd realised so she'd simply decided she didn't trust herself in company, except with the bewildered residents of Glebe Hall, among whom she was entirely comfortable, for they showed no interest in her life at all.

'Did you speak to Dora?' Josie said, changing tack. Annie nodded, and then remembered Josie couldn't see her.

'She told me Finn's a sweetie pie,' she said. 'She told me he's a gentle giant.'

'Ah,' Josie said.

'Course, it's lovely she's taken to him, but she doesn't need to tell *me* what Finn is.'

'No, I suppose not. He's happy, though?'

'She put him on the phone,' Annie said. 'Held the phone to his ear so I could say hello.'

'Ah,' Josie said, again. 'And did you?'

'It would've seemed rude not to. He didn't say anything back, though.'

Now Josie laughed, and so did Annie. 'Dora told me Finn knew it was me, but I'm not so sure. He'd just sit there like a lemon, wouldn't he, while she pressed the phone to his ear?'

'Dear Finn,' Josie said, and their conversation ended in fond reminiscence, which Annie could bear, now she had Lottie.

She was back in the kitchen now, making mince pies: one batch done, one batch in, one batch waiting. The puppy sat at the oven door as if she was watching them bake, but it was her own reflection she was looking at in the glass door; there was a Jack Russell in the oven, she was certain of it. The house was filled with the smell of hot, sweet pastry and there were carols on the radio, turned down low so the sound wouldn't carry upstairs. Annie sang along softly, as far as she was able, anyway; who knew the words, beyond the first verses? Outside, darkness had fallen and through the kitchen window Annie could see dainty pin pricks of white lights adorning the little laurel bush in next door's garden and, on the sloping roof of the house opposite, a lurid Santa Claus flashing red and green. Every year, two weeks before Christmas, up it went, and every year Michael hotly complained, first to the culprits and then to the council. Nothing ever happened, except that Michael got crosser and crosser. Well, his bedroom *was* at the back and the light *did* flash faintly red and green around the outside of his bedroom curtains, and this *was* Michael, who woke up if you dropped a feather on the landing. Still, Annie wished he'd give it a rest. Herself, she welcomed the advent of Santa on the roof. His familiarity was reassuring, and he was something to look at, something festive. In Annie's house you wouldn't really know it was Christmas, except for the bumper issue of the *Radio Times* when it came and, just now, the smell of baking.

There were twelve pies cooling on the counter and she picked one up and nibbled at it gingerly. These could be for Glebe Hall. Well, and the next lot too. There was no point keeping too many here – Michael wouldn't touch them; they were indigestible, he told her, like ice hockey pucks in his stomach, but anyway she'd put a dozen in the tin for herself. He really was a curmudgeon at Christmas. Or perhaps it just showed more at this time of year.

Since Josie called, the phone had rung twice more but Annie had ignored it: floury hands, and anyway there was no one she wanted to speak to. Michael could answer – he was upstairs, doing what exactly she didn't know – but he hadn't bothered either. The answerphone wasn't on, so it just rang and rang until the caller lost heart, but when it happened for a third time Annie decided she'd probably better pick up. Slowly, hoping it'd stop, she washed and dried her hands, then padded to the hallway, closely shadowed by the puppy. For a few moments Lottie looked at Annie and Annie looked at the phone, and then she sighed and lifted the receiver.

'Mum?'

Andrew spoke before she did, and she was utterly astonished to hear him. They talked on Christmas Day, every year, not on 20 December.

'Andrew! What is it? Is Riley all right?'

'Why didn't you answer before?' he said, ignoring her question. 'I know you're in.'

'But I didn't know it was you,' she said.

He gave a sharp laugh, which struck her immediately

as odd. He sounded unlike himself: brittle and a little terse. And close: much closer than usual.

'Andrew, there's no delay on the line,' she said.

'Look, Mum, I'm outside your house, in a car. I brought someone I think you ought to meet and I just wanted to speak to you before I—'

She let go of the receiver and it fell, clattering against the table, knocking against the wall so that Lottie sprang backwards in fright and scampered off back to the kitchen. Annie ran to the living-room window and flung open the curtains and there was Andrew, lit by a streetlamp, helping a woman out of the driver's seat of a discreetly expensive black car. Andrew! Here in Hoyland, not at home in Byron Bay. Annie felt her bowels turn to liquid and her heart threw itself wildly around her chest like a bird in a box. She was afraid to move: afraid to hear his bad tidings, for why else could he be here except to break something to her? It must be Riley. She pictured him dead at the foot of a tree or the bottom of a cliff and burst into tears, and she was crying as Andrew walked down the path, followed by the woman. Who *was* she? In the dark it was impossible to tell, but Annie was still staring, still sobbing, still trying to work things out, when Andrew shouted, 'Mum! Open the door for God's sake,' and she jolted into action. Both of the front doors were locked and bolted and her hands were shaking, but she got the first one open then turned on the little porch lantern that immediately dropped soft yellow light onto her visitors. There was Andrew, in front. Then the woman stepped out from behind him and Annie found she was looking through the glass directly into the familiar grey eyes of Martha Hancock.

It was Michael who let them in, in the end: Michael who heard the hammering of a fist on the front door and accepted, finally, that he must leave off cleaning the hairs of his violin bow and venture downstairs to investigate. It was an extraordinary sight that greeted him: his mother backed against the wall and all tucked in on herself as if she was braced for a bomb blast. She was emitting an unnatural lament, an inhuman, unending moan. Michael had to step around her to unlock and open the door to Andrew. The brothers regarded each other coldly. Michael entirely ignored Martha.

Andrew pushed past him and faced his mother, placing his hands on her shoulders and shaking her, not roughly, but certainly firmly.

'Mum, hush,' he said. 'Open your eyes.'

Martha said, 'It's too much for her,' and her voice seemed to jolt Annie to her senses; she fell silent and forced herself away from the support of the wall. Michael glared at the stranger and said, 'Who the hell are you?' and Martha looked at Andrew, so he spoke for her.

'This is Martha Hancock,' he said. 'My other mother. Mum thought she was dead, didn't you, Mum?'

Annie, ashen, rigid in her miasma of shock, said nothing, then Lottie, emboldened by the sound of visitors, trotted from the sanctuary of the kitchen to sit by her. Gratefully Annie bent to scoop up the soft, warm body in her trembling hands. The little dog licked her face and Michael made a noise of disgust as if this was the last straw in an already barely tolerable situation.

'Let's sit,' Andrew said, pushing open the door to the living room, and Michael, on principle, turned to go back upstairs but Annie reached for his arm and said, 'Please, Michael,' because she really needed him now; needed to shelter behind his instant dislike of the stranger, Martha. To face her alone ... well, Annie couldn't, she just couldn't. Michael looked startled to be called upon and widened his eyes at her as if to say, '*Now* you want me,' but he didn't resist, only shook his head soberly at Andrew like a disappointed teacher at an incorrigible child, although his brother was beyond being rattled by such minor taunts. After all, Andrew had discovered that his mild, devoted mother had lived much of her life believing herself to be guilty of manslaughter. He'd discovered that she'd left Martha Hancock unconscious in a stretch of river in Coventry. He understood, for the first time, why the family had bolted from the home he'd loved to this one that he never loved and never could. He was shocked, profoundly shocked, at the layers of secrecy and denial, and when the four of them filed into the living room it was Martha he chose, sitting beside her on the sofa, near enough to her to indicate a certain closeness, a fledgling understanding. Michael stood by the fire and fidgeted, poised for flight, and Annie sat in an armchair with the puppy on her knees for added courage, looking at Andrew who wouldn't, at the moment, look at her.

Martha said, 'This must be the most terrible shock,' which didn't sound like the opening gambit of a woman bent on revenge, so Annie turned her pale blue gaze upon her nemesis. The younger woman had aged, but serenely, gracefully, the delicate lines on her face only emphasising the refinement of her beauty. There were no pouches or jowls, only elegant angles and gentle hollows. Her hair was much shorter than Annie remembered, falling just below her jawline and expensively cut into a thick waterfall of layers, and although there was grey in it, there were other colours too, shades of blonde, dark to light, framing Martha's lovely face. There were no scars, or none that Annie could see. She'd have liked to look away, but she found there was a siren pull in those grave grey eyes and Annie could only stare; she was careful to fix her expression into one of neutral detachment.

'Right,' Andrew said. 'We're going to talk about everything.'

They look like a team, thought Annie: Andrew and Martha, side by side on the sofa, with the same beautiful mouth and the same expressive eyes and the same self-assured way of holding themselves. It would have been a long drive, from Durham. The pair of them must have talked and talked and talked. Well then, Annie thought: it's over. Time to let go.

35

Martha Hancock hadn't died, that much was obvious. But even so Annie could barely believe her story: not dead in the mire of the Sherbourne but only briefly unconscious, with a wound on the left side of her head and – news to Annie, this – a broken wrist and a badly wrenched ankle. She'd come to in the concrete tunnel of water, crawled along it until she smelled fresher air, hauled her broken body up the bank, and dragged herself back to her lodgings. It shouldn't have been possible, but the human spirit isn't easily snuffed out, Martha told Annie, with a sort of pious wisdom.

'No,' Annie said, 'I suppose not.' She was thinking of Vince, not Martha: now *there* was a flame that guttered but wouldn't die.

'It all came back in dribs and drabs, but not for a long while,' Martha was saying, utterly composed, as if she was catching up with an old friend. 'At first I couldn't remember anything much, but anyway I seemed to know where I lived, when I crawled out. I just limped back to the lodgings. A man tried to help, but I ignored him, and anyway he didn't try very hard.'

She'd probably got herself back and into a hot bath before she, Annie, made it home with the fish and chips.

All those years! She'd been so certain that Martha was dead, but now she wondered if she'd simply willed it to be so.

'Looks like you botched it, Mother,' said Michael, but no one paid him any notice.

'What about the police?' Annie said.

Martha shrugged, and even after half a lifetime, Annie recognised the gesture. 'They didn't get involved. Well, I didn't report you, so they wouldn't, would they?'

'Why? Why didn't you report me?'

Martha looked at Andrew with a sort of wistful regret. 'I decided to give up,' she said, looking back at Annie. 'I was young, and the fight just seemed to leave me, and I couldn't remember any more why I was so set on taking him off you. Also, I thought Vincent might come to find me if I had Robert. I mean, Andrew.'

'Oh, he would have,' Michael said, 'if he hadn't lost his marbles. Instead we were stuck with him.'

'But the bones?' Annie said. 'The bones in the Sherbourne?' She was barely making sense, but Andrew must have filled Martha in on all the details.

'Some other poor soul,' she said.

Her voice had altered in these intervening years, thought Annie. She'd lost the Durham lilt and now you wouldn't be able to guess where she was from, north or south. The harshness was gone too, the indignant, mocking anger of her younger self; now, she kept her voice steady and soft, as if she was telling this tale of her resurrection in a library or by a loved one's sick bed. She seemed possessed of infinite patient understanding: a martyred saint. Annoying, thought Annie; at least the furious anger of the young Martha had felt authentic.

She wondered about Alf: wondered if she should tell him he could close the case again, and then she remembered that he'd only re-opened it in her fevered imagination. She wondered whose those bones were, now she knew whose they weren't.

Meanwhile Martha kept talking in her low, wise voice. She went back to Middlesbrough, she said, took A-levels at night school, studied English literature and French at Durham University, worked for the British Embassy in Paris. Andrew watched her with rapt attention, but he must have known all this stuff already, thought Annie, who was rattled by the story of unmitigated success. She glanced at Michael, and he caught the look and rolled his eyes, so that she knew he felt the same.

On went Martha, and she was moving serenely through the years of her life: met her husband in Paris, had four children – three girls, one boy, all in their thirties now. Madeleine, Eloise, Marie-Claire, Dominic. Andrew's half-siblings, she said with a coy smile that Annie hotly resented. They had a home in Durham, as well as in Paris, but Martha found she was drawn more and more to England as she grew older, especially now she was alone, since Jean-Luc, her husband, had died: a heart attack, ten years ago, on the Paris Metro.

'Rush hour?' Michael said. He looked very glad he'd stayed.

Andrew scowled. 'Apologies for my brother,' he said to Martha. 'He's extraordinarily unpleasant.'

Martha said, 'That's all right,' and she bestowed a generous smile on Michael, who took a step backwards as if her uncommon beneficence might be contagious.

'So, anyway,' Martha said, smoothly resuming the narrative. 'Jean-Luc knew all about Robert.'

'Andrew,' said Annie.

'Sorry, yes, Andrew. The children have always known about you too,' she said, turning to him. 'I told them I hoped you'd come and find me one day, of your own accord. That's why I'm Martha Hancock Guerlin, not just Guerlin. I wanted to make it easier for you if ever you came.'

She said her surname with a rolling, guttural French 'err' at its heart, which sounded pretentious to Annie, as if she, Martha, was advertising her sophistication, her otherness, to Annie Doyle and this poky, provincial front room. Annie wished Andrew didn't look so impressed, but all he said was, 'Do you hear that, Mum? A family that doesn't keep secrets?'

'Well,' Michael chipped in, 'what should she have said? "Here's your beans on toast, love, and oh by the way, I left your real mother for dead in a muddy river."'

'Did you tell your children what happened?' Annie asked.

Martha nodded. 'Yes,' she said, 'but they've been raised in the presence of a forgiving God.'

'Pardon?' Annie said. She remembered Martha's God as more of a hellfire and brimstone type.

Martha dipped her head, lowered her eyes; everyone waited. 'We're Baptists,' she said. 'We follow in the footsteps of Jesus.'

'Oh,' said Annie. She didn't look at Michael but she could feel him smirking. Andrew's expression remained defensively serious. He only smiled when Martha looked at him, and Annie felt a sad nostalgia for her steadfast, ardent little boy.

'Oh right,' Michael said. 'I see. Whosoever shall smite thee on thy right cheek, turn to him the other also. Is that it?'

Annie stared at him, astonished at the things he knew.

'Following Jesus requires faith and surrender,' Martha said by way of an answer. 'There's incredible joy to be found in letting Him take the lead.'

'Right,' Michael said. 'Well, that explains a lot, anyway.'

'Look,' said Andrew, 'this isn't actually about Martha, it's about Mum.'

'And Jesus,' Michael said.

'Shut your mouth,' Andrew said through his teeth, goaded into anger. 'This is all a bloody joke to you, isn't it?'

'Boys,' Annie said, as if they were six and nine, fighting over Lego, and so Andrew turned his fury onto her.

'You!' he said. 'I don't even know you! You behaved monstrously!' Martha laid a calming hand upon his knee, twisting the knife in Annie's heart.

'But she would have taken you from me,' Annie said, simply.

'I would,' Martha agreed. 'I would.'

'You've lived all these years, all these decades, like a woman in hiding,' Andrew said.

'Well ... have I?' Annie said. She looked back now, and her life didn't seem so very strange. Or perhaps it was only that she had become accustomed to its oddness. Mind you, thought Annie, there was nothing odder than this: that Martha was here now, and seemed to bear her no grudge. She must have led a very happy life indeed, after that bad beginning.

'Yes, you have,' said Andrew, 'a life in denial.'

Annie examined the backs of her hands.

'I looked after your father,' she said, 'and all the time he hated me.'

'So?' Andrew said. 'What does that prove?'

'It proves I knew I didn't deserve to be happy,' Annie said.

There was a potent silence, then Andrew said, 'You should get therapy, Mum,' and there was no softening of his tone, no shifting of allegiance. He was livid, thought Annie: furious. He was speaking not from concern for her state of mind, but anger at her entire way of being. 'You must be round the bend. Crazy. Anybody would be, living with all that guilt.'

'Guilt?' she said.

'You have to confront it.'

'I couldn't have loved you more,' she said. 'You were a happy boy.'

'Your secrecy, your guilt makes a mockery of the love.'

'No!' she said, stung by this injustice. 'One doesn't cancel out the other. I did what I did because I loved you with all my heart.'

'Hang on,' Michael said, slowly. '*Tess of the d'Urbervilles.*'

Martha and Andrew both frowned, but Annie understood him.

'Was I there?' Michael asked. 'An alleyway? You told me to count, then I found that book and we had fish and chips.'

Annie nodded. She knew he'd remember, in the end.

'You had fish and chips?' Andrew said. 'You never have fish and chips.'

'Oh,' Michael said. 'Is that why?'

'How could you eat, Mum, after battering Martha senseless?'

'Battering,' said Michael. 'Very droll.'

'Michael, you really are a prize fucking prick,' Andrew said. Martha glanced at him with a sort of painful surprise, but then, thought Annie, what did Martha know about Michael and Andrew? What did she know about the way they were with each other? Nothing. Nothing at all. She knew nothing, really, about any of them.

All at once, Annie found she'd had enough of this enforced retelling of things past. There was simply too much to say; it would've been better to have not even begun. After all, what did any of it matter now, aside from the fact that saintly Martha Hancock was joyously alive and Andrew had found her? She wondered if Martha intended to lead him onto the path of righteousness; there was something in the woman's eyes – a soft, hopeful light – that suggested she would at least try. The saving of Andrew's soul would be Martha's personal mission now, thought Annie, and she stood and tucked Lottie under her arm.

'Well,' she said. 'I really should get on with my mince pies.'

Michael snorted and Andrew said, 'Oh no you don't.'

'Oh no I don't what?'

'Do your usual head-in-the-sand act. You don't get off that easily.'

Annie didn't feel she'd got off easily at all. Far from it. She felt trammelled, wretched, displaced, humiliated and, in spite of all this, rather proud of herself that she was hiding it so well.

'What do you want me to say?' she asked him.

'Sorry might be a start.'

'To you?'

'No!' he said, exasperated. 'To Martha!'

Annie held out her hands in a gesture of helplessness. 'But it wouldn't be true,' she said. 'I'm not sorry. I'm not sorry at all.'

On 23 December, Josie rang again and invited Annie and Michael to Christmas lunch. This was impossible so Annie declined and yet nevertheless there they were, come Christmas Day, Annie, Michael and Lottie the dog, in Josie's round kitchen. How this had come about was nothing short of a miracle. Annie, hoping to please Michael, had told him she'd refused an invitation from Josie Jones to a festive meal that would almost certainly involve Christmas crackers. Michael had said if she'd like to accept, then he would go with her. Annie had stared at him in silence until it became clear that Michael was taking great offence, and then she'd said, well it *would* be nice to see Josie, and just wait until he saw her windmill.

She still didn't understand why he'd agreed to something that went against every dearly held, carefully nurtured anti-social idiosyncrasy he had ever possessed. Annie could only guess – and it seemed, on past form, a wild, unlikely supposition – that he was trying to be more of a son to her, now that Andrew had ... well, what *had* Andrew done? Apart from finding Martha and springing her on Annie like that, he'd done nothing. Hadn't disowned her, hadn't changed his name to Hancock, hadn't sworn never to speak to her again.

He hadn't rung this morning, though, as he usually did: the first Christmas Day for more than two decades that he hadn't phoned at 7am with cheerful greetings and, in recent years, put the boys on to shout Merry Christmas at her from across the world. This absence of contact had stung her into a state of really quite miserable reflection and when Michael said, 'Oh, let him stew,' she'd felt sadder still.

'Do you think I should ring him instead?' she'd said. And Michael hadn't answered, just implied by the straightness of his back and the tilt of his head as he left the room that no, he didn't think she should do any such thing.

And so she hadn't. But she'd felt uneasy with the decision, and still she was wondering, as she sat in the turkey-scented fug of Josie's kitchen, whether she'd been very wrong. A call from her to Andrew might've been an olive branch, if one were needed. It would've told him she was thinking about him. And missed him. And loved him, more than Martha Hancock ever would. On the other hand, she thought, he might not have answered. Or, far worse, he might have answered then hung up. She couldn't risk rejection from Andrew: and yet, in her heart, she couldn't believe him capable of such a thing.

Oh, if only he'd let things lie instead of poking around in the past. It wasn't as if there'd been anything missing in Andrew's life, Annie thought; and what, now, was he meant to do with two mothers? Because Andrew and Martha would see each other again, one way or another, Annie was quite certain of that. Martha would fly to

Brisbane in a heartbeat, make friends with Bailey, fall in love with Riley, and while Annie didn't at all like the idea of any of that, what, after all, was to be done? Cat was out of the bag, as Michael said: worms were out of the can.

'Just you and me now, Mother,' he'd said, when they closed the door on Andrew and Martha and were watching them retreat through the wavy glass: two blonde heads together, in close conversation.

'Oh, well …' Annie had said. 'Let's see.'

'No, look, they're thick as thieves,' Michael said, and it did appear so. Annie had had to turn away and just be grateful that the only thing she now had to fear was Andrew's disapproval.

Now here they were, Annie and Michael, without crackers and paper hats as it turned out, but closeted together in the windmill's festive warmth, and Annie still couldn't quite credit the fact that Michael was seated opposite her at Josie's table, sipping a glass of chilled Viognier, and seeming nearly ordinary, apart from his fringe, which covered his eyes. He peered out from under it like a nosy neighbour behind a net curtain.

Annie drank her wine and considered the future, and it came to her that, actually, she had two simple choices: she could be happy, or she could be sad, and it might just have been the effects of the wine, but she was inclined to choose the former. There was nothing more to be discovered about her, no more dark secrets to be grubbed up, no further skeletons in her closet. This, at least, was something to celebrate. She would fight heartily to stop Andrew drifting away from her and in the meantime, well, there was still Michael. He was strange, yes, and prickly: but he was here, and look at him now, around a table with her friends, almost joining in. And just as she'd lost Finn and gained Lottie, Annie decided, right here and now, to be grateful for what she had. The worst had happened, Martha had come back, and although Annie had thought it would signal the end of everything, it hadn't been so. Martha had even spoken up for her, telling Andrew before they left that day that he shouldn't judge his mother too harshly. 'She was very fiercely protective,' Martha had said. 'She felt you were all she had,' and Michael had said, 'Excuse me?' so Martha had had to quickly apologise. But anyway, that might have been why she and Michael were here now, thought Annie. Her odd older son – for she would always consider herself to be the mother of two boys, not one – was trying to be nice, and she knew full well that indirectly, she probably had Martha to thank for this.

'So,' Michael was saying to Josie, 'Uzbekistan must have a fascinating folk tradition. Do you know, is their music influenced by the Persians or the Mongolians?'

'Oh, what?' Sandra said. She was at the table too, resting her bare feet on velvety Beverley, who was prostrate under the table. Billy was spending Christmas with Trevor and his new American wife Candy, in the Caribbean. Sandra was sour, and a little worse for drink.

'I was asking Josie if—'

'No, Michael, I heard you. I just couldn't believe what you'd asked.' Sandra had had more wine than everyone else. She drank it lustily, as if she was quenching a raging thirst.

Josie looked thoughtful. 'Well it's lutes, fiddles, flutes, that sort of thing,' she said. She smiled at him and he nodded.

'Probably Persian,' he said.

'Do we even have Persia anymore?' Sandra said. 'Isn't it fictional, like the *Arabian Nights*?'

'Any more for any more?' Josie asked. Everyone's plates were empty now apart from Michael's – he'd barely touched his food. Only Annie knew that this was because there was too much on his plate, the turkey cheek-by-jowl with its stuffing, vegetables heaped willy-nilly against each other; red cabbage bleeding into pureed parsnip, roast carrots tangling with green beans. He'd only picked at the food on the outer perimeter of the plate, but anyway, thought Annie, he ate like a penitent monk most of the time; he was probably full.

'I couldn't possibly,' Annie said, patting her belly, grateful that her trousers had an elasticated waist. 'That was delicious.'

Josie acknowledged the compliment with a gracious nod. 'We'll have a break before pudding,' she said. 'Mr Dinmoor said he might join us for some, later on.'

'Well,' Annie said at once, 'we should probably get going.' Michael looked at her, and even though his hair hid his sardonic eyebrows, she could tell they were raised in amusement at her crass transparency.

'No!' said Josie. 'Don't do that. I asked Mr Wright too; he wanted to see how Lottie's doing.'

'Oh,' said Annie, feeling trapped. She drank down her wine, which was delicious. Josie topped her up.

'Wonder what the time is in Barbados?' Sandra said. She pronounced it Bar-bay-dose, like Candy did.

'Four hours behind,' said Michael promptly.

This is one of the things he's useful for, thought Annie.

'Noon then,' Sandra said. 'Probably just ordering

their first daiquiri of the day.' She sounded unutterably gloomy, and Josie laughed.

'Is Mr Wright a friend of yours then?' Annie asked.

'He is now,' Josie said. 'We bonded over the Lottie deal.'

'Was his mother there when you went?' Annie still saw Mrs Wright in the occasional bad dream; always, she was about to pull the furry skin off a litter of golden retriever puppies and it was down to Annie to stop her.

'Poorly,' Josie said. 'She was in hospital with an infection on her lungs, and I didn't like to think of him alone all day long in that dismal farmhouse.'

'What a collection of waifs and strays we are,' Sandra said. She picked up the empty wine bottle and waved it across the table at Josie. 'This seems to be all gone,' she said. 'I do hope there's some more.'

Drunk, thought Annie. But Josie just fetched another bottle.

Alf and Mr Wright arrived at the same time, and there was a frisson of awkwardness because neither man knew the other, and there they were on the threshold of the house, each clutching a gift for Josie. Alf had Stilton in an earthenware pot and Mr Wright had eight lamb chops, frozen and ineptly wrapped in cling film. They'd introduced themselves to each other by the time Josie answered the door but they still came into the room like five-year-olds late to a birthday party, hesitant and self-conscious. Alf wore a collar and tie and his trousers had a straight, sharp crease down the front; a policeman's precision, Annie thought. Mr Wright was just as he had been the last time she'd seen him: dishevelled, grubby, sheep-smelling. His trousers bagged out at the knee and there was a yellow trail of egg yolk on his shirt. Michael flared his nostrils and looked at his watch and Annie thought, *now* you're sorry we didn't leave sooner. Josie made room for them at the table – easier now, since Sandra had fallen asleep, entwined with Beverley on the sofa – and kept the conversation rolling along, light and easy. Alf cast cautious glances at Annie, but she was listening earnestly to Mr Wright, who was telling her about the Jack Russell temperament. 'They're either diggers or runners,' he said. 'She'll be one or t'other, so lets 'ope she's a digger.'

Annie said, 'Oh well, it's all patio so she'll have her work cut out,' and he bellowed with laughter.

A new bottle of wine appeared on the table and Annie had another glass. Her third. Unprecedented, and her vision was beginning to blur at the edges. But Josie's wine was so easy to drink! Like chilled floral honey poured from a tall thin bottle, frosted with cold. Josie called it a pudding wine, and it could pass for dessert all on its own. But there was steamed figgy pudding too, a dark, dense dome, decorated with holly and all ablaze when Josie brought it to the table. Then the holly sprig caught fire and sparks began to fly from the berries, so Alf plucked it from the top of the pudding – fearlessly, with his bare hand! – and dropped it into the jug of water on the table, where it fizzed and died. Annie wasn't sure why she found all this so funny, but she laughed and laughed.

'Pipe down, Mother,' Michael said, but not unkindly.

'I can't!' Annie said. 'Try this.' She pushed her glass of sweet wine along the table and he wrinkled his nose and pushed it back, untasted.

'Suit yourself,' she said, but she smiled at him, suffused with fondness at his fastidious refusal to drink from her glass. He pursed his lips in disapproval but there was the suggestion of amusement in his eyes: what she could see of them anyway.

'I *love* pudding wine,' she announced.

'Evidently,' Michael said.

'Muscat de Beaumes de Venise,' Alf said, bouncing the words out into the room, swirling the golden liquid in his pretty crystal glass and raising it to Annie. She lifted her own, and they clinked.

'By the way, I was wrong about those bones,' she said happily.

'Mother,' Michael said, and raised a warning finger to his lips.

'I'm just saying.'

'Good-oh,' said Alf. He winked at her.

'We really *should* be going,' Michael said, alarmed by the dapper old man and the flush in his mother's cheeks.

'We should,' Annie agreed, nodding fervently. 'We should. But on balance I don't think we will.'

Michael folded his arms and closed his eyes, which might just as easily have been passive acceptance as protest. The room, Annie noticed with interest, had begun to buzz with pleasure at her decision to stay a little longer: not the people in it, but the actual room itself, its curved walls of dove grey, the mellow wooden fixtures and fittings, the Middle Eastern trinkets in brass and pewter, the crockery in all the colours of the spectrum. It was mesmerising: extraordinary. The kettle on the hob whistled a message of goodwill and there were glad tidings in every creak and sigh of the furniture, but when Annie looked around the table to marvel with the others at this dazzling phenomenon, she saw from their faces that she was the only one hearing it. What a shame, she thought, and then she wondered – languidly, without any real concern – if understanding the language of a kettle meant she was, in fact, not quite right in the head. She sipped her wine and considered the question, but Mr Wright had cracked open a chocolate orange and was offering it around, so almost at once she was distracted from her purpose. Then Josie went out of the room and came back with an ancient fiddle and bow of uncertain provenance. Perhaps Baku, or possibly Tashkent, she said; she didn't know where exactly, or when, but years and years ago, anyway. Michael opened one eye, interested.

'Do you think you can coax it into life?' Josie asked. She offered him the instrument and her bangles slipped musically down her arm like a temptation. Annie held her breath, waiting for him to rudely refuse, but Michael took the fiddle almost graciously, tenderly blew off the dust and caressed the strings with the old bow. He winced at the wheeze and scrape, and on the old leather sofa Sandra stirred, and Beverley raised her elegant head, pricked up her pointed ears. Betty the collie moved and stepped out of her basket. She had a tinsel bow on her collar.

'Ooh, go on then,' Annie said to Alf, who was proffering the muscat. He poured, and the light danced through the wine as it flowed, as if even this simple function was touched by magic. She raised her glass in a general, inclusive, encouraging way. 'To Josie Jones,' Annie said, 'and the perfect roundness of her kitchen.'

Her toast echoed around the table, and Betty gave two

pleasant barks, which sounded a little like 'hear hear'. The laughter was more intoxicating than the wine and amid it all Michael threw out a few perfectly rendered bars of 'Jingle Bells'.

Annie thought if she had the power to conjure a good dream, it might be exactly this, here and now. She felt the swell of interest around the table in her strange, clever son, felt the warm weight of the puppy in her lap. There was a woozy lightness in her head that would probably carry a price tomorrow, but oh, the sheer joy of it all! She basked in the knowledge that in this moment, on this enchanted night, she was immersed in the sort of ordinary happiness that had only ever belonged to other people, never to her. When she looked up, Alf was watching her, and he met her eyes with a smile.

Epilogue

Formby Point seemed a different place in the June sunshine. Everywhere Annie looked there were people walking dogs and loafing about on tartan rugs. Behind her, children whooped and charged about in the dunes and in front of her they dug holes and drew lines in the flat, hard sand of the beach. In the distance the sea glittered under a blue sky.

'Shall we walk all the way to the water?'

This was Alf. He had Lottie on a lead and a cool bag over his shoulder, stuffed with picnic food. Annie smiled at him and reached down to scratch Lottie behind her ears.

'We could have something to eat,' she said, 'and see if the water comes to us.'

'I like your thinking.'

Annie scanned the beach, shielding her eyes from the sun with a hand. 'I can't see Dora,' she said. 'We probably shouldn't start without her.'

But Alf had passed her the lead and was already kneeling in the sand, spreading out a big, threadbare beige bath towel, which was the closest thing he had to a picnic rug.

'She'll be here like a shot when I get this food out,' he

said. 'Our kid can sniff out a pork pie from two miles away.'

Still, Annie stayed where she was, gazing left and right, and it wasn't really Dora she was looking for. Finn was out there somewhere, running with the terriers.

'We shouldn't have agreed to meet on the beach,' she said now. 'It's too busy. I was picturing it empty, like it was before.'

'Annie, sit down,' Alf said.

'She'll never see us,' Annie said.

'She will, we're not thirty feet from the car park; she can't leave this beach without falling over us.'

But anyway Annie set off away from Alf, and Lottie trotted mildly alongside her. She was a tidy little dot of a dog, with an endearing habit of treating everyone she met as her favourite person, apart from Michael, who she'd quickly realised was a lost cause. Josie and Sandra were besotted, though. They were sharing her when Annie went away next month: two weeks each. And while Annie was gone, the builders were making a start on the loft conversion, where Michael would have his own bathroom, his own small kitchen and a wide, low bedroom.

Annie had fretted, naturally. 'What will you do, though?' she'd said to Michael. 'There'll be dust and debris and no end of racket.' But Michael had only shrugged and said, 'I'll steer clear by day, and I trust they won't be working through the night?'

He had altered, by degrees, over the past six months. There was a careful cordiality about him; it smacked of effort and concentration, and no one could have mistaken him for a ray of sunshine, but still, Annie privately cherished and celebrated the small advances. When she'd told him she was flying to Brisbane, that Alf was flying with her, that she'd be gone for a month, staying with Andrew and Bailey in Byron Bay, he'd said, 'Rather you than me,' but he'd said it with a smile, and she'd taken that as acceptance, or the closest to it she was going to get.

She didn't think she'd walked very far down the beach, but when she turned to look back at Alf, she was shocked by the distance between them. He looked so small and far away, sitting there on his horrid old towel, waving at her. She waved back, allowing herself a moment to savour the joy she'd found, so unexpectedly, so late in her life. His kindness to her seemed fathomless, as if he'd been stockpiling it for years, only waiting for someone to share it with.

Annie turned again so that she was facing the sea and beside her Lottie sat squarely and searched the beach too, though she couldn't have known who they were looking for. They wouldn't walk any further, thought Annie. She felt too far away from Alf already; she didn't wish to put any more distance between them. In any case, it was a hopeless quest. Finn could be anywhere; he could be in the dunes behind her, or all the way down the distant reaches of the beach, to the right or to the left. She'd imagined, as they approached the beach from the lane, that he would find her the moment she stepped onto the sand – her scent on the breeze, perhaps – but she knew now that was foolish whimsy. Chances were, he wouldn't even know her any more.

'Come on, Lottie,' she said, and she turned to walk back, and then suddenly there he was. Finn, trotting purposefully towards her, head up, tail high, threading expertly around the strangers with a broad smile on his face, because there was his best and oldest friend, waiting for him on the sand.

This Much is True

Reading group notes

Q&A with Jane Sanderson

It's an interesting title – what inspired it?

Good question! It can be so tricky, naming a book, and I did start with another title altogether, so when Orion first alighted on the manuscript, my novel was called *The Dog Days of Annie Doyle*. But there was a feeling in the team that this didn't do justice to the dark heart of the book: the twists and turns of the plot, and Annie's tenacious dependence on a buried past. But being asked to re-name a book when for two years you've known it as something else is a bit like re-naming a baby a couple of years after the christening. Nothing struck the right tone. Then a friend of mine, aware of my difficulty, texted me to say she was going to see Tony Hadley in concert, and might there be a title for my book in the lyrics of 'True'? Well, this was genius, for which I remain completely indebted (to my friend and to Spandau Ballet!). There's something so perfect about *This Much is True* that I feel it must have been waiting for me all along.

Why does the title work so well, do you think?

It sums up Annie Doyle, somehow. She's a complex character, who can only deal with the misery of her life by ignoring it. But by degrees she is forced to confront her past, as if in spite of her deeply private nature she's ultimately made to sift through the lies to reveal the truth. I wanted her new friendship with Josie and Sandra, and their dog walks together, to be a catalyst for change in Annie's life. Just spending time with these women leads Annie down a different path, shows her a different way of being. But also, I'm interested in the lines we don't cross in our friendships: the things we know about each other, the things we don't know, the stuff we share and the stuff we'd never talk about. I think we protect our secret selves in all our relationships, although not – I hope – to the extent Annie feels compelled to do. All of this is reflected in the book's title.

Annie's life, on the surface, is completely ordinary but there are secrets – potentially destructive ones – at the heart of her story. It's a brilliant premise, but did you find it difficult to balance?
It was a challenge, certainly, to stay true to the two versions of Annie: the one she allows her friends to see, and the one we see through the flashbacks to her earlier life. The difficulty lies in not giving away too much too soon, but not giving away so little that the reader loses interest. But this dichotomy between her public and private persona is so often the case in real life, so I wanted it to slowly become clear, as the novel progresses, that there's far more to Annie than we at first realise, and that her own sense of guilt and shame and – to an extent – defiance is as important a part of who she is as her ordinary, everyday respectability. Writing this book has made me look at older people and think, what are you not telling me? Everyone has a story to tell, and the older we are, the more secrets we keep.

Martha is such a pivotal character in the novel but she is largely a mystery throughout. Can you tell us about how you decided to have Vince mention her on his deathbed then allow the novel to build to a dramatic climax.

Annie knows what Vince knows; she believes that he's the only person in the world who could blow her cover, and she feels protected, to a large degree, by his advanced dementia because any fragments of the past that emerge when he speaks can be put down to the ramblings of a befuddled mind. The reader, too, might recall things he said to Annie in the early pages of the book, and realise that Martha's existence was in fact hinted at from the beginning. Annie would like him to die as soon as possible, and take her secrets with him, which is why – I hope – his mention of Martha on his deathbed has such dramatic impact. But also I think it's entirely plausible that the fog in his brain might clear for a moment and allow him to reveal a truth to the family; advanced dementia sometimes offers up crystal clear glimpses into the distant past. For Annie, Vince's moment of clarity is a personal disaster because it shines a light on decades of meticulously denying her own history.

The novel looks at the difficult side of family relationships, particularly the flashbacks to Annie's childhood and relationship with her parents. Did you find these difficult to write?

No, on the contrary, I found Annie's dysfunctional past very easy to write, which was a relief because I felt it was a crucially important aspect of the story. The segments in her early childhood, her lonely girlhood and her ill-advised marriage as a young woman to Vince, were all intended to shine a light on the buttoned-up, socially uncertain elderly lady Annie has become when we meet her. I always knew there was a danger that readers might not warm to her, but she had a place in my heart from the very beginning. I grew up in South Yorkshire and I knew women just like Annie Doyle, with nets at the windows and a mistrust of friendly strangers. I wanted to explore the idea that all sorts of secrets may lurk behind an utterly respectable façade, and that everyone has a story to tell, however dull their life may appear to be on the surface.

Apart from Annie, did you ever consider having another character's point of view?
No, I wanted us – by and large – never to leave Annie's side, to view the action through her eyes. This way we become more intimately acquainted with what makes her tick. If Josie and Sandra had shared centre stage I think the strength of Annie's narrative would have been watered down.

The novel has a very strong sense of place. Can you tell us more about the locations that are featured?
I do like to use real locations in my writing, because then I find the dialogue comes more easily – I can hear the characters' voices, especially when we're in Yorkshire, where I grew up. But there are a mixture of locations, and while most of them are real, some of them are imagined and others are a combination of both. Hoyland exists – my own hometown, sitting in what used to be the mining belt of South Yorkshire, between Barnsley and Sheffield. But

the details of the place – street names, outlying villages, the precise geography – are often altered, because after all this is a work of fiction. The reservoir where the friends walk their dogs exists, as does Ecclesall Woods. But Wentford, where Josie lives, is invented, as is Wheatcommon Lane, which is Sandra's address. The same applies to Coventry, where Annie lives as a girl, and where she meets and marries Vince. The geographical details are slightly fudged here and there, although there *is* an underground river in Coventry called the Sherbourne, and I must say I found this a fascinating and inspiring detail.

Do you have a writing routine and a favourite place that you prefer to write?

I am a most undisciplined writer, fitting in this work between all the other commitments and distractions that rise up to fill an average day. Dogs to walk, dinner to prepare, parcels to be signed for, washing machine to empty or to load, grass to cut, chickens to feed … I'm just not one of those writers who can shut themselves off from domestic concerns to write for solitary hours on end. However, when I do write, I work quite quickly – I believe my years as a journalist are to thank for this – so even though it's a haphazard process, the books do seem to get finished. I always write on my laptop, at a small desk facing one of our bedroom windows. There's the most magnificent view of Hay Bluff and the Black Mountains, but I can't see it, because if I open the shutters the light seems to bleach the computer screen, and anyway I'd start to think how grubby the windows look, and how tatty the paintwork, and before I knew it I'd be abandoning the writing yet again.

Do you have any advice for aspiring writers?
Make a start. You can't edit an empty page, but you can always improve upon a first draft. And keep reading other writers' books: good ones, bad ones – they all serve as inspiration, one way or another.

Who are your favourite authors and are there any books that inspired you to write?
When I was writing my first three books, which were set at the turn of the twentieth century, I used to keep at hand a copy of *Wolf Hall* by Hilary Mantel, as a masterclass – when I was bogged down in my own plot lines – in how to imbue the distant past with freshness and originality. But other than that, I suppose everything I've ever read has inspired me to write – even the ones I didn't enjoy, because it's always helpful to believe you can do better than an already published author. As for favourite authors ... well there are so many. Time and again I go back to Jane Austen for her sly and brilliant comedy, but currently featuring in a pile by my bed are Carol Shields, Elizabeth Bowen, Muriel Spark, Carol Birch, Karen Joy Fowler and Anita Brookner. A thousand apologies to all the others that I love and haven't mentioned.

Questions for discussion

• As Annie Doyle's story unfolds, it becomes clear that she's lived a life of guarded secrets and repressed emotion. Do you think this lack of openness is typical of her generation and is it ever justifiable?

• There are some fraught family dynamics in the novel, particularly between Michael, Andrew and Annie. What – or who – do you think lies at the heart of their problems?

• Annie can be difficult: prickly, defensive and over-anxious. But the flashbacks to her childhood and early married life show that she endured much loneliness and rejection. Does this help the reader to understand the less acceptable aspects of her behaviour?

• This novel's central plotline concerns the extreme lengths to which Annie was prepared to go in order to keep Andrew. Does she lose the readers' sympathy along the way, or retain it?

• Do you see Annie Doyle as a victim? Or do you regard her as a survivor, made stronger by her suffering?

• Is Annie's relationship with Josie, Sandra and Alf somehow key to the unravelling of her carefully guarded life, or is it simply an additional layer to the narrative? Discuss the theme of friendship in the novel.

Further Reading

The Food of Love
Amanda Prowse (Lake Union)

A Life Without You
Katie Marsh (Hodder & Stoughton)

I Found You
Lisa Jewell (Century)

The One Plus One
Jojo Moyes (Penguin)

Leaving Time
Jodi Picoult (Hodder & Stoughton)

The Husband's Secret
Liane Moriarty (Penguin)